Praise for *Theatre

"Enticing. . . . Readers will cheer on this gutsy heroine [and] vibrant cast. . . . An accomplished first novel from a bright new talent."
—*Minneapolis Star Tribune*

"Richly evocative and glittering with atmosphere."
—Stacey Halls, bestselling author of *The Familiars*

"*Theatre of Marvels* is a fascinating, empowering story of a young woman's search for identity and justice in Victorian London, a world that Lianne Dillsworth evokes so richly."
—Jennifer Saint, author of *Ariadne*

"A dazzling tale of self-discovery with a cast of vivid characters. I loved it."
—Laura Purcell, author of *The Silent Companions*

"A startling, original, and utterly compelling novel that subtly navigates the core issues of race, gender, and class."
—Mary Chamberlain, author of *The Dressmaker of Dachau*

"Thrilling, eye-opening, and absorbing."
—Lizzie Pook, author of *Moonlight and the Pearler's Daughter*

"I fell in love with Zillah and her theatre world. I was gripped from the opening pages—highly recommended."
—Louise Hare, author of *This Lovely City*

Theatre of Marvels

Theatre of Marvels

Lianne Dillsworth

HARPER ● PERENNIAL

NEW YORK ● LONDON ● TORONTO ● SYDNEY ● NEW DELHI ● AUCKLAND

HARPER ● PERENNIAL

A hardcover edition of this book was published in 2022 by HarperCollins Publishers.

HarperCollins books may be purchased for educational, business, or sales promotional use. For information, please email the Special Markets Department at SPsales@harpercollins.com.

FIRST HARPER PERENNIAL EDITION PUBLISHED 2023.

Designed by Emily Snyder

Library of Congress Cataloging-in-Publication Data has been applied for.

ISBN 978-0-06-327153-1 (pbk.)

23 24 25 26 27 LBC 5 4 3 2 1

For my grandad Ambrose W. Dillsworth,
who always told the bestest stories.

And for Nana and for Mama. I love you very much
and all I ever want to do is make you proud.

Contents

I

The African in
the Audience

Go to the theatre much? No, nor me. At least not before I became an actress. I know what you're thinking. *Actress*, eh? But you can keep your dirty-minded thoughts to yourself. I trod the boards and no more. Doesn't mean I don't have a story or two to tell, mind. Would you be kind enough to indulge me if I talked about the old days? Hard as it was back then, I can't say that if I had my time again I'd change it.

That feeling you get before the show starts. Whether you've been up Drury Lane once, twice, or ten times, I reckon you'll know it. It comes up on you as the lights go down. The fizzing in your belly conjured by cheap gin and jellied eels at a farthing a pot. Keep your eyes hard fixed on the curtain in front of you. Those red velvet folds, with their heavy gold trim. You're so eager at the thought of the performance to come, you tell yourself you saw it move. But if you really want first peek it's best to look to the left of the stage. Time it right and you might just see the actors looking out at you.

Not at Crillick's Variety Theatre, though. Back in the late forties, if you'd have found yourself sitting in the stalls you would have looked in vain. Doesn't mean we weren't there, just that you didn't see us: redheaded Ellen and right alongside her with the wild black curls? That would be me, Zillah. I know it's strange to think that we watched you before you watched us, but both of us had our reasons. Each night, Ellen searched the audience for a scout, someone with the power to pluck her from the Crillick's stage and take her to the Theatre Royal, Covent Garden. She fancied herself a soprano. I was more concerned about seeing what mood the punters were in—if they were at the stage of drink where they would join in a singsong or so far gone they'd turn violent and throw things at us. Every crowd was different, but there was one September night, the year the Queen was delivered of her daughter Louise, when one man in particular caught my eye.

The first thing I noticed was his hat. It stood out a mile among the flat caps and bowlers, and he had the frock coat to match. It's not often you get a man in a topper at Crillick's. Don't mistake me, Marcus Crillick's show is more than a few rungs up from a penny gaff, but the quality don't like variety. They prefer to keep things pure. So straightaway I was suspicious. Then I clocked the colour of him.

"Him over there. What do you make of him?" I said to Ellen.

She squinted in the direction of my pointed finger.

"The African, you mean? Don't often get one of yours in."

He sat on the benches, three rows back, his right leg stretched out on the aisle. Even from here, peeking out behind the curtain, I could see that he was handsome and broad in the shoulders. Around him sat our usual regulars, the shop boys and navvies already half-cut and impatient for the show to start. The sour tang of their sweat was sharp on the air. Beyond them were the tables for the better sort, the clerks with women worth the price of dinner and a show. The ushers weaved around them, touting trinkets and sweetmeats, competing for the pennies in their pockets. Up above, the box where our proprietor often sat was in darkness. Crillick liked to keep an eye on what was happening in his theatre, but for the time being he was away on business in France.

Ellen, satisfied that she had the measure of the African, delivered her verdict. "Selfish bastard, I reckon. Getting above himself. No call to be wearing a hat three minutes before the curtain."

I was glad she was talking to me again. Things had been frosty between us for a couple of weeks, ever since Crillick had made me the headline act and cut Ellen's solo from the bill to give me more stage time. It wasn't my fault, of course, and she knew it, but that didn't stop her being miffed. I suppose I would've been too, in her position, seeing how green I'd been when I started.

I'd joined Crillick's company nine months earlier, at the new year. Ellen had been one of the first people I'd met backstage. She was the only one to welcome me, to pass the time of day while I got to know my act. Straightaway the others hated me, and didn't trouble to hide it. When I entered a room, they snickered behind their hands. Just a drop or two of colour was enough to make me an outcast in their eyes. But Ellen, coming from Galway as she did, knew just enough of what it was to be different to see that we could be allies. She'd been kind, and all she'd got in return for her troubles was to be demoted. She could ill afford it too, what with all her money being sent back home. I did my best to be nice as I could, let her know I wasn't trying to displace her. We'd always had a laugh together. I didn't want us to feel like rivals.

All this time Ellen had been straining her eyes to look at the African.

"You recognise him?" she said.

"No, why would I?"

"I only asked."

I shouldn't have snapped. It felt like all the Irish people in town knew one another so she probably meant nothing by it. But I didn't know him, had never seen him before in my life. He wasn't "one of mine" like she'd said. I had no one.

But I didn't want me and Ellen to be on the outs anymore. I had enough battles to fight so I squeezed her shoulder to say sorry.

"He's unsettled me is all."

"Then tell the boys to kick him out," Ellen said.

"I couldn't."

I didn't know what it was about the African that threw me off but I didn't want to see his evening spoiled, not on my account. Especially as I knew it must be my act that he'd come to see. Not just him, mind. When I'd started off at Crillick's, I'd been bottom of the bill but now I was the main draw. Over time I'd seen off Aldous the magician and Guillame the mime artist, and now the Great Amazonia was the headline act. I'd even been reviewed in the *Illustrated London News*—"a savage spectacular," they'd said. "Here is one Amazon that has carried all before her." I looked out at the African in the audience. If I performed well enough to fool him, Amazonia might remind him of his homeland. If he'd ventured into Crillick's on his own, he must've wanted to see her very badly. I felt an urge not to disappoint him. I wanted him to like my performance. To like me.

I didn't know where it came from, this sudden feeling of kinship. There had been other Blacks in the crowd before, of course, but this was the first time I'd felt drawn to one. I was half-caste, white as well as Black. Moreover, I was London born and bred, while most of the other Blacks—and mainly they were men— were from somewhere else. The soldiers at the palace who played the drums at the Changing of the Guard were brought in from Africa for their musical talents. I was nothing like them, their smart uniforms bright against their dark skin. Nor was I like the sailors and former slaves that hung around the docks. Buckled and broken down, they had mostly arrived from America. Unlike them, I'd always been free.

"Here now, what's this?" Ellen said.

We watched as one of the ushers approached the African, leaning down to whisper in his ear. The African nodded as he spoke but the look on his face was grim. The usher put a hand on his shoulder and I tensed, waiting for a shout, or a punch to be thrown, but then the African turned back toward the stage and removed his hat. Underneath, his hair was cut close and the tight curls smoothed with a shiny pomade.

"I thought it was about to get tasty there. He's definitely not one of the regulars," Ellen said. She was right; it was rare that a whole night at Crillick's passed without a fight breaking out in the audience.

"You should tell Barky if you're worried," Ellen said. *Or stop your whining,* she could have added, but didn't.

"Let him be. You can tell he's not in the market for any trouble."

Barky was the stage manager. He'd never talked behind my back like I knew Ellen sometimes did and, though he was careful not to show me any favouritism, of all the people at Crillick's I trusted him the most. There was no reason for him to look out for me, but I was glad that he did. Lean and mysterious like a shadow, his greying dark hair cut convict-short, Barky took seriously his job to look after the performers. He moved quiet as a cat. I was never sure how long he had been somewhere before he announced himself. He saw himself as an uncle and liked to call us his family. I suppose we were in a way. All families row and fight and secretly hate one another, don't they? That's what it was like at Crillick's. All those performers with their own high pride and jealousies. Barky always checked up on us before a show so we did not miss our cues.

Now, right on cue himself, he appeared behind us in the wings and tutted to see Ellen and me in dressing gowns and drawers.

"Come on, girls, you should be in costume by now. You know who'll get the rollicking if you're late."

He made his usual noise, something between a cough and a snort. It came out when we annoyed him, which was often. The strange sound had led to his nickname but he didn't seem to mind that that's what we called him. It never occurred to me back then to wonder what his real name was.

"There's a man . . ." Ellen began but trailed off when I shook my head. It felt wrong to bring the African to Barky's attention. The stranger may have rattled me but he had done nothing wrong, and it was reassuring that he hadn't caught Barky's eye. If there had been anything untoward in the crowd, I knew Barky would have spotted it.

"No more dallying then," Barky said and clapped his hands to shoo us along.

Ellen jumped to it but I couldn't tear my eyes from the African. His head was bent over his programme now. He traced a finger down the page, studying the acts to come. Ballerinas, acrobats, a magician, and then: the Great Amazonia. Barky's arm stole around my shoulder. From another man the gesture would have made me cringe, but all the girls felt safe with Barky. He was the only man among the theatre workers that never made lewd remarks, nor lingered while we girls got changed.

"What's got you spooked, girl?"

I desperately wanted to tell him, but I barely understood it myself. Back then I didn't realise that the impression this African had made on me would be the start of something lasting, that it would change the way I lived my life and how I saw myself.

"Nothing wrong with a spot of nerves," Barky said.

He gave me a searching look, but didn't push it. After a moment, he steered me around and gave me a gentle shove in the direction of the steps that led backstage. Ellen hadn't bothered to wait for me.

II

Making Ready
to Perform

The dressing room came with the privilege of being Crillick's headline act. It had a table, chair, and gilt-framed mirror, but for all that it was clear it had started out as a broom cupboard. It didn't bother me that it was still used to store the props. Coming from the slums of St. Giles as I did, this amount of space all to myself could only ever be a luxury. *If only you could see me now, Mother.*

I'd moved in two weeks before and had insisted that Ellen share it with me. I'd even made a den in one corner for her tan-and-white spaniel, Bouncer, who featured in my act. I knew it wouldn't make up for losing her solo but it had helped to improve things between us. I picked my way past the magician's birdcage, the balls and batons used by the clowns, and a rope swing for the trapeze artist. It smelt of dustcloths and floor polish and the vinegar used to clean the stage.

Wooden boards known as flats and painted for all manner of backdrops were leant up against the walls. Snow-tipped mountains, foam-flecked waves, and, my new favourite, the English countryside with rolling green meadows, complete with daffodils and delicate little rosebuds. That rural greenery was a world away from St. Giles and the cramped buildings that I'd grown up among. Most of my life I'd lived in broken-down hovels with not a pane of glass between them. Rooms where the walls were held together with rags and dirt, and where a body might die and no one notice for days, let alone lay it out and say the prayers. There was a time before that, but I tried not to dwell on it too much.

After I arrived for my performance and before I was due to start getting ready to go onstage, I had taken to sitting before that countryside board and imagining myself in those meadows with Lord Vincent Woodward. I pictured him sitting alongside me, his hand twining in my hair, while he pointed out that all the land we could see was his, and would be ours when we were married. If I concentrated hard enough, I could almost feel the tickle of the soft grass against my bare legs, smell the freshness of the strands I'd pulled up in tufts, hear the sound of sparrows chirping and church bells in the distance. I've never been much of a believer but those bells were probably the most important part of it. The ones I heard every Sunday from St. Paul's could be those same ones that carried on the gentle breeze in my imagined meadow. Their chimes were the sole thing that connected the place where I wanted to be with where I was now. You see, St. Giles may be where I was coming from, but I had no intention of staying. Crillick's and the Great Amazonia were my path out of there. I'd make sure of it.

Ellen always teased that I was away with the fairies when she found me sitting there, but she had her own dreams. When I'd first started at Crillick's, one of the very first things she'd told me was about the cousins in New York that she would go to as soon as she'd raised enough money to get her mum and sisters out of Galway. It was what had made me warm to her, that ambition to get on that burnt in me too. I judged her to be around twenty-five or so, five years older than myself. It was clear she knew her way around and, though I was streetwise enough, I saw

in her someone who could help me learn the ways of the theatre. I'd not expected her to still be around, but nine months had
passed since the day we met and here she still was, and talking
about America less and less.

There was no time for dreaming now, though. The band had
struck up, which meant that the curtain would soon rise. I strained
my ears for its heavy velvet swoosh while I wriggled into the skins
Amazonia wore. Ellen handed me my feathered cloak and beads.
I pulled them on and sat down to chalk the soles of my feet so I
wouldn't slip on the polished boards of the stage. Bouncer had
been sleeping, but now he sat up and wagged his tail, sensing that
things were about to start happening.

As soon as I was dressed, Ellen helped me paint my arms and
face. I sat numbly as she smeared over me the mix of grease and
soot, basting my arms and legs like a stuffed goose, so my skin
gleamed dark. She murmured Crillick's instructions in a singsong
while she worked—"Here you go then, blood of yer fallen enemies"—stabbing two fingers into a pot and drawing them across
my cheeks to create twin pairs of dripping "tribal marks." The
stuff inside the pot was made from poppy petals and thickened to
a paste with water and flour. Where did Crillick get this idea of
the tribal marks anyway? Would they mean anything to the Black
man who sat waiting in the audience for the show to start, or anyone else in Africa either? Ellen made one more line down the center of my forehead for good measure. The skin puckered and she
dabbed her finger to my face to correct the smudge, while I stood
silent. Satisfied, she stepped back and looked me over.

"You'll do," she said.

Growing up, I'd hated how dark I was, how an afternoon in the
sunshine would make the colour in me glow. Now it turned out I
was not Black enough. In order to convince as the Great Amazonia, I must be the deep, rich colour of mahogany. The darker tone
combined with the natural hazel of my eyes would increase my al-
lure. At least, that's what Marcus Crillick had told me.

"There can't be a hint of the East End about you. What you need to be is Black as pitch. What was your father? Let me guess. An English gent, I think? We must remove every trace of him for the act to succeed, and no one can ever know of your deception."

My deception? It was Crillick that was paying me to do it. I'd felt the warmth rise in my cheeks and looked away so he wouldn't see. It wasn't embarrassment. There were more bastards than me in St. Giles and more almond-shaped eyes and thick black hair than could be explained away by God's rich tapestry. Still, it was none of his business who my mother and father were, and anyway, what difference did it make? I had only myself to rely on now.

"Can I help you with your makeup?" I asked Ellen and pointed to the pot of burnt cork on the dressing table.

"Not with those nails." Ellen grimaced. At Crillick's request, she had helped me file them the previous week to wicked points. I regretted it already, used to being able to discard the things that made me Amazonia, but one of my rivals at a show on Shaftesbury Avenue had filed teeth. I drew the line at that, but Crillick's Variety was not to be completely outdone.

"My face won't take a minute, then I'll do Mikey and Bob," Ellen said.

The two men played foot soldiers to her cupbearer. Ellen never said so but I couldn't help but wonder if they were cousins of hers, those three seemed so thick with each other.

I looked into the mirror over her shoulder at Amazonia, the woman who was me and not me. In the programme she was described as "a dangerous savage from darkest Africa" but beneath Ellen's cunning paint I was still Zillah. Ellen turned and her pale, freckled face appeared alongside mine in the glass. Soon she too would be transformed for the performance. She and the boys who acted as my worshippers used a pot of Stein's to blacken their hands and faces. I hated the smell of the burnt cork, but it was cheap and it worked, and for them there was no need for pretense, the black so obviously grotesque and the red smiles painted on. I didn't like that the line between me and Amazonia was so blurred. She was a savage. I wasn't.

"Get on with you, Zillah. I'll be along in a minute," Ellen said. "Now you're the headliner, it's not only Barky that gets blamed if you miss your cue."

III

The Great Amazonia

It was the compère's job to introduce me to the audience. To tell them what my story was while I stood silent, waiting in the wings with Barky at my side. He started with how I'd been found in the jungles of Africa, captured by an intrepid English explorer. Crillick said it was an essential part of making me seem like a real savage, and the crowd fell for it every time.

"She was brought to London for your delight," the compère said. As if anyone had ever thought about what a collection of clerks and shopgirls might want.

What did the African make of it all? I wished I could still see him but the lights were down. He was dressed up like a gent, but did he recognise these tales of the jungle? As the compère jabbered on, nerves started to harden like a rock in my stomach. It was the last thing I needed, especially tonight when it was so important to me to be at my best.

The drumbeat that signaled the start of my performance began. I felt it at the back of my throat, the steady thump, thump, thump. The pace increased and a feeling of fullness worked its way to my chest. Every beat was a blow and I cringed as they landed. The rhythm grew faster and entered my mind. It crowded out all other

thoughts, and the memory of my dance steps fled. The audience
had paid handsomely to see my performance. I must show them
something. The African, sitting three rows back—I wanted him
to be impressed. The panic built and the drums beat faster still. I
covered my ears with my hands like a child, but the beats had gotten into my soul. Now they throbbed inside me.

"Go on, girl, let it out," Barky whispered at my side and I
screamed in response, the sound high and wild and frightened.

Barky slapped my behind and jolted me forward onto center stage. Stunned silence and a moment of blinding light as the
spot lamps picked me out. I cast off my cloak and the audience
gasped. This is what they saw: a Black woman, tall and fearsome.
Tribal marks on her cheeks and a string of beads and feathers at
her throat. Barefoot, her limbs slick with grease. The scandalous
shapes of her body barely hidden beneath a close-fitting leopard
skin. I couldn't see the audience but I felt their reaction: the surprise and wonder, a little fear. A low murmur built as the punters
whispered to one another. Looking out over their upturned faces,
my nerves melted away. I felt powerful, until one man, bolder than
the rest, shouted out, "Turn around then, let's see the goods."

He thought I was like the Venus. The woman with the big behind that had been so famous at the start of the new century.
I was glad I couldn't see his face; his hard eyes as they tried to
bore through my clothing, the smirk on his lips as he imagined
my private parts. The heckling was the one bit of performing onstage that I'd never gotten used to, even after all these months. If I
got catcalled on the street I could brush it off. But as Amazonia I
could never answer back and it made me feel vulnerable. I fought
to keep my hands by my sides, when all I wanted was to hide behind them. But Crillick had always made very clear that I had to
let the punters gawp, let them wonder. It was what they'd paid for.
The whispering grew louder. I heard a snicker and my eyes began
to burn, until I remembered the African. How straight and tall
he sat. I drew up my body and looked out, proud as the warrior

queen I was supposed to be, chin raised and a sneer on my lips as though it didn't matter what they thought of me.

Ellen's light footsteps sounded to my left and then she was before me, a handmaiden flanked by two henchmen, their faces painted charcoal black with huge red smiles. The men carried burning torches. I felt the heat of the flames on my face and smelt the ghost of the animal whose skins I now wore. It was time for the Great Amazonia to receive a live sacrifice. At a smarter theatre it might have been a real goat, but the Crillick's crowd got Bouncer, Ellen's tan-and-white spaniel that she'd trained to play dead. Ellen whistled and Bouncer trotted onstage. There was a collective ooh from the audience and he wagged his little tail to acknowledge them. She bent and lifted him up for my approval. When I nodded my head, she put him down before me, and Bob handed me a spear. At the moment Ellen clicked her tongue I plunged it down and Bouncer keeled over, his plump little body small and still.

I turned my back to the audience and leant over Bouncer to the pot of vermilion mixed with flour and water that was kept at the rear of the stage. I thrust my hands in and smeared it around my lips and on my chest. The audience liked to think I'd killed the dog and drunk his blood. It was the part of the show they always wrote up in the papers. When I turned back around, face dripping red, a woman screamed. I took it as my cue to dance.

The drums began again, but this time I welcomed the thumping rhythm. I closed my eyes, and did what the beats told me to, abandoning myself to my well-rehearsed steps. In response to their command, I rolled my shoulders and wound my hips. I lifted a foot and stepped to one side then the other, in time to the drum. I spun and twisted, crouched down and jumped up. I'd always enjoyed losing myself in the routine but lately I was feeling as though I needed to in order to get through it. The cheering of the audience spurred me on, but it had been harder to feed off their energy in recent shows. I put it down to the extra pressures that came with my top billing. *Throw yourself into it, Zillah.* I whirled 'round and 'round and 'round, faster and faster until I felt dizzy. As the faces of the audience blurred, the dance felt like freedom once more, and a laugh came to my lips, high and unnatural. My movements grew wilder, more frantic, until the sweat ran down my face, streaking through the grease and the fake blood to pool in droplets at my chin. Then my surroundings fell away. I was in the dance and all was feeling.

The lights came up and I was back on the Crillick's stage. I stood breathing heavily as the crowd cheered and stamped their feet. My eyes darted to row C but the place where the African had sat was empty. Was that him making his way up the aisle?

"Come back," I called, but the words wouldn't form. All that came out was the plaintive whine of an animal.

"Zillah, you're unwell. Lean on me."

It was my handmaiden. No, Ellen, her whisper urgent.

"He left," I said.

It wasn't unusual for a performance to leave me feeling strange. But tonight, it was more than this. I felt hollowed out. I sagged into her arms, and when the curtain closed for the interval, she half pulled, half dragged me from the stage.

∞

I opened my eyes to Ellen's troubled face.

"You're back, then," she said and I felt her drop my hand, which she'd been holding. I raised my head slowly and paused while the room righted itself. I was propped up on the wooden chair in our dressing room, chilled and shivering despite the thick woolen blanket on my knees. I couldn't remember how I got there.

"Take this."

I shook my head but Ellen was firm and I ate the stale biscuit she offered, the crumbs gritty in my dry mouth. Barky entered with a cup of small beer and I drank it down gratefully.

"A bravura performance, Amazonia."

"Don't call me that."

"You actresses are always so precious."

Barky rolled his eyes. He may have been joking, but nonetheless I wanted to shake him. He thought I was being a prima donna, but it wasn't that at all. I threw myself into my performances, but since I started headlining, it had felt more and more important to make sure the gap between me and my act was clear. I wanted to explain it, but my mouth felt cottony and I couldn't find the words.

"No need to talk. You did very well tonight," Barky said.

He smiled at me but I saw him glance at Ellen, one eyebrow raised, questioning why I wasn't quite myself.

"I'll call Lord Woodward," he said.

"He's been sending the carriage for her," Ellen said, not troubling to hide the note of resentment in her voice.

"I want her accompanied when she leaves tonight," Barky said.

Vincent, coming to collect me? The thought of him now cut through the fog in my mind, but my limbs still felt floppy and loose. I couldn't let him see me like this.

"Help her, Ellen," Barky said. "Get her cleaned up."

He wasn't bothered about how good I looked for Vincent, but he was always on the alert that one of the audience would work out that I was Amazonia. Without the makeup and the costume and with my hair tied back, the resemblance was slight, but I was the only Black member of the company, and to be fair to him, someone sharp might put two and two together, especially if they noticed my filed nails. It was why Barky always ensured I stowed my costume and Amazonia's effects at the theatre, and had advised me to put on my gloves before I left.

Ellen took charge but the direct order from Barky must have riled her, because now she didn't trouble to be gentle. If I'd been strong enough, I would've pushed her away, done it myself. She was always pettish when Vincent came for me, but I could hardly blame her. As long as she'd been seeing Crillick, he'd never dreamt of sending a carriage for her, let alone picking her up himself. She sponged down my face, and scrubbed my body, wiping away Amazonia with strong strokes that left me feeling raw. When I was clean, she helped me on with my drawers and skirt, buttoned my corset, and scraped back my hair. I'd told her the tight curls weren't meant to be brushed, but she forced her way through the tangles from top to bottom and I ignored the pain as she weaved two plaits and jammed in a handful of pins to stop them unraveling.

"There. Happy now?" she said.

I stood up slowly, testing myself. *Definitely more tired than usual.* My own fault. I'd pushed myself hard, and all for nothing when the African hadn't even stayed to the end to appreciate it. Ah well. He wasn't anything to me. I looked in the small glass and pinched my cheeks to bring out the roses in them. I couldn't let Ellen's jealousy get me down. If Vincent was coming for me, it was important to look my best.

IV

The Language of My Forefathers

Vincent, or Viscount Woodward to give him his full name, was part of Marcus Crillick's set. Crillick often had people in to watch the show from his private box, and Vincent, who had been staying with Crillick since he and his father had a falling-out, frequently joined the fun. On the night Vincent first saw my act, he'd begged Crillick to introduce us. That was back in March, a couple months after I joined the show. I was only third on the bill then but just starting to draw the rave reviews that would see me become the headliner. He wasn't the first to want an introduction to the Great Amazonia, by any means. Crillick usually put my admirers off, however hard they pleaded. He couldn't run the risk of them knowing I was a Londoner, but he was different with Vincent. They'd been friends since school and Vincent had that aristocratic charm about him that meant he always got what he asked for.

Vincent was brown-haired, tall, and dashing. The men of St. Giles were often short, their bodies stunted from lack of food or twisted with carrying heavy loads, but even without the clothes he wore, you could've told that Vincent was quality just from the manner in which he stood. He had an easy way about him. He'd never had to be on his mettle, I suppose. Even without Ellen's warnings ringing in my ears, I knew not to fall in love with him. I'd tried that before with Eustace and it had ended badly. I wasn't willing to risk my heart again.

My act at Crillick's was my ticket out of St. Giles. I had to put my all into that. Too many women had let themselves be distracted by a cut-glass accent and a pretty face. I was determined not to be another. But it was lonely at Crillick's—more so as my success grew and the other performers wanted less and less to do with me. And Vincent was very handsome. More than that, he was kind and he treated me like a lady, though Lord knows it wasn't on Marcus Crillick's account. Still, I just had to keep my wits about me was all.

I stepped out into the narrow corridor and closed the dressing room door behind me. It was dim and gamey where the tallow candles that lined the walls had burnt low. Still shaky, I trailed my hand along the wall for balance as I made my way to the foyer, ready for Vincent to collect me. The foyer was a square room, big enough to hold fifty people as they waited for the doors to open before showtime, with a bar running along one side. The chars hadn't been in to do their cleaning yet and it smelt strongly of spilt beer. The walls were papered with brightly coloured prints of previous shows and star turns. The first one, gaudy in pinks and blues, read CRILLICK'S AMAZING VARIETY, with a drawing of three acrobats. Even though it was a few years ago now, I remembered that show.

I'd been desperate to see it, but I was on my own by that point and all the money I had went on rooms that would keep me off the streets and out of the Blackbirds' clutches. When food felt like a luxury, three whole pennies for a few hours' entertainment was out of the question. Still, that poster kept on calling to me every time I walked past it, and so one night I snuck in around the back of the theatre. In the corridor that I now used myself, I lost my nerve, terrified I might accidentally burst onstage, so I never actually saw the performance. Instead, I lurked just out of sight, ready to flee if anyone came along, listening to the gasps and cheers of the audience and imagining what it was they might be seeing. Crillick's had a different troupe of acrobats now. They were the second act onstage, so I was always in my room getting ready when they were performing, but I made a point of watching them practice for the girl I'd once been, who'd wanted to see cartwheels and kicks and tightrope walking, but hadn't been able to afford it. I moved on to the next poster, which was dominated by a drawing of Aldous in his black cape. The magician had been the main attraction since the autumn of '46, but as Crillick said, the times had changed, people wanted something new nowadays.

It was understandable that my swift rise had put my fellow performers' noses out of joint—that and my colour—but I couldn't do anything about either of them. The better I'd done, the more modest I'd become, but I'd grown tired of trying to make myself smaller, knowing that however humble I was, the dancers and the chorus and the set dressers still wouldn't accept me. I wouldn't get too many chances in this life. When they came along, I had to grab them with both hands. And no one could deny how hard I'd worked for it. The crowds we drew each night proved that I deserved my headline spot, and their fascination with my act knew no limits. Hopefully in time they'd realise backstage that we all benefited when Crillick's was successful, whatever our place on the bill.

I paused before the giant poster that announced THE GREAT AMAZONIA, the biggest one of all. A smaller version was sold in the intermission. My name—*her* name—was picked out in swirly black letters. Dense type explained that I was an exotic plucked from the jungle, a cut-down version of the spiel that the compère gave out before I went onstage. It said that the young queen herself had come to see me. That was cobblers, of course, but Crillick said it wasn't the show but the tale that you told, and he was right.

I felt a tickle at the back of my neck that alerted me to the fact I had company. I'd been too lost in looking at the poster to hear the footsteps. I turned, expecting Barky, but the lean, familiar figure of the stage manager wasn't there. Instead, there stood a broad, upright man in a black hat.

"*Buwa*, Amazonia, *kahunyaina?*" he said.

It was the African.

❧

He was around the same height as me, and his skin was like ebony. His coat was woolen, open just enough so a fine, amber silk cravat poked through. The Black drummers in the regiments, they out-did themselves in their turbans and braided tunics. But this man was no show pony. He looked like a merchant—and a prosperous one at that.

"*Buwa, kahunyaina?*" he said again. Was this the language of my forefathers?

"*Bawo ni ore mi?*"

I shook my head and he tried again.

"*Sisi wami kunjani?*"

"I don't understand."

He was affronted. I couldn't tell from what he'd said but it was there in his eyes and in his tone.

"You're English. Aren't you?"

Strange. I'd never heard someone say it like it was an insult. Something I should be ashamed of. The knot of worry from before the performance rose again, twisting my stomach.

"I should have guessed when I saw you perform," he said. And then a little bit under his breath, but loud enough so I would hear, "*gaffed.*"

"What did you say?"

"I called you what you are—a counterfeit," he said.

I cast a quick look over my shoulder but thankfully there was no one else around. Did this African not understand the danger in what he said, the reaction of the punters if they discovered my deception, not to mention the police?

"You shouldn't go around making accusations like that," I said. "You don't know the trouble you could cause for me, for the theatre."

"You are no African. What have I said that is not true?"

How dare he talk to me like that? I bristled while his eyes raked me, but I did not move. I was accustomed to being looked at by men fascinated by my body, but the African's gaze went deeper, through my skin, right into my soul. I sensed his disappointment.

I shifted to block his view of the poster that stood behind me. Less than an hour before, he had watched me dance Amazonia's dance, but now I couldn't bear to lie to him. I wanted him to see me, Zillah. My eyes burnt with the effort of holding his gaze. There was a small scar beneath his right eye. The result of a fall in childhood, I guessed.

"You speak like a gentleman. Are you not English too?"

"You don't have to be English to be a gentleman," he said.

The irritation in his eyes was gone, replaced by pity. Who was this man that felt he could look down on me? I was the main act at Crillick's Theatre.

"I am a son of Africa," he said as if I'd spoken out loud. "You may be gaffed but I would still help you."

He held out his hand to me but dropped it to his side when I kept my arms folded tight across my chest. What on earth made this arrogant merchant think I needed his help?

"Will you not shake my hand, Amazonia?"

"Don't call me that."

He held up the programme I had seen him poring over while he sat in his seat waiting for the show to start.

"Is that not your name?" He cleared his throat and read in a mocking showman's voice as good as the compère, "'The Great Amazonia—a savage woman from darkest Africa.'"

"My name is Zillah."

He chuckled to himself. "Is that so?"

I didn't know what that meant, and I couldn't bear to ask him. It was impossible to work him out. One minute he seemed angry, the next he was mocking. I hated how he wrong-footed me. I'd learnt to rely on my wits, but when I reached for a retort there was nothing there.

Finally, he stepped away from the poster and leant his elbow on the bar. I breathed easier with a little more space between us.

"We should begin again. Good evening, Zillah. Lucien Winters at your service."

He made a half bow and held out his card. I felt my knees dip as I bobbed, unwillingly, into a curtsy to this man who moments ago had scolded me. There was something about the way he stood, his presence, that demanded deference. The card was printed on stiff white paper with rounded edges. I peered at it but folded my hands behind my back so I couldn't take it from him.

"It says you're the proprietor of Winters the Grocer's."

He nodded and smiled but I looked away again. I'd never known a Black like this. The ex-slaves, I had the measure of them, but this Lucien Winters was something different altogether. This Lucien wore scent; there was a smell of cedar about him or maybe it was danger. I took a step back and then another until I felt the wall against my spine. *Come on, Zillah, you can handle him.*

"Where are you from?" he said.

"Up the road from here." I never mentioned St. Giles if I could help it. People would assume I was a Blackbird—one of the Black criminals that had made the slums their home.

"Where are you really from, originally?"

"Out west," I said, not willing to name Mayfair where I'd been born, but we both knew it was not what he meant. When he spoke again there was the warmth of teasing in his tone.

"Your mother and father, then—where are they from?" He clearly wasn't going to give up and though I usually hated it when people asked me this, I wasn't sure I wanted him to.

"My mother was from Barbados. But I was born free."

Once more, I saw pity forming in his eyes. "I *am* free," I repeated. I wanted him to know it; it was what made me different.

"Mark me, Zillah," he said. "I want you to think about tonight. About the part you play." He held up a hand when I would've interrupted him. "When you have thought on it, I want you to come to the address that is printed on my card. If you come to me, I will save you."

He laughed when I shook my head. The cheek of it. He was acting like I was some damsel in distress. Hadn't he seen my name on the bills outside the theatre and the crowds who came for me? Of course, I was being courted by a viscount too, but something told me he wouldn't be impressed by that.

"I'm sure you'll remember the address," he said, but still he tucked the card into the front pocket of my coat, his hand briefly connecting with the top of my thigh through the layers of material.

Smug bastard. But—*Winters the Grocer's, 41 Charles II Street*. It was already burnt into my brain. Before I could say more, there was the sound of footsteps outside the back door.

Vincent.

Lucien looked toward the door but didn't move. It was strange. I needed him gone before Vincent came in, but part of me also wanted him to stay. He seemed to feel the same.

"What I said, it means 'Greetings, how do you do?'"

"All of it?"

"Yes, in Mende, in Yoruba, and in Zulu. I have made it my business to learn useful phrases and I wanted to see if you had any knowledge of your heritage at all."

Another rebuke, but I didn't snap back like I usually would.

"*Buwa, kahunyaina*," I repeated. I liked the way the words felt on my tongue, I wanted to remember them. Lucien smiled at me then, a real smile that crinkled his eyes at the corners, before he headed for the back door.

"No, not that way," I called. But he'd already gone.

I leant my head back against the wall, tired again. The smell of cedar lingered. My head ached with the encounter, but I had barely time to think on it before I heard again the rumble of Lucien's deep voice and Vincent's Surrey drawl in response.

The back door in the foyer opened out onto an alley that ran alongside Crillick's and went all the way from the Strand to the river. It was where I had sneaked in, in my failed bid to see the acrobats four years before. The performers came in and out that way during the day when Crillick's wasn't open to the public, and Barky often went out there to smoke. Crillick and his friends used it too. Now Lucien had run into Vincent there. I edged toward the door and peered out, quiet so they wouldn't notice me. It hadn't rained for days, but there were puddles on the uneven ground. The alley was so narrow that even the autumn sunshine couldn't squeeze in to dry it out. Vincent blocked Lucien's way. He'd come up from the river, which meant he'd spent the evening at Pascoe's, his club. There was only space to pass if one man would give way to the other. Vincent was an inch or two taller but Lucien was stockier. I didn't doubt he'd had more cause for fighting than Vincent and shuddered as a small thrill of fear ran down my back. I wished Lucien had gotten away before Vincent came. Why hadn't I warned him to use the front entrance? Was Ellen still around? She'd know what to do to stop a scuffle.

"Excuse me," I heard Lucien say, his voice pleasant but no "sir" or "please." Couldn't tell what Vincent was or didn't care. It was hard to see from where I stood, barely daring to breathe.

"What are you doing here? This entrance is for the performers."

I didn't want Vincent to know we'd spoken. *Please don't say we talked, please don't say we talked.*

"I must have gotten a little lost," Lucien said.

Vincent was using his sternest voice, but Lucien was smooth, unruffled.

"Indeed. If you're here for a job, you should ask for a man named Barky," I heard Vincent say. "I'd call him for you, but he'll have gone home by now. You'd best be off and try another day."

"I am no performer, sir." I could hear the laugh in Lucien's voice. His words weren't disrespectful but something about his tone was. It was clear he wasn't cowed by rank. Vincent wouldn't like that. He was used to a tugged forelock—but then Lucien was a gentleman too, of sorts.

"A shame. Strong specimen like you. Be sure to come back if you change your mind."

Lucien was dismissed, but he didn't leave, and once more I felt the dread that had come upon me when the usher asked him to remove his hat before the start of the show.

"Please go," I muttered under my breath. Lucien could not have heard it but he may have felt it because he raised his hat, ready to walk away.

"Good night, Mister . . . ?"

"Viscount. Viscount Woodward," Vincent said.

Lucien bowed low from the waist. I'd seen less elaborate bows on the stage. He was brave to mock Vincent like that.

"Lord Woodward," he said in acknowledgment. Vincent stood to one side and Lucien brushed past him. His footsteps echoed a little and Vincent watched him all the way until he disappeared into the shadows. Did Lucien have any inkling that Vincent and I were involved? It was no business of his, but somehow I hoped not.

"Zillah, what are you doing there?"

"Lord, you made me jump."

It was only Barky. As usual he'd managed to sneak up on me. I wondered how long he'd really been there. Had he seen me talking to Lucien? I'd need to find out, but for now I put my finger to my lips and he peered around to look into the alley.

"The viscount is coming," he said.

"I was in my dressing room. I just got here," I said and he gave a quick nod to show he understood what I was asking.

"Look sharp, then."

He shooed me away and I was just in time to scurry back from the doorway and turn as if I'd only that minute come into the foyer.

"Darling."

Vincent swept through the door and as he came in and pulled it to, the late-night chill blew in with him. Vincent was what I knew. I felt relieved to be back on solid ground again. He was dressed handsomely in a navy tailcoat, and beneath the matching waistcoat his white shirt was crisp. A maroon scarf had been thrown hastily around his neck. He crossed the foyer in two strides to where I stood and caught me up in his arms.

"Are you well?"

I nodded, my head against his chest. Beneath the cigar smoke I could make out the smell of starch on his shirt.

"You're not wearing an overcoat," I said.

"A runner came to the club and said you weren't feeling well so I came immediately."

He pushed me back away from him slightly so he could examine my face. There was concern in his gaze, and I dropped my eyes so he wouldn't see the guilt in them. I'd done nothing wrong by talking with Lucien but Vincent might not see it like that.

"Is there anything I can assist you with, Lord Woodward?" Barky said. On another night he would've melted away into the shadows, but he was still trying to work out what he'd missed between me and Lucien. I prayed he wouldn't give me away.

"Ah yes, Barky. I'm glad you're here. You've been keeping an eye on Zillah for me?"

"Soon as she knew you were on your way, she wanted to wait in the foyer for you, sir. I thought it was best to keep her company."

I looked 'round at him and smiled. I'd have to get him a little thank-you gift for this favour. He was partial to a pinch of snuff —that would do it.

"Good man. There was a fellow I just ran into outside. Something about him I didn't like. This back door must be kept locked, do you hear? There are far too many undesirables about."

Was it only his skin, then, that made Lucien, well dressed as he was, an undesirable? I pushed down the treacherous thought. Vincent was only trying to protect me.

Barky nodded. "Can I assist you to the carriage, sir?"

Vincent looked over at me. "What do you say, Zillah?"

I needed a walk to clear the thoughts that swirled around my head.

"I'd prefer the fresh air, if you don't mind."

"Of course," Vincent said. "Is that all you have for a coat?"

"It's enough," I said. Though the weather had been getting steadily colder, it wasn't as if I was used to sables, but Vincent tutted and unwound his scarf.

"Here, take this." It smelt of him, of cigars and influence and money. It was enough to drive away the remaining hint of cedar on the air. He arrayed me in it like armour. I suppose it was.

"Let us go now," Vincent said. "We will walk along the Strand."

V

A Walk Along
the Strand

The Strand was quiet, no carriages rumbling past, no match girls calling out their wares, nor horses' hooves clip-clopping. Big Ben chimed, and kept going. It was much later than I'd thought. On the opposite side of the street a decrepit old beggar counted out the coppers he'd been thrown. He wore a hat that marked him out as a former sailor. Perhaps he was one of the Blacks that had sailed the slave ships when there had been human cargo to carry. Whatever his past, now he'd be classed as one of the Black Poor that all the newspapers complained about. He looked up and saw us and called out to me but I pretended I hadn't heard. I may have felt some form of curious kinship with Lucien Winters but it didn't extend to this man on the street, whatever he might think. Being born free made me different, and Lucien was set apart by his manner and bearing. I'd never met anyone like him before.

Up ahead another couple strolled arm in arm, but apart from them we had the whole of the Strand to ourselves. We made our way along in silence. I liked our time together most when we weren't talking, when I couldn't hear the accent that said Vincent wasn't for me. Or the stories of the places he'd been where I could never afford to go and where my colour would make me unwelcome if I did. It was in these quiet moments that I felt most confident about the future I imagined we might have together, but tonight was different. Tonight, all I could think of was Lucien Winters saying he wanted to save me.

"Vincent?"

"Hmm?"

"What would happen if it was discovered I was gaffed?" To say it felt like swearing.

"That's such an ugly word, Zillah. Where has this come from?"

"Something I heard tonight at Crillick's. The others were talking about me again," I lied.

"They're jealous of you, Zillah. You should ignore them."

Vincent had little time for my fellow performers. He looked down on them, especially Ellen, even though she and Crillick were in a relationship of sorts. I couldn't help but think it was because she was Irish. He'd called her a Fenian, whatever that meant.

"Would I be in a lot of trouble?"

Vincent stopped short and turned me to face him.

"*Gaffed* is a horrible word, Zillah. I don't want you to use it to refer to yourself again. There's no reason for your secret to come out, is there? It's in everyone's interest to keep it. Marcus wouldn't want it known that his star act wasn't everything he said. They'd call him a con man, maybe even take away his license. There's no one you suspect would give you away, is there?"

I thought of the members of the cast. Of Mikey and Bob who appeared onstage with me. It was certainly in their interest to keep things quiet. But what about Aldous, who used to be top billing before I came along? What of the dancers? I wouldn't put it past Ellen either. I thought of her as a friend but I knew she could be rash, especially if I angered her.

"I wish I could get you away from there," Vincent said. "You can't imagine how much I hate it."

I shouldn't have been surprised at the force in his voice. I knew he wanted me to quit the variety show. Never having had to work himself, he didn't understand why my job, however unusual, was so important to me. From time to time he spoke about our future, but until he reconciled with his father, he had not the money to make his own choices. He didn't even have a place of his own in London. Ever since I'd known him, he'd been staying at Marcus Crillick's house.

"I'll start collecting you personally after every performance. You should wait in your dressing room for me."

"I can look after myself," I said.

"But I want to do that for you."

We were nearing Trafalgar Square. The great fountain was still on, sending plumes of water high into the air.

"You were at the club tonight?" I said, eager to change the subject, to hear about how he had spent his evening.

"I was, and guess who turned up. Crillick. I wasn't expecting him for another week or so but it seems he concluded his business early."

That brought me up short. I'd not missed Marcus Crillick since he'd left three weeks before. Whilst he'd been on business on the Continent, I'd been staying with Vincent in Crillick's house. I'd have to go back to my room at St. Giles now.

"You should still stay with me," Vincent said, as if he knew what I was thinking. "We don't need to go back to meeting at Pascoe's if we want to spend time together."

That was a relief. Being invited into a home rather than Vincent hiring out a room for us at his club had been a welcome surprise that he was serious when he said he saw our relationship growing. Over these last three weeks it had definitely put us on a different footing.

"Marcus knew I was planning to have you over while he was gone. It might even have been his idea," Vincent continued.

It was probably true, but not for the reason that Vincent thought. A friend since their schooldays, he was blind to Crillick's nastiness, his need for power and control. Vincent explained it away as japes or thoughtlessness. If only Vincent had his own house where we could be together.

"Nothing from your father?"

Vincent ground his teeth. I should have known better than to bring up his father when he'd been drinking.

"We are both used to getting our way, but I will not give in to him, however difficult he tries to make things for me."

Ha. Vincent thought he had it hard. We'd met after his father had cut him off. I knew his allowance had been stopped and he wasn't welcome at their London house in Park Lane, but he'd never explained why. Still, he could rely on his friends, and though he stayed with Crillick he still had plenty of money for carriages, for his gig, and for gifts. When I showed Ellen the trinkets he brought me, she said, "You should enjoy it while it lasts. Time may come when you can sell those things."

Ever practical, there was little romance in her, but she did have one blind spot, which I liked to tease her over when we were on good terms.

"Have you ever sold anything that Crillick gave you?"

The look she gave me was so shocked I thought she might cross herself to guard against such an unholy thought.

"That's different, Zillah," she said.

I wasn't sure quite what she saw in him. I was grateful to Crillick for my job but I couldn't bring myself to like him. To me, he was the sort of man you never wanted to be alone with if you could help it, but Ellen didn't mind. She'd called him her "little scrapper" once—his ruthlessness, I suppose, was what she liked the most. If I'd have pushed her, she would have said she saw herself in him, or vice versa. Give Crillick his due, he hadn't come from money like Vincent. His money was pure trade. Ellen thought this made him gettable, but the truth was he wouldn't do anything stupid like marrying a girl as lowly as her; he'd need someone who could sweeten the smell of his background, maybe even someone with a title.

I'd have expected Ellen, sharp as she was, would've seen that. She was quick enough with her advice on how best to manage men. It was something she prided herself on, so I let her have her say. She didn't know about Eustace and that I'd sworn I'd never fall in love again after him.

Like all oracles, Ellen rarely followed her own rules. "Don't be available every time, don't cheek him, don't sleep with him straightaway," she'd said to me when Vincent had first shown an interest. I'd nodded along, trusting myself to know what was best, part of me surprised and grateful that any man could inspire some affection from me, but there was one rule that we agreed on —never get pregnant. Ellen said it would be the fastest way to lose Vincent's favour, but I had other concerns. A baby would mean being dismissed from my job, and I wanted more for a child of mine than to be raised in St. Giles, always worrying about where the next meal was coming from. I loved Mrs. Bradley, the woman who had brought me up, but I still believed that a baby's place was with its mother.

My musings had taken us more or less the whole way to Crillick's house. It wouldn't be long before we were inside in front of a roaring fire. As it had gotten later, it had grown chillier. I burrowed my hands deep into my pockets and felt Lucien's card, rubbed a finger along its rounded corners. The wind was strong. I imagined myself taking the card out, holding it lightly between my fingertips, and letting the wind take it away. But I didn't do it.

‌‌ ∾

Crillick kept his home at 25 Northumberland Avenue. Despite the lateness of the hour, lights blazed from the windows, the servants scrambling to make ready for the early return of their master.

"Go in, Zillah. I want to check that the carriage made it back."

Vincent disappeared around the side of the house, but instead of walking up the steps to the front door as he'd told me to, I waited for him. He didn't think about how strange it would feel for someone like me to use the front entrance, nor the reaction I would get. That I'd be as likely to climb Ben Nevis as I would the five steps to the black-painted door with its imposing lion's-head knocker.

Vincent returned smiling, oblivious to my hesitation.

"All is well. I told Coachman to return to Pascoe's. As Crillick hasn't made it home already, I wager he'll spend the night there and will need it for the morning."

I smiled back at him but inside my heart sank. From tomorrow I'd see Crillick not only at the theatre but when I spent time with Vincent in the evenings. It was too much. I'd have to find a way to help Vincent and his father reconcile so that his allowance would be restored and we could find rooms together.

Vincent led me up the steps. Before he even had a chance to knock, the door opened in front of him. Sikkings the butler bowed low, but when Vincent told him to take my scarf, he held it between the very tips of his fingers as though it were infested. Vincent didn't seem to notice and waved him away when he asked if we wanted anything further.

"The lady and I are retiring to my room and are not to be disturbed," he said. Knowing how Sikkings's mind worked, I felt my face flame with embarrassment. I tried not to kid myself about what it was between me and Vincent, but having spent whole days together in these last three weeks, we'd learnt that we enjoyed each other's company outside the bedroom.

Vincent's room was done out in pleasant greens. There was a desk for him to work at, and I'd taken over the small chaise longue and dressing table. Vincent and I had been playing house in Crillick's absence. In the last day or so, I'd caught myself wanting to think of things as belonging to us. *Silly girl.* Crillick's return made it clear that I could take nothing for granted.

The center of the room was dominated by a large canopy bed.

I undressed and slipped between the covers, for though the fire had been lit, the high ceilings meant it was chill and drafty. The cold reminded me of the various rooms I'd rented in St. Giles, but apart from that there were no other similarities. Vincent climbed into bed after me and swore softly as his foot connected with the warming pan. The servants must've forgotten to remove it. I couldn't help but laugh, but instead of being angered he only slapped at me playfully.

We lay close, drawing from each other's warmth, my head nestled on his bare chest.

"Do you think I'm wrong to play Amazonia at Crillick's?" I said.

Vincent sat up. "You're asking lots of questions tonight, Zillah. I do wish you'd tell me if something has happened to upset you."

"Nothing has happened."

"Then shhh, my love. Let's just be together."

"I can't help thinking about it."

Vincent let out a sigh. "Why shouldn't you play her?"

"It's dishonest, isn't it?"

"It's acting is all. No different from that fellow Aldous and the tricks he performs."

It made sense, what Vincent said, but if I'd been pulling rabbits out of hats, I doubt that Lucien's words would have affected me quite so much.

"Do you think the punters—the audience, I mean—do you think they believe the story about me being from the jungle?"

Vincent yawned widely and I felt his arm snake around my back. His fingertips at the base of my spine were cold and I shivered slightly.

"Of course they do. They wouldn't pay their half shilling to come and see you if they didn't. You shouldn't worry. Crillick will make sure your secret is safe. He won't want it to get out."

This was true. It cheered me somewhat. My fellow actors might feel little compunction about shopping me, but to do so would mean getting on the wrong side of Marcus Crillick and none of them would want that.

"You know what I think? I think you're a princess. Princess Zillah. You cannot deny it has a ring to it."

He sat up straighter and made an elaborate half bow. "Your Royal Highness, *I* am *your* humble servant."

I blinked at him for a moment, then, seeing the joy on his face, decided to play along. I climbed to my feet, wobbling badly on the down-stuffed mattress. Vincent got to his knees and we clung to one another for balance. Once I was steady, I held out my arm as though it were a sword and touched my wrist first to his right shoulder and then to his left.

"Arise, Viscount Woodward."

"But I am already a knight?"

His tone was puzzled. Had I taken the game too far? I made to sit back down, but thinking my ankles had buckled, he held on to them so I could stay upright.

"Steady?" Vincent said.

He was gazing up at me. When I glimpsed the strength of feeling in his eyes, I had to force myself not to look away. The moment stretched, and as I let go of the breath that I'd been holding, his smile broke out again.

"Now you are one of *my* knights," I said. "You will be my private guard?"

"Madam, it would be my honor."

Vincent doffed an imaginary hat while I tried my best not to giggle.

"I solemnly vow to serve you, my lady."

He pulled me down so we were both kneeling. He was only a little taller than me and his grey eyes shone with laughter.

"I beg leave to kiss Her Royal Highness," he said.

"It is granted."

᯽

After he had loved me, we lay in bed and I looked up at the canopy, my eyes following the swirls embroidered into the dark green fabric. As soon as Vincent slept, I would douche myself as a precaution, but for now I was content to lie in his arms.

"You need some time away, Zillah. I'll take you to the countryside and you can forget all about your wretched act. How does that sound?"

It sounded perfect. A day away from Crillick's would do me good. I'd never been to the country before. Maybe it would be just like the scenes on the painted boards I sat before in my dressing room.

"Could we go to a meadow? Somewhere with flowers and a stream?" It wasn't exactly the best time of year for it, but even so I could picture us there.

"Flowers, a stream. I might even be able to rustle up a folly for you." Vincent was nuzzling my ear. Thoroughly sated, he was in the mood to grant me anything.

"We could get a steamer to take us out eastward. We could sail along the River Lea."

Vincent stopped abruptly.

"Why there?"

I'd said something amiss, I could tell from his tone. I turned around, but he looked away stony-faced.

"Ellen said she was going to ask Crillick to take her out that way, that's all. She went once before. We don't have to go there. We could go to Richmond instead, or the gardens at Kew." I was gabbling in my haste to undo whatever it was that I'd done wrong. "You should choose where we go, Vincent, I'm sorry."

When he heard the catch in my voice, his eyes softened.

"There's no need to apologise, Zillah. I just don't like that part of London. I've made it a rule never to go there. Richmond is best. The air on that side of town is sweeter and there are deer in the park."

He lay back down again. When I nestled into him, he put his

arm around me, but made no attempt to break the silence. That was fine by me. I wasn't going to risk saying the wrong thing again.

ↄ

I slept fitfully—perhaps it was no wonder after all that had happened. Lucien Winters had put me off my stroke and then things had gone downhill from there. Crillick back, and then Vincent making strange. It was all too much.

Not that His Lordship seemed too affected by it all. Beside me Vincent slept on, his breaths long and even. Sometimes it irked me that he slept so deeply. You could tell he'd never had to get up and flit at a moment's notice, never had to wonder who might have blundered into his room by mistake because he shared a house with five other families all doing whatever it took to earn their bread. But it was hard to stay irritated by him when he looked as handsome as he did now. His chest rising and falling. What did it matter whether we went east or west down the river? He'd never offered to take me out like this before, and when it came down to it, that was what counted. I'd been holding him at arm's length but it was six months now since he'd first asked me out. Maybe it was time to stop clinging to the past and see if I could love again. Not in that same heedless way I'd loved Eustace. But I liked Vincent and not just for his money.

I climbed out of bed and picked up the clothes he'd thrown on the floor. Mrs. Bradley had been a laundress. It had become a force of habit to notice the degree of starch that had gone into every item of clothing, to protect all garments from unwanted creases, but as I folded his shirt I heard a voice in my ear—my mother's. *Never be a maid*, she'd said, and I let the shirt fall from my hand again. Tonight Vincent had called me his princess. If that's how he saw me now, there was no call to play the servant. My overcoat was draped over the back of a chair. I felt in the pocket for Lucien's card and drew it out. *Winters the Grocer's, 41*

Charles II Street. I knew that road. It was a twenty-minute walk
away. Less if you cut through the park. Vincent stirred and I threw
a quick look over my shoulder, but thankfully he hadn't woken.
He'd have wondered what I was doing with the card and I didn't
want to explain it to him. Whatever had come over me last night
talking to Lucien meant nothing. I tore the card in half, then half
again, and kept going. When it had been reduced to more than
twenty pieces, I threw them on the fire. For a moment I watched
as the flames turned the tiny strips of paper into ash, then I made
my way back to bed.

Vincent rolled over and I cuddled up against him. Stupid to
keep that card when he was so good to me. To think, half-caste me,
in the arms of a viscount. And next week he was taking me out,
right into the countryside, in the daytime too. That meant something, that he was happy to be seen with me. I pressed my lips to
his forehead and he opened his eyes.

"I didn't mean to wake you, I'm sorry."

We lay side by side and I felt his fingers burrow into my hair. I
knew my curls fascinated him. He liked to twirl them around his
fingers. It made me self-conscious, thinking that he'd never seen
hair like mine so close before, but things had been too shaky between us tonight for me to turn away.

"I shouldn't have been short with you earlier," he said.

I waited for him to explain exactly why my suggestion we go
east had upset him, but he didn't and it wasn't the time to push.
Instead, I closed my eyes and focused on enjoying his caresses. I'd
been foolish to let the African disturb me. I didn't need saving,
not when I had my act and Vincent besides. I tried to picture the
meadow that Vincent had described, imagined us together there.
There'd be no trips to 41 Charles II Street for me.

VI

Rehearsal

Crillick's return meant extra rehearsals. When I woke up the next morning there was a note telling me that my day off was canceled and I had to be at the theatre by ten o'clock. Vincent didn't care about Barky's schedule, though. By the time I arrived it was five and twenty past eleven, but even though Barky complained, I let it wash over me. Crillick was back, it was true, but Vincent had called me his princess and promised to take me out; surely that was worth being late for just this once.

The dressing room was empty, but I found Ellen on the main stage. She wore her chemise and her waist-length red hair was pulled roughly into a horsetail. Barky had disappeared for a moment so while I waited for his instructions on which scene he wanted us to practice, I took a seat in the front row on the men's side to watch her. It wasn't the best view in the house—I had to crane my head back to see the whole of the stage—but I could make out the concentration on her face and the embroidery on her bodice. You didn't get that in the dress circle. She was stretching, as I knew she did every day, both before and after the performance. She could've gotten away without it for the parts she played, but "performers must keep themselves limber" was what she'd told me. When it came to her work, she was all business. I had to admire that about her. She practiced her scales every day and I knew she hadn't given up on her own dream of headlining. She was there waiting in the wings for the moment that I faltered, and she had Crillick's ear too. It hadn't stopped him from giving me top billing so far but it meant I had to be constantly on my toes.

She sensed I was there, and looked up, a frown crossing her face. "Well, look who it is. Nice of you to stop by."

"Where is everyone?"

"Gone already. Barky said they could knock off early. The dancers have done their rehearsals, and Aldous. It's only our scene left to do."

"Which one are we doing today?"

There were three different routines that I performed as Amazonia. Blood sacrifice, the one I'd done last night, was the most popular, but there was a war dance too, when Amazonia fought off the dancers led by Ellen. The third was a series of tableaux, static poses against a variety of painted boards. It was the first one that Crillick had put together for me when I was just getting started and needed to build up my confidence.

"You better choose, seeing as you're the one in charge now," Ellen said.

I could see why she was narked. I would've been if it were her that had kept me waiting.

"It was Vincent," I explained, hoping she'd understand.

"You shouldn't let him take liberties with you, Zillah. It's your job he's messing with. You've got to keep them at arm's length for as long as you can. Though I suppose that's a bit late for you and His Lordship."

She would've jumped at the chance of a lie-in with Crillick, we both knew it, but tiresome as her jealousy was, I didn't want a row. Best not to say anything about my day trip with Vincent either. The mood she was in I doubted she'd be pleased to see how our relationship was growing.

"Don't be glaring at me, Zillah. I hope you were careful at least? You know I only say it for your own good."

That, and she couldn't refuse to have a dig. She knew I was careful—you didn't grow up in St. Giles without knowing that a vinegar douche would keep your courses running—but the night with Vincent had left me in too good a mood to be spiteful.

"You must be happy Crillick's back?"

"I'm sure he's missed me. Speak of the devil."

I turned, and there he was, striding toward us.

〜

Marcus Crillick was thickset but not particularly tall. There was a coarse look about him which couldn't be disguised, no matter how much money he spent on tailoring. His hair was fair, with a tinge of red; the whiskers that covered his cheeks connected by a thin moustache. He'd always put me in mind of a fox, especially when he smiled.

"Well, well, well. My two favourite girls," he said by way of greeting. My eyes flickered across to Ellen. I knew she wouldn't like that and, sure enough, her teeth were clenched but she smiled sweetly at him. She knew not to show him her temper; I had no doubt that someone would catch it, though.

"We've been practicing to make sure things were perfect for you," Ellen simpered.

"That's right. I asked Barky to call you in. My trip was very fruitful. I've got lots of new ideas for the show, and some presents too, but first I wanted a reminder of your performance. It's been a while since I've seen it."

"Mikey and Bob aren't here," I said.

"We'll have to manage without them then," Crillick said. Of course, he wasn't that bothered. It was Ellen and me that he wanted to ogle. "Aren't you going to open your gift first?"

He jerked his head at a heavy leather trunk on the left-hand side of the stage. I knelt down before it, unbuckled the straps, and eased back the lid. Layers of tissue paper. There was something delicate in here, but I was hesitant to go further.

"Go on, Zillah," Ellen said. I could tell she was curious but I picked up the sharpness of jealousy in her voice too. I hoped Crillick had bought something for her as well as me.

The first thing I took out was a bone. It was long and thin, the surface yellowy and smooth. A wave of sickness washed over me. *Pull yourself together, Zillah.* It must belong to an animal. More tissue paper. I wasn't sure I wanted to see what else was in there, but I gritted my teeth. The next thing out was a shield made of skin stretched tight over a wooden frame. It was something like a child's kite only without the string. There were stains on it. Surely not blood. But what else could they be? I stood up and hefted it. It was heavy. I reached back into the trunk and drew out a spear. The point was wickedly sharp. Was this what killed the animal whose only remains was a bone? My God, had these things all belonged to someone? Where was that person now? I dropped the items to the floor as if they were burning hot.

"Props to make your act more authentic," Crillick said. "You should be more careful. Those things don't come cheap, you know."

It was back, that feeling that tightened my chest when I was heckled onstage. Crillick called these things props, but they were no fake theatre pieces. They had a history. There was no way I could wield them. I looked from them to Crillick and back again, hating the cruel glint in his eye. Ellen must have noticed how he stared at me because she interrupted.

"Can I give you a song, Mr. Crillick? I've been practicing the aria from *La Sonnambula.*"

"The Bellini? But that's almost twenty years old. I've told you before. That's not your strength. Forget your arias. The bawdy songs are what suit you best. If you want to get to New York one day, you'll need to carve out your own niche."

Ellen smiled gamely but I knew this was the worst thing that he could say to her. She didn't want to sing bawdy songs, but New York was her dream so she wouldn't argue back. Not when I was there. Probably not even when I wasn't. She never complained to him, never pulled him up, no matter what his actions cost her. No doubt she told herself that he was oblivious, but I couldn't help but think he was shrewd enough to see beyond her brave face. He knew when he was hurting her, he just didn't care enough not to.

"Give me the one about the wife who discovers her husband with the maid. A couple of trills from you will give our Amazon just enough time to get into her costume and try out her new things."

He turned to me and moistened his lips, and Ellen's face darkened in anger.

"The paint takes almost an hour, sir," I said. "I wouldn't want to keep you waiting."

Crillick checked his pocket watch and pouted.

"So it does. I suppose I shall have to be a good boy and wait until tomorrow with the rest of the audience. Well, let's have Ellen do her song and then you can make your entrance, at least. It's been a while since I've seen your act."

⁓

It's become my act. That's how I think of it now, but it was mostly Crillick's idea. Open auditions were held at Crillick's Variety Theatre on Mondays and Tuesdays, the days the cast spent on fittings and rehearsals. I'd gone along at the start of the new year, not quite sure what to expect but knowing I needed the money. I'd already been turned away from a handful of more salubrious establishments. That very morning, I'd seen a sign in a milliner's asking for an assistant, but when I inquired the proprietress had taken one look at me, then shooed me away like a stray dog. I'd been out of work since mid-December and things were getting desperate, but I'd heard it said that some of the theatres weren't too fussy about who they took on. It had to be worth seeing if Crillick's had something for me.

I was surprised to learn it was Crillick himself holding the auditions, but there he was and younger than I'd thought, thirty or thereabouts.

"What have we here?" he'd said when I walked in.

He was sitting alone at a round table before the stage. Something about his tone made me want to turn on my heel and leave. But I could see he wasn't the sort of man to show weakness to, so instead I raised my chin and strode right up to him. That made him sit up in his chair.

"I'm Zillah," I said and stuck out my hand for him to shake.

He took it, held it just a little too long. A lady might have snatched her hand back but I sensed he was testing me. I must've passed.

"Oh, that will never do; we'll have to think of something better. You sing, dance?"

I needed this job so I said I did both.

"Show me, then."

My mind was blank. I opened my mouth but no sound came out. *Come on, Zillah.* I started to sway from side to side. It wasn't dancing as such but maybe it would be enough to get me a part in the chorus. Marcus Crillick has a mean streak, but that day he must have been feeling merciful because he didn't let me carry on for too long.

"That's enough of that," he said. I could see his disappointment. He'd formed an opinion of me based on my appearance and I hadn't lived up to it. He reached into his pocket for his tobacco. When he unfolded the leather pouch, I got a waft of wood mingled with cherries.

"I'm an actress more than anything, sir," I said. It wasn't strictly true but I spent enough time wishing I were someone else, and I loved Mr. Shakespeare, knew all the lines. I had Mrs. B to thank for that.

"Are you now? Give me something, then."

"'If by your art, my dearest father, you have put the wild waters in this roar, allay them. The sky, it seems, would pour down stinking pitch, but that the sea—'"

He held up a hand to stop me. "You know Shakespeare, do you?" He seemed bemused.

"Told you I was an actress, didn't I?"

He laughed. Good, I had judged him right. Always better to be saucy with a man like this and above all to keep your guard up.

"I can't see you as Miranda."

No surprise in that. It was a daily struggle to be myself when people didn't know what to make of me. Neither wholly Black nor white, coming from St. Giles but not one of the Blackbirds, no schooling to speak of but able to spout Shakespeare. I've never been one thing nor the other, that's why they couldn't pin me down. So he couldn't see me as Miranda. I knew I wasn't Caliban either but I guessed that would be easier for someone like him to accept. Besides, it would give me a chance to show some spirit.

"'This island's mine, by Sycorax my mother, which thou takest from me. When thou camest first, thou strokedst me and madest much of me, wouldst give me water with berries in't, and teach me . . .'"

I was halfway through when Crillick clapped his hands for me to stop. He hadn't liked it as much as I thought. What time was it? Three o'clock. Still time to try somewhere else if I left quickly.

But Crillick held out his hand. "Get up on the stage, girl. I want to see if you can project."

I'd gotten away with it. What luck! If there was the chance of a job here for me, I had to take it. If I came away without employment today, my only option would be in service. I knew how to do a maid's work—Mrs. B had been a stickler for keeping our tiny space clean—but my very soul revolted against it. Not just because at any time my mistress might find out that I was from the St. Giles slums and fire me for it, but because I'd promised my mother that I would do all I could to avoid becoming a servant, where a woman is dependent on the kindness and restraint of a master. *Come on, Zillah. You can do this.* I almost ran to the three steps that led to the stage. I took my place in the center. To my surprise, it made me feel powerful.

"Start from the beginning," Crillick called up to me.

I began again. The stage was my island; I flung my arms out as I declaimed to show my ownership of it.

"'Had it pleas'd heaven to try me with affliction, had they rain'd all kind of sores and shames on my bare head—'"

"Louder," Crillick said. With each line I delivered, he backed farther and farther away. It was like he had my voice on a chain in his hands because, as he stepped back, he pulled more and more out of me. My words soared, they filled the space. If the roof-scrapers had been in, filling the cheap seats up in the gods, they would have heard me. By the end I was quite spent and crouched down for fear I would faint. I had no idea where this performance had come from.

Crillick clapped heartily as he walked back toward me.

"Very good. Very good. Wholly unexpected, but I have to say you do it well."

"Are you planning to put on a play, sir?"

I'd walked past Crillick's Variety Theatre enough times to know it wasn't famous for its classical acting. It had acrobats, a magician named Aldous, dancers, and some popular comedians. Crillick put his head to one side and stroked his chin, looking wilier than ever.

"I have something a little different in mind. Something new.

You're quite tall, aren't you, girl, well built. Lift up your skirt." I froze. I knew what they said about actresses. I wasn't that desperate. Not yet.

Crillick was looking at me expectantly. He must have read my face, however, as he sighed impatiently. "Only to the knee."

I did as he said, wondering what it was he had in mind for me. The elastic that I'd used to hold up my stockings had left a ring of dents in my skin.

"Good legs," Crillick muttered to himself. "Tell me, have you ever been to Holman's House of Wonders?"

I laughed to myself. As if I'd ever had the money for that. A whole shilling for an hour's show. I knew what it was, though. I'd often walked past it, the big building that took up one whole corner at Piccadilly Circus, with its curtained windows. At minutes to seven there was always a queue outside. Sometimes it stretched for two hundred yards or more. Men and women and their carriages waiting a little farther down.

"It's a freak show," I told Crillick.

"That's right. Lot of money in freaks nowadays."

"But there's nothing wrong with me."

"You said you were an actress. Can't you play the part?"

&

Things have changed now, of course, but back then there were three sorts of freaks on the London stage. There were the ones that were born that way: the dwarfs and the giants and the ladies who would be the very pattern of femininity if it weren't for their beards. Then there were self-made ones. Men who'd crippled themselves to make money begging or the ones who'd drawn over their bodies with needles to make pictures from their scars. And finally, there were the exotics. The cannibals from the jungle with their spears and poisoned darts. Obviously, I was none of these. What Crillick was asking me to become was a fourth variety, a gaffed freak. Someone who was just pretending.

He saw it didn't sit right with me. I could tell because his voice started to sound coaxing.

"It could be your greatest role, Zillah."

It would be my only role but no need for him to know that. He didn't strike me as a man you wanted to tell your secrets to. Besides, he didn't give me a chance. He hefted himself up onto the stage and patted the boards to show I should sit down beside him. I did as he said, leaving a gap between us, but it wasn't long until he'd shuffled closer, his thigh pressing against mine. I wrapped my arms in front of my chest and looked straight ahead. I could feel his eyes boring into me but I didn't turn to look at him.

"You were a warrior," he said. "No, not just a warrior . . . a *queen*, a savage queen, with a whole tribe to worship you. I think you were captured in the jungle—no, that's not right. You were injured, and two explorers found you and brought you to England."

"People will know it's a lie."

"I'm not so sure of that," Crillick said.

As much as I wanted to argue with him, he was probably right. For some reason exotics had become all the rage among the quality. It made no sense to me. There were hundreds, thousands of Blacks in London, especially down by the docks. But that wasn't what the people wanted. Your common or garden Black was no good and, to many, half-castes like me were even worse. I'd had enough dirty looks and been denied enough jobs to know that. It was the savages they yearned for.

"What if they find out it's a lie?"

I'd spoken more to myself than to him, but Crillick heard and answered sharply, "That *will not* happen, Zillah." He stared at me hard. "It must never happen, you understand."

I nodded, a bit uncertain, but he schooled his face into a smile as if he'd realised he was scaring me.

"There'd be consequences, my girl. For you, for me. But you shouldn't let it trouble you. Remember that there are no lies in theatre, only performances. You must make the audience believe."

I came to remember that conversation many times, but I don't want to get too ahead of myself. Back then Crillick got up and walked around me. I heard the click of his knees as he crouched on his haunches at my shoulder. I should've just jumped down from the stage, but it didn't occur to me then, even though I didn't want him where I couldn't see him. Instead, I reminded myself how badly I needed this job, forced myself not to turn around when he stood behind me, even when he reached out and stroked my hair. It was plaited and pinned. I felt his fingers penetrate the curls. He tugged until he broke their resistance, there was the pattering of hair grips falling to the floor, and I felt his fingertips against my scalp as he drew his hand down from the crown to the base of my neck. I had to turn. Too close. His lips were moist and slightly parted. The cherry smoke from his pipe lingered on his breath. If I tried to move, he'd grab me. In any case, the door was too far. I wouldn't make it.

"Could she be called the Great Amazonia?" I'd said.

I needed to say something, anything to distract him. That was the first thing that popped into my mind. I didn't know where I'd heard it. I liked it for the z, like in my own name, but different. I didn't want this savage to be known as Zillah.

"What's Africa got to do with the Amazon?" Crillick had said, but when I insisted, he'd let me keep it. "It's close enough, I suppose. Besides, the punters won't know any better than you, will they?"

I knew he was laughing at me, even if I didn't know exactly why. But I had to make my own mark somehow.

ے

Ellen had finished her song. Crillick's hand claps brought me back into the moment. He called over to me.

"Come on then, Amazonia. It's your turn."

He sat back in his seat with his arms behind his head and his left ankle resting on his right knee. Slowly I picked up the shield and the spear. Every fiber of my body protested against it, but what could I do?

"That's right," Crillick called up to me. "Go offstage and then I want you to burst on. Maybe some dancing."

It was what I did in my performance. So why did it feel so difficult now? *Come on, Zillah. It's just a few extra props.* But it wasn't. It was Crillick, eager to see me perform, Ellen looking sullen, and the things in my hands. Crillick was sitting in row C. That was where Lucien Winters had sat. *Get on with it, Zillah.* I took a deep breath, ready to let out Amazonia's war cry, when I heard Crillick say, "What's this?"

His voice was irritated. I stepped back out where I could see him. Barky was at his side bearing a note. Crillick read it and the look of annoyance on his face changed to a sly smile.

"Very well. I'll leave now." He called out, "I'll be in my box to see you soon, Zillah."

My body sagged with relief and I let the shield and spear fall to the floor with a clatter. Crillick looked up sharply at the noise, but said nothing as he shrugged on his coat.

"Thank you for getting this message to me so quickly," he said to Barky. "It is excellent news."

Barky handed him his hat. He was ready to go now.

"I'll see you soon. There's a surprise for you in this note."

Ellen walked to the stage. "Goodbye," she called out, but Crillick was already gone, the doors at the back of the auditorium swinging in his wake.

"Did you hear that? He's got me a surprise." Ellen turned to me, a look of challenge in her eyes. I was happy for her to claim Crillick's remark. I'd had enough of his gifts. There was nothing I wanted more than to think he had been addressing her, but something told me it was me he had spoken to.

"You're welcome to be on your way, girls," Barky said. "I only called you in for Crillick but there's no need to stay now he's gone."

He walked away and it was just me and Ellen again.

"I liked your song," I said. "Crillick seemed very pleased with it."

She gave me a curt smile. "Don't patronise me, Zillah."

"I was trying to be nice."

"Well, don't bother. I don't need it."

Ellen stalked away. It seemed like we were at odds again and Crillick had only been back a day. She was annoyed with him and taking it out on me. It was definitely just as well I'd said nothing about Richmond. She would've been fuming.

I sighed to think of myself back at St. Giles, but in just a few moments Crillick had forced me to remember why it was I couldn't live with him. Better the dirt and grime of the rookery than having him letch on me. There was nothing I could do about it when I was at work, but I didn't have to put up with it outside of that. I'd need to invent a good excuse for Vincent—he wouldn't want me to go—but if I stayed Crillick might come between us, and I wasn't having that, not when he'd already driven a wedge between me and Ellen.

VII

A Handbill for the Black Poor

It was still light when I left Crillick's so I wrapped a scarf around my hair as I hit the Strand and kept my head down until the theatre was a good five hundred yards behind me. I barreled along, only half hearing the muttered curse of a costermonger as I brushed past him, but I couldn't outrun the feelings that swirled around my head. I always looked forward to my day off on a Thursday, but being called in for the extra rehearsal had spoiled it. It was Crillick that had unsettled me. The props he had bought and his eagerness to see Amazonia had made me feel unclean. I knew Ellen had seen the way he looked at me. How could she stand it? She wasn't the only one, though. Vincent overlooked his friend's bad behavior too. *But Crillick hasn't changed*, came the voice in my head. True, he'd always made my skin creep. If I was honest with myself, he wasn't the only thing that had thrown me off, so what was it? *Lucien Winters*. I'd ripped up his card but he was still in my thoughts.

Until Lucien had questioned me, I'd been able to ignore the slight discomfort I'd been feeling when I performed, but with the return of Crillick and his wretched props, my unease had crystallised. I'd worked hard for this and now it was tainted. I needed to keep my focus. I was earning enough to make my own way. When I had as much money as Lucien, maybe I'd be able to afford to think on these things more deeply.

"Excuse me, miss. Excuse me."

The voice sounded officious and my stomach flipped. *Keep going, Zillah. He might not have meant you.*

"Miss, I'd like to talk to you."

I picked up my pace, but he only called out again. Couldn't be anything to do with the theatre. I was well away from it now. No, it was probably a bobby wanting to feel powerful. It wouldn't be the first time I'd been stopped for just going about my business in an area where I was one of few that looked like me. I stopped and waited for the man to catch up to me, knowing there was little point in making a scene. His hand on my shoulder was heavy but as I turned to face him it wasn't the police officer I'd expected but an earnest-looking man in a suit. Just a do-gooder. I could have cried with relief. Sure enough, he pressed a handbill on me.

"There's a lecture at Exeter Hall the Tuesday after next, miss, the first of October. It's something you might be interested in. I do hope you'll consider it."

It wasn't often someone called me "miss." Certainly not a gentleman like this one. I looked down at the handbill. The black letters swirled and righted themselves. BLACK POOR, the headline read. I thrust the piece of paper back at him.

"I'm not interested."

He looked at me askance, as if I couldn't know my own mind.

"It's about Sierra Leone, miss, on the Grain Coast of Africa."

I didn't care what it was about. The title proved it was not for me. This man with his sad eyes thought I was one of the Black Poor, did he? If only he knew the truth.

"Let me call over one of my colleagues. Perhaps he can tell you a little more about it," the Do-Gooder said.

He looked over his shoulder and it was then that I saw Lucien

Winters. He was talking to a Black man in beggar's clothes and with no shoes on. Thankfully he hadn't noticed me.

"I've got to go," I said.

I didn't want to see Lucien right now. Not when I was feeling so jangled. I wondered how long he'd been in the area. He must've been giving out handbills when he saw the posters advertising Amazonia's performance. I started to walk away and the Do-Gooder kept pace with me for a couple of strides.

"You're sure you can't stop for a moment? There is a lady you could speak to instead if you could wait just one minute. There are plans for a settlement and support will be given. At least keep hold of the information, won't you?"

I stuffed the handbill in my coat pocket to appease him and at last he dropped back and let me go. As soon as I turned the corner, I'd chuck it. I might be one of the Black Poor to the Do-Gooder, but that wasn't how I saw myself and it wasn't how I wanted Lucien Winters to think of me either. Lectures, settlements, Sierra Leone. Whatever it was all about, it was nothing to do with me.

Breakfast
with Crillick

A week had passed since Crillick's return. Mercifully, he'd
been largely absent from the house, out on business in the
daytime and at his club of a night. It meant I could continue to
put off my return to St. Giles, but whenever he was around, I was
reminded that I needed to be on my way soon, however hard it
would be after the luxury of Northumberland Avenue.

I'd managed to avoid being alone with him, but the house felt different when he was in it. Crillick was so brash it rubbed off on the
servants. The undercook's grumblings could be heard even when
the kitchen door was closed. The maids shouted to one another as
they went about their chores; even the fires crackled louder. It was
as though the house had slept while Crillick was away, and now he
was back, it had roared into life. The noise left me feeling edgy. I'd
gotten too used to the calm and quiet of life with Vincent. His low
voice, the expensive swish of his fine clothes, the way everything
he touched seemed to yield to him. I supposed it was for the best,
though, as I couldn't afford to get too soft. A girl like me had to
keep her guard up. But today wasn't the time to be worrying about
that. It was my Thursday off and soon Vincent and I would be in
Richmond, for a wonderful day, just the two of us.

I walked along the corridor and pushed open the door to the morning room. There were Crillick and Vincent seated at the heavy oak dining table. They were deep in conversation, their heads bent over a massive sheet of blue paper, and I paused on the threshold, too shy to interrupt. Crillick sat at the head of the table. I'd known him to be on horseback but he was dressed for riding in a tweed coat with brass buttons. The outfit looked new and he shifted from time to time as if to stretch out the seams. I thought of Mrs. Bradley and what she'd say if she were here. *Don't want to spill any grease on fabric like that. Nightmare to get out.*

Vincent's smile when he glanced up and saw me gave me the courage to walk into the room. I knew I looked well in my new pink carriage coat and the expression on his face confirmed it. He'd bought me this, and an emerald hairpin, in the last few days. He always chose bright colours for me because he said they set off the shine of my skin. I wasn't sure about that, but maybe I didn't need to worry about the effect that Crillick's return would have on him as much as I had. It was clear he wanted me just as much as ever. Our trip to Richmond could be another step forward in our relationship. It was there in Vincent's eyes as he stood up to pull out a chair for me.

"Good morning," he said out loud as I sat down, and then, a little quieter so only I could hear him, "my exotic princess."

The paper Crillick and Vincent had been looking at was almost see-through. It took up practically the whole of the table and was covered in the sort of neatly ruled lines you only get with a sharpened pencil. Squares, triangles, and one or two words. I twisted my neck trying to read them upside down but Crillick saw me and rolled the paper up, tying it tightly with a piece of black ribbon. He wagged a finger at me.

"All in good time," he said. As if I should care what was on it.

Vincent summoned the butler with the merest nod of his head. I'd been on the receiving end of a gesture like that myself once or twice. That was how they got things done, the rich: all nods and winks. Vincent could achieve more by raising an eyebrow than I could've done with an army at my command. I determined to enjoy the bowing and scraping from Sikkings, however grudging it was. Might as well make the most of it, especially if it wasn't going to last too much longer. I moved my elbows off the table as Sikkings laid a place for me: napkin, knives, forks, and spoons, one after another.

"Just tea," I told him when he offered me a drink. He was lucky I wasn't petty; it would have served him right if I'd been demanding all sorts, seeing how it galled him to treat me like a lady.

Smoked salmon, cold ham, eggs, and a wooden board of cheeses, and all before ten o'clock. There was something shocking in such a feast. Back in St. Giles I would have eked out this amount of food for a week, but Crillick wasn't one to do things by halves. I helped myself and let the talk between him and Vincent wash over me.

"We're going to get left behind if we don't make some changes. The frogs are way ahead of what we have here," Crillick said.

"They have villages, you say?" said Vincent.

His grave expression was at odds with Crillick, who was almost bouncing on his chair with excitement.

"Whole villages, and not just one of each type but three or four men and women, children too. There's money in it."

"But that is not what you went there for?"

"Oh, no. That can come later. There's another road that I'm much more interested in, but I won't say too much, old man. All will be revealed."

Crillick looked up at me and gave a sly smile.

"Pretend you've heard nothing, Zillah. I'll be throwing a party on Sunday evening and nothing should get in the way of what I have planned. I told you I had a surprise."

So the comment he'd made at last week's rehearsal had been aimed at me and not Ellen. I could tell he was in the grip of his new scheme. An act, no doubt, but how it would fit into our current show, I could not even guess. Vincent didn't seem to know too much of it either, but I wished I'd acted a little more grateful for the props. If I lost top billing so soon after gaining it, my fellow cast members would love it. I'd have to find a way to get ahead of what was happening. Maybe Barky would know more. Perhaps this had to do with whatever the note was he'd brought Crillick that day at the theatre.

"I'll be seeing your little friend tonight," Crillick said to me.

I smiled awkwardly. He may have been trying to make me jealous, but in truth I was pleased for Ellen that she'd be seeing him soon. I knew it had been bothering her that he hadn't sent for her since his return.

"We'll all be here tonight, then?" Vincent said.

Crillick was scornful. "Oh, no. None of that. I'll take her to Pascoe's. Capital service there."

I felt a pang for Ellen that Crillick wouldn't have her at his house. No wonder she got snippy that my relationship with Vincent had moved past that stage, especially seeing as how she and Crillick had been together so much longer than us.

"They keep a room for me," Crillick continued. "Alexander was there last night. He asked after you. I told him I was planning a soirée for Sunday evening, said he was welcome to bring his sister along with him. Ma Alexander will be there too, you know."

"Oh?" Vincent said.

He sounded disinterested but he'd clenched his jaw and the tips of his ears had reddened. I'd heard him mention Alexander before. He'd told me he was a friend from Oxford but maybe they'd fallen out, for he seemed none too happy that he'd be at Crillick's party. Not just Alexander, his whole family. Vincent had never said anything about a sister. I wondered what Crillick had planned. He often had get-togethers but usually only for the gentlemen. He must have something special in mind if there were going to be ladies present.

"Your tea, madam," Sikkings hissed from just over my shoulder, but before I could answer he'd already started to pour. I wasn't sure I was hungry—the smell of the grease was turning my stomach a bit—but I picked up my fork. There'd been too many times without dinner for me to waste a meal.

Sikkings bent down and briefly whispered at Crillick's ear. Whatever he said made Crillick smile.

"Good man, exactly what I wanted to hear. Have the carriage brought 'round forthwith."

The butler clicked his heels and melted away.

"Come, Woodward, we have business," Crillick said, throwing down his napkin and pushing back his chair from the table.

Vincent shook his head, looking meaningfully at my plate, but Crillick was unrepentant in the face of the silent reprimand.

"Zillah's a big girl. She can eat alone. Besides, business waits for no man."

Vincent himself still had a full cup of coffee to drink. I waited for him to explain that we were off to Richmond today. Instead, he avoided my eyes.

"Right you are," he said and pushed away his plate, ready to leave. My mouth was too full of scrambled egg to allow for protest but Vincent had seen my hurt expression.

"Go ahead, I'll follow shortly," he said to Crillick.

"The carriage will be 'round in five minutes," Crillick said. He rose and walked over to the door. "You're looking very done up today, Zillah. I hope you have something nice planned."

I heard him chuckling to himself as he disappeared down the corridor. He'd known we had plans, the bastard. How could Vincent let Crillick get away with it?

Once Crillick had left, Vincent bent down to me and rested his forehead lightly against mine.

"You didn't forget, did you?" I said.

I could see he hadn't. More like he'd chosen to put it out of his mind when Crillick needed him. He could lie to himself all he liked but I wasn't fooled.

"Did we say something about Richmond?" he said.

Just like that, as if it were just a day trip. Maybe that's all it ever had been to him and I had read too much into it.

"I don't think we'll be back too late. We can go out this afternoon instead," he said.

There'd be no point by then. Richmond was a good hour from Westminster at least, and the days were already starting to draw in. Vincent tried to take my hand, but I snatched it back and turned away when I felt tears of frustration form in my eyes, annoyed for letting myself care so much. Vincent's hand caressed my cheek and gently he turned me back to face him.

"Come now. Don't upset yourself. What about if we go next week instead? I can send to Fortnum and Mason for a picnic?"

The thought of one of those little hampers dampened down some of my anger and made me see sense. I should try to be more reasonable. Crillick was only just back and we'd been staying in his house. To complain that he wanted to spend time with Vincent could only make me seem churlish.

"Will you order the beef tea?"

"My love could have champagne or even game, prawns, or poultry in aspic. Instead, she wants beef tea."

It hadn't even occurred to me to ask for those things. What did I want with game?

"Beef tea will do just fine. I've had a hankering for it lately."

"Then that is what you'll have."

Vincent placed a kiss on top of my head.

"I'll make it up to you, Zillah, I promise. And we'll be together tonight," he said.

This was my chance to ask him about Alexander but there was a commotion in the hallway and Crillick poked his head in at the door.

"Come, man, don't want to keep the horses waiting."

Vincent tensed obediently and prepared to leave.

"We'll speak later," he said to me, and with a final kiss he was gone.

I trailed my fork through the scrambled eggs. The pieces stuck together and my stomach turned, my appetite gone. Sikkings re-entered with the maid and the two of them set to clearing the table, not caring that I'd yet to finish.

"I imagine you'll be more comfortable in the kitchen, madam."

If I told Vincent about these slights, the man would lose his job. But he was counting on the fact that I wouldn't, and of course he was right. Besides, it *was* much easier for me in the back rooms or the servants' quarters, where I was less of an outsider. I was never truly comfortable in the morning room. I rose and left, dragging my feet as I made my way down the corridor and up the stairs to the first-floor room I shared with Vincent. The housemaid, Grace, would've been in the kitchen, and sweet as she was, I wanted to be alone.

Shutting the door behind me, I threw myself down on the bed. My special outfit chafed against my skin. I closed my eyes, but I had too much pent-up energy to stay mooning about the house, and after a minute I sat back up. From what Crillick had said, it seemed like the spoiled day trip was the least of my worries. I didn't like the sound of the party he'd planned at all. It meant something for my act, I was sure of it. Barky had to know if my position at the theatre was under threat. I'd go down to Crillick's and ask him.

I fingered the hat that Vincent had bought me. A curved feather poked up from its brim, orange and white with a rounded glossy black tip. He'd told me it was from a lyrebird. I said I'd never heard of one but he explained it was wild and exotic just like I was. What was there between him and Alexander's sister? He'd looked too sheepish for there not to be anything. *Got to be more careful. Vincent was lenient with you today, but it won't do to show him too much of your temper*. He knew I wasn't the dutiful type, of course. It was one of the things he liked about me, but it was a fine line to tread.

I went to the wardrobe, ready to change back into my usual clothes, but holding up the dull brown serge of my coat against the pretty pink fabric gave me pause. Such a shame to waste this outfit, especially when I'd managed to get my hair just so. I might as well wear it to the theatre. Barky wouldn't care—he never noticed what any of the girls wore—but I knew it would make one or two of the dancers jealous. Maybe even Ellen. She was supposed to be there today. I put on the hat and dabbed a little scent at my temples.

Outside it was a little chillier than I'd expected. Not really picnic weather at all, and I was glad I'd worn my overcoat too. Maybe it was as well that we hadn't gone to Richmond. I burrowed my hands in my pockets and felt a piece of paper. I drew it out and recognised it as the handbill that had been pressed on me as I'd walked back from rehearsals the previous week. I'd forgotten all about it. When the Do-Gooder had given it to me, I hadn't gotten beyond the headline, but now I paused to read it. Sending Blacks to Africa, that's what it was about. I bristled. As soon as I'd seen the headline, I'd known it wasn't for me, and I'd been right. What I couldn't fathom was why Lucien Winters was one of the people handing these out.

A little way behind me I heard the chimes of Big Ben. Still only eleven o'clock. Barky wouldn't thank me if I interrupted him in the midst of rehearsals. Best to try and catch him when the performers took their break around lunchtime. That meant I had a couple of hours, and Charles II Street where Lucien kept his shop was not far from here. I could satisfy my curiosity about him and the scheme for the Black Poor in one fell swoop. A little visit couldn't hurt if no one found out about it.

IX

A Visit to
Charles II Street

Charles II Street was just off Haymarket so the walk from Crillick's house took less than twenty minutes. Close as it was, I'd never been there. Usually, I tried to avoid this part of town. It wasn't that it held memories as such—I'd been young and my recollections were hazy—but it felt strange knowing that I had once lived around here when my mother was in service. Maybe once I'd known the name of the road, but I didn't now, and since Mrs. Bradley had died, there'd been no one I could check with, even if I'd wanted to.

The house had been tall, five stories at least. That much I could recall. I'd played a game, seeing how fast I could run up and down the back stairs before the second housekeeper shouted at me for making too much noise. We hadn't gone out much, hadn't been allowed to. *Don't dredge up the past, Zillah.* Whatever had happened then, I was walking around freely now and in a fancy outfit no less.

I walked along past number 19, number 30. As I got closer, I slowed down. It wouldn't do to arrive glowing and breathless. *What does it matter if you're not trying to impress him?* Butcher's, milliner's, and there it was just as he'd said, a double-fronted shop with his name on the sign above the door in gilded letters. I'd never known a Black to have his own shop, especially in such a nice part of town. Who was this Lucien Winters, really? He certainly wasn't one of the Black Poor that his handbill had been addressed to. But then neither was I, and though we'd shared barely a moment a week and a half ago, it felt important that he knew that. I couldn't think of another reason for him to feel sorry for me. I set my shoulders and went in, determined to satisfy my curiosity.

Inside, the shop was cool and a little dark. It reminded me of Crillick's cook's store cupboard with its smell of tea and coffee and spices. There were two mahogany counters. The one to the left was for everyday things like beeswax and brimstone and lampblack. The other was directly opposite the front door, packed with jams and pickles and dried fruits stacked up behind it, and standing there was the shop's owner. He had his head bent down over a ledger and I coughed loudly to get his attention.

"Excuse me, madam—" he began and then stopped. He'd recognised me.

"Good morning, Mr. Winters. I was passing your shop and thought I would stop in."

I made a show of walking around, inspecting the goods he had on display. I'd never afford anything like this on my own wages, but there was no need for him to know that. Let him think I always wore kid boots and hats with feathers in them and could buy what I liked. It would teach him for thinking he could rescue me.

"What may I get for you, madam?"

So formal, but I could tell from the half smile on his lips that he remembered me. I hadn't thought of buying anything, though. Did I even have any money on me? I cast a quick glance around. Everything looked expensive, but how galling if he knew I'd come in just to see him.

"I'd like some sugar, please," I said, the first thing that came to mind.

"I'm sorry, we do not stock that here."

A funny sort of grocer's that didn't stock sugar, I thought, and then it dawned on me. It was a remnant from all the protests over the slave trade. Lucien stepped out from behind the counter and removed his white apron.

"You're looking very well, Miss . . ."

"I told you before to call me Zillah. It's all the name I need." I raised my chin, ready to stare him down if he asked me how come, but was relieved when he didn't. Any surname would mark me out as someone's possession. Because I was free, I chose to go without.

"Ah yes, of course."

"Why do you smile to hear it?"

"Because it means shade, shadow, darkness. I wonder who named you."

That felt too personal. He could wonder all he liked, but it was less than none of his business.

"What does your name mean?" I shot back. It didn't seem to rile him as it had me, but I think he got the message. He didn't answer, though.

I looked down at the counter before me. A tray of marchpane shaped into tiny fruits caught my eye.

"Are you sure you won't pick something out for yourself? It would be my gift," Lucien said. "Anything you want."

I was no stranger to a gift from a gentleman, but when Vincent bought me things, he consulted his own taste. It was a bit of a thrill to choose for myself. I bent down closer to get a better look at the sweets. There was an apple, a pear, a peach, all hand-painted down to the tiniest detail. Then I made my mind up.

"One of these," I said, pointing to a strawberry.

Lucien reached into the counter and drew one out for me. He would have placed the sweet in a bag but I stopped him.

"I'd like it now."

I pulled off my right glove, held out my hand, and he placed it in my palm. For a brief moment his fingers connected with mine. We both stared at the strawberry as I raised it to my lips and bit into it. The taste of almond exploded into my mouth, and I looked up just in time to see him turn away.

"It is my usual custom to take a walk around the square at this time. Would you like to join me?"

I hadn't heard him mumble before, or maybe it was just because he was facing in the opposite direction, reaching for his hat and coat, which hung on a stand near the door.

This was taking a chance. All well and good coming to see his shop, but was it wise to go for a walk with him? *Careful, Zillah.* But while my head said one thing, I heard my voice say out loud, "Yes. I don't have long, but a walk would be pleasant."

≈

We walked down the road, crossing over Haymarket, and on until we reached St. James's Square. Through the glossy black railings that surrounded it, I saw neat lawns and flower beds of lilac-petaled pansies and bell-shaped salvias. I never usually went into places like this. The gate, the railings with their spikes were, to me, a warning to keep out, but if Lucien noticed he wasn't troubled by them.

"I find a turn around this time sets me up for the afternoon," he said.

I nodded, only half attending, my thoughts returned to the comment he had made about my name. Shade, shadow, darkness. My mother wouldn't have chosen that for me. Compared to hers, my skin was fair. Did that mean it was my father who had picked it? A little joke he'd indulged himself with, perhaps?

I'd stopped without realizing it and Lucien looked at me with concern in his eyes.

"Are you well, Zillah?"

"I was just thinking, that's all."

He waited for me to say what about but I didn't feel like telling him. I didn't like to talk about my mother because it forced me to think of how she'd abandoned me. Mrs. Bradley always told me I shouldn't see it like that. She said that all my mother had wanted was to do her best by me. She was probably right, but that didn't stop it from hurting.

Lucien led me to a bench set a little back from the path.

"You find it painful to think about your mother?"

How did he know that?

"I was born free," I said. It was a reflex action but Lucien didn't seem impressed by it.

"You told me that before," he said.

I didn't like his tone.

"You were a slave, then?" I threw back at him.

"I was."

The way he said it, so matter-of-fact, took the wind out of me. He could see that.

"It's nothing to be ashamed of, Zillah."

Wasn't it? How could it not be?

"I . . . My . . . my mother was a slave." There. It was out. I'd never told anyone before, never said it aloud.

Lucien nodded, as if this wasn't news at all. "She came from Barbados, you said."

"She did, and she worked in a house not far from here." It was my voice but it sounded like someone else speaking and from far away. A slammed door, a walk up New Oxford Street, half running, looking back over our shoulders, and my gloved hand in hers, clammy from being held too long.

"You lived nearby?"

"I grew up in St. Giles. I've . . . I've lived there most of my life."

Not with my mother, though. When I was seven years old, she'd taken me to the house of her friend Mrs. Bradley and left me there. I hadn't seen my mother since. Didn't even know whether or not she was alive. I wasn't enjoying this conversation. I'd lost control of the thread, and I preferred it when I was the one asking all the questions.

"Tell me about Sierra Leone," I said.

"It's a country on the west coast of Africa. The capital is Freetown."

Freetown. I liked the sound of that.

"I hear that's where the government want to send the Black Poor," I said, not wanting to let on that I'd seen him giving out the handbills.

"Not just the poor. It's open to anyone who wishes to go. I have been distributing information on behalf of a philanthropic committee, with some other concerned people. Had I known you might be interested, I would have brought one with me."

He spoke faster than in our previous conversations, his face more animated. He was excited about this scheme, so what was I missing?

"The government is paying passage for as many as want to go and will give support for three months on arrival besides. They're providing lessons in Mende, clothes, tools, whatever is necessary. You should consider it."

"I don't need handouts, thank you."

"That's not what it is at all, Zillah. The payment is an acknowledgment of the restitution that is owed to Black people in this country. There is a lecture this coming Tuesday at Exeter Hall. You should consider attending. There are people I could introduce you to. One woman in particular I would like you to meet is a Quaker by the name of Elvira Masterson."

I hadn't been planning to go when I read the handbill, but now that he was inviting me maybe there was something in it. To think, he wanted to introduce me to people. I felt myself smiling back at him, caught up in his enthusiasm, but I wasn't going to make any promises that could give him the wrong impression. I'd only come on a whim and would have to rush if I still wanted to catch

Barky on his break and find out more about what Crillick had planned for his party. I stood up and smoothed down my dress.

"I'd best be getting back."

"Not to work?"

"Actually, I have Thursdays off."

"You're still performing at that theatre, though?"

"I am."

"I told you to come to me when you'd thought about the role you play. Have you done so?"

"I didn't come looking for you. I told you, I was just passing."

He caught my eye and held it. I had to look away. "The offer still stands, Zillah."

"I'll think about it."

It was like he was challenging me, but for once I didn't know what else to say. We stood opposite each other. The moment called for something but I wasn't sure what. I held out my hand to him. Vincent would have kissed it but instead Lucien shook it, firm as if we'd concluded a business deal, like I was his equal.

"I'll let you be on your way."

"Yes, I should go now," I said, but neither of us moved.

"Would you like to know what you would say in Mende at this point? It is what you say to bid a temporary farewell to someone. *Ngewor e bi mahungbea.*"

I practiced and Lucien smiled.

"What does it mean?" I said.

"Take care, or may God watch over you."

"Will you teach me more?"

"Yes, next time," he said.

I backed away from him for several steps, then waved my fingers before I turned. When I reached the edge of the square and turned back to wave again, he was still in the same place, watching. I still wasn't sure I would go to the lecture, but he was right —there would be a next time for us.

X

Overlooking
the Thames

Crossing Trafalgar Square and back onto the Strand, I felt much more comfortable. This was my London. I knew these streets, so much busier and more raucous than the quiet and genteel part of town I'd just come from. In the future, I wouldn't avoid St. James's like I had done, though. From today, its associations wouldn't all be with my mother. Now they'd be with Lucien Winters too, and the nutty sweetness of marchpane.

"What are you doing here all done up on your day off, then?"

I hadn't spotted Barky standing behind the empty foyer bar as I walked in 'round the back of the theatre. He dusted his hands off on his trousers as though he'd been moving boxes, but I thought it more likely I'd caught him about to take a sniff of brandy.

"Nice to see you too," I said and he gave his customary snort.

"Not come to distract Ellen from her work?"

I shook my head. I wouldn't mind her seeing me in my nice outfit but it was Barky I really wanted to speak to. There was no one there to overhear but I leant over the bar and dropped my voice, just in case.

"I wondered what you knew about the surprise Crillick's been talking about. You took a message for him the other day when he came to see Ellen and me rehearse. It's not a new act, is it?"

"Worried for your billing, are you?" Barky said shrewdly. "I was just about to have a smoke. You can walk down to the river with me."

We went outside and I followed Barky down the alley toward the Embankment, until it widened out to a ledge where we could stand side by side, overlooking the grey waters. The stink of the Thames was high, even as the weather cooled. Sometimes I heard people complain about the smell: horse dung and cat piss, rotting vegetables and dirt. That was when I knew they weren't real Londoners. To me it smelt like home.

There were some stairs that led down to the river's edge, but no one ever used them and they were green and slick with algae. As usual, the river was busy ferrying people up and down, its fleet of steamboats cheaper and more convenient than a horse and carriage. I watched one boat go by and wondered where it was headed, who the passengers were that it carried, and what they had planned for the day. Vincent and I would've been in Richmond by now, but I didn't feel as upset about it as I had done earlier.

"So it's definitely an act?"

"I'd have thought so, but all the message said was that Crillick's goods had arrived," Barky said.

"It might be a mime artist? There's been nothing like that since Guillame left," I said.

Barky shrugged his shoulders. "Can't be nothing like that. If it were, I'd have known more about it. There'd be preparations to make. Set dressings and props to buy. Speaking of props—"

I held up a hand.

"You're going to tell me off for not being more grateful, I know. It's just . . ."

What was it? I still couldn't explain it.

"Old Barky's just keeping an eye out for you. If it helps, I don't think he'd be buying things to improve the act if he was going to replace you."

It was a good point. As usual, speaking to Barky had made me feel better. He reached into the inside pocket of his jacket and withdrew a slim silver case, just a little bigger than my palm, and engraved with a tobacco leaf. He opened it and held it out to me, shrugging when I shook my head. He struck a match and twisted the end of his cheroot from side to side over the flame until it caught.

"Important that they burn evenly," he said, noticing that I watched him closely.

"Vincent smokes them. Your case is almost as nice as his."

"You're not the only one with fancy friends, my girl," Barky said.

The dancers often gossiped about who Barky's mistress might be. I suspected she was a rich widow.

"You can't keep her a secret forever," I said, wanting him to say more, but as usual he chuckled to himself and kept schtum.

Barky liked to know all about us but it was rare for him to give away anything about himself. I stored up the information to ask him about one day when he had his guard down. For now, I held out my hand and he gave me the cheroot. I sucked on the tip and he laughed as I exploded into a fit of coughing. Eventually he slapped me on the back.

"I thought if you'd seen His Lordship smoke, you'd know not to inhale."

"That's vile."

"It's all the rage among the quality. Got to keep up appearances, ain't we?"

We watched the river for a little longer. There was something floating in it half wrapped in a cloth and I forced myself to look away before I could make out exactly what it was.

"Have you ever heard of Sierra Leone, Barky? It's in Africa."

"Can't say as I have. I know nothing of Africa. What about it?"

"It's just a place someone told me about, that's all."

Lucien had seemed so excited, I wondered if everyone was talking about it and somehow I'd missed it, but apparently not. If Barky knew nothing, Ellen certainly wouldn't, and it felt wrong to mention it to Vincent, seeing as how I'd found out about it.

Barky hawked and spat into the river.

"Who was that Black I saw you talking with the other week?"

"Nobody," I said, widening my eyes to try and look innocent, but he saw right through it.

"What you playing at, girl? You haven't seen him again, have you? His Lordship fawning over you and you're taking stupid chances."

"He's hardly fawning. We were supposed to go out today but he went out on business with Crillick instead. I hardly know Lucien."

I didn't dare tell Barky that I'd just come from Charles II Street. Not when he was looking at me so disapprovingly.

"Lucien, is it now?" He shook his head. "You want to steer clear of him, Zillah. You're lucky to have Lord Woodward's attention. I'm surprised you'd risk throwing it away."

"He was supposed to take me to Richmond, Barky."

He raised one eyebrow.

"I didn't know it was serious as that. It's a good sign, even if you didn't make it this time. A viscount out with the likes of you. It's not to be sniffed at."

I summoned something close to a smile and Barky gave me a pat on the shoulder.

"You're a treasure, Barky," I said. He waved the compliment away but I meant it. He kept it hidden from the other cast members but he did more than a lot to look out for me. He pulled his watch from his pocket. It was a beauty too, another thing of silver. Just the case and the watch alone were worth hundreds. A gift from a friend, he'd said. She must be a very close one to give him something as valuable as that.

"You need to be getting back?" I said.

He nodded. "Aldous sent off for a new magic contraption. It arrived just before you did. We need to test it before tonight. Where you off to now?"

"I'll go back to Westminster and wait for Vincent to come in. He said he wouldn't be out all day."

We walked back up the alley, Barky stopping halfway to enter the theatre.

"Go well, Zillah. If I do hear anything, I'll pass it on."

I carried on until I reached the Strand. I still didn't know what Crillick had in store but I felt reassured by what Barky had said. Not only about my act, but Vincent too. *If he is right about that, isn't he right about Lucien, though?* I almost wished now I'd told him that we'd met. I needed to talk it over with someone. Not Ellen —she was too close to Crillick. It would get back to Vincent in a heartbeat. Not that I'd really done anything. I'd been to a grocery shop. What could be more natural? But I was lying to myself that there was nothing more to it. He'd managed to get me talking about my mother. I never did that. I gave myself over to the memory that had been lapping on the edge of my thoughts, the memory of the day we'd left for St. Giles.

I'd had to skip to keep up with her back then, my seven-year-old legs struggling to match her pace so she half dragged me along. She'd kept looking over her shoulder, but once we'd gotten to Endell Street, she was calmer and finally willing to answer my questions.

"We're going to a place called St. Giles, Zillah. To see Mama's old friend Mrs. Bradley."

She'd packed up all my things into a little cloth bag.

"Are we going to stay with her now?"

The cramped streets of St. Giles had been frightening after the wide, tree-lined avenues of St. James's. I'd pressed close to her as we walked along.

"Mrs. Bradley used to live with us, but she left when she had her son, Eustace. He's only a year older than you. You'll be able to play together."

Oh, Eustace. Thinking about my mother had led to thinking about him. Maybe I'd been fooling myself that I was ready to move on, even though it had been four years since his death. Better to leave it all in the past where it belonged. I was almost at Northumberland Avenue. Hopefully Vincent would be there and I could forget about everything else.

XI

Party Preparations

When I arrived at 25 Northumberland Avenue, I found the back door to Crillick's house wide open. A horse and cart had pulled up outside, and I watched as its driver struggled in, bowed by the weight of two heavy boxes. I walked over to the cart, wanting to lift the sacking that covered it and see what else he had inside, but as I reached out a hand I heard a shout.

"Clear off, girl, or I'll call the Peelers on you!"

It was a lad—the carter's apprentice, I guessed from his age and the homespun trousers and leather apron that he wore. He stood in the doorway of the tradesman's entrance. Grace must have offered him a drink while his master was working.

"I was only looking."

I walked up to the door and indicated for him to step aside, but he made himself bigger, blocking off the entrance.

"Get on. You'll not be pilfering anything here."

"Out of my way. I live here, you know."

He didn't believe me. There was a tense moment while we faced off with one another, while he waited for me to slink away, but I was going nowhere. Here I was, dressed in my best, but he hadn't even hesitated to order me away. Beggar, thief, whore. He saw my colour and couldn't imagine I was anything more than that. On cue, Grace came out and nodded in my direction.

"Can I get you anything, miss?" she asked.

The apprentice looked from one to the other of us, his face clouding in confusion. Then it came, the down-mouthed dismay and horror that I'd been waiting for, and I fancied his head whirring through the consequences of not paying me the respect I deserved.

"I have all I need, but please leave me the name of this trader. I doubt we'll be using him again."

Grace nodded and spoke to the apprentice coldly.

"Cook's just settling the bill with your master; he'll be along in a minute."

The boy sloped away, looking sheepish. So why was I the one left feeling like I'd been bested? I might have taught the boy a lesson but little good it did me to have the love of a viscount if I needed a servant to vouch for me in order to enter his home.

The kitchen table was piled with covered baskets, punnets of fruit, and jars of preserves. There were almost as many groceries as I'd seen in Lucien's shop.

"Is this all for the party?" I asked Grace.

Crillick never did things by halves. There was lots to dislike about him, but you couldn't begrudge him that. I was so busy nosing through all the items Crillick had bought, I didn't notice him enter the kitchen.

"Zillah, what have you done with my friend the viscount?"

Grace jumped up and curtsied to her master, but he ignored her.

"He went out with you, remember?" I said.

"So he did, and spoiled all your plans. I'm terribly, terribly sorry," Crillick said.

There was a laugh in his voice and I hated him for it. A fishy smell about him too, which I recognised but for the moment couldn't place.

"Now I think about it, he'll probably be out for the rest of the afternoon. Said something about seeing his father this evening. We could have dinner à deux if you like."

Ugh. The thought of it. And Vincent definitely wouldn't like it. If ever I hinted at how much I hated Crillick, Vincent defended him, told me I had his friend all wrong, but for all that, he still didn't like me to be alone with him. Much as he protested, I'm sure there was some part of him, maybe even unknown to himself, that had the true measure of Crillick, knew he was dangerous.

"I thought you were having dinner with Ellen tonight?"

"Ah, your friend Ellen. A common little baggage, but there is something I like about her. Always hungry, isn't she?"

Poor Ellen. She was looking forward to her dinner with Crillick and this was how he spoke of her. The man was poison.

"I'll order dinner for seven, then," Crillick said.

I could tell he wasn't going to take no for an answer and, as long as I was in his house, if he insisted on dining with me, I couldn't very well refuse him. The only way to avoid spending the evening with Crillick would be to return to the rookery. I'd known I would have to once he came home from his business trip. It might as well be tonight.

"I only came here to tell Vincent that I was going back to St. Giles, actually."

"Are you now? I'm happy to give you a ride in my carriage if you like."

Part of me wanted to take up his offer out of spite. I doubted his carriage would last five minutes in St. Giles before it would be stripped of its hubcaps, but even the satisfaction of that wasn't worth being alone with him.

"Grace, you'll tell His Lordship that I'll see him soon, won't you?"

It was wrong of me to put her in the middle of things, but it was clear that my best bet was to leave.

"I'll see you at the theatre tomorrow, then," Crillick said.

I nodded. At the theatre I could cope with him. There I had power. I was the headliner, after all. He needed me as much as I needed him. Here in his home, it was a different story, especially if Vincent wasn't there. I turned and almost bumped into another trader.

"Not there, man, there," Crillick commanded as the poor man tried to place down his burden.

Whatever he had planned, it was something big.

✎

St. Giles is the worst kind of slum, but if I didn't want to sleep under the same roof as Crillick, it was the only place I could bed down for the night. Sometimes you read things in the papers and know it for a pack of lies, but when they say that the rookery has more pubs than houses, that poverty forces men and women who don't know each other from Adam to sleep side by side as many as ten to a room, and that the rats are bigger than the terriers brought in to catch them, it's all true. It'd been weeks since I'd been back there and, as I crossed over from New Oxford Street, I whistled the tune of the Blackbirds to make them think it was one of their own returning to the roost. The high note, something like the sound the colly birds made at first light, followed by two slow ones, told whoever was listening that I was no intruder, nor yet a mark for them to prey upon. Eustace had taught me that. After what had happened to him, I'd determined that I'd have nothing more to do with the Blackbirds, but at times like this knowing a little of their ways suited me.

This was the longest I'd ever been away from St. Giles since that day my mother dropped me off, and for the first time, on entering the narrow warren of streets, I noticed the smell. Animal fat, sour milk, and the ooze of rainwater and God knows what that clogged the gutters. It was disgusting but familiar, and I paused to take three deep breaths in until it no longer affected me. In my best hat and coat, I no doubt looked like a visitor, but the truth was that this was my world, however long I stayed at Northumberland Avenue.

A young child shambled past me, yawning and exhausted from a hard day's work. Slow as he was, I watched him overtake a woman with a babe on her hip and a bottle in her hand. There was a movement at my side and I batted away the hand of a pickpocket. Sometimes people romanticised this life, as if the poor never stole from each other, but in St. Giles anyone was fair game. Strange. Here I could be robbed at any time but I felt safer, more at ease, than anywhere I'd ever been with Vincent.

I headed toward my old rooms, though with little hope of finding them available. Sure enough, they'd been taken. I'd been away three weeks and had paid enough rent to last the month, but no one here would care about the whys and wherefores of that. The woman who answered my knock sent me packing and I didn't have enough about me to argue the toss with her. Tomorrow I would reclaim them but for now I needed a bed for the night. It was getting on for four o'clock, and soon all the best lodgings would be taken. I paused for a moment, unsure what to do. I needed to make a decision quick. Only the brave or stupid would hang around dressed like I was. That they wouldn't know what to make of me might buy me some time, but likely they'd assume I was new here, someone to be taken advantage of. Now my room was gone, there was only one place left that I could hope for an undisturbed night, but I had to get there quickly.

Clarke Street was the Mayfair of St. Giles. You needed money for a place there but it came with the knowledge that you most likely wouldn't be robbed while you slept. There were no guarantees, of course, but I wanted to make sure that when I woke up the next day, I still had all the same possessions as when I'd closed my eyes. Cold as it was, it'd be no bad thing to sleep in my clothes. Eustace and I had always planned to live on Clarke Street. That's when I thought I'd stay in St. Giles forever, but since he was gone, and Mrs. Bradley too, I knew the best thing for me would be to leave and start again, away from all the memories.

I made my way through the rookery, dodging the deeper puddles of filth and keeping my eyes down. Though it would soon be teatime, there were still children out, sitting on front steps, lurking in doorways. I doubted many had parents to call them inside and, if they did, there was no cozy room awaiting them, no meal ready on the table.

I'd been lucky. Mrs. Bradley had kept her word to my mother and done her best by me. There wasn't much, but whatever she had she shared, and she'd instilled in me a love of music and Shakespeare too, the things she had enjoyed with her aristocratic lover until she'd become pregnant and he'd thrown her out. I thought of her now. Her kind face and the rings she wore on almost every finger. Paste jewels, I realised now. With the money I'd made as the Great Amazonia I could have bought her something nicer. Not a diamond, nor even a ruby, but a gold locket, with a miniature of Eustace inside.

With my room paid for, Clarke Street was the safest place I could be. I was glad to be off the roads. I didn't want to run into anyone I knew, least of all a Blackbird. The best thing would be to keep myself to myself until I could get away again. I lay down in my bed for the night, swatting at the fleas that fed on me and wondering about the other people who had rested their bodies on this mattress. The sheets showed signs of stains, something that had never bothered me before, but now I knew what life was like outside St. Giles, it was harder to come back here.

How had she managed, my mother? She'd lived in St. James's, but as a slave, a servant, so she wouldn't have known what it felt like to sleep in a room like the beautiful one I shared with Vincent. Or did she? Had she been taken to a room like that when

I was conceived, lighted candles and promises made, or had she been accosted while going about her duties, forced into a stairway, defiled, and then made to carry on with her chores—cleaning, making up fires, serving tea—while all the time my father's seed slickened the inside of her thighs? She'd never said who he was—the master of the house or his son, maybe even a guest—but one thing she'd always told me was never to be a maid. When she'd left me here in St. Giles, she'd been clear on that. My conversation with Lucien had brought it all back.

We'd followed many twists and turns to find Mrs. Bradley's house. When my mother had knocked, it took a while for her friend to answer, but when she pulled back the door and saw us, she clasped my mother into a long embrace and the two of them clung to one another.

"You left them, Beulah, well done," I heard her say.

She ushered us into the house and my first impression was that it was small and cramped, nothing like the home I'd known until now. It smelt strongly of starch and the air was damp and heavy with drying clothes. We followed Mrs. Bradley down the passage into the main room and she cleared a pile of laundry from an old easy chair so my mother could sit down.

"Come over here, child, let me see you," Mrs. Bradley said, but I held on tightly to my mother's hand and wouldn't go to her.

"She's like you, Beulah. No face for serving, far too pretty. How old now?"

"Seven, just a year younger than your boy."

"His too?" Mrs. Bradley asked, but my mother acted like she hadn't heard and Mrs. Bradley gave a rueful smile.

"Tell me how you got away?"

"I didn't. I'll have to go back but . . ." She turned and gave me a strange smile. I didn't know what it meant, but Mrs. Bradley did because she sat back in her chair and gave a doleful sigh. She looked old then, older than my mother, but at that time she would only have been about twenty-seven or so.

"Eustace," she called out and a scruffy-looking, black-haired boy came in. "Take little Zillah outside to play, will you?" she asked him.

I didn't want to go, but my mother gave me an encouraging push and I followed him outside to the bit of scrub that passed as a back garden. As we closed the door behind us, I heard my mother say, "Hannah, you must help me."

I wanted to know with what and hung back for a second.

"Aren't you going to come and play?" Eustace said. "I've got some marbles I found the other day."

This was treasure, indeed—a toy and someone to play with. I looked back behind me and could see that Mrs. Bradley had pulled over her chair and now she and my mother were sitting side by side. I knew they were going to have a private conversation, but even if I couldn't understand it, I wanted to know what they said.

"You can have first turn," Eustace said.

He pressed a clay marble into my hand. Its surface was smooth and brown and speckled like a bird's egg. I looked from him to my mother and back again. Mrs. Bradley—Hannah—was holding her hand now. I wasn't wanted in the house. Mama had told me to go and play, and so I followed Eustace for a game or two.

It was getting dark when my mother called me back in. She stood at the back door with the light shining behind her like a halo. I went in reluctantly. I'd been enjoying myself with my new friend and wanted to tell Mama all about it, but her face looked grave and suddenly I was scared. She'd put her hat and coat back on and I scrabbled in my pocket for the gloves I'd discarded during my play with Eustace.

"No, Zillah. You're going to stay here with Mama's friend. You had a nice time with Eustace today, didn't you? You can play together every day if you stay here, what about that?"

Her voice was bright but brittle. It was the tone she used on the rare occasions when the mistress asked her how she did, but never before had she used it with me. Going and leaving me behind? She couldn't mean it. I tried to take her hand but she drew it back out of my reach.

"I'm ready to go now, Mama," I said.

My mother knelt down and disentangled me from her skirts, which I clutched like a limpet. We were on eye level now and she wrapped her arms around me and spoke low into my ear.

"I wish I could stay with you, but if I leave, they will come for me. Hunt me down and find me. They'd put adverts in the papers to say I was a runaway, and every time I went abroad I'd fear that they were watching me. They own me, body and soul, but you were born free." She sat back on her heels and I could see her face was wet, but her voice was strong.

"Say it after me, Zillah. Born free," she said.

"I was born free," I hiccuped out through my tears, too young to grasp the full meaning of what it meant but understanding that it was something most important.

I felt someone behind me and turned to see Mrs. Bradley. She placed her hand on my shoulder and gave a comforting squeeze.

"You're sure, Beulah?" she said, and my mother nodded. "Best go now then. You'll be in enough trouble as it is and there's no need to make it worse." She gave my mother a fierce hug. "I'll do my best by her, for your sake, but it's not an easy life."

"I'm not naive," my mother said. "She may not be much safer here, but whatever chance I can give her, I will. She was born free but in that house they will treat her as if the law has not changed. You will teach her to look after herself?"

"As if she were my own daughter, don't you worry about that."

My mother bent down to me once more.

"You will be a good girl for Mrs. Bradley, won't you, Zillah?"

I'd stopped crying, knowing somehow that my mother needed me to be brave. She untied her scarf and wound it around my neck. It smelt of her.

"Take this to remember me by and, above all, promise me one thing. Never forget that you are free and that means you can go where you like and make your own choices. Do what you can to avoid serving others. Say it again for me."

"I am free. I was born free."

It was my mother who made me feel that to be born free made me special. Which meant that slavery was a sin, a sign of shame, was it not? Lucien Winters had said different when I'd walked with him around St. James's Square. He'd given me a great deal to think about.

§

By seven o'clock the next morning I was ready to leave. St. Giles ran on its own time, so many of its inhabitants worked at night and slept through the day, but I clung to the routines of Vincent's world. *Your world too now, Zillah,* I reminded myself. I had to think myself deserving of it, or I'd never learn to claim a place there. I'd barely slept, the sound of the rats scuttling beneath the floorboards and the hunger pangs in my stomach too insistent to be ignored. There was no place to wash, no water— hot or cold—and I'd slept in my clothes. In one sense, all I had to do was get up and walk out, but my past had a grip on me that couldn't be as easily discarded as an old coat that no longer suited me.

It was a relief to get to the theatre. When I sat down at the table in the dressing room I shared with Ellen, I could've wept. There was a knock at the door.

"Come in, Barky," I called. But it wasn't the stage manager that walked in; it was Vincent.

As often as he'd met me at the theatre, Vincent had never been backstage. I saw him take in the props leant up against the walls, and the mess of jars and pots on the dressing table, and felt an urge to shield them from his gaze.

"So, this is where the Great Amazonia comes into being," he said.

He stepped forward to embrace me. He smelt of soap and cigar smoke, but I backed away. His face turned grave. He thought I was angry with him over Richmond, but I was worried that the fleas I'd picked up last night would burrow into his woolen coat and his freshly washed hair.

"Where have you been? I told you to wait for me at Crillick's last night."

"I . . . I couldn't. It's not the same now he's back."

Vincent made an impatient sound.

"Don't be silly, Zillah. Come back with me when you've finished here tonight. I'll be watching from the box and we'll go home together in my carriage."

I nodded and his tone softened.

"Good girl. I missed you last night."

"You went to see your father?"

A look of confusion flitted across his face. "Why would you think that? I was at Al—" He caught himself. "I was at dinner with a friend."

Clearly, he'd been with Alexander. Had his friend's sister been there too? But before I could ask any more, Vincent said he must be going. He pressed a swift kiss on my forehead and left me wondering what had happened at dinner that he was so eager not to talk to me about. *At least he said he missed you.*

A few minutes later, Barky came in.

"You're early?" he said and then, when he noticed how I scratched at my arms, "Spent the night at the rookery, did you?"

"I'll be back with Vincent tonight," I said. "He was here just now."

"You can't take him for granted."

"I won't, Barky."

The night in St. Giles had reminded me how lucky I'd been to find a way out. Only three short weeks away and I'd let myself forget what it was like there, how squalid it was, how full of memories. Vincent was my path to better things. The feelings I had for him were nothing like my love for Eustace, and would never be, but I wasn't a foolish girl waiting for her head to be turned. I was a survivor who needed to be practical. If Crillick had a new act, I would fight to keep top billing. If some debutante was making eyes at Vincent, I'd see her off. I knew what I wanted: to carve out a life for myself away from the slums, and from now on, I wouldn't let anyone get in the way of that.

XII

Crillick's Surprise

Sunday rolled around, the day of Marcus Crillick's party, and despite my best efforts, I was still no nearer to finding out what his surprise was to be. All I had gleaned was that it was to be the high point of the evening after drinks and a buffet dinner. The day before I had even asked Ellen, but though she knew nothing about it either she'd had quite a bit to say about the guest list.

We'd been gossiping about Crillick and Vincent as we got ready for the evening's performance. It almost felt like old times, but she couldn't resist putting in one of the barbs that, by now, I should have become accustomed to.

"You know who'll be at the party tomorrow night?"

From her tone I knew she was aiming to get a rise out of me and so I tried to head her off.

"No one God-fearing, seeing as it's on a Sunday."

"Marcus gets bored on Sunday evenings—you know his set don't care for the conventions," Ellen said.

There was silence for a minute, but when she realised I wasn't going to answer her original question in earnest she burst out, "Henrietta Alexander will be there."

This was the woman Crillick had mentioned at breakfast, who

Vincent had maybe had dinner with earlier in the week, but I refused to give Ellen the satisfaction of seeing that she had me worried.

"Should I know who she is?"

"Only one of the most beautiful women in London, and an heiress to boot. Marcus says she has her eye on Vincent."

This I could not ignore. Vincent and me were in harmony once more after the postponement of our trip to Richmond but we hadn't settled on a new date yet. I wondered if it had anything to do with this Alexander woman.

"If I was you, I would have to ask him about her, Zillah."

It was all I could do not to laugh out loud. Crillick could and did do whatever he wanted and Ellen would not make a peep. There had even been a rumor that he'd slept with one of the chorus girls and still Ellen would not have a word said against him.

"I trust him, Ellen."

"Do you? There comes a time when all men need to settle down. Maybe now he's had you, his wild oats have been sown."

𝒞

Back at 25 Northumberland Avenue, the conversation played on my mind while I watched Vincent get ready for the evening.

"I wish we were going together," he said.

"Going where? The party is downstairs. It is not as if it's a big affair."

"Everything's a big affair with Crillick. The fellow can't help himself," Vincent said. "You can't imagine what he's laying on."

I'd seen it all a few days before: flour, spices, and sugar to make pies, puddings, and jellies, and there'd probably been other deliveries since.

"Tell me who the guests will be tonight?"

"I'm glad you ask, Zillah. Stop fussing with that and sit down, will you? There's something I want to say."

His voice was so serious I put down the cravat that I toyed with and perched beside him on the bed.

"Henrietta Alexander will be here tonight, and I saw her when I went to Alexander's for dinner the other evening."

He didn't have to say anything about her to me. It must be a good sign that at last he'd volunteered it.

"Your friend's sister?"

"That's right. Alexander was with me at Oxford. It's not just Henrietta, though. It's her mother."

I swallowed down the anxious feeling in my throat and tried to put a brave face on it.

"The old lady has designs on you? Let her try and come between us."

"Be serious, Zillah. She wants me for her daughter, and she is a most determined woman. Alexander himself has warned me."

Vincent stroked back a stray curl that bobbed on my forehead. "I tell you this, Zillah, because I'll be spending most of the evening with them. Alexander is good fun and his sister too is lively and vivacious. If you see me acting the gallant with her, you must not set too much store by it."

He hadn't needed to explain himself, but I was glad that he had. Surely this was proof of how much he cared for me. I just wished he'd described Henrietta Alexander with less admiration.

"I understand. If I see you with them, I will not scratch their eyes out."

"That's my princess."

"Besides, I'll be out of the way up here," I said.

He stood and paced once, twice across the room before kneeling at my feet and taking my hands in his own.

"I must have you there tonight, Zillah."

My heart sang. Paving the way to declaring us a couple would take time. Vincent would suffer for it as well as me, so having me in the same room as his friends was surely a good sign. It didn't matter that we hadn't gone to Richmond after all. *What do you think of that, Ellen?* I thought, perhaps a tad spitefully. But what would I wear? The party would start in less than an hour. I jumped up to look in the wardrobe, wishing I had something in there even half suitable, and Vincent smiled.

"It will be a difficult night for you, but I'm glad that you agree."

He understood. That was so important to me.

"Here, I borrowed this for you, from that maidservant you like."

We were the same size, but what could Grace possibly have that would be suitable for a party? She had even less than me. As I stared at the outfit in Vincent's hands, I realised what he wanted. I wouldn't be at the party as his guest at all. I would be there in the guise of a servant. He held up a black dress and white apron.

"Is something wrong, Zillah?"

The red flea bites on my arms were still fresh; the itching reminded me of why I must keep my temper. *Stupid girl. Be glad that he wants you there at all.* But I knew I couldn't do it. My mother had not given me much, but I felt compelled to abide by the one rule she'd handed me: Never be a servant. It was a maxim I'd lived my life by. Even in the leanest times, I'd ignored the listings in the paper for kitchen maids and maids of all work. Instead, I'd got myself the role at Crillick's, built on my performance until Crillick saw fit to make me the headliner. Vincent wanted to undo all that work in a moment just for his own comfort.

"It's only for an hour or two. It would mean a lot to me to have you there. You can tell me what you think of everyone."

It was all a game to him and I knew how it would be. I'd serve drinks to his friends, and when he thought no one was looking, he'd touch me where he shouldn't. But tonight I wasn't playing. I couldn't.

"You don't need me there. You can tell me all about it afterward. I'll be up here waiting for you."

Vincent pouted. Maybe it was a mistake to leave him to his own devices at the party, but my pride was one of the few things I had. I wasn't ready to compromise it.

"You'll deign to choose something for me to wear at least?"

It was like him to be peevish when he didn't get his own way. I wasn't going to back down, but I didn't want to send him off to the party feeling like he wanted to spite me. I picked out a velveteen jacket in palest blue. He knew it to be one of my favourites. That I was willing for him to look his best showed that I had confidence in him.

"Are you sure it should be this one, Zillah? Even though you know I am hunted."

"I trust you," I said, and he spun me 'round and kissed me.

&

I did trust him, didn't I? This was what I was thinking as the evening wore on. I had watched out of the upstairs window as the carriages arrived. Vincent had said drinks and a light supper, but some of the women were expecting to dance, based on the gowns they were wearing. The light, bright notes of Mr. Brahms wafted up from downstairs and I could hear the hubbub of chatter. There could be nothing wrong with taking a closer look.

I leant over the banister just as the butler announced the Alexanders. My view wasn't great, but I could see just from her extravagant hairpiece that Henrietta Alexander was likely as striking as Ellen had said. I slunk back to Vincent's room wishing I'd stayed put. The maid's outfit was where he'd left it, draped over the chaise longue. I picked it up and held it against me. Could I? Grace was skinnier than me, so it would be a little tight, but it wasn't the fit I was worried about. Could I betray my mother like that?

She left you, Zillah. She wasn't willing to fight to keep you with her. They were ugly thoughts, and many times Mrs. Bradley had tried to explain why my mother judged it best to leave me, but though she always said how much Mama loved me, I struggled to believe it. I pulled on the costume. With memories of my mother in my head, I felt as uncomfortable now as I did when I dressed up to play Amazonia. Why was it that I was always compelled to be someone else and never truly myself? There was a looking glass on the dressing table and I stood before it. Did I look like her at all, the woman who had brought me into this world? I stepped out onto the landing and followed the music downstairs.

❧

Crillick had invited more than twenty people to celebrate his return from the Continent. They were gathered in the drawing room, where the furniture had been pushed to one side and the rugs rolled up to make space for dancing. A buffet table had been set up and groaned with food, a three-tiered pink blancmange decorated with tiny flowers taking pride of place. I hovered two steps into the room, watching the guests as they stood talking in threes and fours, crystal goblets in hand. Some of the men I recognised from parties in the past. George Fayers, tall and dashing, often visited for cards and billiards. And there was Graham Alexander with a sharp cravat, his hair dark with Macassar oil. No doubt they knew Vincent had a mistress, but they wouldn't have reason to know it was me. Crillick had always warned me to stay out of sight in case anyone probed Vincent on how we'd met and made the connection between me and Amazonia. Crillick called these people his friends but he didn't think enough of them to trust them with his secrets. I should go in, but once I entered, they'd have every right to call on me to freshen their glasses, to paw at me. I needed to get my courage up before I subjected myself to that. The guests were the least of my problems, though. It was Sikkings and the other servants that I was most reluctant to see. It was hard enough getting their respect as Vincent's mistress, but now I wore a uniform, I knew Sikkings would take a cruel delight in ordering me around. I'd just have to make sure I stayed out of his way.

The ladies in the room were like a flock of birds in their bright dresses. I tugged at the bodice of the maid's outfit. It was so tight I was almost spilling out of it. I looked up and my eyes caught Crillick's. He'd been holding court on his recent travels to a pair of girls about my own age. Now he blinked and a slow smile spread across his face. A horrible suspicion came into my mind. Had he put Vincent up to this? It was just the sort of thing he'd get a kick out of.

It took a while to spot Vincent in the crush, but then I saw him on the far side of the room, next to the piano. It shouldn't have surprised me—he loved music, and the young woman who had commandeered the instrument played prettily, the light notes rising and swelling above the chatter. Of course it was Henrietta Alexander. The stout matronly woman who sat close by her, decked out in furs despite the warmth of the room, must be her mother. Between the two of them, they had Vincent cornered. It would be nigh on impossible for him to escape, if he even wanted to. I watched as Vincent leant down and turned the page for the piano player. He'd hinted I had nothing to fear from her, but how true was that? It was just as well I was here to stop him getting too distracted by her. Maybe Ellen was being kind to warn me about her after all. Either way, I wished I'd given more thought to the outfit I'd picked for him. He was easily the handsomest man in the room, with his moustache neatly trimmed, his wavy hair parted on one side, and on his lapel, his family crest. I felt a sort of pride in him, as if —ha!—I could ever truly claim him as my own. I could not tell from where I stood, but I knew his boots were polished to a sheen. Seeing him here among his friends, and me dressed in the maid's outfit, brought it home to me how fragile my hold on him was. He was only ten steps away but in social terms it may as well have been ten fathoms. I couldn't compete with the Henrietta Alexanders of this world. Not on money nor clothes, but at least I had my wits to rely on.

And he called you his princess.

Vincent must have felt my eyes on him, because he looked up and smiled. I never got over his smile. I'd seen it much less often lately. The friction with his father had been distracting him and he refused to explain exactly what the problem was, insisting that it would only bore me. If only I could've been here as his guest and not as the maid! *What do you expect, Zillah? He's heir to half of Surrey.* The matron at Vincent's side, seeing him smile across the room but thankfully not realizing it was for me, tapped his arm to reclaim his attention. He cocked his head to hear what she said and then they both looked across to the piano. Henrietta played energetically, her head nodding to punctuate the breaks in the music. It was hard not to admire her.

🙰

Outside in the corridor the oil lamps had been dimmed and it was cooler. I leant against the paneled oak wall. The hard ridges of the moldings dug into my back but I wanted the discomfort, wanted my body to match what I felt inside my head. I took one deep breath and then another, steadying myself as Ellen had once taught me to do before a performance. On the opposite wall a collection of oil-painted ladies and gentlemen leered down at me. They must have come with the house, as they couldn't be Crillick's ancestors. He was from trade, his money and connections brand-new. Enough of both, though, to have bought his way into society. I stepped forward to read the nameplate of the nearest lady, depicted Grecian style with a playful spaniel at her feet. Her name was Arabella. Henrietta, Arabella. These were the sorts of women that a viscount should be associated with. *But he wants you,* I told myself. *He could have a woman like these for the asking and yet it is you he has chosen to have by his side. Even if it means you must play a part to be near him.* The thought made me feel better. If he was going to make love to the Alexander girl, he would not have asked me to be there with him, even in these wretched maid's clothes. Once Vincent and I were alone together, all I'd have to be was Zillah. *He loves you for who you are. Your skin, your history, they mean nothing to him. Don't you forget that.*

&

I turned to reenter the drawing room as Henrietta came out. I only just avoided bumping into her and she gasped, pressing a hand to her chest, before she got over her surprise, and gave a weak laugh.

"You quite frightened me, lurking there in the shadows like that. I barely saw you!"

I tensed, waiting for the command for water or champagne, but nothing came. Instead, she snapped open her fan with a flick of her wrist and waved it back and forth. Her eyes narrowed for a moment, searching my face, before brightening again.

"That's much better, isn't it? So warm in there." She held out a gloved hand to me. "It's Zillah, isn't it?" She laughed at the puzzlement on my face. "Marcus told me to look out for you. I'm Miss Alexander."

I frowned again, wondering why my name would have come up in a conversation between her and Crillick. How much did she know about what I really was to Vincent? I made a movement somewhere between an awkward bob and a curtsy. I wanted to get away, to find a place where I could see Vincent, but she blocked the doorway into the drawing room.

"I won't let you run away from me. Now I've got you, we must be friends."

"I believe His Lordship wanted me."

She raised an eyebrow. "I'm sure you call him Vincent, don't you? No need to pretend. You might be wearing a maid's outfit but I know about you. All men have their follies when they're young. Vincent's getting a little too old for it really, but frankly I see no need for him to give you up if it saves me from certain unpleasantness."

She looked me up and down, for all the world like she was one of the punters at the theatre. I could see the same fascination in her eyes.

"I bet your mother was a slave, wasn't she?"

The heat rose to my cheeks. How dare she? For a moment, I wished I really was Amazonia in her skins, ready to rip her bloody like a dog. Henrietta wouldn't dare question me then. *But it's true, though, isn't it?* came the voice inside my head. *You're slave stock, and you can be with Vincent all you like but that won't change it.*

It's nothing to be ashamed of, said another voice. Lucien's.

"You weren't a servant at the Woodward house to begin with, were you? I've been there, you know. Darling little place," Henrietta said.

I shook my head, but said nothing. Vincent had told me his family home in Surrey had four floors and eighteen bedrooms. How rich was this woman that she would speak of it like a costermonger's cottage? *And who am I to think myself a rival to her?*

"I spent all my summers there when I was young. Our families have always been close," she added.

Her face was smooth but she pasted on her paint quite thick. I guessed she was slightly older than me. Twenty-four or twenty-five years old perhaps, a little younger than Vincent—old not to be married, though, in her circles. Her blue eyes were sharp and knowing. She moved closer and lowered her voice, though we were quite alone in the dim corridor. Over her shoulder the light shone from the drawing room and there was a burble of conversation. I wished I had stayed safe upstairs in the bedroom.

"What I really want to know is how you get away with it."

I was taller, stronger than her, but as long as I played the maid she had the better of me. This was why my mother had insisted I make my own way.

"I don't know what you mean," I said.

"Why, your act of course. The Great Amazonia, they call you, don't they? Crillick tells me you're quite the draw at his Variety Theatre."

I froze, unable to keep the hate from my eyes.

She smiled at her victory. "What would happen if it was known that you were a fraud, Zillah? That you'd been taking all those poor audiences in with your lies, prancing around up there half-clothed on the stage."

When I still didn't speak, she added, "You can tell me. I don't gossip."

I'll trust the devil before I trust you, I thought. I didn't like the closeness of her gaze, the calculating look in her eyes.

Vincent appeared behind Henrietta in the doorway. His half smile dropped when he saw the two of us together. Following my eyes, Henrietta turned and gave him a brilliant smile. How could she go from threatening to sweetness and light? She was a far better actress than I was.

"My mother let you go?" she said to him.

"I needed a drink," Vincent said lamely, his eyes flicking in my direction, as if I were a real servant. Henrietta played along.

"Oh yes? This one is very helpful. Mother always says a good maid is worth her weight in gold. Even one as big as this. We're becoming great friends out here. You want to be careful we don't poach her. Though we'd have to do something to fix those finger-nails. Couldn't have her snagging all my fine fabrics."

Embarrassed, I tucked my hands behind my back. I hadn't realised she'd noticed them. Her little speech had made Vincent uncomfortable too. He grimaced at what she said, but I knew he wouldn't pull her up on it.

"Come back into the drawing room, Hen. Marcus is about to unveil his big surprise," he said.

"Very well. Zillah and I will have to find another opportunity to continue our conversation."

"Yes, ma'am," I said and bobbed a proper curtsy this time, though Lord knew who I was doing it for.

Henrietta raised up her hand for Vincent to take.

"You can escort me back in to my mother."

He bowed and did as she said.

XIII

The Leopard in the Library

The perilous ting of solid silver on crystal halted the low hum of conversation. When Crillick knew the eyes of the room were on him, he put down his knife but kept ahold of his glass and took a hearty swig.

"Ladies and gentlemen, your attention, please."

He swayed slightly. Must've had a skinful already, but when he spoke there was no hint of a slur.

"When I invited you to my house tonight, I promised a surprise. You've been very patient and now it is ready. Come. To the library."

Alexander was standing directly behind Crillick. I saw him give a sly smile. He was in on it, then. No one else, though, from the expectant looks on their faces and the way they whispered to one another. Even Vincent didn't seem sure. Crillick strode from the room, and after a moment his guests began to follow him. The breaking up of the party brought Vincent to me.

"You know what this is?" I asked him.

He pulled me to one side, away from the current of people that swirled around us. The ladies bunched up by the doorway, not caring if their gowns got crushed. It wouldn't be them up all night with starch and a sewing kit.

"It will be some frolic—you know Marcus," Vincent said, but his eyes were wary.

I did. It was precisely that—knowing Crillick—that had me worried. He was only ever happy at someone else's expense, and all night he'd worn a grin that nigh on split his face. What exactly had he been up to on the Continent? A grim fascination took hold of me and I moved to join the line of guests as it snaked down the corridor. It was Vincent's hand at my waist that stopped me.

"Vincent!" I hissed, startled, but there was no need. No one had noticed. Maybe they wouldn't care. Maids were fair game for the gentlemen of the house, after all. Now Vincent stood inches from me, so close it made it seem like it was just us two, center stage, and the remaining guests in the drawing room around us extras, props.

"You don't look so pretty when you're frowning, Zillah. What's wrong?"

Vincent was looking at me intently. He could see that something troubled me, but what could I say to make him understand even half of it? I fiddled at the corset that I was bound up in, but it was laced good and tight. All the fine breakfasts and dinners I'd been eating since living with Vincent were starting to show.

"What were you talking to Hen about?" he said.

"Nothing much. She knew my name and asked how we'd met."

"That's all? You must stay away from her."

I couldn't read what I saw in his eyes. I was ready to ask him, but before I could speak, Crillick was back to round up the stragglers. He poked his head into the drawing room.

"Well now, what's all this?" he said and I stepped back smartly, feeling guilty though I'd done nothing wrong.

"Come, my man, the show's about to start," he said, without a glance at me.

"Right you are," said Vincent.

Crillick disappeared again.

"Come on," Vincent said. "There'll be no rest until he's made his show."

He took my hand and pulled me along after him. I wasn't as convinced as Vincent was that the surprise was the end of what Crillick had in mind. To me it felt like a beginning.

⌒

The library was sumptuous. Down in St. Giles a room of this size could hold four families but here in St. James's it was home only to books. Shelves lined the walls, floor to ceiling, and each was tightly packed, the volumes bound in leather and their titles etched in gold. Usually, a large globe stood in the center of the room. When Crillick was away, I had wandered in here a few times, liked to stroke the globe's smooth surface and watch it spin, but tonight it had been pushed to one side. In the space left behind, wooden dining chairs were set out in four rows of five, all facing toward the far end of the room, where a low stage had been made up from half a dozen wooden shipping crates.

Letting go of Vincent's hand, I ducked into a window alcove at the back of the room, but stayed on my feet. Half-hidden behind the curtain, I wouldn't have a great view, but something told me it might be dangerous to get too close. At least no one would question me being here in my maid's disguise. Vincent hadn't noticed me fall back, and he took a seat in the front row. I saw him look around for me, but Henrietta stepped in front of him so he didn't see me wave. She sat down next to him with a toss of her golden hair. From the way he'd spoken, it sounded like he had little time for her but now her fingertips rested lightly on his arm. I knew that trick, that feather touch, how it would make him think of her as dainty, delicate. *Don't fall for it, Vincent. Don't fall for it.* How close had we been only a second ago and yet you'd never know it now.

I forced myself to look around over the heads of the seated audience. Watching Vincent with that woman would do me no good. Nor would it help to watch the mother either, the old bird in her feathered turban. She mustn't know about us. As fragile as my standing was, it gave me a petty pleasure to think the man she wanted for her daughter was already in love, with an actress no less, and a half-caste one too.

It wasn't so different to being at Crillick's just before the show began. Same excitement, same chatter, but somehow the room felt a little less alive. Like the action was happening behind a pane of clear glass. At the theatre it was rowdy. By this point in the proceedings, drinks would be sloshing. Here they were sipped. We'd been waiting awhile now—ten minutes since Vincent and I had been the last of the party to enter the library. By now the crowd of punters would be drumming their feet on the floor of the theatre. Here the air beat with the rapid movement of ladies' fans.

"Excuse me, would you?"

It was a slender, dark-haired woman I had not noticed before. She moved carefully past me and sat in the next window seat along. The hand I'd felt when she brushed past me was cold; she must have just come in from outside. She was dressed as fine as the other guests but there was something different about her, less frivolous; the dove-grey silk of her dress more sober than the pinks and greens of the other women. Maybe she was a little older. Judging by her looks, she definitely wasn't one of Crillick's cronies, but if that was true, then what was she doing here?

Now that all the guests had taken their seats, I felt an air of expectation descend on the room. The attention of the audience was drawn to the makeshift stage, which was two crates high and about nine yards across. For now it was empty, giving no clues to what we would be presented with. Barky was right. Surely if it was an act with the scale to displace me as headliner, there'd at least be a prop or two and some scenery? While I tried to reassure myself, the oil lamps were dimmed. I gave a slight shudder as if the temperature in the room had been lowered as well as the lighting. For two long minutes we waited in semidarkness while the vague shapes of servants shuffled and scraped as the stage was dressed.

The lights came up gradually to reveal a small metal trolley. I craned my head to see what was on it and made out a set of scientific instruments: long metal pincers, a needle, and three glass tubes filled with coloured liquids. The pink-filled tube gave off a thin strand of smoke, and underneath the smell of pomade and tipsy people talking, there was a waft of cleaning alcohol. Now Grace and Alice, the maid of all work, filed onto the stage holding a white sheet up between them. I suppose I should have been grateful that my servant's disguise for the evening hadn't required me to partake in the spectacle, whatever it would be. The thin material bulged and twitched as if something behind it moved, and I saw Grace flinch. Her plain face was pinched and even stolid Alice looked nervous. Could it be some sort of animal behind the sheet? My heart began to hammer and I picked at the back of my corset again. A little pop and one of the ties surrendered to my pointed nails, allowing me to take a grateful gulp of air.

Crillick had melted away when his guests took their seats, but now he reappeared, in eyeglasses and a long white coat. He must've taken it from the theatre. In the strange getup he had everyone's attention. Chatter ceased. We watched as he inspected the tools on the table. He touched the back of his hand to the smoking tube, which had just begun to bubble. You could have heard a matchstick snap. Crillick turned to us and smiled, rubbing his hands together.

It was showtime.

"Some of you will know that I've been away on business," he said, "but I also made time for pleasure."

Some of the men chuckled and he leered back at them before continuing.

"I stopped off in Paris and picked up a little something that I just had to show you. It's exceeding rare, let me tell you. Before tonight, its like has not been seen in London. No mistake, what you are about to see will make you gasp. Some of you ladies may feel afeared, but do not worry. The men here will protect you."

Right on cue, there came a small cry of fright and I turned to see that in the front row, just below the stage, Henrietta now clung to Vincent, while he murmured softly into her ear. The brief exchange I'd had with her told me she was more than capable of looking after herself if she chose, but what of Grace and Alice? I couldn't believe they were so given to dramatics, but there was no doubting how frightened they were. Crillick must have got ahold of a snake, or maybe even a panther. Only a wild animal could inspire this sort of dread.

The room was poised. Crillick had us in his power. There was a thin sheen of sweat on his face. I recognised the look in his eyes, the brightness that came when you had an audience hanging on your every word. He surveyed us all and his gaze lingered on me a little longer than the others, until I shrank still farther back into the alcove. Was that a frown that crossed his face when he saw the woman sitting along from where I stood? I looked over at her but she sat perfectly still, watching intently. She held a tiny notebook in her hand, her face eager as all the others to take in everything that happened. Did I recognise her? I thought I might have seen her before, but couldn't remember where.

Crillick placed his hand on top of the sheet that Grace and Alice held. This was it. My hands were knitted together at my chin, my body braced to see the animal I was sure Crillick had brought home.

"I present to you the wondrous . . . Leopard Lady!" Crillick cried.

He whipped the cloth from Grace and Alice's hands with a flourish. The two girls immediately fled the stage.

And there she was, her eyes wide and staring in fear. The strangest woman I had ever seen.

❧

She wore a close-fitting cream shift that was only just decent, the hem skimming her knees and leaving her arms bare. Her skin was dark, darker than mine, save for a great patch on the left of her face that was almost pure white. The patch circled her eye and stretched as far as her earlobe. I looked again and saw her arms bore the same markings. Did the strange pattern continue all the way up to her thighs and across her torso? It was as if someone had thrown paint at her. Her tightly curled hair was clipped short and was mostly black but there too I noticed a colourless streak. Not grey with age, but white, as if all the pigment had been bleached out of it.

I'd underestimated Crillick as a showman. He let us look our fill—no patter, no pronouncements. I'd been on the receiving end of this gaze. In the moment when Amazonia threw off her cloak, I'd interpreted the wide-eyed stares as admiration, told myself that the audience's attention conferred on me some sort of power, but from this vantage, I saw it for what it really was. The men and women who came to see Amazonia at Crillick's were not marveling at a wonder; they were gawping at a monster. Worse still, I could sense it in myself, this way of looking as I took in the woman before me, my eyes roving, questing, probing, greedy to consume her.

In the quiet Henrietta's whispered question was loud as a shout. "What is it, Mother?"

Crillick stepped forward.

"You see before you a creature taken from a jungle tribe, the *Leopardus tribus.*" He ignored a guffaw that came from one of the middle rows on the right and continued. "This primitive race can be found only in Africa. Strong, sleek, like the big cats they are named for, but this one was doubtless the runt and had been discarded."

It was the typical freak-show turn. The spiel was not so different from how I was introduced. Until now I'd dismissed it as part of the game, knowing it wasn't really about me, Zillah. It was about Amazonia, someone else entirely. I wondered who the Leopard Lady really was, what products she used on her skin and hair to produce such strange effects. I peered more closely, trying to work it out, and then her eyes connected briefly with mine. In them, I saw the very depths of her confusion and fear, and it hit me like a hammer blow. She wasn't gaffed as I was.

What must she be feeling? All I could do was pray that she didn't understand English, nor that Crillick had named her for a dangerous animal and stolen her humanity. Standing there listening to it, I felt ashamed, not just for myself, but for this aristocratic audience. Educated, worldly, and yet they lapped it up.

"Who found it?" a male voice called out.

"A treasure hunter. He came across her quite by accident. She'd been abandoned by her mate," Crillick said. "We've made her presentable, of course, but in the wild she wore no clothing of any kind."

"Is she dangerous?"

"Find out for yourselves. Which among you brave souls will be first to approach her?" Crillick said.

Henrietta, next to Vincent in the front row, had leant forward in her chair for a better look. Crillick beckoned her to the stage. "Come, Hen. You can touch her."

Henrietta stood up slowly and squared her narrow shoulders. Just a moment ago she had pressed herself into Vincent in mock fear. Now she was courageous enough to confront the Leopard Lady. Crillick held out one hand to assist her onto the stage. In the other he now grasped a stick, thick as a broom handle.

"Go on. It's quite safe."

Despite the reassurance and the weapon he carried, Henrietta was nervous. I could tell by the way she stretched out her slender arm as far as it would go, rather than get too near. It was the way a child might approach a dog, scared it might turn vicious and bite at any moment. Up on the stage, Henrietta circled the Leopard Lady, each time getting a little closer. When she felt quite safe, she reached into her bag. She found what she wanted in a moment. From where I stood, I couldn't make it out at first. Then I realised it was a pair of gloves. She drew them on one by one, slowly and carefully, for the cream lace was delicate. Her hands protected, Henrietta extended a forefinger and drew it down the Leopard Lady's arm, from black to white to black again. It was what a painter might do to mix grey, but the colours refused to bleed into one another. Puzzlement registered on her face and she tried again, rougher this time.

"Is it a trick?" Henrietta asked.

All the while the Leopard Lady stood motionless, her eyes averted from Henrietta, her face temporarily blank.

"Rather noble, isn't she?" I heard a man in the row of seats ahead of me mutter, but all I could see in her was terror. The so-called Leopard Lady was bracing herself, but what did she think was coming? She might do all she could not to see what was happening, but I knew there was nothing she could do to stop feeling it.

One of the gentlemen rose from his seat. He was middle-aged and wiry, and his lilac waistcoat hung loose like it had been made for someone else. I did not know him but I had seen him in the drawing room earlier in the evening. He climbed onto the stage and the Leopard Lady's eyes grew wide as he loomed over her. Henrietta pulled a face as the man spat into his silk handkerchief. He wiped it across the Leopard Lady's cheek as though her colour was dirt that could be lifted off. When this had no effect, he scratched at the black skin with a fingernail and the Leopard Lady flinched.

Crillick watched on, a half smile on his lips. He gestured to the table of instruments.

"Here I have lemon juice, soap, acid. None of these will remove the colour on the flesh, nor can it be scraped away with these." He held up the pincers. "Come, see for yourselves."

Others approached the stage, tugged at her clothes to see if the patches covered her whole body. She clung to the thin straps of her shift as it was pulled down her shoulders. Vincent was not among them, thank God. But he didn't do anything to stop it. I shifted from foot to foot, not sure what I could do to help but knowing I must try something. I took one step forward before a single thought halted my progress. What if they tried to pull me onstage too? My legs gave out from under me and I slumped back into the alcove.

"Now, now, ladies and gentlemen. Any damage you cause will have to be paid for," Crillick said, but he was clearly enjoying the reaction he'd aroused in his audience.

"Why is she like that?" "How old is she?" "Can she speak?" The questions came thick and fast. Three men stood over the table of instruments, consulting one another about which to try first. Next to me, the woman in grey rose, the only other person not caught up in the excitement. Her face grim, she began to pick her way determinedly through the rows of chairs to the stage. The set of her shoulders told me she was not getting closer just to gawp; she was going to put a stop to it. I willed her on. Could she intervene where I had failed?

When Crillick saw her approach, he hurried to reclaim the crowd's attention. "You have not seen the best of my Leopard Lady yet."

He motioned Henrietta and the others to return to their seats. Then he turned to the Leopard Lady and barked a command at her. She hesitated and he manhandled her to the edge of the stage. Again, her eyes darted around and I tried to catch her eye, in case a friendly face might make her feel safer. In the moment, it was all I had the strength for.

"Go on," Crillick urged.

The Leopard Lady opened her mouth and out of it came the purest sound I ever heard. It wasn't singing but a moan that set the hairs on the back of my neck to standing. It was a cry. In that sound I recognised her pain, writ plain as if I'd read it in one of the leather-bound books that surrounded us. Or maybe it was clear because it was my pain too. I'd wanted to help her, but when the moment came I was petrified as she was. All my bravery, all my smarts, had counted for nothing in the face of the terror that I might be called to the stage to stand alongside her.

A woman I'd heard announced as Lady Martins was the first of Crillick's friends to walk out; maybe she felt something of the Leopard Lady's pain too, a plea beyond mere sensibility. She squeezed past the others in her row and made for the door, and the other women followed after her. The woman in grey was the only female guest who remained, now standing at the front of the room, by the stage. Crillick sensed the change in the mood. He had not expected it; that was clear from the way he bellowed at the Leopard Lady to stop.

"That's enough for tonight, I think. Consider this a preview. Two weeks from tonight, this siren will be appearing in my show and, for those among you who might want to examine her at your leisure, I will be holding private viewings for up to twelve at a time. See me before you leave and we can discuss the terms."

He had to raise his voice to be heard as the rest of his guests shuffled out. Angrily, he turned to the Leopard Lady, who cowered a little before the stick that he gripped in his hand. From the table behind him he took a rope, tied it around her wrists in a sailor's knot, and handed the end to Grace.

"Hold tight to this, you hear me," he said.

"Marcus Crillick? I'm Elvira Masterson."

The bold voice belonged to the woman who had sat along from me. I recognised that name. As Miss Masterson held her hand out for Crillick to shake, it came to me where I had heard it. She was the philanthropist friend that Lucien had wanted to introduce me to. It was she that had been among the campaigners giving out the Sierra Leone pamphlets a week or so earlier. She stepped up onto the makeshift stage so she was on a level with Crillick. He took her hand limply.

"I don't recall . . ." Crillick began.

"My invitation must have gone astray," Miss Masterson said. Crillick rallied a little.

"I wouldn't expect to see a Friend out on a Sunday evening."

"The Lord's work can be done at any time," Miss Masterson said. "I want you to explain what you mean by this . . . this *display*. I won't call her 'Leopard Lady.' What is her name? Speak up, man."

Crillick mumbled again. I couldn't make out the words but he sounded like a sulky child. I wanted to hear what more Miss Masterson had to say to him, but I couldn't miss my own chance—I knew I must speak to the Leopard Lady if I could. The spell of my own fear had been broken. Grace and Alice were ready to lead her away. I had in my head that I could comfort her somehow and approached the stage. Close, I could see that her skin was cracked and ashen, her eyes dulled. There were open sores at her wrists. It seemed tonight was not the first time she'd chafed against the rope. Bile rose in my throat at the thought of what she'd been through.

"Are you well?" I called up to her, but her head was down and she didn't turn. I needed to get her attention somehow. I searched for the words that Lucien had said to me. The Mende that I had felt in my core.

"*Buwa, kahunyaina?*"

No response. "*Sisi wami kunjani?*" I tried instead.

The Leopard Lady raised her head, looked around. Our eyes met and her face that had been so waxy and still came alive.

"*Indodana yami,*" she cried. "*Uthathe indodana yami!*"

What did it mean? She needed help? She was in pain? I repeated her words to myself, desperately trying to commit them to memory.

"*Sisi wami kunjani?*" I said again, hating that I knew no more.

Miss Masterson and Crillick had stopped their argument. The Leopard Lady dashed forward, almost wrenching the rope from Grace's hands.

"*Uthathe indodana yami!*" she said again. The distress on her face was unbearable, but I had no response.

I reached out a hand to her, but Crillick's voice slapped it down like a whip.

"Get it out of here," he said, and Grace and Alice hurried to obey his command.

"Come away, Zillah."

It was Vincent. He'd been sitting in his front-row seat the whole time, watching but taking no action.

I couldn't quite read the tone in his voice—he sounded upset, but I didn't know if it was at me, at Crillick, or at the whole ugly scene that had just played out.

"That woman needs me."

He gripped my arm so hard it was almost painful.

"Come on, Zillah. Miss Masterson will take Crillick to task."

He pulled me away, but I looked over my shoulder as I left the room. Miss Masterson had returned to remonstrating with Crillick.

"That poor woman," I heard her say.

"I don't know what you mean. She will be paid handsomely, this is a good chance for her. They don't feel pain like we do," Crillick replied.

Vincent shut the door and the rest of the conversation faded away.

"Go to my room, Zillah."

Surely, he couldn't be angry with me? All I had done was try to speak to the Leopard Lady in the midst of her distress.

"Go," Vincent said again. "The party is over."

He was right about that. Ahead, the hallway was busy with servants running to and fro to fetch cloaks and summon carriages. If I lingered, I'd be called upon to help and I couldn't face it. Not after what I'd just seen. I looked around for Henrietta, but there was no sign of her or her mother.

"Vincent?" I said softly, but he didn't seem to hear me.

I hovered by the library door for a moment, but though I could hear the row between Miss Masterson and Crillick went on, I could not make out what they said. I was glad the Leopard Lady had a champion in Miss Masterson. I hoped she knew she had one in me too. I felt connected to her, through my act and through the Zulu words she had called out to me.

"Zillah, are you coming?" Vincent called over his shoulder. He strode away from me toward the stairs. I trailed after him, unable to go any faster, weighed down by what I had witnessed.

XIV

The Empty Kitchen

It was a relief to get back to the bedroom. I opened the door to find that the maids had been in to straighten everything since we'd dressed. With all that was going on downstairs, how had they had the time? The bed was neatly made, the lamps turned on, and the fire stoked. On the dressing table there was a steaming ewer and a bowl and towels laid out so we could wash. It was all so civilised, but not ten minutes ago a woman had been paraded before an audience that questioned her humanity, then led away at the end of a rope. I had been just five when Wilberforce claimed his victory. Fifteen years on and he must be turning in his grave.

Vincent shut the door behind us. The decisive click as he turned the key in the lock said "enough." If only a closed door could keep out thoughts as well as people. Henrietta, Crillick, Miss Masterson, Ma Alexander. Their voices rang inside my head and the cry of the Leopard Lady was the melody that carried them. I pressed my hands to my temples, but it was not enough to still the clamor in my mind. Too tired even to ask him to help free me from the maid's corset, I perched on the edge of the chaise and watched as Vincent undressed. First his cravat hit the floor, then his waistcoat and jacket. He gave no thought to where they landed, too used to being picked up after. The carelessness of it rankled.

"You should have spent more time with me tonight," he said.

He was down to his breeches before he noticed that I'd made no reply. By then I'd lain back, too weary to stay upright. The bones of my corset weren't quite so sharp when I was on my side.

"I hope you're not sulking about our day trip, Zillah. I said I would make it up to you."

How could he think about Richmond after what we had just witnessed? It was almost as if the last half hour hadn't happened. I couldn't keep the anger from my voice.

"I don't care about that. I'm worried for that poor woman. She spoke to me, Vincent."

There was the sound of water being poured and Vincent's voice was muffled behind a flannel.

"What could you possibly know of that gibberish she spoke? Besides, Elvira has already kicked up quite a fuss. Marcus will not be happy about it."

It was the one bright spot, the way Miss Masterson had barreled down to the front of the room to accost Crillick. I would've been scared myself if I'd seen her coming for me with such fierce intent, but I was glad the Leopard Lady had someone like that in her corner.

"You know her well?"

"Oh yes. She's heiress to the Masterson fortune, but she won't marry now. She has causes instead, lots of them. She's quite formidable."

There was a sneering tone to his voice that I didn't like. It reduced Crillick's treatment of the Leopard Lady, and Elvira Masterson's reaction, to a spat between two people with opposing views. I raised myself up on my elbows to see him. He ran the flannel across the back of his neck and then returned it to the water. He seemed to be simply washing away the evening like any other.

"Did you not see how they touched her?" I said.

The pale, spindly fingers of Lord this and Sir that had been everywhere. I shuddered to think of the way they'd prodded, pinched, and poked, and the women no better. Worse, in fact, for surely many of them would know the sickening feeling of hands where they didn't belong.

"She's a novelty, that's why. Besides, when she goes onstage no one will get near her. Barky will see to that."

"Crillick's not going to show her at the theatre, is he?"

"He hasn't told me much of what he has planned, but going by tonight, I think he'd be confident that the crowd will love her."

I thought of the men and women who came to watch our show. How they bayed if there was the slightest delay and broke out into fights when they got bored in the interval. A funny sort of love, that.

"I hope you're not jealous," Vincent said. "I see how you and Ellen snipe at one another sometimes, so don't pretend you're above it. The Leopard Lady is no rival, though."

Why not? Because she was a real freak and I was a gaffed one? Because I could change my clothes and scrub off the paint? Besides, did he really think my concern here was only about my own standing in the theatre?

"Did you not see how scared she was, Vincent?"

"She will get more comfortable with time."

You did, he could have added but didn't.

His ablutions done, he walked over to the bed, pulled back the sheets and blankets, and got in, lifting the heavily embroidered eiderdown up to his chin.

"Come to bed, my love."

"I'm not tired," I said. It wasn't true. I was weary to my bones but I felt restless. I rose from the chaise and sat at Vincent's desk. On a piece of paper I wrote down the words that the Leopard Lady had called out to me. There was no chance I could forget them now, but it didn't get me any closer to understanding what she'd meant. Maybe if I could see her there'd be some clue. I could take her one of the creams I made up for myself from the ingredients in Crillick's kitchen, some ointment for the sores on her wrists.

"Is he keeping her in the house?" I said.

"I imagine so. Where else would she go at this hour?"

"I want to see her."

Vincent lifted his head so our eyes connected over the bed-covers.

"Don't be silly, it is late. The best thing you can do is come to bed."

"I want to see her," I repeated.

"You should wait until the morning, Zillah. She'll be in bed herself, I'm sure."

I couldn't deny the sense in this. It must be past midnight now, but I knew that even if the Leopard Lady had been given a bed, she would not be sleeping. Who could rest after that? I decided to try another tack. I stood up and crossed the room, sitting down on the bed with my back to Vincent so he could unlace me. His fingers were nimble as any lady's maid's and I pushed away the thought it was something he'd done many times for other lovers before me.

"It upset me to see her tonight, Vincent. Not because I am jealous, but because she is hurting."

An appeal to his better nature always worked. Now my dress was unlaced he pulled the back sections apart and I wriggled out of it before folding it in half.

His voice softened in agreement. "It was distasteful, I grant you. I don't hold with all that nonsense about science. I would rather they hadn't talked of examining her like that."

"Do you think they would have gone through with it if it wasn't for Miss Masterson?"

Vincent's silence told me what he thought. He turned me

around to face him and wiped away the tears on my cheeks with the pads of his thumbs.

"Don't cry, now."

"Will you help her?"

"I don't know what you want me to do about it, Zillah. You should put it from your mind."

That's what he was doing. Acting like it hadn't happened. Maybe once I could have done that too. Didn't I put Amazonia from my mind when I came offstage and removed the leopard-skin costume? This felt different, though. The woman tonight—this "Leopard Lady"—had appealed to me as one woman to another. The remembrance of the catch in her voice made me cry all the harder.

"Please, Vincent, you must help her," I said again.

"I would do anything not to see you sad."

"Speak to Crillick, then. Tell him he can't treat her like that, like an animal. Tell him she's not to be experimented on."

"I will, but only if you promise to get into bed now."

He shuffled back to make room for me and raised the covers so I could crawl under them. His body was warm and I felt comforted wrapped in his arms.

"Thank you," I said, and turned my head to plant a kiss on his shoulder. He'd closed his eyes and his breaths had evened out but I knew he wasn't sleeping.

"You'll talk to Crillick tomorrow?"

"Yes, Zillah, I said I would. I didn't like it any more than you did."

There! I knew he had been disturbed, as I had been. How could he not have been? I waited for him to say more, to condemn his friend, to help me make sense of what we had seen. But no.

"Sleep now, will you?" was all he said.

I closed my eyes obediently, still troubled but calmer than I had been. Vincent would speak to Crillick in the morning and the

Leopard Lady would be safe. It would not change what she had been through tonight, but it would mean she would not have to face a crowd like that again.

᭚

It was still dark when I awoke and the house had the quiet of the early hours. I was desperate to relieve myself and climbed out of bed to hover over the chamber pot. Through the half-open window, I heard Big Ben chime for two o'clock. I had been asleep for little over an hour. My business done, I pushed the pot back under the bed, but I wasn't ready to lie down again. The Leopard Lady's face had haunted my dreams. I had to see her. I leant over the bed to watch Vincent for a moment, but he was dead to the world. I would be glad of his help tomorrow but I knew my rest would be fitful until I had visited the Leopard Lady for myself. Was she able to get to the pot? Had Grace left her some water? I needed to find out.

I slipped Vincent's dressing gown on over my nightclothes. Late as it was, I couldn't be certain that all Crillick's friends had left. There were none that I'd want to encounter without the protection of corset, stays, and Vincent at my side, especially now they knew me as a servant and would think themselves free to take any liberties they might want. Off the kitchen there was an unused servants' room where I imagined Crillick would have had Grace house the Leopard Lady for the night. It would only take a minute to check on her. I put a jar of cream in my pocket and a pomade I'd made from bear's grease and almond oil. She could use it on her hair.

I eased the bedroom door open and poked my head out, but the corridor was quiet. The gas lamps had been dimmed, which meant the guests were gone or retired to their bedrooms. I closed the door softly behind me and crept down the stairs reassured that if any of Crillick's friends had stayed over, they were fast asleep now.

The kitchen was at the back of the house. Mostly I entered the house that way and waved to Grace when Vincent wasn't with me. When I pushed open the door, I saw that a candle had been left burning and the fire was banked. The embers gave off an orangey light that was just enough to see by. It should have been comforting, but the draft from the open door made the flames gutter, and jagged shadows danced against the walls. I stepped into the room and sucked in a breath at the cold of the flagstones beneath my feet, the shock of it made worse after the opulence of the thick carpet that lined the hallway.

The room was dominated by the kitchen table. It was where the undercook weighed ingredients and chopped vegetables before handing them over to be boiled or fried or baked at the range. It had been scrubbed down and two china bowls set out ready for Cook to prepare Crillick's breakfast. I skirted around it, past a large dresser that half-covered one wall, and made for the small room on the far side of the kitchen, where I knew there was a cot as well as a table and shelves full of pots and pans. The door creaked open but when I looked over to the makeshift bed, it was tidy, the covers neatly made. No one had slept here tonight. I looked around, puzzled. There was no chance that Crillick would have given the Leopard Lady a guest room. Where else would she be?

For a moment I wavered, knowing that the most sensible thing to do would be to go back to bed. I'd not run into anyone so far but I didn't want to push my luck. I stood still, straining my ears for the noises of people moving about, but there were only the nighttime sounds of the house settling. Yes, Vincent would be annoyed if he woke to find I'd disobeyed him, but I wasn't ready to give up on the Leopard Lady yet. Grace would start her chores in less than an hour. After last night's event, she would no doubt begin in the library. I would wait for her there and ask where the Leopard Lady was being kept.

The library door swung back at the push of my fingertips and I saw that the room had not been righted since the performance. The chairs remained in loose rows, but some had been scattered as their occupants got up to touch the Leopard Lady, or to storm out at the end of the night. Others had been turned to one side when members of the audience whispered to their neighbors, trying to work out what she was. There was a haze of fruit-scented cigar smoke, and discarded glasses lined the mantelpiece. A sadness descended on me. I'd never be here again without feeling the Leopard Lady's presence, remembering the vacant terror as she looked out from the stage at the men and women to whom she was nothing more than a curiosity.

The little trolley of medical instruments was still there, by the side of the improvised stage. Better not to know exactly what was on it, but I couldn't resist the pull. A long thin needle—Lord knew what that was for. A scalpel. They'd tried to remove her colour with saliva and the scratch of a fingernail. Was the curved blade of the scalpel the next step? I grazed it lightly against my arm, wondering what it would feel like.

"Careful, Zillah, you might cut yourself."

It was Crillick's voice. There was a distinctive way he lingered over the double *l* in my name, like he was tasting it. But where was it coming from? I spun 'round, the scalpel still gripped in my hand.

"Did you enjoy the performance this evening? I especially wanted you to like it."

Crillick rose from the window seat where three hours earlier I had stood to watch him reveal the Leopard Lady. I'd been in the library for ten minutes at least. He must have watched me all this time. His cravat was loosened, he'd pulled out his shirttails, and as he weaved toward me, I saw his eyes were glossy with drink. I could slice him, dig the blade in, twist it, watch him bleed. The rush of thoughts, the violence of them, scared me and I let the scalpel fall.

"She cannot write, if it's an autograph you came for."

I pulled Vincent's dressing gown close around me, and crossed my arms against my chest. Grace should be here any moment. Until then, I'd have to play for time. Please, God, don't let her come along, hear his voice, and walk away.

"I doubt you know what she can and cannot do."

"On the contrary, I assure you, I know exactly what she can do."

He leered as he said it and I tasted the bitterness of bile at the back of my throat. It was not enough that he exhibited her on-stage; I suppose I should have guessed that he'd defiled her in that way too. I couldn't leave her to his mercy. Somehow, I would have to get her away from him. He moved toward me and I stepped back to keep the distance between us, but now he stood directly between me and the library door.

Crillick put on the showman's voice that so grated on me earlier. "She can sing, she can dance." He reverted to his usual tone. "You should look to yourself, Zillah. You might lose your job."

I often told myself that Crillick and Vincent were not alike, but perhaps they were more similar than I wanted to imagine. Both assumed that I was jealous or territorial about my role at the theatre, but this wasn't about me.

"She can feel too, or do you choose to ignore that?"

"I was warned the ladies might be tiresome, and so it has proved."

Crillick spoke more to himself than to me. Was this my chance to leave? He would be able to cover any move I made toward the door, but he was drunk so maybe that would slow him down.

"Miss Masterson is right. You treat her like an animal."

"Perhaps, but others won't be so squeamish. You saw them. They want to touch, to poke, to prod. Weren't you fascinated too?"

I thought of the white patch in the Leopard Lady's hair. He was right. I had wanted to touch her, but not like them. They looked to find difference. I wanted to know how we were alike, if her curls were soft like mine.

"I want to see her," I said.

"You had your chance earlier. Now you must wait and pay your shilling like anyone else."

"Where are you keeping her? You must let me see if she needs anything."

Crillick looked at me quizzically. *Careful, Zillah. Don't make demands.* But it wasn't that. My distress had tickled him and now he was more determined than ever to deny me. He became business-like, almost as if he wasn't as drunk as he'd first seemed.

"She's quite safe and being very well looked after. You have me all wrong, Zillah. You act as though she were my prisoner, but she is one of my staff. As are you."

His warning snuffed the fiery words on my tongue. I would do well to heed it. Vincent's protection allowed me some leeway. Crillick wouldn't want to offend his influential friend, but I didn't want to push either man, didn't want to make them choose when I couldn't guarantee that I would come out on top, however much Vincent said he cared for me and no matter how many punters I brought to Crillick's theatre. Wealthy men, I had learnt, could be relied on to stick together.

Crillick beckoned me with a crooked finger, but he was cracked if he thought I'd go within two feet of him. There was danger in him most especially when he'd been drinking.

"There's more to come, you know."

The excitement in his voice made me cringe. More from the Leopard Lady? Or, God forbid, more freaks?

A scene built in my mind. It was Crillick's theatre, but with all the seats removed so it was more like an exhibition hall. And there was Marcus Crillick himself in the center, dressed as he had been tonight in the white coat of a scientist. At his feet crouched the Leopard Lady and all around him were cages and cages and cages of men and women and children. I knew I should leave but I was locked into the horror of it. Dimly I heard Crillick say, "Some will come for the tawdry display, to feel the delicious thrill of fear that such creatures exist, but most of all I want to cater to those who wish to experiment."

The image shifted. Now I saw the Leopard Lady laid out on a table, bound by ropes at her ankles and wrists. Crillick hovered over her, a needle in his hand, while four men in tweed looked on and a fifth scribbled furiously in his notebook. While the waking dream played before my eyes, Crillick crossed the room and crowded me once more.

"I see you're worried, Zillah. But you've no need to fear. I won't throw you over. We've done very well together, have we not?"

He reached out and ran the side of his finger along my cheek. I held myself completely still.

"I'm sure you saw that some of the chaps tonight were quite excited, but I'll always prefer your kind, I think. You mulattos have the same appetites, all the curves, and yet you're so much more feminine."

His finger continued its trail. The nail, ever so slightly too long, grazed my neck. Soon it would reach my collarbone.

"Your act. It's inspired by a real one, you know. I met her when I was twelve years old. She was from the Dahomey tribe. Have you heard of them?"

At the base of my throat Crillick withdrew his hand. I struggled to hold back a cry of relief.

"She had not a stitch on from here to here." He traced the tip of his index finger from his neck downward. His fingers skimmed over the fine buttons of his dress shirt until they reached the waistband of his breeches. It was where he would've touched me were it not for Vincent's tightly tied gown. I shuddered at the thought.

"She was not as tall as you, but a fine figure nonetheless. She was with her mate and three others. A whole tribe to be had on contract. The bidding for their services was something fierce but my father didn't raise his paddle once. I couldn't understand why, and he wouldn't say. I thought of her several times over the years, and then when I saw you, it came to me. I could re-create her."

That day when I had auditioned for Crillick's. I had gone there expecting to be a chorus girl at best. I remembered the way Crillick's eyes had lit up when he saw me. How he had demanded I show him my legs and forced his fingers into my hair. I hadn't been auditioning for Crillick's public show, but for his private fantasy. No wonder he had been so eager to give me a part despite my lack of experience. And he had built up my act to the point where I was headlining. My outfit, the dancing, even down to the props he'd brought back from his trip. All designed to stoke his desire. And I had played right into it, believing somehow that it had to do with my own abilities, my talent and independence. Oh, the shame. In this moment, I knew that whenever he came to watch me, I'd feel dirty. And now he'd not only be thinking of the Dahomey woman, but comparing me to the Leopard Lady too. I had to get us both away from him.

"If Vincent wakes, he will wonder where I am," I said. I hated how small my voice sounded.

"You should go to him, then."

As if he would've let me before now. It was the touching. It had stirred him and, in doing so, it'd told him that he'd gone too far. Crillick held open the door. I hesitated, knowing that I would have to squeeze past him. It need only be for a second. I stepped forward but, as I did so, he did too. I was trapped, the doorframe hard on my left and Crillick with his front pressed against my side, his mouth at my right ear.

"Remember who's in charge here," he said and I flinched from the stale warmth of his breath. "My house, my show, and Vincent is *my* friend."

"What would he say if he saw you now?" I managed.

"Why don't you scream, see if he comes?"

I considered it, but only for a moment. Vincent said he loved me, but he ignored the things he didn't want to see. Shrugged them off, like he'd done with the Leopard Lady tonight. Maybe he would choose to ignore the evidence of his eyes. It might suit him to see me as a wanton, rather than to confront the fact that his friend was a villain. As Crillick said, we lived in his house, but in that moment I longed to be back in St. Giles, for all its squalor, where the villains had knives and knuckledusters—the sort of weapons you could recognise.

When Crillick knew I would not make a sound, he pressed against me. I felt the full weight of his body: his strength and my helplessness. It was less than ten seconds before he stepped back to let me pass, but we both knew he'd only let me go because I, his proud Amazonia, was beaten.

I half ran down the corridor and back upstairs, throwing glances over my shoulder, but Crillick had no need to follow me. Why should he? He could get to me anytime. If only Vincent had the funds for an apartment of his own. Damn his father for beggaring him. I reached the bedroom door and wrenched it open. Inside, I locked it, the key rattling as my hand shook. I sagged back against the door, needing its solidity to keep me upright. Vincent still slept. He lay on his side, his head resting on his hands. My breaths were so harsh and ragged I feared he would wake, but soon my heart slowed and finally I was calm. I put my ear to the door. Not a sound was to be heard, but that didn't stop me pulling the chaise half across the door to make sure no one could get in.

I tiptoed over to the bed and, instead of taking off Vincent's dressing gown, I wrapped it tighter and huddled down under the covers. Though it wasn't cold, I trembled from head to foot as though I had the ague. My left hip was sore where Crillick had crushed it against the library doorframe. I'd only gotten away because he'd let me.

I started, but it was only Vincent's arm that snaked around me, and I felt him bury his face in my hair. He hadn't fully woken, but perhaps some part of him sensed my fear because he held me tight. For now, I was safe in his arms, but Crillick's challenge still echoed in my ears. *Why don't you scream?* he'd said, knowing that, as long as I was in his power, I couldn't make a sound.

I didn't know where the Leopard Lady was, or even if she was safe, but I was more determined than ever that I must help her. If Crillick could make me feel so powerless, when I had my act and Vincent to protect me, I didn't dare to dwell on what danger she must be in when left alone with him.

XV

A Game of Billiards

They say it's dishonorable to eavesdrop, but listening at doors has often served me well. You don't always learn much from hearing two gentlemen talk — with them it's grunts and harrumphs and the occasional sniff of snuff — but Crillick was a commoner at heart and tended to say too much. I knew that if I timed it right, I could learn where he was keeping the Leopard Lady. I didn't have to wait too long.

Vincent and I were eating dinner on Monday evening, the day after the party. He'd loved me as the sun came up, but since then we'd been a little strange with one another. Vincent had had a letter from his father so I knew what was preoccupying him. It was the Leopard Lady that was still on my mind, and now I was certain that Crillick was keeping her elsewhere. He'd barely been at the house since returning from his business travels and something told me it was to do with her. *More to come*, he'd said. I needed to find out exactly what. More freaks? Or did he have further horrors he intended to inflict on her, specifically?

"Are you well, Zillah? You've been listless all day."

"A headache is all."

"You must go and lie down," Vincent said. "I promised Crillick a game of billiards tonight, so I'll be late. When I come up, I'll try not to wake you."

I crossed my knife and fork over one another and stood. He captured my hand and pressed it to his lips.

"You are sure you're not ill?"

"I'll be fine once I've slept."

Vincent knew how my rest had been disturbed. I had dreamt of the Leopard Lady and woken up whimpering. But she was not alone in my dreams. I was there with her. Sometimes I *was* her. And when I woke, I remembered what Lucien Winters had said: *Mark me, Zillah. I want you to think about tonight. About the part you play.* He'd said he would save me and I had laughed at him. Now it was all beginning to make more sense. I *did* need him—not for me, but for her. For all that I remained wary of the strange power he seemed to have over me, I realised it was time to pay him another visit.

"I haven't forgotten about Richmond," Vincent said, and I blushed to be caught thinking of another man when the one I thought I'd been falling in love with was making plans for us.

⌒

The chance to listen in while Vincent and Crillick played billiards was too good to pass up. Once I knew Crillick was home and had had the time to wash and eat, I tiptoed along to the billiard room. Sure enough, I was rewarded. Inside I could hear them talking and, better yet, they'd left the door a touch ajar.

The clack of billiard balls told me they were in the midst of their game. Sometimes their voices were closer, sometimes further as they moved around the table to take their shots. It was Eustace who had taught me how to play most games. As children we liked cards—whist, écarté, and loo—but billiards was a gentleman's game. It wasn't until Vincent that I'd been introduced to it.

Of all the places in the house, the billiard room was most clearly

Crillick's, but while he was away Vincent had taken me in there for the first time, determined that I would learn the game and help stave off his boredom after dinner. It was a small room, all dark wood and furnishings, the only spot of colour the big table with its felted green top. Vincent's attempt to teach me had failed, but we'd enjoyed it. How much better it had been without Crillick in our lives.

I pushed the door open a little wider so I was able to see in without giving myself away. My view wasn't perfect—I could only see one end of the billiard table—but that didn't matter; the most important thing was to hear what they said. Here was Vincent, though. I enjoyed the sight of his lean figure stretched across the table. "Are you happy with how it went last night?" he was saying to Crillick as he leant low over his cue to line up a shot.

His eyes were narrowed in concentration and his mouth quirked up as I heard the ball slide into the pocket. Straightening, he reached for the chalk before taking a sip from his glass of brandy. He moved away and Crillick took his place, his eyes flickering over the table, weighing up the options for a winning hazard.

"So-so. Milburn showed a lot of interest, but he only dabbles in science. It's Tonleigh I want. If he comes along, others will follow. He's published, you know."

Vincent again. He placed his drink on the lip of the table and rested his weight on the cue.

"I didn't know that was what you had in mind."

There was disapproval in his voice. Good. Could this be the moment that he impressed upon Crillick the evil of what he was doing? But no. His hatred of confrontation won out because next I heard him say, "The men seemed on board, I think. It's the ladies that you will have to win over."

It was almost as though he was giving him permission. I could imagine what he'd say if challenged—that a man must look to himself to know if he was doing the right thing. But he had influence over Crillick and could've used it if he chose to.

"I could do without that bluestocking bint," Crillick said.

"Elvira Masterson? She's got the beating of you, old man."

Crillick stepped forward and Vincent moved out of his way. Crillick must have made a clumsy shot, for he cursed under his breath.

"You've got to give a chap a little room to maneuver," he said. "It wasn't you that invited her, was it?"

"Not me. It was your affair, after all."

"Didn't stop you inviting your"—he hesitated—"inviting Zillah along. Although I must say it quite amused me to see her filling that little uniform."

Vincent chuckled but it sounded brittle.

"Much good it did me. I hardly saw her all night and when I did she harangued me about how you'd upset her. I told her I'd speak to you."

"You let her take far too many liberties. Sometimes I wish I hadn't introduced you both."

"I'm very glad you did," Vincent said, and I blushed to hear the two men laugh. Of course, he was a man like any other, but somehow I didn't like to hear him leer. That's what you get for eavesdropping, I suppose.

"So, what's it all about, Crillick? Will you insist on this . . . what are you calling it?"

"Top secret for now. Consider your duty to Zillah discharged."

"I think she was expecting a little more than that," Vincent said, but when Crillick changed the subject, he let him. I hated the way he pandered to him. Crillick's behavior was obviously in need of checking, but Vincent always stepped back from a row. Silly of me to think that he would help. There was little point in staying to hear any more. I started to tiptoe away when Crillick said, "You didn't spend much time with Hen."

This got me back to the door.

"I told you she's not for me," Vincent said.

"You could do worse. Bit of cash to fill the coffers."

"I'm not that pressed for funds."

This was news. Vincent had told me he stayed with Crillick because he had no money. All this time he had lied to me? It made no sense. He was as keen for us to have a space of our own as I was. Or was he stringing me along? An Indian shawl, crystallised ginger, a Fortnum's hamper. Gifts and trinkets, yes, but of promises he'd made, how many had been kept? Richmond had been a promise.

"How much did you make from the compensation? Forty thousand, wasn't it?"

What on earth would Vincent have to be compensated for? Vincent stepped up to the table again. I saw he frowned as he always did when money was discussed in any detail. Crillick wasn't watching him as closely as I did, though, for he blundered on, "There's a lot you could do with that sum of money."

I felt anger bubble up inside me. If Vincent had ready access to such a huge sum, we should be living in our own flat. In truth, an amount like that could buy us a mansion.

"It's not my money, it belongs to my father. In any case, I won't spend it. I'll have nothing to do with it. Filthy business."

Crillick looked as if he might argue, but then shrugged it off as if he couldn't quite be bothered.

"All I'm saying is have your fun and have some money," he said.

Vincent shook his head but he was smiling. It was clear what Crillick meant. I was the fun and Henrietta was the money. I knew the longer I stayed the more upsetting the conversation would become—but my anger had me rooted to the spot.

"I know if I were you, I'd have them both," Crillick said. "It's not as if anyone can't see exactly what it is you like about Zillah."

Surely he wouldn't dare talk to Vincent about what he'd called my appetites? Or was it a topic he'd been desperate to broach, and now he'd take the chance to satisfy his curiosity? The atmosphere between the two men had become fraught and tense all of a sudden. Vincent laughed but there was no real mirth there anymore.

Frustrated by my partial view, I pushed the door a little wider still, grateful for the servants who kept the hinges well oiled. There were four balls left on the table, but for the moment the game had been abandoned and the two men faced off across the baize.

"She came to see me after the party, practically in her smalls," Crillick said.

Lies. I'd been wrapped up in Vincent's dressing gown, but Crillick made it sound like I had made a play for him. Vincent had told me to leave it with him. He wouldn't like this at all and Crillick knew it.

"She was pleading with me about the Leopard Lady. 'Promise me you won't hurt her, Marcus' and all that."

I never called Crillick by his first name. Surely this would tell Vincent that his friend was lying, but the jealousy was on him now. I heard it in the chill of his voice and what he said next.

"She's frightened of a little healthy competition is all."

How could Vincent say that? He must think very little of me if he thought all I cared about was my place in the theatre. He knew there was more to it than that. I knew he'd felt the wrongness of it too, even though he chose not to confront it. I did not have that privilege.

"So, should I tell Alexander you'll come with me to his dinner tomorrow?"

Crillick was playing Vincent like a fiddle. Even before he agreed, I knew he would fall for it and my heart sank.

"I don't see why not."

"Good man. Alexander asked me to put a word in, so he'll be pleased. He'd be the perfect partner in my little venture. If you could oblige me by—"

"By marrying his sister," Vincent cut in. "Dammit, you beat all."

Crillick was unrepentant. "Business is business, old man."

I leant back against the wall and there was a clack as another ball was potted.

"That's three hundred points. I make that the game," Crillick said.

"Did you not touch the black when you leant down? I could've sworn it moved."

"Not me. I'm surprised you'd be a sore loser."

Immediately Vincent backed down. It summed him up, really, to know that Crillick was in the wrong but not to take a stand against him. I slunk back to the bedroom and blew out the candle, but I couldn't sleep. There was a sound of banging, sawing not too far away. Who in the neighborhood would be building at this time of night?

When Vincent came in an hour or two later, I kept my eyes shut and he made no attempt to wake me. I felt him looking me over. Thinking about what Crillick had said to him, no doubt. Part of me wanted to defend myself against Crillick's innuendos, even if it meant confessing that I'd been eavesdropping, but another part was angry that he'd let himself get conned, that he'd believe Crillick and his lies over everything he knew about me. Here was proof of what I'd always feared: for all his professions of love, when it came down to it, men stuck together if there was a choice to be made.

Vincent lay on the far side of the bed, not touching me. Let him stew. I knew he'd drop hints tomorrow that he was going to meet Henrietta and I was determined not to rise to it.

When Vincent's breathing lengthened, I rolled over and watched his back. Silly to think I could trust him to get the job done. If I was going to protect the Leopard Lady, I'd have to do it by myself. Lucien Winters would know what *Uthathe indodana yami* meant.

XVI

Stalking Crillick

Vincent had already left when I woke the next morning at half past seven, and I was glad of it. We'd only have rowed and I didn't have time for that.

I had a new plan to find the Leopard Lady—I would follow Crillick and find out where he went to conduct his business in the daytime. Eavesdropping had only backfired, but maybe he would lead me to her if I were careful. Tuesdays were for rehearsals but Barky wouldn't be too annoyed as long as I was there before lunchtime. That gave me a good three hours to see if Crillick's movements would offer me any clues to the Leopard Lady's whereabouts. I filled my pockets with salve and bandages for her. There were no guarantees I would see her today, but if I did, I could tend to her wounds and find a means to help her escape him.

For once Crillick didn't call out the carriage. It was the first sign that things were going my way. If he was on foot, I'd have no trouble tracking him. Perhaps it was the mild weather that had encouraged him to walk. Though it was not yet nine o'clock, the sun was already high in the sky. I felt the sweat form under my armpits as I half ran to keep up with him. From the bottom of Northumberland Avenue, Crillick made straight for the pier at Westmin-

ster and went down the flight of stairs that took him riverside. Of
course he wouldn't use his carriage for such a short journey. I let a
few people pass in front of me before I followed him. It wouldn't
do to get spotted.

Embankment had never sat well with me. I wasn't bothered by
the smell of the river, but the old ships gave off a stink so strong
you could almost taste it: brine, damp sailcloth, and decayed fish.
It clung to me, that smell, caught in my hair and seeped into my
clothes, so that whenever I went there it followed me for days afterward and only scrubbing myself raw and a spray of Mrs. Bee-
ton's rosewater could shift it. I'd caught a nasty whiff off Crillick
when he'd offered to drive me to St. Giles after ruining the plans
I'd made with Vincent. Now I recognised what it was. He'd been
here at least once since his return.

As usual Embankment was bustling, the air noisy with the cawing of gulls and sails whipping in the wind. There were sailors
—Black and white—with nothing to do but drink while they
awaited their next ship, bowlegged baggage carriers hauling boxes
of goods from who knew where, and street children hoping to run
errands for a penny. Crillick jumped onto a boat and I watched as
he headed downriver toward the City.

It wasn't hard to keep sight of him. The river traffic was so
heavy that his private vessel was no faster than the crowded steam-
boat that I'd hopped onto. Most of my fellow passengers were
clerks, but there were one or two other women—servants by the
looks of them—and I stayed close to them, wanting to keep as
low a profile as possible, no easy task when, as was so often the
case, I was the only Black woman there. I had a couple of coins
on me, but I wasn't due to get paid until Friday and I wanted to
keep a bit in case the Leopard Lady needed it. Dodging the captain's eye got harder as we floated past St. Paul's and the numbers
on board dwindled.

"Where you headed to, miss?" the captain said, holding out his
hand as I rummaged in my pocket for the halfpenny fare.

I could hardly say I was following Crillick. He was still ahead of me. But if I didn't say something soon, the captain would think me simple and throw me off.

"The new docks are the last stop," he said, doubtful that I'd be headed there, and well he might be, but it made sense.

"Yes, West India Docks is where I want."

"You're sure? Not with the customs people, are you?" he said and laughed at the very idea of it.

"My master works for the West India Company," I said, with a flash of inspiration. It was the right answer.

The captain was satisfied with that. "Only doing my job to ask, miss. The security is something fierce down there. Seamen, servants like yourself, and customs officials are all that's allowed there unaccompanied, like."

"Naturally," I said. Everyone in London knew that the new docks had been built solely to cut down on thievery. Before business had been transferred, I'd benefited from a few bits and pieces going astray myself. The bolt of cotton for my dress had come from India. Old and well-worn as it was, it was quality and had lasted. No chance I could have paid the shop price.

It was only a little farther and soon I found myself deposited dockside. The whole journey from Westminster had taken around half an hour. I wondered how often Crillick shuttled back and forth. He'd seemed to know where he was headed, and I couldn't help but wonder if this was where he was keeping the Leopard Lady. With so many sailors from all around the world—Blacks and lascars and Chinese—it would be easy for her to blend in as long as no one saw the patches on her face. I could think of no other reason for him being here. He didn't import, and if he was buying materials, there'd be no call to come all the way out to the island. Rum and sugar were stored in quantity at the docks, but all could be sampled in the City.

West India Docks was just like the pictures I'd seen printed in the *Illustrated London News*. Set a little farther back from the water were a couple of two-story buildings marked Customs and Excise, a row of smaller offices where the exporters had set up shop, and huge warehouses for keeping timber and mahogany. It wasn't a place for anyone delicate—the noise and the numbers of unsavory people saw to that—but I felt more and more convinced that Crillick was hiding the Leopard Lady here. I'd hoped for a clue to where she was but, with any luck, he would take me straight to her.

I'd have to find him first, though. For now, I couldn't see him and cursed myself for losing him. I didn't have long to spare if I wanted to make it to work on time. After a minute I spied him talking to a thin, rat-faced man who had the look of a survivor. When the two men had finished speaking, Crillick moved off. That he knew where he was going was clear, for he didn't waver or pause. I could follow him, but something told me I should speak to Ratface first.

Ratface was overseeing the loading of barrels onto a cart, but I felt his eyes on me as I walked up to him. Close up, I could see his skin was pockmarked, his teeth rotten. It was nowhere near lunchtime, but when he spoke there was rum on his breath.

"That man in the tweed," I said.

"What about him?"

"I want to know what you talked about."

"Want to come here and ask me my business, do you? Man's talk ain't for the likes of pretty little things like you. Now piss off."

I jingled the remaining coins in my pocket, hoping to make it sound like there were more than there were. I had little enough to spare, but if I had to pay for information, then so be it.

"I don't need all the details. The gist will do me."

Ratface turned away and called over to the loaders who'd slackened from their work while he'd spoken to me. I needed something else to make him talk.

"It's for my master," I said. It had worked well enough to get me down here.

Ratface looked me over, weighing up who my master might be. "One of Black Bill's girls, is it?"

I flinched at the name, and Ratface smiled, believing it was confirmation that he'd guessed right.

Bill Dixon was the leader of the Blackbirds, celebrated in the penny bloods as the King of St. Giles. He ruled with an iron will over the rookery's alleys and its cathouses, its pubs, and its slums. If there was any racket going from Bow to Kensington, you could be sure him and his gang were behind it. Housebreaking and thieving were the Blackbirds' special skills. But Bill wasn't above getting his hands dirty. He wore a leather belt with a sharpened silver buckle, and word had it that his crew and enemies alike feared its gouging lash. *Don't think of Bill; you know what it leads to.* But it was too late. Eustace's face was also in my mind now—not cocky and handsome, as I liked to remember it, but swollen and purple as he fought for breath at the end of the rope.

"I should've guessed by the looks of you," Ratface said. "You can keep your pennies. But mind you tell him it was Stivers from down the docks that done him this favour."

Bill and the Blackbirds had cost me dear. If they hadn't enticed Eustace into working for them, he'd still be alive now. For the sake of what they'd led him to, I'd determined to leave St. Giles, work as hard as I could to take myself beyond their influence. But this wasn't about me. Could I risk using Bill's name if it got me closer to finding the Leopard Lady?

"Yes, one of Bill's girls," I heard myself say. I'd just have to pray that word of this didn't get back to the man himself.

"You should have said up front," Ratface muttered. I wasn't imagining that some of his swagger had gone, and I felt a chill steal over me. By invoking Black Bill I'd put myself on dangerous ground here, but it was done now. *And if he were still here, Eustace would understand why I'd done it.*

"I know it was Marcus Crillick you spoke to. I just need to know why," I said.

"A shipment came in with his name on it. Some livestock, you might say."

My stomach roiled. Livestock meant people. Only the credulous thought slavery had truly ended, regardless of how the liberals congratulated themselves. They could pass all the laws they liked in Parliament, but I wasn't convinced that the richest abided by them.

"How many?"

"Handful, that's all. He's not in the volume game. Too much risk nowadays. Something a little more specialised."

There's more to come—that's what he'd said. More freaks like the Leopard Lady. The half dream I'd had came back to me and I tried to blink it away. Ratface jerked his head to the left. "Over there. That's where Crillick keeps his cargo."

I turned to look where he pointed. A lockup made of corrugated iron. Crillick stood outside it. Surely he didn't need a whole warehouse? The thought of how many people a space like that could hold made me queasy, but Crillick was about theatres, entertainments.

"He owns it?"

"Not him. I forget the name but I could get it for you."

"Will you tell me who's been in and out?"

He leant into me. "Anything for Bill," he said, his breath on my face.

It took all my strength to stand my ground and not take a step back. With men like him you could never show your fear. He was another Crillick but without the tinge of respectability.

"Tell me what you want to know," he said. "I've seen a fair few things in the last week or two. Things that could make your hair curl."

He must mean the Leopard Lady, but who else might Crillick have brought there? I looked into his smirking face; he was so pleased with his little joke. But I wasn't going to let that intimidate me.

"That's given me enough to go on," I said.

"A pity. If you do want to know more . . ." He left his words hanging but his hand passed over his crotch. It was my cue to go. I made a note of where Crillick stood. I would come back later when he wasn't there. I was sure now I'd find the Leopard Lady inside, but what state she might be in I dreaded to think. It was always chilly by the river, especially at night. Would Crillick have provided blankets, an oil lamp? I couldn't be sure. He'd called her his staff. That was the one thing I clung to, that he wouldn't run the risk of her being too unwell to perform. But I couldn't shake the memory of her skin so raw and cracked and her hair all matted. The sooner I could get to her the better.

It was growing late and I turned to leave. There was a boat heading back to the City. To stay here any longer would only attract attention, and I'd already seen two of the dockside police look over to where Ratface and I stood. I hoped Black Bill's name meant something to them too, if I needed to protect myself.

❧

The journey back upriver was slower. We were fighting against the tide, but I was grateful for a minute to collect my thoughts. If the Leopard Lady was being kept here, she must have done this journey several times herself. What did she think as she was ferried back and forth? Now I knew where the Leopard Lady was, I could return and free her. It was just a matter of working out how. The docks were well guarded. They had their own police, but if I was careful . . . *What, Zillah? What will you do? Break in? How on earth would you get away again?* I needed a plan, and I had to hope that Lucien would be willing to be part of the rescue as well as translating what she'd told me.

XVII

Winters the Grocer's

Charles II Street was busier than on my previous visit. It was half past eleven now. I was definitely going to be late for work again. I'd have to beg Barky not to dock my wages. At least it was a rehearsal, not an actual performance, though. Hopefully he'd take that into account.

Two smart carriages idled outside the dressmaker's, and I imagined daughters inside with their mamas picking out the latest fabrics. There was a queue outside the fishmonger's where housekeepers and the wives of City clerks waited, straw baskets in hand, to select the choicest offerings. In the window of the butcher's, three whole pigs were hung by their mouths from a row of hooks. The only time Mrs. Bradley went out to buy meat was at Christmas but it was nothing like this. I'd waited while she haggled over a bit of scrag end, pleading for a penny off, and we'd taken it home with the blood dripping from a slice in the brown wrapping paper where the piece on offer had been cut in half so we could afford it. I felt very out of place here. There were no other Black people that I could see on the street, even servants, and I wondered how Lucien managed here, whether his colour affected his business.

I took a minute to compose myself before entering Winters. There was a bakery next door and my mouth watered at the sight of the currant buns and crusty golden loaves piled up in the window. I'd missed breakfast in order to follow Crillick, but though my stomach rumbled, there wasn't time to eat.

Lucien looked up as I entered, and smiled to see me.

"Well, who have we here? I didn't expect to see you so soon, Zillah."

There was a warmth in his voice that suggested he was remembering our last conversation, when he'd said he'd like to know me better, but I wasn't here for that.

"I need your help," I said.

I saw the eagerness light up his eyes. All my life, I'd had to depend upon myself, but for once, I knew I had to let myself be vulnerable. This wasn't about me, after all. Lucien stepped out from behind the counter, removing his shopkeeper's coat as he did so. Underneath, his shirt was white and crisp. A great deal of starch had gone into that. Good on half an hour with a heavy iron, fingertips flicking drops of water at its base until it hissed and steamed. His pointed shoes were highly polished. Who'd done that for him, then? He'd never mentioned a wife. *Focus on why you came here, Zillah.*

"There's a woman who needs saving. A freak."

It felt wrong to say it, like swearing in church, but I'd learnt a lot since the last time I saw him. A freak. That was what she was to them.

He cocked one eyebrow. *Not you?* He might as well have said it aloud.

"It's not me."

The bell over the door tinkled and drew his gaze to a customer entering the shop.

"One moment, Zillah. We will talk somewhere more private."

He stepped over to the customer, greeted him by name. There was a short conversation before Lucien directed the man to browse and instructed his assistant, a fair-haired lad of about fifteen, to help if needed.

He led me back to the counter and opened up the wooden hatch. "Come through here."

I hesitated for a moment. Going behind the counter meant entering Lucien's home. It would be difficult to explain away to Vincent if I needed to. *But you asked Vincent to help and he wouldn't.* I looked into Lucien's eyes. I found him hard to read, but one thing I was certain of: he wouldn't compromise me, even if there was a part of me that wanted him to make an advance. I was doing this for the Leopard Lady. But I'd be lying if I told myself it was the only reason.

Lucien parted the beaded wooden curtain behind the counter. The strands knocked against each other and he smoothly captured them in one hand to clear the way. The room he showed me into was small but cheerful, with a low table and two armchairs arranged before a fire.

"I'll be with you shortly," Lucien said.

He didn't give much away in his person, so I had hoped maybe his home would tell me more about him, but here again were few clues. The furnishings were modest, nothing out of place. Then I saw it. The thing that marked him out as different: a floor-to-ceiling bookcase that covered the whole of the far wall. There were at least ten dozen books here. Not far off the number Crillick had. I had not realised there was so much money in groceries. After the Leopard Lady, I thought I'd struggle to be in a library again, but the similarities between the two rooms started and ended with the books. I ran my finger along their leather spines.

"Sit down, Zillah."

I hadn't heard him come back in. His tone was gentler than before, but suddenly I was unsure of myself. Cozy as the room was, the air felt different. Yet I could hear the assistant opening and closing drawers not three feet away. The bell tinkled as another customer entered. I couldn't walk out of his private space now, not if the shop was full. I took a seat and he did likewise, folding his legs one over the other. I pushed away the thought that it was how Vincent sat too.

"Do you read a lot, Zillah?"

"Mrs. Bradley taught me," I said without thinking. There was silence for a minute and I raised my eyes to his, realizing that he wanted me to say more. "She was the woman who brought me up."

"Very good. Not many of our people have been educated."

He had been. I could tell by the way he spoke. Proper, like Vincent and Crillick. I was glad that he hadn't pushed me further on Mrs. Bradley. It was too much after the thoughts I'd had about Eustace. It had felt a lot to admit to him that my mother was a slave, but one day I would tell him more about that last time I'd seen her, when she had taken me to St. Giles. A maid came in now with tea. She set it down on the table that lay between us and withdrew, but not before she cut her eye at me. He thanked her and she bobbed a curtsy at the door. Thank God. There had been a moment when I wondered if she might linger to eavesdrop on our conversation.

"Last time you left in quite a rush. I wasn't sure if I'd disturbed you?"

He had, and in more ways than one.

"I'm late for work again today, so I cannot stay too long."

"Tell me why you came here," he said.

"Marcus Crillick has a woman; he calls her the Leopard Lady. He means to display her."

"Men, women, and children are being displayed all over town. What is so special about this one?"

Is this the question he asked himself before he came to see the Great Amazonia? I wondered. *Concentrate, Zillah.* How could I explain my moment of connection with the Leopard Lady?

"I want you to help me put a stop to it."

He steepled his fingers together and placed them under his chin.

"You think this woman is in danger?"

"I am worried for her. She attempted to speak to me, to give me a message, but I could not understand what she wanted."

"Do you remember the words she said?"

Of course I did. They were imprinted on my mind.

"I said to her: *Sisi wami kunjani?*"

"You spoke to her in Zulu?" Lucien said. There was a sense of pleasure in his tone and I felt an answering consciousness bloom on my face.

"The only words I know are those you addressed to me at the theatre. I thought it might comfort her to hear them."

"You claimed her as your sister, Zillah. It would have encouraged her mightily."

It was what he had tried to do for me. It was more than a mere greeting for him, it always had been, and now I was using it too. Of course, *sisi* was sister. I should have realised.

"What did she say in response?" Lucien asked. When I told him, the smile fell from his lips.

"*Indodana yami?* You're sure that was it?"

The words had haunted me so much, I was sure I had them right, but I reached into my pocket for the piece of paper where I'd written them down and read slowly and carefully, "*Uthathe indodana yami.* What does it mean, Lucien?"

"It means she has a child. A son. And they have him too."

⁓

Lucien and I sat side by side on his sofa, while I recounted what had happened that night in Crillick's house. Speaking it out loud made it worse. I was forced to see it anew. I did not mention Vincent—there was no need; he had done nothing—but as I told it again my feelings toward him hardened. He'd acted as though ignoring the problem would make it go away, but here were Lucien and I discussing it now and he was listening to me, really listening, asking how I had felt, how she was. It was a terrible thing to confront, but we didn't have the privilege of looking away.

"There is one thing more: Elvira Masterson was there. The woman you said you wanted to introduce me to."

"Miss Masterson is a good woman. It does not surprise me that she was there to take this woman's part. She does what she can and more besides."

Here was another possible ally. I should have thought of her before, but how would I have reached her?

"I think that Crillick is keeping the Leopard Lady in a warehouse at West India Docks. Perhaps her child is there too."

The warehouse was huge. There'd be no need for Crillick to keep them from each other. But I'd been worried when I thought the Leopard Lady was there. How would a child fare in those conditions?

"I am due to see Miss Masterson tonight. I can speak to her on your behalf if you wish."

"I'd like to speak to her myself if you'll introduce us. Where is it you're due to meet her?"

"At Exeter Hall. The Sierra Leone lecture I mentioned when you came to my shop last week. It's planned for tonight."

"I'll be there," I said.

"Can you find out for certain if the woman is being held in the warehouse as you suspect?"

I looked at the carriage clock on Lucien's mantelpiece. Almost one p.m. Barky was going to be so angry with me.

"Not in time for tonight. I have to get to work now for a rehearsal, but tomorrow morning I could try and find out, or on Thursday—that is my day off, you remember?"

Lucien frowned when I mentioned my work. I was glad he didn't raise it with me directly. What could I say to him about it? The affair with the Leopard Lady was bringing home what he had seen in my act, though I still clung to the notion that my performance was different from hers. *Why, Zillah? How?* But I ignored the voice in my head. Right now, I had to put the Leopard Lady first.

"I won't keep you any longer, Zillah. Until tonight, then." He thrust a pamphlet into my hand. "Do read this if you have a moment."

I put the pamphlet under my arm and rose to leave. Lucien pressed my hands in his by way of farewell.

"I'm glad you came to me, Zillah. We will help her together," he said.

XVIII

A Meeting at
Exeter Hall

Exeter Hall was nestled among a parade of shops along the Strand, with two stone pillars at the entrance. I'd hung around at the theatre after rehearsal, practicing my steps on my own to show Barky I was sorry for being late, and arrived just before six o'clock. I'd seen the hall busier, but there were still three carriages waiting outside, the drivers down from their boxes smoking pipes by the curb and the horses, reins loosened, chomping at their feed bags. It was five minutes before the lecture was due to start. There were Black men and women streaming in through the doors and I let myself be pulled along by them.

"Zillah, there you are. I was watching for you."

Lucien was standing to one side of the entrance to the main room and I stepped out of the crowd to join him. In his left hand he carried a cane. The gilt handle was carved into the shape of a lion's head, and when he saw me look at it, he smiled.

"It felt fitting for this evening's lecture—Sierra Leone, it translates as Lion Mountains," he said. "Did you find a moment to read the literature I gave you?"

"I'm here to meet Miss Masterson," I reminded him and then felt a little mean when his face fell. The Leopard Lady was my primary concern but I didn't want to seem ungrateful. Not when he'd helped me with the translation and now the introduction.

"I'm expecting her in time for the second half. As soon as she arrives you can make her acquaintance."

He offered me his arm and together we entered the lecture theatre.

❧

I'd thought Exeter Hall was grand from the outside, but inside the main room was stunning, bright from the light of two large chandeliers and big enough to hold a thousand people or more. Crillick's Variety was tiny compared to this. Straight ahead was a raised platform with an iron railing around it. Steps led up to it from left and right and there was a gallery too, which had started to fill with people. I was conscious of my brown woolen coat. It was a bit shabby but hopefully there'd be no call to take it off as the dress beneath it was no better. I'd best keep my gloves on too. I regretted my filed nails and I doubted Lucien Winters would be keen on them either.

"We could sit on the platform," Lucien said, "but it's better if you stand. Your first time here you must get the full effect of the speakers. Here will do."

He planted himself in the middle of the floor, taking up space just as he had at Crillick's when he'd sat in the pit to see me perform. He didn't care where anyone might think he should or shouldn't be, only that he got the best view. There was something daring in it.

"Look around, Zillah, aren't you curious?" Lucien's voice whispered at my ear. He was so close I felt the tickle of his whiskers.

"A lady doesn't gawp," I said.

I looked into his eyes. The mocking expression from when he'd first introduced himself to me was back. Eyebrows raised and lips quirked into a half smile, he said, "Tonight, you are among friends. You must be yourself."

Was he insulting me? I couldn't quite tell, but his smile suggested not. Maybe there was no game here and he had no expectation that I'd be anything other than who I was.

The hall had grown busy while we talked. The carriages outside must be double-parked now for there were many ladies and gentlemen clustered in groups with drinks in hand. Lavender and rose petal. Not the usual sweat and hair-oil stink of the Crillick's crowd. The majority of the Blacks were rougher looking—the so-called Black Poor that they were trying to entice halfway around the world—but one or two of the men were well dressed like Lucien, and I noticed that he acknowledged them with a nod. He'd never struck me as a man who had many friends, so I guessed they were business associates. He saw me looking and offered to introduce me, but I shook my head. All well and good, shaking hands, but what if they asked where I was from or, worse still, what I did? It wasn't just a matter of preserving my secret. The idea of admitting that I played the role of Amazonia, the thought of them seeing me cavorting at Crillick's, made bile rise to the back of my throat. If shame was water thrown from a bucket, it couldn't have drenched me more completely.

"Shall I get us some punch, Zillah?" Lucien said, unaware of the turn my thoughts had taken and looking over to the far side of the room, where a table had been set up with drinks and food.

"No, don't leave me."

It came out before I could help it. My arm clutched his, the sharpened nails digging into the tweed of his jacket. For a second his forehead creased in a frown. But then he stepped a little closer and I felt the warm pressure of his hand over mine before he gently loosened my fingers and gave them a comforting squeeze.

"You're right, of course there's no rush. The talk will last about an hour. We can take refreshments together when it's finished."

I smiled at him. He couldn't know what I was thinking but he'd sensed my fear and protected me. I wasn't made of china and wouldn't last too long if I acted that way, but every so often it was nice to be treated like it. *Vincent would be like that, Vincent would take care of you,* came the voice in my head. I hoped rather than knew it to be true, but regardless I couldn't imagine a place where we could be seen together like this.

᠋᠋᠋᠋᠋᠋᠋᠋᠋᠋

It was time for the lecture to start. A hush descended as three men walked out onto the platform and took up their seats. One was white, two Black; all gentlemen from their clothes and air. The white man, angular and sallow, came to the front rail and looked out over the audience.

"That's Martin Johnson, he spearheads the cause," Lucien said.

"Who's next to him?"

"Ade Bankole, and after him Oscar Gbeho. You should know them, Zillah."

Johnson thanked the audience for coming and introduced the speakers for the evening as writers and abolitionists. Nothing like the guff that the compère used to announce me. How strange to see Black people onstage introduced as themselves.

"I want to thank those of you who have already contributed to the relief efforts for the Black Poor that have been so successful," Johnson said. "And to introduce the Sierra Leone Resettlement Scheme."

There was a round of applause. This was a much easier crowd than I was used to if a mere introduction could earn you a clap.

"Some of you will know of the scheme already," Johnson continued. "That the government is paying fourteen pounds to all members of the Black Poor who volunteer to go to Sierra Leone and start a new colony. The first boats have left London already and are making their final preparations at Liverpool, but there is one more due to depart in two weeks on the sixteenth of October."

I couldn't help but show my surprise, and Lucien chuckled

to see it. He'd said that payments were being made but fourteen pounds was a large sum, more than three months' wages. The size of the crowd made so much more sense now. I hadn't recognised anyone from St. Giles and wondered if the Blackbirds had taken steps to keep news of the scheme out of the rookery. They'd struggle to find and retain members for their gang if they were competing with these sorts of figures—and all legal too. I wondered what other gems might be hidden in Lucien's pamphlet. I'd been dismissive of this Sierra Leone scheme, but it had my full attention now.

Martin Johnson described the country. The sandy beaches and mild climate seemed a world away from the autumnal weather outside. He talked of an abundance of wild game and fish, and drawings were handed around the audience of native species: an ox and what looked like a fleeceless sheep. I looked around and saw Black men and women as interested as I was. I wondered if the talk of grain and soil meant anything to them. It didn't to me, a Londoner born and bred, but some were nodding. Lucien too was paying close attention. He'd been giving out the handbills, surely he must know all this, but he was rapt all the same.

Johnson moved on to the journey itself. A hum of chatter broke out; it was something that people were worried about. Beside me Lucien took a sharp breath and I was vaguely aware of him pulling a handkerchief from his inside pocket. He must have been about to sneeze. Johnson, continuing, spoke of the ports the ship would call in at to take on supplies on its way to Freetown. Madeira, Tenerife, Gorée, Bathurst—I'd barely ventured beyond the West End and hadn't heard of any of these places. Would the boat stop for long; would there be time to get off and look around?

We'd reached the interval, and the second half of the evening was reserved for personal testimonies from Bankole and Gbeho, who had recently been to the new colony and would be taking questions.

"You look as though you enjoyed that," Lucien said, smiling over at me. "If you wait here, I will bring us some punch."

Within a minute or two he was back at my side. He handed over a goblet and something small and brown the size of a chestnut.

"This is a kola nut," he said. "They have set up a table of the produce that grows in Freetown."

I weighed the kola nut in my hand, full of questions, but before it had passed my lips, we were interrupted.

"Mr. Winters, it is so good to see you," a cool voice behind me said.

Much as I wanted to learn more about Sierra Leone, I welcomed it. Elvira Masterson had arrived.

⁓

Only two days had passed since I'd last seen Miss Masterson. In the brighter light of Exeter Hall, I noticed how handsome she was. Before, I'd judged her to be around thirty years old, but when she smiled she looked younger.

"Miss Masterson, good evening," Lucien said.

"Please introduce me to your friend," she said, turning toward me.

"I'm Zillah," I said, stepping forward and sticking out my hand.

"Elvira," she replied as she took it in her own and gave it a firm shake. For a moment she frowned but then her face cleared.

"I've seen you before, haven't I? You work as a maid for Marcus Crillick?"

Lucien knitted his brows together, puzzled. He hadn't thought to ask why I'd been at Crillick's house when the Leopard Lady was exhibited but well might he wonder. He knew I was the Great Amazonia, so how could I be a servant too?

"I was covering for a friend who was ill, but usually I work elsewhere," I said.

I knew I sounded guarded, defensive even, but I was on shaky ground and thought it best not to say too much. Elvira sensed my awkwardness because she didn't push any further.

"I'm glad to meet you," she said, smoothing things over, and I felt a little more at ease. I'd have to think of something further to say to Lucien later, though. He still looked like he was trying to work out if he'd missed something.

"Tell me what you thought of the lecture," Elvira said.

"I liked it very much. I hadn't heard a lot about Sierra Leone before this evening," I admitted.

"We think it could be a very important scheme, don't we?"

Her question was aimed at Lucien and he nodded. He hadn't said it in so many words, but I wondered if he was determined to go, and the thought of it left me feeling a little deflated. I had so many questions about Sierra Leone for Lucien. I wanted to hear more about it from Elvira too, but the second half of the evening was due to start soon and I didn't want to miss my chance to ask for her help.

Lucien, ever polite, offered to fetch Elvira a drink. As he melted away into the crowd, we both started to talk at once and then laughed.

"I hope I did not make you uncomfortable when I mentioned that I'd seen you before?" Elvira said.

I shook my head. There was nothing wrong in what she'd said, but it was important to me that Lucien didn't learn too much about my standing at Northumberland Avenue, nor get any inkling of my relationship with Vincent. I knew he already judged me for appearing as Amazonia. I'd rather he didn't know I was mistress to a viscount too.

"That was a dreadful night at Marcus Crillick's house," she said. "That poor woman. I have not forgotten her."

"Nor I. I've determined to save her, and I wondered if you might help me."

Elvira's eyes glinted with excitement.

"Of course I will help. What would you have me do?"

I hadn't expected such a quick agreement and was a little taken aback.

"I have no plan as yet, but as soon as I do, may I come to you?"

"I hope that you will, Zillah. There is a woman who works for me, Ethel. I am sure she will wish to contribute too."

I wondered if she'd been about to say more, but Lucien was back with her punch, and before Elvira had taken one or two sips, she was called away to another group who wanted her opinion on their discussions.

"She agreed to help?" Lucien said.

"She did." I was about to explain when an announcer called out that the second half of the evening would shortly start.

"Bankole and Gbeho will be taking questions, but if there is anything you wanted to ask, I'm sure I could help," Lucien said. "Shall we go for a walk instead?"

❧

It was nice to be out in the cold evening air.

"I can escort you to St. Giles if you wish?" Lucien said.

"I'd prefer it if we walked around the fountain."

"It's no trouble," Lucien said, and I wondered if maybe the exchange between Elvira and me had piqued his attention. Whether he wanted to know more about my living arrangements without directly asking. Well, I wasn't going to get caught up in that. I started toward Trafalgar Square and he followed me.

"How many people will go to Sierra Leone?" I said as we took a slow turn around the fountain, the wind blowing the spray back onto our faces from the plumes of water it threw up.

"There is space for a little over two hundred souls to travel in a fortnight's time."

"And will you be one of them?"

"I haven't decided yet."

"But one day you will return to Africa?"

He didn't answer, but I felt him nod and then he began to speak.

"I was a child when I came to England. I don't remember much about the journey here, but it was hard. Harder than they acknowledged tonight."

I'd been right. He had reacted when they'd spoken of the passage. I kept quiet and after a minute he carried on speaking.

"It was in a coffeehouse that I was gifted."

I didn't quite understand. I already knew he'd been a slave. "Don't you mean you were sold?" I said.

I still found it hard to believe. *Lucien, a slave?* This proud man before me had been bound, gagged. I couldn't think of it, pushed away the thoughts of my mother that suddenly began to crowd in. I squeezed my eyes shut before I could stop myself. *I have always been free*, I reminded myself. *I have always been free.* I knew now that slavery was nothing to be ashamed of, that being born free meant I was lucky, not special, but horror was still my gut reaction.

"I didn't misspeak. My owner gifted me to the wife of a friend. She kept me like a sort of pet."

"Like a lapdog?"

"Like one of the pages you will have seen in the park."

I realised I knew what he meant. It wasn't quite the fashion now, but there'd been a time when I was young when every lady took an African child with her when she went out in public, the darker-skinned the better. Eustace and I had gone to Green Park and seen a young boy, done up in gold with a turban on his head. He'd been sat alongside a woman in a phaeton. To see him cross-legged on a cushion eating cakes, and hungry as we often were, we'd been a little jealous. I couldn't square the memory of that boy with the man before me now. A young Lucien would have been just like him.

"My mistress was good to me at first," Lucien said. "She took me everywhere because the darkness of my skin made hers appear fairer. She'd take me into company and place my arm against hers to show the difference."

Had not Vincent done that same thing—held his arm against mine for comparison while we lay in bed?

"She got bored after a time, and I grew up. What had charmed her when I was a child scared her in a man. She had a daughter. We had played together, but when I was fifteen my mistress ordered me out of the house. It was lucky my patron took me in, otherwise I might have ended up in a very different place. He was a rich man. He saw potential in me and had me educated. When he died, he gave me my freedom and left me the funds to start my own shop. He wanted me to be self-sufficient."

Thank God he had. Otherwise, there was every chance that Lucien could have ended up as one of the Black Poor. Brought to England and then left with nothing when, in the eyes of their masters and mistresses, they'd fulfilled their usefulness. Was it any wonder so many were forced to beg on the streets? It was why the Sierra Leone Resettlement Scheme had first started. I'd spent years averting my eyes from the Black men begging in the gutters. How many had been in Lucien's situation?

"Doesn't it make you angry?"

"It did, but I remind myself that not all the English are bad. Yes, my mistress threw me out, but my patron took me in, left me money in his will. I would not have Winters without him." Lucien's face was serious. "I want you to know all about me, Zillah. Would you like that?"

He had opened himself up to me. Could I be completely honest with him in return? He knew about my mother, but could I tell him about Eustace? About Vincent? Is that what he really wanted? I stared into his eyes. His expression was sincere.

"I would like that," I said.

Lucien gave me a slow smile. "I am glad of it," he said.

XIX

The Warehouse at
West India Docks

I made sure I was good and early for work on Wednesday evening. Ellen was surprised to see me seated at the dressing table when she walked in with Bouncer at her heels and burst out laughing.

"I see someone doesn't want another bollocking from Barky today."

She was right. He'd not been pleased when I'd turned up so late for rehearsals the day before. Unable to tell him the true reason why, the excuse I'd given had been feeble and I could see he was hurt by the lie as well as angry.

"It was just one of those things," I said.

"Feels to me like it's getting to be quite a habit," Ellen replied. She hummed to herself as she began to get ready. "You know I'm going to perform an aria tonight?"

She stood up and executed a near-perfect pirouette in her excitement and I listened as she described in detail her entrance. How she would wave to the left, give a knowing glance to the right, a cheeky wink in the direction of the boxes. I put her dig about my timekeeping to one side and let myself get caught up in her enthusiasm, pleased that she was finally getting her chance. After all the work she'd put in, no one could say she didn't deserve it, but it got me thinking. Was there ever a time when I'd felt like that about being Amazonia? When Crillick had first hired me, I'd felt relief more than anything else. Out of work for weeks, I'd been less occupied with the role and more with which of my debts I'd be able to pay off.

Making headliner had been different. There was no getting away from the excitement of everything that went with that: the appearance of my poster in the foyer and the handbills that Crillick had made up. He'd paid a group of urchins a farthing each to give them out to people walking down the Strand. On my first night as top billing I had felt triumphant and the whole of the next week too. How different things felt now; but it wasn't the theatre game that had changed. It was me. For far too long I'd been kidding myself. At last, it was time to face up to it.

Much ado about nothing, I'd told myself when I first saw the outfit Crillick demanded I wear. *They don't mean anything by it,* when I'd seen the dancers snickering as my feet refused to perform Amazonia's dance. *Nerves, Zillah, that's all, totally natural,* when I'd balked at my first night before the baying crowd. Unable to name what I was feeling, I'd dismissed it. It had taken Lucien to rouse me. Before that night when I'd first seen him from the wings, I'd been able to ignore how dressing up as Amazonia had made me feel. I'd focused instead on my achievements. Look at me: orphan Zillah from St. Giles, a headline act! Lucien had helped me to see that it wasn't just about me. Not for the first time since last night, I found myself hoping that he wouldn't join the boat that was due to leave for Sierra Leone on the sixteenth of October.

"Zillah, are you even listening to me?"

The irritation in Ellen's voice cut through my thoughts.

"I asked if you were coming to see the punters?" she said. "Crowd should be in their seats by now."

It was our tradition to look out at the crowd before the show started. I'd never missed a night since she'd asked me to join her when Crillick first hired me. But I couldn't face it. Not now, know-ing what they really thought. It had been bad enough watching it directed at the Leopard Lady. I couldn't bear to be on the receiv-ing end.

"Not tonight. You go."

Ellen frowned. "You're all right, though?"

I nodded, and although unconvinced, she left.

"I'll let you know if there's anyone interesting in. Maybe your fancy African's come back."

I started. She couldn't know I'd been thinking about Lucien, but it was uncanny how she seemed to put her finger on what-ever was preoccupying me. Surely she didn't mean anything by it, though. There was no way she could've known I'd seen him last night. I kept my eyes down, away from her scrutiny, just in case. "I should be ready by the time you get back," I said.

But when she returned fifteen minutes later, I was still in my chair.

"We've got a lively crowd in tonight and no mistake," Ellen started to say and then realised I wasn't dressed. "What's wrong with you, Zillah? You're proper out of sorts. Come, I've got ten minutes before I'm due on; I'll help you."

Putting on the skins Amazonia wore was torture. Though they were light, I felt trussed up, and Ellen, looking at me critically, pulled down hard to stop them from rucking up and looking scan-dalously short. I hadn't understood before. To me they had been a costume, much as Ellen wore her burnt cork and grass skirt, but there was more to it than that. In the skins, I assumed not just clothing but the persona of an African, and until now I had not done it justice.

Ellen looked toward the door. She would miss her cue if she didn't leave now but still she hesitated, genuinely concerned for me.

"You're sure there's nothing wrong, Zillah? It can't be that His

Lordship is giving you gyp? You know you can tell me anything?
I won't judge."

Before I could answer, there was a tap at the door and Barky
walked in.

"What's this, girls? Have to come and get you now, do I?" he
said.

"We were on our way. Zillah wasn't feeling right."

"Well, come on then, Zillah, you're almost up."

I tried to stand but there was no strength in my legs. Barky leant
over to haul me to my feet but my body flopped back against the
chair. I couldn't stir myself.

"This isn't the time for silly buggers," Barky said. "Get up." But
I couldn't.

Barky knelt in front of me.

"You all right, girl?" he said. I hadn't noticed before how dark
his eyes were. A deep brown. The expression in them was troubled.

Ellen joined him. "I did tell you, Barky. She's not been right
since she came in."

"Do you know what it is?"

Ellen turned away from him and shrugged. "She was in early
but I've hardly been able to get a word out of her."

They were talking about me as if I weren't there and I coughed
to clear the lump in my throat.

"I can't go on tonight."

"What do you mean, you can't go on?" Barky's voice had an
edge of anger suddenly. "You're not playing the prima donna with
us, are you?"

"No, it's not that," Ellen said. She took my hand and chafed it
between her own. "Feel her hands. They're freezing."

Barky sighed, his eyes kind again. "She's going to have to get
out there. The crowd won't have it if she don't appear. Let me
juggle the lineup. She can go on last at the end of the second half.

I'll ask Aldous to eke out his bit; you can do an extra song or two, can you?"

Ellen nodded, pleased at the prospect of more stage time.

"Let's go, then," Barky said to her. He turned to me. "Zillah, I'll be back at the interval in half an hour. You've got until then to sort yourself out."

I was glad they were gone. *Was* I being a prima donna? No, he knew me better than that. *Come on, Zillah. Get it over with.* My eye fell on the box where the makeup was. There was a blue glass vial in there. It was Ellen's. A "livener," she said it was. I'd seen her use it when she came in tired from a previous night. Must be laudanum or similar. I usually stayed away from stuff like that, as St. Giles was littered with opium eaters. I'd seen the state of them: skin all scabby, clothes patched and torn. The lengths they would stoop to for their next hit were disturbing, even in a place as depraved as St. Giles. But if it helped me get through tonight, surely it was worth it? There was no way I could be Amazonia, not tonight, without something to take the edge off.

I looked over to the door; it was pulled to. Just as well, as I didn't want Barky to see me, and I couldn't imagine Ellen would be too pleased either with me sneaking her stuff. But if she'd wanted to keep it to herself, she should have hidden it in her bag. I poured a cup of water from the jug on the dressing table and tapped the vial over it. A brownish powder floated onto the surface of the water and I stuck in my finger to swirl it around. It would be bitter, but I had no sugar available. I glugged it down in one, surprised that it wasn't as bad as I thought. Definitely not laudanum, then. Either way, I hoped it would kick in quickly.

ⵌ

I'd rarely seen Barky angry. Now he was furious. I tried to school my face into seriousness but I couldn't help but giggle. He'd said he'd be back at the interval. How could that time have passed so swiftly? Ellen came in full of excitement after her performance, but when she saw me she pulled up short. Barky turned to her accusingly.

"Did you give her something, girl? I've told you before, I don't want none of that in my theatre."

Two spots of colour appeared high in Ellen's cheeks. I thought she was embarrassed, but no, she was angry.

"Not your theatre, though, is it?" she spat.

"It is as far as you're concerned," he said and she backed down, went sulky.

"She's not had nothing off me. Not unless she stole it."

She rummaged around in the box and found the blue glass vial.

"Did you take this, Zillah?"

I wanted to tell her yes, but all that came out was helpless laughter.

"She's hysterical," Barky said. "What in God's name is it?"

"Laudanum."

Barky gave one of his snorts. He was right not to believe her.

"Give it here," he said, and when Ellen hesitated, he snatched it off her, tipped a little onto the back of his hand, and inhaled it like snuff.

"That's no laudanum. What is it, eighty percent pure? Christ knows what effect it will have on her. Take it away. I don't want to see it here again."

Ellen took it back and put it into her bag.

"I'm ready to go on now," I said.

It was true. I'd felt lethargic before, worried about the faces of the audience and what I might see in them. Now I didn't care. Everything was hazy, like I was floating. As down as I'd felt before, I was closer to joy now. I couldn't have said why. It was just me and Amazonia together, and I made one of her trademark leaps. The dressing room wasn't big enough for it really, but though I stubbed my toe on one of the painted boards, I felt no pain. It was like nothing could touch me.

"See, Barky? I'm ready to do her dance," I said.

"I bet, but I'm not letting you. Not in this state. You're going to go home, Zillah. Sleep it off tonight; you're not due back again until Friday. When I see you then, I'm expecting you to be in top form and we'll say nothing more about this."

He turned to Ellen. "You won't go telling tales to the boss either, or I'll see to it he knows about your little bottle there."

She flounced out. Barky gripped my shoulders. It was almost painful.

"You need to clean up your act, girl, and fast. Headliner or no, you won't last too long if you can barely stand up straight. Turning up late to rehearsals and now this. I expected better from you."

He put his face in mine and sniffed.

"Gin too? Sit down a minute. I'm going to need to think of the best way to deal with this."

Yes, there had been gin. I remembered now. A tumbler. There'd been a big order from the brewery and there wasn't room for it all behind the bar so a few extra cases had been stored in our dressing room.

I sat down on the floor. Before the flats. The meadow one was uppermost, with its rolling hills and dots of pink and yellow flowers.

"Vincent was supposed to take me, but we didn't make it. Stayed in London instead. The Leopard Lady, she was dancing. Crillick's party — you remember it?"

Barky's face was worried.

"They were going to strip the skin off her, Barky."

Tears brimmed in my eyes. I could see her face: the fear, the pain.

"Beautiful skin she has, you know, but there were patches."

"I've told you to be careful around Ellen. Crillick will hear of this," Barky said.

Part of me wanted Crillick to hear. If I was sacked, then I

wouldn't have to be her again. *But how will you eat? How will you live?* No, Crillick couldn't find out about this.

"You'll have to go now, Zillah. I'd rather not send you off in this state, but I don't want the others to see you like this. I'll say you were taken ill tonight, but you'll need to be better by Friday."

Barky's tone sobered me a little.

"Yes, Friday," I said.

"Best to make your own way, and then, by the time you see His Lordship, the worst of it will have worn off."

He wet a cloth and gently wiped the half-done makeup off my face. From inside his jacket he produced a bit of string and made me turn around so he could tie my hair back for me. A strand fell across my face and he took a hair grip from the dressing table and pinned it up out of my eyes.

"Get changed, then go out the back, walk from there, the fresh air will help. I'd go with you if I could but I'll have to tidy things up here."

"Thank you, Barky," I managed.

The joyful feeling had worn off a little. My head had started to ache and my toe felt sore. I had banged it, hadn't I? I pulled on my skirt and blouse, my fingers fumbling over the buttons. All I wanted was to be between soft cotton sheets. I had sought one type of oblivion but now I was ready for another—sleep would put me right.

&

Cold, so cold. I huddled into my coat. Maybe the opium hadn't worn off as much as I thought. At least Northumberland Avenue wasn't far. Again, I thought of the comfort of Vincent's bed, but another thought popped up too. The Leopard Lady. Was she in the warehouse tonight? And what about her child—was he with her too, the pair of them huddled together for warmth? Thank

God for Lucien. With his support, I could rescue her, and Elvira Masterson would help with what came next. She'd need somewhere to stay.

A light rain began to fall and I almost slipped on the steps that led down to the river. I shouldn't be here. Was supposed to go back to Vincent. But my feet had brought me here. Oops. There was a boat waiting, not too busy.

"Skipper, over here," I called out to the boatman. "You going down toward the docks?"

ϡ

The daytime bustle of the docks had dwindled, but when I jumped off the boat, I was careful to keep to the shadows. The breeze on my face as the boat traveled downstream and now being back on solid ground had sobered me a little, and with what I knew about the security arrangements here I didn't want to draw attention to myself. There were a couple of porters with wheelbarrows full of goods. A group of sailors gathered 'round a barrel drinking rum and yarning to one another. I could just about handle myself if one of them spotted me, but if I was caught by a customs officer, I'd have no excuses.

When I got to the warehouse, it was in total darkness and no windows to peer through. If I was going to confirm the Leopard Lady was here, I had no choice but to go inside. I looked over my shoulder but there was no one to see me. The sailors had started singing shanties—something about a drop of Nelson's blood. I reached into my hair and pulled out a pin, remembering with a pang the night Eustace had taught me this Blackbird trick. The corrugated-iron door screeched as it swung open, and I froze, terrified that someone had heard. But no. The only sound was my breathing, harsh in the quietness of the night. *Courage, Zillah.* I slipped inside and closed the door softly shut behind me.

Inside the warehouse was even bigger than I'd thought, the size of Leicester Square and then some. Crillick could fit hundreds of Leopard Ladies in here. I remembered the conversation he and Vincent had had over breakfast—something about tribes and villages—and I felt a shudder ripple through me. There were one or two boxes here and there, but in the far corner there was something more, though it was hard to make out from where I stood. As I walked toward it my footsteps echoed on the ridged concrete flooring and I heard the sound of rats scurrying into their hidey-holes. When I got closer, I called out, but I could already tell I was the only living person here. That had not always been the case, though.

There was a group of twelve chairs arranged around a make-shift stage, just as there had been in Crillick's library, but much more intimate. He must have exhibited the Leopard Lady in this place. *Who on earth to, out here on the docks?* I picked up a discarded oil lamp and lit it with some lucifers I found on one of the chairs. The light the lamp gave out was faint but it showed an offcut of rope on the floor and a piece of paper. I put the lamp down and bent to pick the paper up—but what was this? Two, no three, rust-coloured drops had soaked into the concrete. They could only be blood, and my stomach heaved at the thought of what could have happened here. There was a screen to one side. I forced myself to look behind it. A blanket dropped on the floor, a dish of water and straw. Straw! Like she was an animal. And here, a piece of sacking stuffed and sewn shut, with a crude face drawn on. Mrs. Bradley had gotten Eustace to make me something like it, to amuse me when I'd first moved in with them. It was what I had most feared—a clue that, yes, the Leopard Lady's child was with her, and likely he'd been exhibited too. My hunch that she'd been here was right, but where was she now? Had she been moved? I wondered if Ratface had given me away, let Crillick know some-one was onto him. I was too late. I hoped her son was still with her—he must be young if they were trying to comfort him with toys. I picked up the paper, but as I held the light up to it, I heard a noise. There must be a night watchman. I turned down the oil lamp and stood very still, hardly daring to breathe. I'd been lucky but I could not afford to stay here any longer. I stuffed the paper into my coat pocket. It was time to get out of here.

Outside the warehouse I stretched my arms and took three huge breaths, thankful to be in the fresh air. I wanted this for the Leopard Lady, and for her son, and there was no time to lose. I headed back to the jetty. There were no boats waiting and I cursed myself for coming here so late without thinking about how I might get back. Of course the passenger boats didn't run all night. A rough timetable had been posted up. I was trapped here until at least five o'clock tomorrow morning, when the first boat was due to leave. That was hours away. Vincent would be looking for me, but with luck he'd never find me here. Even the sailors had cleared out. Was it safer to take my chances on the jetty or return to the warehouse? Either way, I was risking my skin.

Despairing and unsure what to do for the best, I sat down in the doorway of one of the exporters' offices and waited for dawn.

XX

A Gift
from Ellen

A ray of autumn sunshine warmed my face but I kept my eyes closed and clung to the meadow that I'd been dreaming about. Soft grass, butterflies. It was no good. The clang of a poker brought me back, like a child summoned by her mama. *Mama.* I had been thinking of her so often lately.

But then I remembered the jetty. I had to catch the boat! My eyes sprang open and I saw where I was. The green room I shared with Vincent. Just as it had always been but now with a bouquet of cut flowers on the dresser. How did I get here? I blinked, but they were still there. Red roses, and white. Like blood and bandages. I heard the poker again, at the fireplace.

"Grace?" I hadn't seen her much since Stratton's party. I was sure she'd been avoiding me.

"Oh, miss. You're awake. I'll call His Lordship."

"No, Grace," I started to protest, but she'd already dropped her cloth and run from the room. Through the door she'd left ajar came the sound of sawing and cutting. Far away but close enough for me to make out. I recognised it from my dreams.

"She wakes," Vincent said and I turned to see him at the door.

"I've told Grace to give us a minute. Do you need anything?" he asked. "Some wine, of course."

Vincent poured a cup from a small decanter on the mantel and brought it to me. I tried to sit up to take it from him but my head swam.

"Slowly, Zillah. You have been unwell."

I couldn't remember anything since falling asleep at the jetty. Had I gotten on the passenger boat after all? When did I get to bed? "What day is it?"

"Friday."

"My performance," I gasped, throwing back the covers. I'd promised Barky I would make sure I was well by Friday. It was our busiest night, and Barky liked us in early. By the looks of things it was getting on for eleven o'clock and I still needed to wash and eat before making my way to the theatre.

"Stay where you are, Zillah," Vincent said. "There is no question of you performing tonight. Crillick knows you're unwell and has given you the rest of the week off. You don't have to go back until your regular rehearsals on Monday."

Hesitantly, I leant back against the pillows, grateful that I could stay beneath the sheets, but confused again about the lost time. Vincent placed his hand on my forehead briefly and brushed away a stray curl. As he did so, I heard the carpentry work again.

"What do you remember?" he said.

"It sounded like hammering. Sawing, maybe," I said. "Like building work. I heard workmen shouting to one another."

Vincent looked confused. "I mean what do you remember of the docks?"

I froze. When I didn't speak, he continued, "I asked you not to go there, Zillah, didn't I?"

Had he? I had to cast my mind back before it came to me. And then I remembered how adamant he was about not heading eastward when I'd suggested we go out that way for our day trip. It had struck me as odd at the time.

"If I ask you not to do something, I expect you to obey me. One of the exporters found you huddled in his doorway when he went to work. He said you were a little confused where the cold had gotten to you. Thank God you had the presence of mind to give him my name."

Vincent was rarely stern with me, and there was no call for it when, by his own omission, I'd been unwell. I had been waiting for a boat. The opium and the gin and the cold must've gotten to me, but he hadn't finished yet.

"What were you doing there, anyway? I went to collect you at the theatre and Barky said he'd sent you home feeling poorly. Well, Zillah?"

I rarely cried, but I brushed my hand across my eyes to let him think he'd upset me. While he was ranting, it was impossible to gather my thoughts. The artifice worked. Vincent stopped pacing and came and sat down on the bed by my side. He was still angry but made an effort to soften his voice.

"Let's not dwell on it in any case, Zillah. There's no need to cry. I want to take you out today, so hurry and get dressed. I promised to take you to Richmond. Maybe if we'd had our day together, then you wouldn't have been so exhausted. That was why you collapsed, wasn't it?"

Better he think that than find out about the opium.

"I'm so thankful you made it home safely. I dread to think what could have happened to you. Promise me you'll be more careful. I was worried."

This was more like him. But it still niggled at me, why he was so keen for me to keep away from there? I could feel the answer just beyond my reach and tried to force myself to concentrate.

"I'll send Grace in to help you get dressed. You'll find a new outfit in the wardrobe."

My head was still swimming as I got ready. Vincent had arranged for a new dress, an Indian shawl, and even gloves, but as much as I wanted to get excited, I couldn't. Grace fussed around me.

"You look like a real lady, miss," she said. She meant it kindly, and maybe a couple of weeks ago I would have taken it as a compliment, but today it didn't feel like it. The smartly dressed woman who stared back at me from the mirror was no more me than Amazonia was. I didn't want to offend Vincent, not after he'd gone to all this trouble, but if I could've gotten away with wearing my usual sprigged muslin dress, I would have done.

"There's one more thing, miss. A bonnet. One of the trimmings was a little damaged so I was working on it last night. I left it in the kitchen. I'll run and get it now."

She was back almost as quick as she left and found me combing almond oil through my curls.

"You can leave it on the bed for me, Grace," I called.

"Yes, milady, very good" came the mocking reply. It wasn't Grace at all. It was Ellen.

It felt strange to see Ellen here at Crillick's house. She'd been angling for an invite for so long and now she'd gotten one. She'd obviously dressed up for the occasion in a yellow shot-silk dress that I hadn't seen her in before. It looked pretty against her red hair. She must be hoping to see Crillick himself afterward, maybe. Ellen pulled over the armchair and sat down.

"Why aren't you at the theatre?"

"It's not only you that can skive," Ellen said, but she winked to soften the harshness of her words. "You know I'm only joking. Aldous is on tonight."

I grimaced.

"I wouldn't be too quick with that face. You might be the headliner but the show must go on."

"Who's covering tomorrow night?"

"Yours truly," she said triumphantly. "It's exactly the sort of experience I need for when I go to New York." She stood up before launching into a burst of song. She hadn't said much about her dreams of America lately, but she hadn't forgotten them.

"Very pretty," I said. It was what she'd wanted for so long. I couldn't blame her for being excited.

"You were in a bad way, Zillah. Lucky that exporter found you. Down by the docks it could've been anyone. You should've known better than to go there on your own like that. What on earth were you doing? Has it come back to you yet? Takes a while, it does. You must have had enough to knock out a horse."

I remembered the sun coming up, being wrapped in a blanket. There was a man and his wife. I remembered now. They'd found me shivering whilst I waited for the first boat back upriver. The man had been kind, but the woman had asked if I was a runaway.

"I thought it was laudanum," I said.

"I trust it's taught you not to steal from me," Ellen said. She accompanied it with a laugh, but not an entirely kind one.

Ill as I'd been, she wasn't above a dig. There was something reassuring in her spikiness. I'd had to grasp and fight and strive for the little I had, so when Vincent called me his princess and treated me like cut glass, it could throw me off balance. I was not a woman who'd been brought up to be treasured. That's one of the things I had loved so much about Eustace. That before we were lovers, we were friends and he treated me as such.

"It'll come back to you in dribs and drabs," Ellen said, helping herself to one of the breakfast rolls that Grace had left out for me. I hadn't been hungry when I woke up and even now I felt queasy.

"Bet your stomach's been a bit dicky too, has it?" Ellen said. I finally realised: she was enjoying this. I'd been crouched over the pot, my stomach cramping, and I felt my face heat with embarrassment.

"That'll wear off soon enough. The worst is the day after and you've gotten through that now. Why did you end up there, though? Barky asked me and I couldn't work it out."

I hadn't told Vincent about the Leopard Lady and the warehouse. I wasn't going to tell Ellen either. How close I'd been to getting the Leopard Lady away from Crillick. I'd thought exhibiting her bad enough, but now that Lucien had confirmed she had a child and I'd seen those spots of blood on the warehouse floor, I knew it was so much worse. I cursed Vincent's plans for this day trip. I'd already lost a day. I should be trying to find out where Crillick had stashed the Leopard Lady now. And her child. I'd gotten lucky following Crillick on Tuesday, but would he lead me to her again? If he didn't, I couldn't imagine where I'd start. I closed my eyes, concentrating on what I'd seen. The mattress, the straw. And there was a piece of paper. *The paper!* I almost jumped up, desperate to dig it out of my pocket, but I wanted to look at it when I was alone. Please, God, don't let Grace have thrown it away. It might be my clue to where the Leopard Lady was being kept now.

"Barky's not too angry with me, is he?" I said, hoping Ellen wouldn't notice that I'd ignored her question.

Ellen shook her head and mimicked his snorting sound to make me laugh.

"There now, it's good to see you smile. And it's just a few nights you'll have missed. I'd best be on my way. I was only after seeing how you were. You wouldn't know the best place for me to find Marcus before I go, would you?"

"You could try his study. It's on this floor. Take the corridor on the right when you reach the landing."

"Been there." She pouted. "I'll just have to catch him another time."

"You did me good, Ellen."

She'd wrapped her shawl around her shoulders and moved over to the looking glass to check her appearance before leaving. She dipped a finger into one of the creams on the table.

"I didn't know how well set up you were here."

"You know Vincent likes to buy me things."

There were five or six pots laid out. Ellen picked them up one by one, unscrewed their lids, and gave them a sniff. Then she opened the drawers and riffled through them.

"You enjoying yourself there?"

"You don't begrudge me a little look, do you?"

After purloining her opium, I couldn't say much if she decided to swipe a cream or two.

"You're welcome to it, Ellen."

"Do you think you'll be coming back to the theatre next week?"

Ellen's voice was casual but I knew she'd been working up to this, wondering if her headline slot could be made permanent.

"I'll be in on Monday. I was only given this week off."

"More than the rest of us would get, though, eh?" Ellen said. "Not that it hasn't worked out quite well for me, if I'm honest. I'd best be going, then. I've left a little something for you. Hair of the dog is the best thing. Don't let Barky know, though. He'll have my guts. You mustn't overdo it."

She shuffled toward the door and I heard the telltale knocking of the things she'd helped herself to in her pockets. She grinned at me, knowing that she'd given herself away but not caring. As she pulled the door open, I heard it again. The sound of building work.

"Do you hear that sawing?"

"Next door but one, I think. I saw a brickie outside there."

It sounded closer than that, but I was glad she'd acknowledged the noise at least. Vincent had ignored me when I'd mentioned it.

"Goodbye, Ellen," I said and she waved her fingers and closed the door behind her.

❧

I went over to the dressing table to see what Ellen had left me. She'd definitely taken a bottle of scent and my comb, but I was glad to see the pearl clip that Vincent had bought me a couple of weeks back still nestled on the cushion in its navy velvet box. She must not have seen it. And there was the blue glass bottle. The rest of the opium. I took it up quickly and hid it in my pocket— it was too dangerous to leave it lying around. Hair of the dog—or was she trying to get me hooked? It was an uncharitable thought, but if I was out of my mind on opium, the chances of Ellen getting a bigger part at Crillick's increased. *Don't be ridiculous.* Still, if Wednesday night was anything to go by, I'd be needing something to get me through my performances. Now the penny had finally dropped, how could I possibly continue as Amazonia? I'd have to get away from Crillick's. Have to. As soon as the Leopard Lady and her son were safe, I would find a way to leave. Until then, gin would have to do.

"Here, miss, I found it. Right beauty, ain't it?"

Grace stepped into the room and stopped.

"Are you really well enough to go out, miss? You still look a bit peaky. I told that girl not to overexcite you."

"Don't fuss, Grace," I said, taking the broad-brimmed straw bonnet that she held out to me. It was in the French style, trimmed with lace and ribbons and butterflies cut from silver paper. It was so delicate, made of the finest, lightest cotton.

"His Lordship is in the drawing room when you're ready." Grace bobbed a curtsy and turned her attention to a pile of freshly laundered clothes ready to be put away.

"Grace, my skirt—you haven't cleaned it, have you?"

"Oh yes, all the laundry was done yesterday while you slept. Everything washed and pressed and all in the cupboard waiting for you."

The paper I'd found at the warehouse and stuffed into my pocket was gone. Rubbed away, no doubt. I growled with frustration. What was it that it had said? I'd never know now. Might as well leave. I was halfway out of the door when Grace called me back.

"There was one thing, miss. I found this in your pocket. Wasn't sure if it meant something to you?"

Grace held out a small scrap of white paper in her hand. It hadn't been destroyed after all. I almost snatched it from her. It was folded in half and when I opened it there were two words on it.

"'The Odditorium,'" I read aloud.

"What's one of those when it's at home?" Grace said

I wasn't exactly sure myself, but it seemed that Crillick had big plans for his new show. It scared me to think that his exhibition of the Leopard Lady wasn't even the half of it. But at least now I knew exactly what it was I was searching for. I had a name that I could give to Elvira and Lucien and maybe others who might help me. *The Odditorium*, I said to myself, hoping that the more I said it, the more the fear the very sound of the words sparked in me would lessen. For now, I didn't know where it could be found, but I was determined to be the one to track it down. *Hold on, my sister. I'm coming.*

"Will you be leaving now, miss?"

"One moment."

The paper on which "The Odditorium" was written bore a crest I hadn't noticed at first, but that I had definitely seen before. The name was all too familiar.

"Don't forget Lord Woodward is waiting, miss," Grace said.

Woodward. That was the name at the top of the paper. Woodward Trading. It's not an uncommon name, I rationalised. But crests were unique to each family.

"Can I help you at all, miss?"

I was at the wardrobe now, pulling out the items one by one and throwing them on the bed until I found what I was looking for. The pale blue velvet jacket that I had picked out for Vincent to wear at Crillick's wretched party. I looked from the design embroidered on its lapel—two lions bearing a laurel wreath—to the paper I held in my hand and back again. I willed them to be different but they were one and the same. Grace was staring at me as though I was cracked. I'd had such strange dreams while I recovered from the mix of opium, drink, and bitter cold, but this waking nightmare was real. Woodward Trading was Vincent's company. The warehouse where Crillick had kept the Leopard Lady belonged to him too!

"Come on, Zillah. It's time to go."

It was Vincent himself at the door. I scrunched the paper into a ball and stuffed it in my pocket.

"Won't you hurry up? The carriage is waiting."

I stood blinking at him before he stepped into the room and grabbed my arm and said, "Come on, you goose."

As he prattled on about the picnic he had bought for us, I stumbled in his wake, struggling to understand the enormity of what I had learnt. Vincent the owner of the warehouse where the Leopard Lady was kept. However many times I turned it over in my head, I couldn't quite believe it.

XXI

A Picnic at Richmond

The parkland stretched as far as the eye could see. But though it had the flowers I'd imagined, the feeling it gave me was not a patch on what I'd felt when I sat before the painted flats at Crillick's theatre. Maybe it was the October weather—the sky grey with a threat of rain to come—or perhaps it was because the Zillah who had wanted all it had to offer was no more. *Vincent has been helping Crillick hide the Leopard Lady all along.* We sat on a tartan picnic blanket, its corners weighted down so it wouldn't blow away in the wind. Cucumber sandwiches with bread sliced thin as paper, a selection of cheeses, even a pork pie. We ate it all in silence and every morsel was like a mouthful of cotton wool.

"You're so far away from me," Vincent said. He patted the ground beside him, encouraging me to shuffle over, but we both knew that was not what he meant.

"Why can't things be like they were a few weeks ago?" he said. It was the first time I'd thought of his voice as whiny. A few weeks ago, I'd been made headliner and Crillick was in France. It felt like a different lifetime. Before the Leopard Lady, I'd been a different Zillah.

"I've been thinking, it's past time I got a place of my own," Vincent continued in the face of my silence. "You could live there with me. What do you say?"

Not too long ago, I would have given my right arm for an offer like that; now all I could bring myself to say was "Maybe."

Vincent turned me around to face him.

"You're angry with me, Zillah. I shouldn't have reprimanded you earlier. Talk to me, won't you?"

I didn't know if I was right to say what I knew but I couldn't be in his presence any longer without confronting him.

"I want to know why we had to come here instead of going east. Why you couldn't bear the thought of going anywhere near the docks."

"Don't you like it here? I know we haven't seen the deer yet, but we're sure to spot some soon. It's their mating season, you know. If we're lucky, we'll see them rutting."

I turned away from him, pulling up tufts of grass. I had imagined us sitting together in rolling fields but never that I could feel toward Vincent the way I did now. At last he said, "You know, don't you?"

❧

I was laid back on the blanket, my eyes fixed on the murky grey sky. Vincent sat by my feet, his head bowed. I knew he was building up to an explanation, so I waited, and sure enough he soon began.

"The warehouse is my father's, Zillah. I've never been there and we no longer have interests in the West Indies. I want you to believe that."

"But you did?"

"Everyone did. There is nothing unique in that, Zillah. When the time came, we gave our interests up."

"When your slaves were taken away, you mean."

Vincent blew out the air in his cheeks.

"My father owned an estate in Guyana, another in Barbados. He had nine altogether, and to work them he had one thousand two hundred and fifteen slaves. When the act was passed, it was ruled he was owed £69,760 for setting the slaves free. There's not one member of the landed gentry that has not received a payout, a large proportion of the middle classes too."

I lay very still, trying to figure the vast sums that he described. It was an extraordinary amount. This was what Crillick must have meant when he talked in the billiard room of compensation, but this was more money than even he had reckoned on.

"You could buy . . ." I started but my voice trailed away. What couldn't he buy with that amount?

Vincent gave a bitter laugh.

"A railway, ten railways, mansions in every county, and yet they say human life is priceless."

Not if you were working class, it wasn't. Around by St. Giles, life was cheaper than chips.

"It's not all been paid, Zillah. It won't be, not for a hundred years or more. The money comes through monthly in installments, but so much is owed that it will take several lifetimes to pay it."

Several English lifetimes maybe, but how many slave lifetimes? Maybe thousands.

"But you live with Crillick?" I said. It made no sense to me.

"Yes, Zillah, I live with Crillick. Though I am a viscount and heir to one of the foremost estates in Surrey, I live on the charity of a school friend. That is the consequence of the choice I have made not to benefit from reparations. The money is all in my father's name. I have not taken one penny of it."

He might not have taken the reparations but he'd benefited from the trade all right. From birth his family fortune was based on the backs of slaves. He carried on talking, his voice a tiny hammer knocking at my temples, and the flatter and more even his tone, the madder I became.

"The warehouse stands empty, Zillah."

He was still lying to me. The audacity of it brought me to my feet and I shouted down at him.

"There was blood on the floor, Vincent! The Leopard Lady was there not two nights ago."

He looked up at me, confusion on his face.

"This is all about that woman who upset you the other week?"

"It was on Sunday, Vincent, and she didn't upset me; you did. You and Crillick. I asked you to make sure she was well and then I find you not only haven't done that but you've been a part of hiding her from me all along!"

I was really shouting now. Vincent jumped up and gripped my shoulders. I would have turned away from him, but he held me tight, so instead I shut my eyes to the desperation I saw in his.

"In the warehouse? I didn't know, Zillah. I didn't know."

"Liar," I spat. "I suppose you'll tell me you know nothing of her child either."

Vincent blanched. "What child? There's a child involved? You're right, Zillah. That I don't know."

I badly wanted to believe him, but after he'd lied to me for so long about his family's slave-owning past, I knew I'd never again be able to trust anything he said.

The wind had picked up while we argued. The paper that had been wrapped around the pork pie skittered away across the grass, followed by the parasol he had bought me. We let them both go.

"You choose *not* to know, Vincent."

His face was livid. I tensed, waiting for him to slap me, but instead he bent down and started bundling up the picnic things.

"Get off the blanket. It will rain any second."

I did as he said, gently packing the china plates into the wooden picnic basket while all the questions in my mind crashed against each other.

How could he say he didn't know? He must have given Crillick permission to use the warehouse. How else would Crillick have gotten the key? But did he know the whole of what was going on there? I paused, watching him chase after the parasol as it bounced across the grass, lifted and discarded by the wind. There was a rumble of thunder. He'd been right; the rain was coming. The first drops splashed onto my cheeks and I dashed them away as if they were tears.

While Vincent collected up the last of the picnic things, I took shelter under a tree as the heavens opened.

"I sent the driver away to get himself a drink, but now he's seen the weather I'm sure he'll be back soon enough."

Vincent looked bedraggled and defeated, his hair and clothes dripping wet and his shoulders slumped, but I couldn't let myself feel sorry for him. Those spots of blood on the floor of the warehouse were more important than his pride. How many pints of blood had been spilled there over the years? His own inaction had been a part of all that hurt, and not just the Leopard Lady's.

The rain continued to pelt down. This was no mere shower. Awkwardly we waited for the carriage in silence, both looking desperately over the horizon, willing it to reappear. After twenty minutes Vincent sat down. His breeches would be covered in mud when he got up.

"It's not easy, you know."

I wasn't in the mood for his self-pity. I could've been looking for the Leopard Lady back in London, but here I was out for a picnic with a man I realised I no longer liked.

"I've tried to do the right thing, Zillah. I didn't like seeing what happened to that woman any more than you did, but what could I do about it?"

I knew he'd been affected by the performance, but he acted as if he were powerless. I was a lowly actress and I was doing something about it. How come he—a viscount, no less—found the effort too much for him? *Because he doesn't care.* No, that wasn't right. He did care, but it was all jumbled up. He wouldn't accept his father's money—that was good—but then he made no attempt to stop Crillick. How could he make a stand on the one and turn a blind eye to the other?

"I've lost my family over this, Zillah. I don't speak to my father, and he won't let my mother speak to me. I am her only child. Can you imagine what a wrench that is for her?"

Did he want me to be . . . grateful? I couldn't quite tell. There was a small part of me that felt for him, even after I had seen the dirty blanket and the straw and the rust-coloured droplets that spattered the warehouse floor, but try as I might to give him the benefit of the doubt, in everything he said there was some parallel to the Leopard Lady, and all I could think of was how much worse her situation was than his. He was separated from his mother, but the Leopard Lady was likely being debased in front of her son. Much as he pleaded poverty, Vincent was safe and warm and comfortable in Crillick's house. His mother might miss him but she knew he was safe. The Leopard Lady didn't have that luxury when it came to her little boy.

At last, the carriage appeared, rolling along the path just as the rain eased and the sun came out. There was a weak rainbow in the distance and the driver was full of apologies. He'd gotten lost on his way back, he said, but Vincent brushed away the excuses as he handed me in, climbing up beside me and rapping on the roof to signal we were ready. I shivered, my dress soaked through. Wordlessly he handed me the picnic blanket.

"My mother was a slave, you know."

I felt him flinch. I waited for shock, sympathy, questions, anything, but after a few moments of silence I realised he refused to ask me anything more. *Typical Vincent.* When something was too painful, he just didn't want to know. Briefly, he squeezed my hand, then withdrew to the far side of the seat and trained his gaze on the view beyond the window. We trundled back through the park and I gave my body up to the rocking motion of the carriage, concentrating on the clip-clop of the horses' hooves and the large wheels on the gravelly road beneath us. There were nine long miles until we were back in Westminster, and I knew this was the last time I'd ever be alone in Vincent's company. It was over between us.

XXII

A Place to Stay
at Holborn

Barky lived at 23 Lamb's Conduit Street with a whole floor to himself. It wasn't that far from St. Giles in terms of distance, but his rich curtains and the window box he'd filled with daisies made it seem a whole world away. The residents of the rookery had merely made themselves a place to stay. Here Barky and his neighbors had true homes, humble as they might be. I'd asked Vincent to drop me at High Holborn, unable to imagine another night under the same roof with Crillick. I'd walked down from there, hoping I was remembering the address right. Barky had only let it slip by accident one night, and I doubted he'd want anyone else to know it. He'd always been one to keep himself to himself.

I knocked on the door and waited. Barky would have been at the theatre this morning, making preparations, supervising props and cleaners, but he always popped home in the afternoon before returning an hour before showtime. It was past five now so I hoped I hadn't missed him. I put my head down as a couple passed by, not wanting them to see a Black woman in their exclusively white area. As I'd walked along, I hoped Barky was in. Now I was here, I wondered if he'd welcome me. He'd never invited me, but after the silent journey back from Richmond I needed a familiar face so badly. If he took pity on me and agreed to put me up for the night, even better.

The door swung back and there he was, tying his housecoat. I saw his eyes flick over me in surprise and remembered that I was wearing the outfit that Vincent had bought for me. I was glad someone appreciated it. After today I wouldn't be wearing it again. Barky looked over my shoulder, but the street was empty.

"What are you doing here?"

I knew if I spoke the strains of the day would overwhelm me, and Barky must have seen it on my face.

"You'd better come in, hadn't you?" he said.

ᘓ

Before I'd moved in with Vincent, I would've thought Barky's two poky first-floor rooms and the smoking fire absolute luxury. I knew better now, but even so I felt more at home than I had done in weeks. He led me into the main room. The table in the corner, stacked up with pots and pans and cup and bowl, showed it served as kitchen and dining room both.

"You might as well sit down now you're here," Barky said. "You going to tell me what's gone on?"

"I won't be staying with Vincent any longer."

"The drugs, was it?"

"No, not that. I found out . . . some things about him that I didn't like."

Barky looked puzzled. Well he might. Perhaps it was absurd that someone like me might turn their nose up at Vincent, but it was precisely because I was starting to know myself that I'd walked away. In the carriage, as we'd crossed over Waterloo Bridge, Vincent had called out to the driver to head straight for Northumberland Avenue. He was taking it for granted that I'd go with him, but I couldn't do it. Better to be on my own than with someone I couldn't trust.

"I'd have said he was one of the good ones, Zillah."

Sad to say he probably was, but I didn't want to talk about it anymore. There'd been too much talk today already and the effects of the opium still lingered. A yawn took over my face. All I wanted to do was lie down.

"I suppose you'll be back at St. Giles tonight."

I looked at the floor. The thought of trying to find a room at the rookery was unbearable. I still had the scabs of the flea bites from my last stay there.

"I don't suppose . . ."

"Oh, you're trying to wheedle yourself into staying here, is that it?"

"Please, Barky. You know I wouldn't ask unless I was desperate."

There was a time when I might have called on Ellen, but we weren't as friendly as we'd once been.

Indecision floated across Barky's face. I knew he liked his privacy, that his neighbors would hate it, thinking he'd lowered the tone of the area if they saw a Black girl coming and going. At last his better self won out.

"I'll put you up until you find your feet," he said and I slumped with relief.

"I won't outstay my welcome. You'll hardly know I'm here and I promise not to make a show of myself."

"That's right. Headscarf in and out and no one from the theatre can know. I don't want all and sundry turning up if they fall on hard times."

"They'd never guess I'd come here," I said. "But I know you've always looked out for me."

I squeezed his hand and he patted my head awkwardly.

"None of that. I've got to get back to work, you know. Aldous is on with his rabbits tonight."

"I can give you some money when I get paid?"

"No, keep your pennies. You'll be short after missing all these nights and being late for rehearsals."

I hadn't even thought of that, and any money I did have I wanted to keep in case the Leopard Lady needed it when I found her.

"You're not back at work until next week, I hear? Very jammy. That was Vincent's doing. Not mine. I'd have called you in and had you scrubbing the stage as a punishment. You owe him."

"Hmm," I said. I was still too angry at Vincent for all that he'd withheld from me to acknowledge any debt.

"I thought I would come in tomorrow, Barky. Not to perform —maybe I could look over my costume."

It sounded lame. We had a seamstress to look over our things, but a plan was forming in my mind for how I might find out where Crillick's Odditorium was located. He had an office at the theatre. If I could find a way to get up there, I could see if he'd left any information lying around. It wasn't just the Leopard Lady and her son who needed me now. It was his other prisoners too.

～

Barky went into the other room to get changed before he headed back to the theatre. We carried on talking, the walls so thin we didn't even need to raise our voices.

"Crillick can't have realised what made you ill, then. I'd thought Ellen would be the first to tell him. Still, glass houses and all that. And she won't be doing too bad out of you being away for a night or two. You know she's got top spot tomorrow night?"

"She came and told me this morning. And she said I wasn't your favourite anymore."

Barky snorted. "Twenty dancers I have in the ballet corps and yet I don't get half the grief from them that I do with the pair of you."

"Everyone's allowed one slipup, Barky."

"I suppose you're right." He looked me over. "No bag, I see."

"It was all spur-of-the-moment. This is all I've got with me," I said, pointing to my fancy outfit.

Barky shook his head. "And you say it wasn't him that kicked you out? I'll see if I can get a message to one of the servants, get your things for you."

"Don't worry, Barky. It's probably best that he doesn't know I'm here."

He pursed his lips but saw the sense in it. I wanted my sprigged muslin back. All the rest of the things were Vincent's, really. If Barky would take the outfit I wore now to the fripperer's I could exchange it for a whole week's worth of things. And the balm I used on my hair, it would be easy enough to make some more. It was a shame that I'd lost the creams and bandages I'd taken for the Leopard Lady, though. They must have been stolen the night I slept at the docks.

"I can make you a bit of dinner if you've got something in?" I said.

I might not have enough money to pay Barky for my keep right now, but maybe I could look after him a bit.

"I'm off out now. It was lucky you caught me. See to yourself. There's a bit of bread, some cheese I think, a slice of ham. I'll be back in the morning."

And he left the room before I could ask him where he'd be all night.

XXIII

Inside Crillick's Office

The next day, Saturday, I arrived at the theatre at ten o'clock in the morning. Most of the other performers wouldn't be there for another hour or so and it helped that I wasn't expected. No one would be looking for me or wondering where I was.

My plan was to search Crillick's box before the show started. He had commandeered the two to the right of the stage at the level of the dress circle. In the first he had installed a desk and treated it as his office. The second he used for entertaining. It had been from that second box that Vincent had first watched me. He'd told me later that's where he'd fallen in love with me, but the Zillah who had loved him back felt long gone. It wasn't just how his father made his money, or even that he'd kept it from me—Vincent couldn't help his background any more than I could help mine. But good intentions or not, he was a coward. The Leopard Lady's plight had shown that, when it came down to it, I couldn't count on him.

As I'd hoped, the theatre was quiet. Only Barky seemed to be in. He must have come straight here from wherever he'd spent the night. I would quiz him on his mistress later. As I walked through the empty auditorium, I heard him harrying the rigging man who helped Aldous with his special effects. Aldous—there was one man who wouldn't be pleased to see me back. It had been strange to see his name chalked on the boards when I arrived. Ellen's would be front and center when they were updated for tonight's performance.

I climbed the stairs to the dress-circle level, my feet sinking into the thick carpet. Backstage it was all bare floorboards, but this was where the better-off took up their seats and it had been furnished accordingly. With no windows, it was gloomy, but I knew that from seven o'clock the gas lamps would be turned on, the band would be in full voice, and the excitement of the audience would be running high. The door to Crillick's office box was open. I ducked inside and closed it softly behind me. *No need to act all furtive, Zillah. There's no one here.* But I couldn't help it. It would be a disaster if I got caught.

Inside the box was roomy. The chairs had been removed and the desk pushed up against the barrier so that, when Crillick sat down to work, he could look out onto the stage below. I untied the curtains and let them fall. That way there would be no chance of any of the acts looking up and seeing me while they rehearsed. The desk was made of oak and inlaid with leather. There was a writing pad and, to one side of it, a small bottle of India ink. I'd been hoping that Crillick would have papers out, but no, he kept his business affairs tidy. I sat in his chair and pulled open the desk drawers one by one. I doubted the Odditorium was like the variety show. If Crillick was using acids and scalpels on his acts, there'd be no handbills. More likely it would be advertised by word of mouth, whispers passed from one ear to another at Pascoe's and the other gentlemen's clubs. It was probably too much to hope for a card even, so I riffled through the papers without quite knowing what I was looking for.

To the right of the desk was a small bookcase. There was a

cloth-bound volume that looked well used, and sure enough, it was Crillick's accounts. I'd seen him carrying it around with him before, cradling it to his chest like a vicar would his Bible. I took pleasure from how much he'd hate to see me flicking through the pages, but I forbore from focusing on what the other acts were paid. I skimmed down the entries, wondering if any of them would signify the place he had the Leopard Lady hidden, but there was nothing. Any of these payments could be connected to her, or none at all. I sat back, frustrated, not knowing what to do next, when I heard a noise. No, it couldn't be. I jumped up but there was nowhere to go in the tiny space. The best thing would be if it was Barky come to bring up Crillick's post or something, but it was the man himself, I could tell by his whistle, one of the show tunes that I had heard Ellen practicing. He was getting closer. *Think, Zillah, think.* There was only one option. I perched myself on the desk and waited for him.

Crillick flung open the door.

"Well, well, what have we here?" he said.

∽

Crillick was thickset and the box felt even smaller when he entered. I could only get out now if he let me, and I felt a prickle of sweat form on my neck. He smiled broad enough to show his teeth. How could I put some distance between us? I shuffled backward on the desk, then I remembered. The curtains were heavy but they would not stop me falling. It must be a twenty-foot drop at least. A shiver went up my spine and I gripped onto the wood with my fingers.

"I came in early to rehearse and make sure I was ready for next Wednesday. I wanted to say sorry too, for missing all my nights this week."

He gave me a calculating stare. This wasn't the usual tone of

our interactions, and in the narrowing of his eyes, I could tell he was trying to work out what my game was.

"Not here to ask after Vincent?"

I looked down at the floor and ran my pointed toe back and forth across the carpet to buy myself some time. *What exactly was I doing here? Would I have to seduce Crillick to get the information I needed?*

"I'm afraid I can give you no news of him. He's off to Surrey, that's all I know. He was packing as I left this morning and I couldn't say when he is coming back."

Vincent going home? He hadn't seemed to be planning it, but then again we hadn't talked much after the picnic. He was probably going to make up with his father and get the money after all.

When I looked up, I found myself staring into Crillick's eyes. He was still trying to work me out, but I could see a glimmer of something else there too. His desire for me made me wary of being alone with him, but I would have to exploit it if I was to get away with being caught in his office.

"I'm not sorry he's gone," I said.

"No, you don't look as though you are."

He came and perched next to me on the desk and I steeled myself not to shift along to avoid my thigh touching his.

"You didn't need to leave Northumberland Avenue. I would have been happy to put you up for a little while longer."

His hand crept around my shoulders. *Don't flinch, Zillah. Don't give yourself away.* This was a dangerous game I was playing. It may have gotten me out of the frying pan, but there was no mistake I was in the fire now. I looked toward the door and, when Crillick saw my glance, he rose and crossed to close it. I breathed a sigh of relief that he was no longer next to me but then he turned the key in the lock. I was effectively trapped with him.

"You said you were sorry, Zillah, for letting me down. I wonder if you've thought about how you might make it up to me?

The gate was down this week because of your illness. Ten, maybe twenty pounds I've lost already. It adds up to quite a lot, especially when drinks and things are thrown in."

My mouth was suddenly dry and I swallowed convulsively to moisten it.

"That is a lot of money," I said, my voice sounding small and scared.

Crillick put his hands on my shoulders to soothe me.

"There now, no need to worry," he said. "Why don't we go next door? I'm sure we'll be more comfortable there."

The two boxes were connected by a through door. I knew the second one to be bigger still, with room for chairs and a chaise. Crillick took my left hand. In desperation I reached behind me and swept the ink bottle to the floor. Crillick turned when I yelped as its contents started to spread across the carpet.

"Oh no, I'm so sorry."

I bent down to pick up the rapidly emptying bottle, tipping it slightly to make sure all its contents came out whilst still looking like I was helping. The stain grew larger. I could see Crillick was irritated. He was very careful of his possessions, particularly expensive ones like this, and I was clearly making things worse with my clumsiness.

"Go on through," he said impatiently.

I rushed to obey him, keen to put as much space as possible between us. I stepped forward to the front of the box and looked over the edge to the stage, putting myself in Crillick's place. He hadn't been in much lately but he often came to watch the show.

"It's a great view, isn't it?" he said at my ear. He'd followed me in.

I half turned but he'd put his arms on either side of me and I was caged.

"The ink, I didn't mean to spill it."

"I'll send for someone to clear it up later. We were getting on

quite well, weren't we? No need for a silly accident to interrupt that."

He was pressed close against me. I knew I had the strength to push him away, would do it if I needed to, but that would mean losing my job. It had to be the last resort, but I was getting close to it. The thought of him pawing me made me feel sick to my stomach.

"It's not just the acts I see from here, it's all sorts. The women who sit in with the men, the serving girls who help themselves to a drink on their way to and from the tables. The men who exchange cards, but not for business."

Naive of me to think that he watched the show. All this time it was the life of the theatre that entertained him, the tawdry seediness of it all.

He lifted my hair to put his lips to my neck. "You smell like roses," he said half to himself.

This was it. But just as I tensed to push him off me, I heard a voice that made me want to cry out with relief as much as it caused Crillick to swear.

"Marcus, are you up there?"

It was Ellen.

"Damn that wench," Crillick said. I could sense him half consider whether or not to carry on, but he decided against it.

"Go back into my office for now. I'll get rid of her."

I did as he said and heard him call to her from the second box. "I'm in here."

This was my chance to get away. I stepped over the ink stain and felt a perverse pleasure to see the expensive Turkish carpet all but ruined. I cast one look behind me before leaving and that was when I saw it. A folder of papers. Crillick must have carried it under his arm and I hadn't noticed. Quiet as I could, I opened it. I could hear Ellen and Crillick murmuring together in the next room. The first item that slipped out was a folded sheet of blue paper. I recognised this from the breakfast Crillick, Vincent, and

I had shared when he first returned. The other papers looked like invoices; there wasn't time to take them in, at any moment Crillick might send Ellen away and return for me. But what was this? A page of notepaper filled with Crillick's crabby handwriting alongside inked illustrations. This must be his plan for the Odditorium.

Dare I take it? It was near the top of the pile so Crillick would realise quickly that it was gone. It was risky, but hadn't I already taken a chance in coming up here? With a trembling hand, I extracted the sheet and stuffed it into my pocket along with the blueprint for good measure. I had gotten what I'd come for. It was time to leave. I turned the key in the lock slowly, careful to make as little noise as possible, but it was well oiled and did not betray me. Out I stepped into the corridor. Everything in my being told me to run, but there was no sense in that. I was almost away. I headed for the stairs, took the first two. When I'd heard Ellen's voice before it had been a relief. This time it had the same effect on me that it had had on Crillick.

"Hey, Zillah, is that you?"

Ellen was standing at the door to the box Crillick used for his office. She must have come in just in time to see the door close behind me. I turned around, careful to keep my hands down by my side, covering my pockets in case the stolen papers were poking out.

"I came to see Crillick to apologise for missing my shows this week."

"He's been with me. You went into his office on your own?"

"I . . ." My wits had deserted me, and in my hesitation, she seized on a portion of the truth.

"Did you come to make a play for him?"

I started to protest but she cut me off.

"You little slut. I should've known."

She had raised her voice and it brought Crillick out of the room behind her.

"Now, now, ladies, what's this?" I didn't need to see the smirk on his face—amusement dripped from his voice.

Ellen didn't even turn around.

"This is between me and Zillah," she said.

Her voice was icy with fury. I'd never heard her talk to him like that, and he clearly wasn't used to it either, for it left him open-mouthed.

"You've got His Lordship, but that isn't enough for you, is it? You had to throw yourself at my man too."

"That's not it, Ellen," I said, but I dared not admit I wasn't with Vincent anymore. She'd seize on it as further proof.

"The front to tell me I'm wrong when you're looking as guilty as you do? Dress all askew. It's not wrong what they say about you people, is it?"

"What do you mean, Ellen? Out with it."

"Blacks are loose, oversexed. I should never have trusted you around my man at all."

I was stunned into silence. The pain of this—from her, a woman I had called my friend—was too much. And over a dog like Crillick too. Ellen couldn't believe I'd never wanted him. She was so blinded by love she thought everyone felt the same, though most of the other girls at the theatre were as repelled by him as I was.

"You've always had your eye on him. I've seen you."

How deluded she was. I felt fit to burst with the things that I could say to her. Crillick had barely any time for her. She was convenient to him, that was all. If he hadn't been surprised, I had no doubt he would have taken me in front of her and not cared a stuff about it. But I bit my tongue, hard enough to taste blood. I knew deep down she knew it all herself, and there are some things too terrible for one woman to say to another.

But she wasn't finished. She muttered something as she turned away, something so vile I had to question whether I had heard her right.

"What did you say?"

"I called you what you are, an uppity nigger."

I reeled as though she'd slapped me, and she followed up with an undercut.

"That's right, Zillah. That's what they all call you. Aldous, Mikey, Bob, the ballerinas, and the chorus girls. I've always stood up for you, you know. More fool me."

I leant a hand against the wall to steady myself. It wasn't the first time I'd been called that, of course. Wouldn't be the last. But I hadn't expected it from her. Had she ever really liked me? Either way, she'd shown her true colours now. I wasn't surprised to find the others spoke of me like that. My rapid rise at Crillick's, from novice to headliner in less than a year, had all but guaranteed their enmity, but coming from her, it hurt. More so because she knew what it was like to be different. How it felt to be treated as inferior just because of where you came from. We'd become rivals, but I thought that, when it came down to it, as outsiders we'd always have each other's backs. How wrong I'd been.

She looked down on me from the top of the stairs and began to approach. There was not one bit of remorse in her face. I held my ground, prepared to defend myself if need be, but she only shouldered past me. Once she'd been my friend, but as of today, I knew I had an enemy for life. Crillick looked after her, the smirk still on his lips. He'd enjoyed the confrontation. It might be the only time that he'd had two women fight over him.

"I'd have expected more from you in a catfight, Zillah," he said and I heard him chuckling to himself as he retreated back into his office.

એ

Barky found me in my dressing room. Ellen must have been in before I made it back, and all her things were gone, even Bouncer's blankets. The cases of gin, the painted flats, and the odds and ends of props remained, but without her it felt empty. How could my one female friend have said those things to me? I'd lost two of the people closest to me in as many days. I felt wounded and very much alone.

"What's all this, then?" Barky said.

Thank God I still had him to count on. He looked anxious. I realised he probably thought I'd been at the opium again, but I was just numb from what had happened. I knew there'd be nothing strong enough to take that pain away. To have forever lost Ellen and Vincent within the space of twenty-four hours.

"I know about the fight with Ellen."

"Why ask me about it, then?"

"I wanted to hear your side. She's in the kitchen putting it around that you made a play for Crillick. Your name's mud among the cast."

"Isn't it always?"

Barky pulled out an old leather trunk from among the props and sat down on it.

"Is that the truth of it, Zillah? Is that why you came in today? I thought you hated Crillick."

"It's not about him, Barky. There's someone I need to protect. Going through him was the only option."

Barky scratched at his chin. He was disappointed in me. I wanted to tell him about the Leopard Lady—that it was her plight that had driven me into Crillick's office—but I didn't dare. I needed him to understand, and the thought that he might not was crushing, especially in this moment with Ellen's cruel words ringing in my ears.

"Nothing happened with Crillick. Nothing," I said.

"Does Ellen know that?"

"Ellen believes what she wants. She didn't even see us together."

"You were in his office, weren't you? Not thieving?"

That stung. In a way he was right, but I'd only wanted information to help another. Nothing for myself.

"But you won't tell me what you were doing in there?"

When I remained silent, he shrugged. "I can't help you then, girl, but I tell you: be careful. Ellen is your enemy now, and she's turned the rest of the performers against you."

"You're my friend still, though, Barky?"

"I am, but it won't be enough. You'll need to find a way to get her back onside."

Impossible after what she'd said to me, and though I'd determined never to let anyone at Crillick's see me cry, I felt the tears start to roll down my face.

"No need for that," Barky said. The words were gruff but his tone was kind. He let me cry for a minute, a silent witness to all the hurt. When I was cried out, he handed me a silk handkerchief and patted my shoulder for good measure.

"That's better. Stand up now, Zillah. Walk out with your head high. Don't let them see you cowed."

It was good advice and I was thankful for it. Vincent was gone, my friendship with Ellen was over, but at least I knew who I could rely on. Most importantly, I had more information on the Odditorium. There was no address, no directions, but even so, I felt a step closer to finding the Leopard Lady. I would have to cling to that.

XXIV

The Dog and Duck
at Fleet Street

It was Monday—the first day I was due back at the theatre after Vincent had arranged with Crillick for me to have Friday and Saturday night off. Had he told Crillick the reason I'd needed time away to recover? I very much hoped not. Crillick was sharp and I didn't want him connecting my trip to the docks with my desire to free the Leopard Lady from his clutches. By now he would surely have missed his Odditorium blueprint; I had to hope he didn't realise that it was me who had taken it.

I lay in the bed that Barky had fashioned for me in his kitchen, reluctant to get up and start the day. I knew it would be a hard one, all the performers together for rehearsals and without the presence of the audience to demand we be civil to one another. The best I could hope for was that they didn't talk to me. Being ignored, I could take. I just prayed there wouldn't be any more to it than that. I wasn't afraid of a row but there were a hundred ways they could get at me. Ellen was petty enough to hide my costume or throw me off my cue. I wouldn't put it past her to drop a prop on my foot, even. At least I had Barky's support; that was something.

All the way to Crillick's I dragged my feet, putting off the moment I'd have to walk in, but when I arrived, Ellen wasn't even there. I overheard Mikey say she had a cold and wondered if it was true. Without her there, the rehearsal was much better than I'd thought it would be, but it was still tough. She must've been rubbishing me the whole of Saturday night because each of the chorus girls greeted me with a dirty look. The men just ignored me. While Aldous practiced his latest magic trick, I kept to my dressing room to avoid having to sit with the dancers in the auditorium and only came out when I was required to be onstage myself. It wasn't a full dress rehearsal, something I'd felt grateful for, but seeing them snicker to one another in the audience seats as I marked out Amazonia's steps wasn't easy. Even from where I stood on center stage, I could see the spite in their faces. They'd be planning something with Ellen to bring me down a peg or two, I was sure, but for now there was nothing I could do about it.

At lunchtime, I looked for Barky and found him smoking in the alley that ran alongside the theatre. He was leaning back against the brickwork, puffing smoke rings to amuse himself. As I walked up to him, picking my way past stagnant puddles that weren't wholly made of rainwater, he held out his cigar case, but I shook my head no. I didn't feel like smoking.

"What are you doing out here, then?" Barky said.

"I wanted to get away for five minutes."

"Girls been treating you rough, have they?"

He'd shown no sign of it when he was managing the rehearsal all morning, but of course he'd noticed. Ellen must have done more to keep the others in line than I'd thought. The gloves were off now, though.

"You going to try to make it up with Ellen?"

"Not after what she said." I was surprised he was still suggesting it.

"I was planning to send everyone home early this afternoon as soon as we've run through the encore. After that I've got one or two bits of paperwork to do, but if you wait ten minutes, we can walk back together if you've . . ."

He didn't finish but I knew what he wanted to say. If you've got something to disguise yourself. I pulled out the blue silken head-scarf I used to cover my curls going to and from Barky's house and the theatre.

"What do you think this is for?"

"Can't afford any slipups," Barky said. He blew out a plume of smoke and the smell made my stomach swirl.

"I take it you'll be looking for a new job if you're not going to try and smooth things over here?"

"Soon as I can. I told you, there's something that I need to fix and then I can concentrate on getting out."

"Does the boss have any inkling you want to leave?"

I hadn't really thought about it, but Barky was right. Here was another problem I'd have to find a way around if I wanted to put Crillick's behind me and start again.

"You know what he's like. The Great Amazonia is his headline act. You make a lot of money for him. It'd be silly to think he'd just let you walk away from it. What if you turned up at a rival show? He couldn't have that."

"I don't want to be onstage anymore," I said. It was true, but I'd need to find some way to earn a living. The chances of a new job paying as well as this were few, but maybe I'd get some dignity back. That had to be worth something.

"If you really wanted to get away, I'm sure the viscount would speak to Crillick for you."

"He's left town," I said. "You don't think Ellen would shop me now we've fallen out, do you, Barky?" The thought had just popped into my mind.

"Not her. Crillick would do for her if she did. He's business first, always has been. She knows that."

I hoped he was right, but I couldn't be sure. I'd caught real hatred in her eyes when she pushed past me on the stairs after finding me in Crillick's office. Anyone who held on to that much anger was unpredictable. Maybe she'd think the risk of bringing down Crillick's was worthwhile if it got me thrown in prison. Just last week a group of three gypsies from Bristol had been sent to the hulks for pretending to be African warriors. I didn't want to be next.

"You don't reckon His Lordship will be back, then?" Barky said. "I wondered if the package that arrived for you at the theatre on Saturday afternoon was from him."

"It was the clothes I'd left behind at Crillick's house," I said. Vincent must have sent them on before he left London. I'd put them on straightaway, grateful to be back in my own things. "I can't see him staying in Surrey for long, but if he comes back to London it won't be for me."

Whatever was between us was all in the past. Now I knew about Vincent's family, what was there for us to say to one another? He had distracted me and it had been nice while it lasted, but I'd moved on. Barky, seeing he'd unleashed a torrent of thoughts, sucked quietly on his cheroot and I kicked mindlessly at the wall for something to do.

"Shhh. Did you hear that?" Barky said.

I stood still and strained to listen. Nothing for a moment, and then, just as I was about to tease him for getting jumpy in his old age, there came the sound of footsteps. No one used this alley except Crillick, Vincent, and the performers. In any case, Crillick's was closed to the public outside of showtimes.

"Make sure your hair is tucked in and face the wall," Barky muttered. "I'll handle this."

I did as he said, tying on the blue headscarf, my fingers fumbling the knot beneath my chin. It must be the Peelers. What would they do? What could they do? I didn't even know if Crillick was around to vouch for me, though he'd be in trouble too. *Stay calm, Zillah. They can't prove you're Amazonia just because you're standing outside the theatre.* The footsteps stopped. For a moment all I could hear was my breathing, then Barky made the snorting sound deep in his throat.

"This way's not for you. You'll want the entrance 'round the front," he said.

Just a punter, then? I let out my breath, and as I sucked in fresh air, I smelt a whisper of something woody and sweet and familiar. *Could it be?* I peeked at Barky's face; his expression was stern but carried no sense of danger. It was safe for me to be seen. And sure enough, when I turned around, there stood Lucien. Handsome as ever and carrying his gold-tipped cane. When Lucien saw me, he smiled in relief.

"At last, I've found you. This is the second time I've come looking. After what you told me, I was expecting to see you last Thursday, but nothing."

The last time we had met, I'd strongly suspected the Leopard Lady was being held at the docks, but had no concrete proof.

"Lucien, I've got so much to tell you."

"You two know each other, then," Barky said. I'd forgotten he was there, my whole attention focused on Lucien.

"You remember Mr. Winters? He waited to speak to me after a performance a few weeks back." My words were for Barky but I couldn't take my eyes off Lucien.

"An admirer, then?" Barky said.

Not exactly, but there was something growing between us. At least I thought I wanted there to be, and now I was free of Vincent, I didn't need to feel any guilt about it.

"I heard from our mutual friend," Lucien said to me, "and there's more. If you are ready now, I've thought of a place we can go where someone might have heard of your Leopard Lady."

Barky's eyes were darting back and forth between the two of us. I'd have to explain it all to him later now he'd heard her name.

"Can I finish for the day?" I asked Barky.

He narrowed his eyes and I could tell he was thinking about the encore scene he wanted us to practice, where each act ran on to give a final bow before the audience went home.

"There's always tomorrow, I suppose. You and Ellen would be first up, though, if she comes in."

I wasn't relishing the prospect of that at all.

"Why don't you come with us, Barky?"

"I've work here, Zillah."

Hadn't he just told me that he was almost done for the day? He'd taken against Lucien, I could tell. Only once so far had he addressed him directly.

"Please, Barky?" I said.

"Maybe I will. Where are you going?"

"To the Dog and Duck," Lucien said.

A public house. I'd not heard of it, but Barky clearly had.

"I won't be welcome there," he said. His tone was curt.

"Whyever not?"

"It's Blacks only."

Lucien opened his mouth to say something and stopped. A look passed between him and Barky that I couldn't quite work out. A pub for Blacks only. I'd never heard of such a thing. Barky stubbed his cheroot on the wall.

"I'd best be getting on. Lots to do, as I said." He touched his hat to Lucien. "Good afternoon, Mr. Winters."

He headed back inside the theatre and I looked after him, nonplussed by what had happened. Barky had been nothing but kind to me, had accepted me despite my colour. I'd hoped he'd do the same for Lucien.

"He's not usually like that."

"I understand," Lucien said. At least one of us did. "You've known him long?"

We'd met on my first day at Crillick's. Straightaway Barky had taken me under his wing, but the truth was I knew hardly anything about him. Even living with him had revealed little, his rooms so tidy. Yet I'd seen the trinkets he carried. Knew he went out most nights after ten o'clock and didn't come back until dawn. He had a secret of his own, obviously, but I had yet to find out her name.

"Only since I started here. He's been good to me."

"Well, perhaps it is for the best he didn't come," Lucien said.

I found I badly wanted the two men to like each other, but for the moment there seemed little chance of that. Lucien crooked his elbow and I threaded my arm through the space he'd made for me.

"The Dog and Duck is on Fleet Street. We should be there in fifteen minutes."

❧

It was different walking along the Strand with Lucien than it was with Vincent. There'd only been one time with Vincent, and for every step of the way, even though it had been late at night after I'd finished at the theatre, I'd felt as though we were watched. That anyone who saw us would question how and why we were together. Walking side by side with Lucien, it seemed that no one cared. We were just two free Londoners going about our business. Business was the right word too, for with Lucien it felt like I was going places. Vincent's stride was long and loping. There was a languidness to him, an assurance that wherever he was headed, people would wait for him, that because of who he was, he could never be late. Lucien's confidence was of a different order. It demanded that he be taken seriously, that people would pay him attention. Better yet, I got no sense that it was a front. He truly believed in his right to be anywhere, do anything he wanted. He walked with purpose, face set, eyes straight ahead. He had a good profile. I didn't have to feel ashamed of what people would think if they saw me with him.

Fleet Street was quieter than the Strand. It had fewer shops and more offices, where clerks and hacks worked on getting the daily papers sent to press. We trotted along, past the Old Bailey, past a barber's with its red-and-white-striped pole, past a wig shop where curled, white hairpieces sat on sightless wooden heads. Up in front stood the proud spire of St. Paul's. The wind stung my face, making my eyes water, but I didn't care. I decided that from now on, whenever tears dried to salt on my face, I would remember this exact moment: the bite of the cold, the tapping of Lucien's cane against the flagstones, and the sensation of walking arm in arm with a man and feeling no fear in it.

"You're quiet, Zillah. I thought you had lots to tell me?"

"Where is it you're taking me? The Dog and Duck, you said?"

"It's a little farther down, just past Chancery Lane."

"And they'll know about the Leopard Lady?"

"All we can do is ask, but I feel hopeful, yes."

It was just over a week since I'd seen her exhibited in Crillick's library. She'd been scared then, but not broken. I wondered what had happened to her at the warehouse. The blood droplets could have belonged to any one of Crillick's prisoners, but I desperately hoped they were not the Leopard Lady's or her child's. Please, God, let me find out more about their whereabouts. There was only one more question I had to ask.

"Will I be welcome?"

I hadn't planned on going out. Wasn't dressed for it, in my plain old smock and my heavy brown boots, but that wasn't what I was thinking of.

"Why wouldn't you be?"

"I was just thinking on what Barky said." I hadn't realised it was bothering me, but it was. It made sense that Barky wouldn't be welcome, but exactly how strict was their "Blacks only" policy? How ironic if I was too black to be accepted by my fellow performers at Crillick's and too white for the Dog and Duck. Lucien had stopped and was looking at me, puzzled. He was going to make me explain it to him.

"I'm not Black like you, am I?"

It felt like I was making a confession, or maybe it was just that we'd passed the Old Bailey. It was only recently I felt comfortable to say that I was Black at all. For too long, I had thought of myself as half-caste, neither one thing nor the other.

"That doesn't matter," Lucien said, but I could tell he knew it did.

Not to him, maybe, but there were plenty of Blacks who'd judge me for it. The theatre folk weren't the only ones who'd rejected me. It was a question of being asked to pick a side, though the truth was my colour wasn't a crime.

"You're sure there'll be no trouble?"

"You'll be with me," Lucien said.

He made it sound so simple. The words stirred a half memory. Vincent had said something like it once, but it wasn't the men that paid when a couple went against the grain. It was the women who had to put up with the sly looks and the whispers.

"All will be well, Zillah," Lucien said when still I hesitated.

I could see the Dog and Duck a little farther along the road. There was a man outside. It would be him in charge of enforcing the "Blacks only" policy. If he questioned me, I needed Lucien to understand how hurtful it was and not brush it off.

"I will make sure you feel welcome, Zillah," Lucien said, and I let him lead me toward the door.

ɕ๑

The Dog and Duck was a tall, narrow building with timber beams painted black. The upper windows were gabled and, like the taverns we'd passed already, the lower had that milky-coloured etched glass so you couldn't see beyond them. The doorman sat on a high stool on the pavement outside the entrance. His eyes were sharp but they softened in recognition when Lucien raised his hat.

"*Buwa.*" Greetings, the doorman said. He gripped Lucien's arm

—not the customary dry handshake but a gesture of real warmth, followed by an embrace.

"*Kahunyaina.*" How are you, the doorman said, and I spun around to see him with his hand outstretched to me.

He'd claimed me as family, as a real African. When Lucien had first spoken these words to me, they had stirred something deep inside me. I was glad to greet the doorman likewise.

"*Buwa,*" I said back to him.

He gave me a broad smile.

"Go ahead."

When I was very young, I'd been in and out of the public house to fetch small beer for Mrs. Bradley. It was said that St. Giles had one tavern for every two houses, but to me it had always seemed double that. Mrs. Bradley had sent me along with a jug, and the landlord had given me sweets while I waited for his wife to fill it. The taste of licorice always took me back to those days, prompting memories of the sneaky sips of beer I'd taken on the return home, telling myself it was only to stop it from spilling.

The inside of this public house was different to what I remembered, though. Here was no back room where it felt like you'd wandered into the landlord's home with his wife and daughters sitting in the corner. Instead, there was a long mahogany bar that took up the whole of the back wall. Stools with red velvet seat covers were set out for the solitary drinkers, and for couples and groups there were round tables and chairs, just like in the posh section at Crillick's. High-back booths along the walls offered a little more privacy.

"Take a seat, Zillah. I will bring you a glass of wine," Lucien said, but I shook my head. I'd been made welcome so far but I didn't yet feel brave enough to be left on my own.

The bar had the shine of a French polish. While we waited to be served, I looked around and noted the prints on the walls, all of bare-chested men holding trophies. When it was our turn to order, Lucien introduced me to the landlord.

"This here is Miss Zillah . . ."

He paused, waiting for me to supply my surname, but I'd never had one.

"Zillah is all the name I need," I reminded him.

Lucien smiled at my boldness. I liked that it never seemed to threaten him.

"Meet Augustus McTavert, London's finest fighter."

That explained the prints on the walls and how he'd made enough money for such a luxurious establishment. I smiled at Augustus. He was old but still powerful, with a barrel chest. His face bore the scars of his past, the bridge of his nose flattened and his ears thick and lumpy like cauliflower.

"Pleased to meet you, miss, but you mustn't listen to this storyteller. My prizefighting days is long gone. This one, though."

He raised his fists to Lucien and the two men threw mock punches at one another. I hadn't known that Lucien boxed, but he did have the build for it.

"Zillah is looking for a friend, Gus. I thought you might be able to help her?" Lucien said. "It's an African woman but she has white patches on her face and arms. They call her the Leopard Lady and have been exhibiting her as a freak. Have you heard of her?"

Augustus shook his head in disbelief. His brow was furrowed and the expression in his eyes was pained.

"A bad business. Why will they do that to we?"

My tongue was stuck to the roof of my mouth. Augustus wasn't looking for a reply, but what could I, a gaffed freak, possibly say to that? *Why will they do that to we?* In all this time, it had never occurred to me to ask that one simple question. But before now, would I have had the answer? For the first time it dawned on me.

When the crowds greeted Amazonia's arrival onstage with monkey noises, when they bayed to see her dance or gasped in mock fear to see Amazonia drink Bouncer's blood, it wasn't just about an enjoyable way to spend an hour. My act wasn't harmless; it had never been. Its very success had emboldened Crillick to seek out the Leopard Lady. To rip her from her child and exhibit her. It was why I felt responsible for her. Why I was risking everything to find her.

Why will they do that to we? It was a question I should have asked myself long ago.

Lucien was still speaking.

"We'd appreciate any news that you're able to pass on, Gus. You know my place on Charles II Street. You will send a note if you hear something?"

"If she's in London, there'll be someone in tonight who could tell you. Matthias will be here later. Bill himself, if you're lucky. Soon as I see either of them, I'll give you the nod."

I forced a smile to show my thanks, but inside my stomach churned. Black Bill. Who else could Gus have meant? I'd done everything to keep away from him and his men, but now I was being pulled back into their world. I hoped it hadn't somehow gotten back to Bill that I'd used his name to get information from the rat-faced man at the docks. *It's worth it if it helps the Leopard Lady.* I looked around but didn't recognise any Blackbirds among our fellow patrons.

Lucien handed Gus some coppers before we claimed one of the empty tables in the center of the room.

"I'm surprised Augustus hasn't heard of your Leopard Lady, but don't lose hope," Lucien said. "The men he mentioned are well-connected all over the capital. I am still confident we can find her."

"Your friend, Gus . . . the man he mentioned was Black Bill, wasn't it?"

I tried to keep my tone light, hoping that I'd gotten it wrong.

"What do you know of Black Bill, Zillah?"

I tried to hide the hatred in my eyes. I only knew Bill through Eustace, but I wasn't ready to tell Lucien about him yet, not how I'd loved him or how I blamed Bill for his death.

"You can't grow up in St. Giles and not know him," I said.

That was true enough. All the Blackbirds were well-known, and none better than their leader. Before Eustace had made it clear that I wasn't interested, one or two of Bill's henchmen had tried to recruit me, but I hated that Eustace had gotten himself involved with them and never wanted any part of it myself. I'd seen the impact that being a Blackbird had had on some of the other girls that lived around St. Giles.

Maisie was a few years older than me and lived around the corner from Mrs. Bradley. She used to give me sweets when she saw me—"presents from my gentlemen," she'd say. At nineteen she'd been stabbed by a john and left to bleed out in one of the rookery's alleyways. Rose, on the other hand, hadn't done too bad. She'd lived well for a few years on the profits from housebreaking but eventually the law had caught up with her and now she stayed at Her Majesty's pleasure in Newgate. Swings and roundabouts was the talk in the streets.

Bill was one of the few employers who'd pay a Black man or woman a fair whack for their work, and there weren't too many in St. Giles who could afford to worry about whether what they were doing was legal or not. If a job went sour, it wasn't Bill's fault. But I'd never forget what he let happen to Eustace. I was sixteen when he was hanged. And the blame for that lay firmly at Bill's door.

"He's not a man I like to do business with," said Lucien, "but if you want to find the Leopard Lady, he is our best option."

Lucien was right. No one was more likely to get a tip as to the Leopard Lady's whereabouts than Bill. Much as I hated to accept his help, if I'd have thought of it myself, he'd have been the first person I'd have gone to.

"To finding the Leopard Lady," I said and raised my glass. It wasn't a toast, but a solemn vow, to myself as much as to her.

XXV

An Encounter
with Black Bill

The afternoon wore on into evening. Just as the doorman had said, the pub started to fill as we drank our drinks: red wine for me and whisky for Lucien. It was warm and smoky, and as a steady flow of patrons entered, many stopped to greet each other. Others pulled up chairs at tables already packed. Two women perched together on a single seat. It wasn't clear if it was their fathers, lovers, or brothers who had brought them. I watched the handshakes and the embraces hungrily. I wanted that camaraderie for myself.

"I will get you another, Zillah," Lucien said as I drained my glass.

This time I felt confident enough to let him go to the bar on his own. I watched as he crossed the small space. There were only a handful of other women in the place. One fair like me, the others darker-skinned like Lucien. One of the darker women had a glass of wine too, and she sipped it as daintily as any of Vincent's fine friends. I'd thrown mine down like it was gin. I'd have to pace myself with the next. Already I could feel it going to my head. All four women had noticed Lucien, I could tell, and I felt a burst of pride that he'd brought me here with him. Surely it must mean something over and above the search for the Leopard Lady that he was willing to show me off like this. It wasn't only the women. The men responded to him too. I saw one or two nod to him, another raise his glass. And he stopped to talk to a third before he reached the bar. Once there he told Augustus his order before bending down to scratch the bitten ears of a white bulldog that I'd noticed playing up to the other punters earlier in the evening.

"Excuse me, miss?"

The man who spoke wore a long apron and held a cloth in his hand. One of the Dog and Duck's staff, I guessed, and smiled, but the apologetic look on his face put me on my guard.

"You can't be here," he said.

It was what I'd been dreading. No sooner had I started to feel at ease than I was given a reminder that I didn't belong.

"What do you mean?" I said, my voice sounding small and faraway, but then Lucien was there.

"What's this?" Lucien put down the two glasses he carried in his hands and turned to face the waiter. Instantly I felt better. I could look after myself, of course, but in this pub, where I felt off-center, I was grateful for this one moment when I didn't have to.

"I was explaining that you must move," the waiter said, taking a step back. "There will be dancing now," he added when Lucien frowned at him.

The waiter pointed over his shoulder to where three men were setting up. A fiddle, a trumpet, and a drum. The tables where we sat were being cleared to make a dance floor. I was so relieved, I nearly giggled. Lucien picked up our drinks and moved us to a booth.

"Don't sit down. You want to dance, don't you?"

"I didn't have you down as a dancer."

"Nor am I, but I thought you might enjoy it. You've been pensive."

He was right; I hadn't said much since we'd arrived. I didn't want to seem ungrateful—not after all he'd done to help me—

but even so. I could see the women in the corner. They were watching me intently. If I tried to dance here and now, I would stumble, lose my footing. I'd had all the confidence in the world dancing as Amazonia for the Crillick's crowd, but now, among my own people, I was too scared to put one foot in front of the other. How badly I'd debased myself. All that cavorting, and when Lucien was watching too. I didn't think I'd be dancing for a very long time.

"Bill will be here soon, won't he? I wouldn't want to miss him."

"As you wish."

"We could talk instead?"

"You never said what you thought about the lecture the other night."

"It was very interesting. I'd like to hear more, I think."

In all of the drama at the docks, and with Ellen and Vincent, Sierra Leone had been pushed right from my mind, but now Lucien mentioned it, I remembered how much it had excited me to hear about it. The kola nut he'd given me. It must still be in Vincent's room at Crillick's house unless Grace had thrown it away. That evening with Lucien at the lecture had been the last time I remembered feeling happy, learning about Africa and knowing I could call on Elvira when I needed her. Lucien had told me so much about himself too, as we walked around the Trafalgar Square fountain. I knew how I would have felt if I'd told him all my past and then he'd gone missing. I owed him a confidence if I wanted to get closer to him.

What was the best way to get all this across to him, I wondered, but right now there wasn't time. Gus was signaling to us from behind the bar. Black Bill had arrived.

ဆ

Bill Dixon was of medium height and build. His clothes were plain; he wore no handkerchief, no jewelry. Nothing about him stood out at first glance. Maybe that was how he had managed to evade the law for so long. No one would guess by looking at him that he ruled over St. Giles with his gang of criminals. I hadn't seen him for months, and then only at a distance, but I'd have known him anywhere.

Bill bowled in, his lackeys a couple of steps behind. He headed purposefully toward a booth in the far corner and there was a scramble as the two men already sitting there picked up their pint glasses and made way for him. Bill threw himself against the high-backed seat and I saw him open his mouth to call for a drink, but there was no need. Augustus was already there with a tall glass. It would be boiled water, I knew. Bill may have encouraged his followers to drink, but he never touched a drop himself.

Might as well get it over with. I rose and strode across to where he sat. As I arrived, the two heavies who'd accompanied Bill made to close ranks, but he'd seen me coming.

"No need, gents. I know this one," he said.

Lucien had followed me and slid into the booth next to me as I took my seat.

"Give us some privacy, will you?" Bill said.

His henchmen nodded and moved a little farther away. They turned their backs on us, but I knew they'd be doing all they could to listen.

"I never forget a face. Zillah, isn't it? I've not seen you at the rookery lately. Heard you'd moved uptown," Bill said.

Of course he had. Knowledge: that was the source of his power. That and his deadly belt buckle. I caught a glimpse of polished silver at his waist and swallowed down the fear it gave me.

"I've been around. I've got to work, don't I?"

"Ah yes, I'd heard about that too. Good to hear of a fellow Bajan doing well."

I always forgot that he was from Barbados as my mother was.

"I need your help, Bill," I admitted, though it burnt me to say it.

"Is that right? I thought you'd never accept nothing from the 'Birds."

"I never would. Not for myself. It's for someone else."

"This where you come in, is it?" Bill said, turning to Lucien.

I looked over to Lucien but all he did was shake his head.

"There's an African woman. They call her the Leopard Lady."

"Freaks are big business, Zillah. You know that, though, don't you?"

"This is different. She's real."

Bill splayed his hands out before him and picked at the dirt beneath his thumbnail. I could see him thinking it over.

"What do you want me to do about it?"

"It's just information I need. The show she's in, it's called the Odditorium but I don't know where it is." The sort of things I suspected they were now doing to the Leopard Lady, and possibly her child too, were too gruesome even for the London stage. "It'll be somewhere private, unexpected."

"And if I find out its location, then what?"

"We'll take it from there," Lucien said. The first words he'd uttered since we sat down.

"I don't know, Zillah," Bill said. "I'm not in the favours business."

"I'm not asking for a favour," I said quickly. "I can pay."

I could work out how and with what later.

"Even so," Bill said, returning to the dirt under his nails. I wondered where it had come from.

"There's a child involved," Lucien said.

Bill glanced at him. He sat forward in his seat, taking him in.

"A freak too?"

"We don't know. We've not seen him."

Bill waved a hand and one of the men came over. I held my breath. Was this the moment we'd be escorted from the pub? No. Instead the man took out a small notebook and a stub of pencil and Bill scratched out the word "Odditorium." He held it up to me to see.

"That right?"

"Yes," I said.

"Then meet me tomorrow afternoon at Hussmann's and I'll tell you where it is."

Hussmann's was Bill's place. I'd never known the address, but Lucien obviously did because I felt him nod.

"Four o'clock?"

"Thereabouts," Bill said. He looked over my shoulder and I could tell that we'd been dismissed. Lucien stood and I followed him out of the booth. He took my hand as we walked away, but before I'd gone three steps, Bill called me back.

"I'm glad you came to me, Zillah."

"I didn't want to."

Bill laughed and slapped his thigh. "You haven't changed, have you?"

I bit my tongue against all the things I wanted to say to him. After Eustace died, I'd sworn never to consort with the Blackbirds and I hadn't, not for these five years.

"I'll find your Odditorium for you, Zillah," Bill said.

❧

After the warmth of the pub, the cold felt like a ringing slap. The wine had gone to my head more than I'd thought. I hadn't noticed in the fuggy atmosphere of the Dog and Duck, but as soon as I stepped out on to the pavement, I felt a little wobbly.

"Here, take my scarf," Lucien said, and gratefully I burrowed into it, breathing in his scent. "Tell me where home is and I'll walk you there."

"Lamb's Conduit Street. I'm staying with Barky for the moment."

"The fellow who was concerned about the entry policy?" Lucien said, his voice a little strained.

He wasn't jealous, was he? I started to laugh at the idea of me and Barky, but Lucien's face was serious and so I stopped myself.

"He's a friend—a father figure, really." It wasn't something I'd dare say in front of Barky, but he was old enough and it would stop Lucien getting the wrong idea. "We think he's got a mistress—he's always turning up at work with expensive gifts."

Lucien was still offish, I could tell. It wasn't just about Barky; I was sure he wanted to ask me about Bill, how we knew each other. I didn't want to explain it all. I never spoke about Eustace, I'd tried to school myself not to think of him, and for years I'd been successful. Lately not so much, but as we walked along, I knew that I must if we were to move forward. If I could tell him about my mother, I could tell him about my first love. *You did say you wanted to be honest with him.*

"You want to know how I know Black Bill," I said.

"I didn't ask," Lucien said.

"I want to tell you. I think I must."

He turned and gave me the first smile I'd seen from him since Bill's arrival. He'd been willing to let me keep my secrets, and that made me all the gladder that I'd decided to tell him.

"You know I grew up in St. Giles?"

"With your Mrs. Bradley, yes?"

"That's right. With her and with her son, Eustace."

Lucien's step faltered slightly, but he remained quiet so I carried on.

"Eustace was a year older than me. We never courted, but we were close." Close enough for him to be my first, but he hadn't been the hearts-and-flowers type, so what I'd said to Lucien wasn't a lie. Eustace hadn't made any sort of play for me. We were friends more than anything, and that remained true after we became lovers.

"He was a Blackbird. Started out with some petty thieving here and there, but he was good at it and he caught Bill's eye."

Handkerchiefs, purses. That's how it began, but then he moved on to housebreaking. He tried to give me some of the things he brought home—the odd necklace or bracelet that Bill let him keep—but I never wanted it.

"There was one job he was up for, out Kensington way. One of those four-story houses with the steps leading up to them; it belonged to a judge. He told me it was a 'meal ticket' job, because we'd be dining out on it for years. His mum didn't want him to go. She'd never wanted him to fall in with Bill, but that is how most people eat in St. Giles. You either work for Bill direct or one of his people. Not many are able to get away."

But you have, Zillah. You've gotten away. At least I hoped I had. Please, God, don't let tonight mean I was sucked back in.

All this time Lucien had been walking with his head down. He was listening closely; I could tell he'd made up his mind to hear me out. I wondered what he was thinking. In my head, telling him about Eustace would show him how important he was becoming to me, but he might not see it that way.

"He went out on the job and something went wrong. It's never been clear exactly what, but there was a knifing and the judge died. It wasn't Eustace, I know it wasn't, but he was the one they came for."

How could I ever forget that day when they all turned up, ten constables and just Mrs. Bradley and me in the house? They found the knife after two minutes but they still turned the house upside down, just because they could. I'd never seen it before. They sat with us, wouldn't let us leave the kitchen, and when Eustace came in, they took him. No chance to warn him or even to say goodbye.

"You think Bill planted the knife?"

"That or he fingered Eustace as the one who done it. There were some whispers for a while but they died down quick enough. No one wanted to cross Bill, you see, not for a small fry like Eustace. Either way, it was Eustace that swung for it."

"And what of his mother?"

"Mrs. Bradley died a little later."

There was no money for a doctor, of course, but everyone in the rookery knew it'd been of a broken heart. I was the one that found her and it was then and there that I'd vowed to get out of St. Giles for good, whatever it took.

"Thank you for telling me, Zillah," Lucien said.

"I wanted to."

While I'd shared the story of what happened to Eustace, we'd reached the top of Chancery Lane, crossed over High Holborn and onto Red Lion Street. In fifteen minutes more we'd be at Barky's. I'd expected him to say more in response to my confidence, but we walked along in silence. *You shouldn't have mentioned Eustace.* But Lucien wasn't simple. He'd know I had a past. Not that there was any chance I'd tell him about Vincent, though. A first love was one thing, but I doubted he'd want to hear that until last Friday I'd been mistress to a viscount.

We were outside Barky's neat little home now. There was no light shining from his windows on the first floor. If he'd made it back after work, he'd gone out again and probably wouldn't return until the morning. I unwound the scarf Lucien had lent me. *Please don't take it back.* It would be a bad sign if he did, but no, he let me keep it. It meant I'd definitely be seeing him again. He was wealthy but not enough to give away cashmere.

"Thank you for tonight, Lucien."

"You're welcome. I feel we made good progress."

I hoped there was a double meaning to his words. Progress in our search for the Leopard Lady and progress with whatever it was between us.

"Will you be coming to Hussmann's with me tomorrow?"

Much better to meet Bill on my own, so I was relieved when he shook his head and gave me the directions. "I will come and meet you there when I've finished at the shop. We close at five on Tuesdays."

"I'd like that," I said.

It was a moment where something might have happened,

but I was wary of lingering too long outside the house after the warning Barky had given me. Even with Lucien clearly being quality, his brown skin made him a mark as much as myself. I scrabbled for the key that Barky had left out for me under a clay flowerpot.

"Good night, Lucien."

"*Ngewor e bi mahungbea*," he said. Take care.

⁓

Overcome with weariness, I wasn't careful enough as I stepped through Barky's door and knocked into a low table. The china bowl it held wobbled furiously.

"Shh," I commanded, as though it wasn't me that had done it.

In the room that served as kitchen and living room, there was a plate with a cloth over it. Cold ham. Barky must have left it for me. I wolfed it down, famished.

"Is that you, Zillah?"

I hadn't spotted Barky hunkered down in the easy chair where I'd made my bed for the last two nights.

"Didn't mean to disturb you," I said in a loud whisper, though by now he was wide-awake. "When I didn't see a light on, I thought you must be out."

"Not tonight."

"You were out yesterday, though," I said hoping he'd say who with.

"I was," he agreed, but left it at that.

He wasn't usually so short with me. Perhaps he'd intended to go out and was disappointed.

"You had a good time, then?" Barky said before I could ask him anything else.

"I only had a glass or two," I said, defending myself against the disapproval in his tone. "It was so strange, Barky, you cannot imagine it. I've never been somewhere like that, all those Blacks together. Drinking, dancing, and they made me so welcome. I wish you could have seen it."

"Oh?"

There was a catch in his voice.

"He's a good man, Barky. You had no need to worry."

"You told him about Vincent?"

I shook my head. It didn't matter anymore. I'd made my choice to leave him.

"You're playing a dangerous game, girl."

"Don't lecture me. Not when it's been such a long day already. Besides, there's nothing Lucien needs to know. That's all done with."

"More fool you."

I'd told Barky about the source of Vincent's money and he made it clear that he thought I was mad to throw him over. There was definitely something that had irked him tonight. He was being more than usually crusty. A giant yawn almost split my face.

"You might as well have the bed," Barky said. "You'll feel it in the morning if you don't. I'm comfy enough here in the chair."

He'd spread a crocheted blanket over his knees, and with the fire it was quite cozy. Boldly I bent down to kiss the top of his head and he recoiled. It sobered me a little.

"Just two glasses you said, eh?"

"You don't like Lucien, do you?" I said.

"Are you seeing him again?"

"Tomorrow afternoon. I've got his scarf, see." I knew I should probably explain to Barky about the Leopard Lady, but now Lucien was helping me, it felt like our thing, and I hadn't found her yet.

"He said I should ask you to tell me more about yourself," I said.

"You're right, I don't like him."

"I wish you would, Barky. I wish you would."

"Go to bed now."

I left Barky sitting before the fire. The orange flames cast a warming glow on one half of his face but left the other side in shadow. It was like him, really, only to show one side of himself. I would find a way to make him and Lucien friends.

I hadn't yet been inside Barky's bedroom. It was small and square, with little furniture. Just a round side table and a wardrobe in addition to the bed. I took off my dress and folded it. My boots proved a little harder and I was forced to pull them off with both hands. Down to my shift, I lay back on the bed and drew the covers up to my chin. There was a rectangular patch on the wall where the chintzy wallpaper was brighter. A picture must have hung there until recently. Maybe it was a portrait of Barky's lover, but what would she have looked like? The idea made me giggle. *In the morning I'll ask him*, I told myself, knowing that by then I would have forgotten all about it.

Even though I was tired, I forced myself to keep my eyes open, trying to think through all that had happened. Silly to fight sleep. I should welcome it. It would make tomorrow come all the quicker. The prospect of sitting down face-to-face with Bill was unnerving, but I'd just have to make sure that any fear I felt didn't show. My goal was to learn exactly where the Leopard Lady was being held. If he could tell me that, it would be a good day.

XXVI

Hussmann's
Coffeehouse

Hussmann's was tucked away down a blind alley off Oxford Circus. Lucien had given me the directions I needed last night. Even so, I'd gotten a little lost on my way over from Tuesday rehearsals, and the sun had already begun to dip when I arrived a touch after four o'clock. From the outside it was hard to tell what kind of shop it was, for the windows were clouded with steam. But as soon as I opened the door and the bitter smell of coffee wafted out, there could be no mistaking it. Inside, there was a long wooden table with two benches, enough to seat twenty men. About half the spots were taken, but the customers weren't spread out; they were clustered in the middle, listening closely while one man read from a newspaper. I thought I recognised a couple of Black Bill's henchmen from the Dog and Duck, but it wasn't only Blackbirds, or even Blacks, here. Some of the men looked like costermongers, others clerks, but I guessed they all worked for Bill in one way or another. Two looked up at my entrance, surprised to see a woman on her own, but none questioned me. Hussmann's wasn't the sort of place you went into unless you had business with its owner. They must have realised I was there by Bill's invitation. I took a seat, and within moments a boy appeared with a dish of coffee. I scrabbled in my pocket for some change and clinked two ha'pennies into his hand.

"You can 'ave as many of 'em as you like for that," the boy said.

The dish was brimful with dark syrupy liquid. I picked it up with both hands and took a swig, determined to get my money's worth. Disgusting. It reminded me of nothing so much as drinking soot. Maybe coffee was like cigars—something you had to force yourself to appreciate. They said it helped to clear your mind and free your thoughts. All well and good, but I'd had enough of thinking for the time being. I realised I was drumming my fingers on the table and put my hands in my lap instead. Any woman would feel nervous to meet Black Bill on his home turf but there was no need to advertise it.

Black Bill appeared after half an hour, entering by a set of stairs behind the counter. He must have rooms here above the shop. I saw him look around and take in who was there before his glance fell on me and he strode over. He took up a seat opposite me, looking nothing like the larger-than-life villain they painted in the papers. It was hard to imagine that the man before me wielded so much power, but I knew from bitter experience that he did.

I took Bill's lateness as a subtle show of that power, but his expression when he sat down was businesslike. He didn't look like a man who had come to play games. The boy who'd served me brought over a glass of water, the surface shimmering slightly as his hands shook.

"Where's your handsome friend today?"

"I thought it best if we were alone," I said.

"Scared I'd say something about your viscount?"

Of course he knew about Vincent. After I'd left the pub last night, he'd probably asked around. I doubted there was anyone known to him, as I had been through Eustace, that he didn't keep track of in one way or another. I sat forward in my chair.

"Have you found her? Or the child?"

"I haven't seen them, but I know where your Odditorium is."

"Close by?"

"Here in Westminster."

As close as that! Bill's hand disappeared into the inside pocket of his coat. For a second, I held my breath, wondering what it was he kept in there, but when he withdrew it, there was no weapon, only a scrap of grubby paper between his fingers.

"The address is written on here."

I made to take the notelet from him, but he wouldn't let it go.

"There'll be no charge for the information. You know I've always had a soft spot for you and the Bradleys. Even though your little friend was careless, I could find a use for you. I imagine you'd be quite a good spy now you're used to mixing with the aristocracy."

How dare he speak of Eustace like that. A retort was on my tongue but I bit it back. Bill's lazy smile told me that he was mocking me, trying to get a rise. I would not fall for it. We still held the paper between us. It was the key to helping the Leopard Lady, but by dealing with Black Bill, would I be betraying Eustace if I took it? I thought of Eustace's face. He wasn't handsome like Lucien or pretty like Vincent. With his crooked smile and the unruly black hair that curled past his collar, he'd looked what he was—a ruffian—but I'd loved him regardless. I took the paper but placed it down on the table without opening it.

"I insist on paying you," I said.

I had precious little but Bill wasn't a man I wanted to be beholden to. Then it struck me. There was something I was willing to trade.

"I want you to take this for the information."

I held out Ellen's vial of opium. It had turned out to be of some use to me after all. Curious, Bill took the blue glass bottle from me and opened it. Using his finger as a stopper, he upended the bottle, righted it, and then licked the dab of powder left behind.

"Where did you come across this, then?"

"Never you mind."

He hesitated for a moment.

"Your choice. You know what sort of place this Odditorium is, do you? It's more than a bit of dancing."

The paper was still on the table. I was scared to ask him, but I knew I must.

"Tell me."

"There's an evening show," he started.

I nodded. I'd had a taste of the evening show in Crillick's library.

"But it's the matinee you want to watch for," Bill said. "Starts about three."

He gave a small shudder, no longer smiling or mocking. Bill had seen all sorts and the Blackbirds were not known to shy away from violence. The Odditorium had to be bad if it had this effect on him. What was Crillick putting the Leopard Lady through if an afternoon show could make the likes of Black Bill flinch?

"They're running experiments," he said.

"You're sure?" I asked, but I knew the answer. I'd seen the glass tubes, the acids, and the pointed instruments on the trolley. The blood droplets on the floor of the warehouse. The scabs and sores I remembered were only what was visible. God alone knew how many scars she bore now.

"Are they experimenting on the child too?"

I could hardly bear to ask. I had no idea how old the Leopard Lady's son was, but the thought of what they might be doing to him was monstrous. I'd seen the scientific papers that Crillick had left around the house. There was a theory they could tell intelligence from the shape of a person's skull, but knowing Crillick's cruelty, head measurements were likely the least of it.

"I don't know about that. But this Leopard Lady is not alone. Her name was only one on a list of several."

"Can you tell me exactly how many?"

These nameless others had been worrying me more and more. I might not have seen them, but their plight was every bit as bad as the Leopard Lady's. For all I knew, they might be in an even worse state.

While Bill threw back his boiled water, I unfolded the paper he'd given me. It was the very piece that he'd written the words "The Odditorium" on last night, but now two more lines—an address—had been added beneath.

Bill was getting to his feet but stopped when he heard my gasp.

"Wait. This can't be right." There'd been some kind of mistake.

The other patrons looked up at the sound of my raised voice. Black Bill sat down again, with a stern look. He did not appreciate anyone making a scene.

"Don't call me a liar, girl. My man was there not two hours ago, watching the house. I'd say the show is in the cellar."

"25 Northumberland Avenue?" I said it in a half whisper.

"That's right," he said.

"Vincent lives there."

"You can't trust them, Zillah," Bill said, not unkindly, and I wasn't sure if he meant the English or the quality or both.

He leant back from the table, watching me coolly as I struggled to make sense of what I'd learnt. I'd always prided myself on keeping my wits about me, but I'd let myself become so wrapped up in being an exotic princess in the eyes of a viscount, I'd failed to notice that, two floors below in the basement, the Leopard Lady, her child, and others like them were being exhibited and experimented on in the name of entertainment.

ᐁ

It was a fresh bowl of coffee that brought me back to myself. Bill had left, but I still held the note in my hand. I could scrunch it up, burn it, but that wouldn't erase the truth. The banging, the crashing at Crillick's house. That's what it had all been about. I'd gone searching for the Odditorium downriver but all the time it was being built right under my nose.

I called the boy over to ask what time it was. Half past five. Lucien would be well on his way by now, but I couldn't wait here any longer. I hurried out of Hussmann's, walked up toward the main road, and dimly heard a coachman swear as I crossed over Oxford Street without checking for carriages.

Amid the chaos in my head, as I tried to think how I could save her and the boy as swiftly as possible, I didn't hear Lucien call my name, but I did feel it when he grabbed me before I stumbled into the path of yet another carriage. For a moment I collapsed into his arms, flooded with relief.

"The Odditorium," I stammered. "We have to get there. Now."

"Zillah, what has happened?" Lucien said.

I was looking up and down the street for a cab and he trailed after me.

"She's at Northumberland Avenue," I said.

But he looked at me blankly. He didn't understand the significance of that address. Nor could I tell him too much without the risk of revealing my relationship with Vincent.

"I wasn't expecting somewhere so close to the theatre," I said lamely.

"It is not far from my shop. But, Zillah, you can't think of going there now. It will not be a matter of bursting in and taking her. You said there are others to think of too?"

He was right. I'd gone off at half-cock when I went down to the docks. It hadn't mattered. The Leopard Lady was long gone by the time I discovered where Crillick had first held her, but this time I could not afford to make the same mistake. It meant leaving her at the Odditorium for another day, when even an hour was too much, but I had to make sure everything was in place.

"Black Bill's information was that she's paraded before an audience twice a day. Once in the afternoon and then again late evening. Our best chance will be between her performances."

If the matinee show started around three o'clock and lasted an hour or two, and the evening show was at ten o'clock, that gave us a clear window to get her out, and all the others too. God knows what state they were kept in. We'd need a carriage to get them to safety—maybe more than one.

"Shall we think of a plan together?" Lucien said.

Now that I'd had a minute to calm down, I could see the sense in working out the best way to free the prisoners. It had been a shock to find out where the Odditorium was, but I could use my knowledge of 25 Northumberland Avenue to my advantage. Grace and I had always gotten on well. Could I count on her to help me?

"We could go there tonight to see it for ourselves," Lucien said.

"No," I said, and he looked hurt at the forcefulness of my tone. I squeezed his hand to show that I appreciated him. "I want your help, of course, but we have to be cautious. You have your business to think of. If anyone saw you, it would be too easy to track you down."

And I wouldn't want Grace to let anything slip about Vincent and me, I thought.

"I will go to Elvira," I said. "She promised she'd be on standby to help me with whatever I need, and neither Crillick nor the Peelers would take the liberties with her that they might take with you."

Lucien's cheek twitched. It angered him that he couldn't help in the way he wanted to, but he saw that what I said was right.

I knew Elvira lived in Mayfair. *Could I get there tonight?* I looked at the darkening sky—it was coming up to dinnertime, but this was my best chance. Tomorrow I would have to be onstage, and I couldn't afford to rouse Crillick's wrath by missing any more performances. Not after my unexplained illness. I turned on my heel back toward Marble Arch. Lucien followed after me.

"I can see you are ready to act now, Zillah, but are you ready to talk about what happens after? What comes next once the Leopard Lady and her child are safe?"

I hadn't gotten that far. I was still reeling from learning where the Odditorium was.

Lucien opened his mouth to say more, but before he could go any further, I interrupted.

"I'll get to it, Lucien, I will, but for now I must do what I can to rescue this woman and her child."

We stood facing one another. Lucien had put his hand on my arm to delay my leaving, but I couldn't help looking over my shoulder to the main road. At last, he said, "I understand, Zillah. What I have to say can wait. Come, I will help you find a carriage."

XXVII

To Mayfair

Lucien flagged a hansom cab and paid the driver to take me to Berkeley Square. I was grateful for his help but glad he hadn't come with me. He was throwing up too many complications, and having failed to realise where the Odditorium was, I felt that acting quickly was the best way to make amends.

Before long, the carriage deposited me outside Elvira's house. I'd never had much call to come out this way before. London wasn't that big, not really, but the wide streets of Mayfair were a country mile from where I'd grown up in St. Giles. There was another reason too. Only half-formed but there all the same. A vague memory of a big white house five stories high with steps leading up to a black front door. I had once lived in a house like this. My mother had too. For all I knew, perhaps she still did. Once Mrs. Bradley had died there'd been no one to tell me where I could find her, but part of me hadn't felt able to in any case. Surely if she'd wanted a relationship, she would've come looking for me. I didn't want to run the risk of finding her only to realise she didn't want me.

I knocked smartly on Elvira's imposing door before I lost my nerve. It was opened by a trim woman in a dark dress and matching apron. She looked a little older than me, her fair hair scraped back from her face in a modest bun. I expected to have to explain myself, but no. There was none of the condescension that I anticipated. She merely bid me wait while she fetched her mistress.

As she made her way up the stairs, I took in the entrance. This was a much bigger house than Crillick's. From the outside I'd have expected the hallway to be highly decorated, but it was plain as anything—no ornaments, no flowers. There was a serenity about the house that reminded me of Vincent. I didn't miss him, not really, but this luxury was a reminder of why I'd stayed with him. After so long at St. Giles and those few weeks playing house while Crillick was away, the ease of Vincent's way of living had beguiled me. A carriage to pick me up after every performance, clothes made just for me, a full belly every night. I'd let the comfort of it all distract me. But it wasn't who I was. Or who I wanted to be.

It was less than five minutes before the maid reappeared. She asked me to follow her into the south room, where her mistress was expecting me. *Should've prepared a speech, Zillah,* I thought as I set off after her, but I knew Elvira wanted to help. I'd seen how passionate she was when she'd challenged Crillick in his own house, and when we'd been officially introduced at the Sierra Leone lecture, she'd been more than willing. If I was clear about what I wanted and why, she wouldn't need much persuading.

The south room was large, with a high ceiling. Again, there were no frills nor flounces, and just the minimum of furniture. Elvira was seated on a cream sofa plainly upholstered and free of cushions, but as soon as I entered, she stood up, smoothing down her dress and patting her hair into place before greeting me.

"It is good to see you again, Zillah. I take it you know now what it is you would have me do?"

Straight to the point. I liked that. She led me to a table and gestured for me to pull out a chair.

"I never quite feel comfortable discussing matters of import sitting on a sofa," she said. "Please excuse me for one moment."

When she returned, she wore a pair of gold-wired spectacles and carried something heavy in her hands, a sloping wooden object whose purpose I wasn't sure of. She settled it down on the tabletop and sat directly behind it.

"This is my writing box, Zillah. See, here is the compartment for the ink and the paper. I find myself writing a lot of letters for my causes, so this box has become my constant recourse."

Neat and tidy as she was, I could see what looked like ink stains on her fingers. The role I had in mind for her was probably more practical than she was used to. The maid came in with a tray of tea things, the same woman as had answered the door. It seemed ridiculous that Elvira would have only the one, but I wasn't impertinent enough to ask her about it. Not yet anyway. She'd noticed me looking, though.

"That's Ethel," she said. "I might have mentioned her when we met last week?"

I nodded. She had and I'd been intrigued.

"I took her in when her parents threw her out," Elvira said. "She was let down by a gentleman and now she helps me in my work. She's as much a companion as anything else. We have no secrets. I told her you were coming to us with an opportunity. Now, when we were at Exeter Hall, I believe I misspoke when I said you were one of Marcus Crillick's maids?"

"It was as a maid that I attended Crillick's party, but . . ." I paused, not wanting to come out with it, but hearing what she'd hinted about Ethel, I took a chance that she wouldn't judge me. "I was close to his friend Viscount Woodward."

"Vincent? I knew him well once," Elvira said. "I've not seen much of him since he moved to London. I am not enamored of the company he keeps now. Perhaps the less said of him the better. Now, what do you have planned?"

I'd rehearsed it as the carriage driver had circled round Berkeley Square before coming to a stop outside Elvira's house, nestled right in one corner. It hadn't seemed so madcap then. *Out with it, Zillah. She doesn't seem like a woman who would balk at it.* I sat forward in my chair, my hands resting on the table.

"Ever since that night in Crillick's library, I've been looking for the Leopard Lady. I don't know if you heard, but she spoke to me. Lucien told me that what she said meant 'my son' in Zulu. From then on, I have been determined to track her down. I worried that it wasn't just her they were exhibiting, but her child too."

Elvira had been taking notes as soon as I started talking, but now she paused. "A child? They would do that to a child?"

"I traced them to the West India Docks. Crillick was keeping them in a warehouse there. I think he must have put on at least one more show there like the one we saw. I found a stage, just as there had been in the library. There were drops of blood on the floor too."

"Crillick talked about intimate shows. It must have been one of those," Elvira said.

"I think so — there were about twelve chairs set out altogether — but she cannot have been there longer than a night or two. By the time I got there, he'd moved her and her son on, but that's when I found out that the show he'd built around her was called the Odditorium."

Elvira rang a small bell that Ethel had brought in with the tea things. When the maid came in, Elvira whispered in her ear and gestured to the sideboard, recognizing that the matters we were discussing would require something stronger than tea. Ethel returned with glass tumblers and a decanter and served us both with stiff measures of brandy.

"Stay, Ethel. You will want to hear what Zillah has learnt firsthand," Elvira said. "And take one for yourself."

I'd already warmed to Elvira, and to see the way she treated her maid like an equal sealed it. She was exactly the sort of person I wanted in my corner.

"That was last Wednesday," I said. "But it wasn't until this afternoon that I learnt where the Odditorium was located."

Elvira and Ethel leant in.

"Crillick is hosting the show in the basement of his own house."

"At Northumberland Avenue? Are you quite sure?" Elvira said.

"I have not seen it for myself, but the man who told me was certain. It makes sense, in a way. Crillick has had carpenters in to build a set for him."

Again, I heard the sawing and the banging. Those noises would haunt me now until the Leopard Lady was free.

"It is despicable that he would do this to a woman, let alone a child. I cannot believe that Woodward would stand by and allow that. He lives with Crillick, doesn't he?"

"He's not in London right now. I hear he went to his father's house in Surrey."

"I saw him yesterday," Elvira said. "At Fortnum and Mason."

Vincent back already? No reason for me to know, really, but as Elvira herself had said, how could he allow it? When I'd challenged him about Crillick keeping the Leopard Lady at the warehouse, he'd said he didn't know. Surely, he couldn't use that same excuse now. It made my stomach turn.

"I am hoping that you can help me get her out."

"Tell me what my role would be. Ethel will assist us too."

"You have a carriage? Maybe more than one? I was thinking you might drive her away once I have freed her from the cellar."

Elvira clapped her hands. "That is easily done. After we have rescued the woman and her son, they can stay here with me."

That was the offer I had been hoping for.

"What about the others? I'm assuming that there's at least three more men and women that Crillick has forced to perform, but I do not know them."

"There is room for them all here, at least for one night," Elvira said. "On Thursday I can arrange for them to be taken to my country house, where they can recover."

"That's the day after tomorrow. You think the rescue should go ahead tomorrow night?"

"There's not a moment to lose, is there? But you are taking the job of getting them out of the house all on yourself. Can Ethel not help at all with that?"

Ethel nodded enthusiastically at this idea.

"I would be grateful," I said. "I've seen a drawing that shows the Odditorium is quite large; there is more than one room to it, so it would help to have two of us."

"I'm sure there are others among my friends who would lend you their support, but I imagine you'll want to ensure that the minimum number of people are involved."

"Do you think you would be able to help the prisoners find work?" I said.

"If they want it, yes, but if they would prefer to return to their homelands, then I will arrange for that."

It sounded perfect.

"I have another question," Elvira said. "How will we make sure the way is clear for the rescue attempt? What can we do to guarantee that Crillick is out—ideally you want him at his theatre, don't you?"

I nodded. It was very important to me that he be in his box when I put my plan into action.

"I have an idea for that," Ethel said. "I bet he's one for the ladies, ain't he? His sort usually are. We can send him a letter, can't we, posing as a likely lass saying she'll meet him at the theatre. That should get him there."

"I like that, Ethel, but we'll need him to stay there too. We cannot run the risk that Crillick leaves when his would-be lover fails to materialise."

The two of them frowned, puzzling over how to keep Crillick at the theatre, but I'd already thought of this. What I had planned for my final show would have him transfixed.

"I'll handle that," I said. "I've got just the thing in mind," and I smiled at the thought of it.

"That's all settled, then. I'll go and find some scent to spray the letter with," Ethel said and she left the room.

We had a plan and I felt confident in it. But Elvira had yet another question for me that I hadn't properly considered. The same one that Lucien had posed earlier and that I'd brushed off.

"Have you thought about where you will go?" she asked. "You will not be able to return to Crillick's, I take it. Do you have other work and a place to stay?"

I didn't, and even if I did, what were the chances of Crillick leaving me be? My plan would likely ruin him. He wouldn't let me get away with it.

"I'm staying at Holborn. I'll be safe there," I said. *But will you still be welcome after all this kicks off?* I would have to tell Barky everything tonight. It would be unfair not to. I'd already left it later than I should have done.

"For a night or two, perhaps. But I imagine you'll want to get out of London as swiftly as possible," Elvira said.

Could it be that bad? *Why wouldn't it be?* Crillick would do whatever he could to make me pay. Staying at Barky's could only be a short-term solution, but where else would I go? *Sierra Leone, Zillah.* It was drastic, but there was no denying it would be the solution to all my problems. A fresh start somewhere where Crillick couldn't reach me.

"There is a way I could leave town," I said.

"You're speaking of the Sierra Leone scheme, are you not?"

I nodded in reply to Elvira's question.

"It's a good opportunity, Zillah. You should give it your strongest consideration," she said.

I wouldn't make any decisions yet, but it was something that I'd have to think about. I drained my glass and shook hands with Elvira. She was proving a great ally, but now it was time to head back to Holborn and sleep. I'd need a good night's rest to be ready for all that was to come.

XXVIII

Barky's
Revelation

The moon was up and Berkeley Square was quiet, with only the wind blowing through the trees. The soft whistling sound it made soothed me. I should have been quicker to work out where the Odditorium was, and the Leopard Lady and her child had suffered more because I hadn't, but now I had a plan. *By this time tomorrow night, you'll be free.*

I started the walk back to Holborn, but I'd only taken two steps from Elvira's house when I heard my name called. I turned in surprise to see Lucien walking toward me.

"What are you doing here?"

"You were so distressed after meeting that man at Hussmann's, I thought I would wait for you."

"But that was almost two hours ago. You've been standing out here all this time?"

"I didn't want to interrupt when you were making your plans."

"Forgive me. I was rude earlier. I know you only wanted to help."

He fell into step beside me and we walked along in silence for a moment.

"Last night we spoke of Sierra Leone," Lucien said.

Only yesterday but it seemed as though so much had happened since then.

"I want you to come out there with me."

That brought me up sharp. I'd suspected Lucien might go, wondered if it was why he'd held himself back from me, but to accompany him? That hadn't crossed my mind until Elvira brought it home to me that, after I had rescued the Leopard Lady, staying in London would be out of the question. What had they said at Exeter Hall: *No place so fit and proper?* Could I really go there with him?

I turned around. Lucien had stopped a little way behind me, and I walked back toward him so he didn't have to raise his voice. He breathed heavily from trying to keep pace with me. It was the first time I'd seen him less than in control. I liked him better for it.

"I'm asking you to marry me, Zillah. I wish for the two of us to build a life together in our ancestral homeland."

A proposal? Lucien was proposing to me?

"You want me to go to Sierra Leone with you?"

"To Freetown, Zillah. I will be honest with you. It is something I have been thinking of for some time, but when I accepted my feelings for you, I knew that was where our future lay."

He'd tried to talk to me about it before. At his shop, last night at the Dog and Duck. The half thought I'd had at Elvira's was starting to become real. Lucien stepped close and took up my hands.

"You heard what they said at the lecture. It is a place of convenience, of comfort."

I opened my mouth to interrupt. Thinking of it was one thing, doing it quite another. But Lucien hadn't finished.

"Zillah, it could be *our* place, we could belong there. I saw how you felt last night, surrounded by your own people. Comfortable, accepted, safe. Think of it: every day could be like that, everywhere you went."

The thought of it. No hiding behind a headscarf, nor calculating my every move, nor having to make sure I was always a step ahead. And it would only be worse if Crillick was seeking vengeance. I wasn't sure I could imagine that sort of freedom. But Lucien clearly had. Well as he was doing with his grocer's and his staff, he didn't need it, but I could tell from the shine in his eyes that he wanted it badly.

"What about your shop? Wouldn't it hurt to give it up after all your hard work?"

"I would sell it. We could build another, build it together. Why fight for custom here, when in Sierra Leone I know they would come to me for my produce, not for my novelty value?"

Is that what he thought? I didn't know whether it was true or not, but I could see how something like that could eat away at you.

"Will you give me your answer?" Lucien said.

It was all too quick. A matter of weeks ago, I had not even met this man. *He wants you,* came the voice in my head, but did I really want him? The attraction was there, had been since that first night I saw him in the audience at Crillick's, but that alone was not enough. I thought of the times we had spent together, how he'd taught me to speak in Mende and drawn me out while we walked around St. James's. Only Mrs. Bradley and Eustace also knew about my mother's past, but Lucien had helped me realise that neither she nor I bore the shame of her enslavement. He was offering me his hand and a new life. For that reason alone, I had to consider his proposal properly.

I peered into his eyes, and he held me with the tenderness of his gaze. What I felt for him was a shadow of what I'd felt for Eustace, but our relationship was still new. In time it could grow and our feelings could deepen.

"If you need time to think, you don't have to tell me now," Lucien said when I made no reply.

But I knew the boats would be leaving soon. The sixteenth of October. That's what they'd printed in the pamphlets, and it was only six days away. He might not want to rush me, but no sea captain would delay a trip across the ocean while a girl made up her mind. I wasn't ready to say yes. But my answer wasn't an outright no either.

"We are close to finding the Leopard Lady. I know that is your dearest wish," Lucien said. "Once she is safe, may I ask you again?"

He was disappointed, that much was plain from his voice, but he was prepared to be patient. That he knew what was important to me, and wanted to support me in it, was another good sign.

"I would like that very much," I said.

Barky had left the key under the flowerpot for me again and I slipped in quietly. He was sat at the kitchen table, his head nodding over a half-eaten plate of bread and cheese. He looked tired.

"You want tea?"

He started to get up, but I stopped him.

"I'll make it," I said.

In the cupboard over the sink there was a jar half-full of dark brown leaves. I spooned two measures into Barky's silver teapot and poured on water that had warmed over the fire. I brought the pot to the table and sat down to let it brew. My first sip was perfect. Much better than that coffee muck at Hussmann's.

"You shot off after rehearsals. You weren't out with him again, were you?"

Just "him," not his name, as if it sullied his mouth to say it.

It threw me off and when I replied it came out all defensive. This wasn't how I'd been expecting things to go.

"I went to a coffeehouse," I said, thinking it better not to say which one.

"He took you to a coffeehouse?"

"I take it you don't drink coffee, then?"

Barky sniffed. "Back when it was in style, maybe. I'm surprised; I wouldn't have thought a coffeehouse was a place for the likes of you."

Where had that come from? I expected this from Ellen but not Barky. What *was* for us? Not coffee, not drawing rooms. Where could we go to just be? Barky saw the look on my face.

"The likes of you meaning *women*, Zillah. I'd have known you'd been around that Black even if you didn't tell me. He makes you ever so touchy."

If it were yesterday, I would have let the comment pass to avoid a row, but now that "that Black" had proposed, I wasn't having it. Barky might be in a pissy mood, but there was no need to take it out on me. I couldn't deny I was different lately. But while Barky was right that it was because of Lucien, he was wrong to say I was too sensitive. I was starting to think that until now I had not been sensitive enough. I was seeing things now, staring them down when before I would have turned away. Was one way better than the other? It was true that before Lucien, my life had been easier, but perhaps I'd finally found the narrow gate.

"I wasn't with Lucien at Hussmann's, as it happens. I met him afterward."

"Wait, Hussmann's?" Barky said. He looked up sharply, the frown on his face a mix of anger and worry, and I realised that he must know who owned it.

"Yes, Hussmann's. I went there to meet Black Bill."

"You're getting mixed up with the Blackbirds now, Zillah? I thought you were better than that."

"So I can't mix with the Blackbirds nor Lucien. Who should I associate with then, Barky? It's not as though I have a line of people queuing up to be my friend."

"You're a big girl, Zillah. I shouldn't have to tell you why to steer clear of thieves and murderers. As for Lucien, I just don't like the cut of his jib."

I couldn't fault Barky's honesty. From the first he'd been down on him. But now I thought about it, Lucien hadn't been too friendly himself. I remembered the look that had passed between the two men yesterday when Lucien had suggested we go to the

Dog and Duck. But tonight was a good night. I wanted to get back to how I'd felt when I'd left Elvira's, confident in my plan to save the Leopard Lady.

"You feeling all right, Barky?" I said, deciding that I would be the one to smooth it over.

"Don't know what you mean."

I got up and moved closer to him leaning against the table at his right hand. "You seem a bit crusty tonight, that's all. I wondered if it had anything to do with you not going out last night?"

After the thrill of Lucien's declaration, I wanted Barky to be happy too.

"You know you can tell me about where you go at night, Barky. Who you go with?"

I saw Barky's shoulders stiffen. I knew I probably shouldn't pry, but maybe if he could talk about it, he'd feel better.

"I don't ask you about your business. You best keep your nose out of mine. Don't make me regret having you stay here."

I threw up my hands. If he was in this much of a funk there'd be no getting through to him. I might as well go to bed before he killed my mood completely. I'd just have to tell him my news about the Leopard Lady in the morning. It was probably best he didn't know too much. Just enough not to give me away before-hand. Afterward I knew I could rely on him to help keep me safe until I left the country. I was less certain of when might be a good time to tell him that Lucien had proposed to me, but I hadn't made up my mind yet. There was just one thing that was bother-ing me.

"Why was it that Lucien suggested you tell me more about yourself?"

Barky ignored me. I asked him again, loud enough that he couldn't fail to hear. His eyes snapped up, and in that moment, I saw it. What Lucien had seen when he questioned why Barky wouldn't come to the pub with us.

"You're never . . ."

"Never what, Zillah? Go on, say it."

"Barky, you're Black."

The word lingered on the air between us like I'd cursed him. It made sense now. His kindness to me, but also his concern that no one saw me come in and out. Plenty of nosy people who might put two and two together, and then where would he be? Not welcome in Lamb's Conduit Street, that was for sure.

"I don't believe it. All this time . . ."

"You're not to tell, Zillah."

"Of course I won't."

I was hurt that he thought I might, but no wonder he was wary. I thought of the theatre, of Aldous and Ellen and their faces if they found out he was coloured.

"Does Crillick know?"

"No. Not Crillick, not Woodward, none of them."

"But Lucien knew."

"Appears so," Barky said. His voice was bitter. No wonder he hated Lucien.

"He wouldn't say, Barky. He didn't tell me."

"But we're talking about it now."

There was nothing I could say to that. Barky's hair cut convict short. That made sense now. He couldn't dare let it grow. It might not be woolly like Lucien's but it could be curly like mine. His eyes, the brown so deep; the way he caught the sun. Was that why he was never in his shirtsleeves?

I looked up and he was staring at me. He knew what I was thinking and it made me sad. Sad that he felt he had to hide. I'd felt like that about my mother's servitude, but Lucien was making me see that I had nothing to feel ashamed of. Maybe he could do that for Barky too.

"Lucien says—" I began.

"What does Lucien know?" Barky snapped. "He wasn't born here, was he? When they tell him 'Go back to where you came from' it means something. Where would you go? Where would I?"

"There's no need to get nasty. I was only trying to help."

"I'm not Black. Why should I be? My mother was white, my father half-white. You were taught to figure, Zillah. That makes me more white than Black. Who's to tell me otherwise?"

I got the sense of his argument. There was a logic to it, but there were many who'd disagree with him. One drop of Black blood was enough; he knew it as well as I did.

"It doesn't work like that," I said.

"But why?" His voice was plaintive.

"You carry on like people are cake—half this, half that. But it's more like a gin fizz. Once the measure goes in, you can't separate them."

It felt too simple, talking of something so important as this in terms of food and drink, but I was only just coming to terms with it all myself.

"How can you say that when you play Amazonia? When you switch it on and off?" Barky said.

There was a time when I'd thought I could leave Amazonia behind, but the truth was colour couldn't be discarded. I hadn't realised it, was all.

"Don't tell me you wouldn't pass if you could," Barky said.

Would I? It's not like I'd never thought of it. The things I could do came at me in a rush. The roles I could play, the places I could go. The lives I could live. Barky spoke like he could see inside my head, his voice low and persuasive.

"We could steam your hair, take out the curl. Powder you up, trowel it on thick. What do you say to that, Zillah?"

I could almost see it. An easier life, yes; a more successful one, most probably. But then came the stubborn voice. "It wouldn't be me."

The words sat between us for a moment, until Barky murmured, "You can be anyone you want to."

Was he telling me or himself?

"Barky, you're living a lie."

"Don't you worry, my girl. I'm doubly used to that." There was such bitterness in his voice. If it was to do with his mistress, I wondered why he couldn't at least tell me if he wanted to talk about her. But he carried on before I could ask. "You're in no position to judge me. Even you didn't suspect."

True, I'd never known he was passing, but just because he could hide his colour, it wasn't right he felt he should have to. Lucien would know what to say, but I didn't. I could see why Barky felt like he did. I disagreed, but I didn't yet have the words to say why. Barky rose to go to bed. At the door, he spoke, his voice flat and determined.

"You won't say a word about what you learnt tonight, Zillah. Others have thought about it."

At the threat my temper flared—but like a match, no sooner struck than it burnt out. Barky was forty if he was a day. Maybe even older. It was a long time to keep a secret like that. I wondered what it was worth to him; who were these others that had attempted to expose him?

For a long time, I sat before the fire mulling over what Barky had said. The candle burnt low and it was only when it went out, drowned in its own pool of fat, that I stirred. The fire had gone out too, but as I sat down on the easy chair and wrapped a blanket around me, I knew that wasn't the reason I was chilled. Barky wasn't playing. Next chance I got, I'd tell Lucien to keep clear of him.

XXIX

Farewell Performance

Wednesday morning dawned and I walked to Crillick's with a sense of purpose. Every day for the past few weeks I'd dragged my feet, paused to look in shop windows, taken the long way 'round, and all to avoid my growing awareness of what I did when I played Amazonia. Today was different. If everything went according to plan, it would be my final performance. By the time the curtain went down, ten days since I'd first seen her, the Leopard Lady would be well on her way to freedom and me not too far behind her.

When I arrived at the theatre, I took care to hide my excitement from my fellow performers. I didn't want to make them suspicious, but there was one person I did want to see. Ellen and I had not spoken since she'd caught me coming out of Crillick's box. Yesterday she'd cried off rehearsals, sent a note in with Mikey to say that she was ill, but if she cared enough to avoid me, it was worth a shot to try and end things on a good note. She didn't deserve it really, not after what she'd called me, but now I was leaving I could afford to be the bigger person, and I wanted to make it clear that nothing had happened between Crillick and me.

I found Ellen with Bouncer in the box room the performers

used for a kitchen. She was gargling salt water, one of her many rituals before she went onstage; she'd even made me do it once and laughed when I swallowed some down by mistake. Bouncer trotted over to me and put his wet nose in my hand, but when she saw it was me, Ellen spat out the water and called him back to heel sharply. She made to leave the room, but I blocked the door. There wouldn't be another chance for us to talk properly and I was determined to say my piece.

"You're singing tonight?"

"What's it to you?" she said.

So it was going to be like that, then.

"I didn't sleep with him," I said.

Ellen shrugged her shoulders, making out as if she didn't care, but I could tell she was hurting. Our friendship had always contained more than a dash of rivalry, but surely she knew I'd never let a man come between us, and certainly not one like Crillick. She resumed her preparations, stretching her arms, warbling her scales as if I weren't standing there, and though I'd come to make peace, I started to get annoyed.

"It's fine if you don't want to believe me, Ellen, but Crillick will back me up. You should ask him."

Of course, I knew she wouldn't. She was too afraid he'd leave her to hold him to account. It pained me to think she'd never see that she was too good for him. Ellen stopped what she was doing and spun around to face me.

"How dare you say his name to me, you little harlot."

There was a noise behind us and I turned to see the back of one of the dancers who'd probably come to get a drink, seen us rowing, and thought better of it.

"You see, no one wants to be around you, Zillah. Even a girl as sweet as Marie."

"Everything's my fault, is it? Crillick can do no wrong, but it's fine to freeze me out? I know it's you who told the others not to speak to me."

"You shouldn't have done it, Zillah."

"I didn't. I wouldn't do that to you."

We stood face-to-face, both spitting angry. I could see from the glare in Ellen's eyes there was nothing I could say to convince her. And maybe it wasn't even about me. I'd been ready to punch Crillick before things went any further that day in his office, but she knew what he was like, she'd seen how he looked at me. I hovered in the doorway, knowing I should leave but unwilling to walk away. There had been good times between us, I didn't forget that. But maybe we hadn't been as close as I'd thought. I was sorry we couldn't still be friends, but I couldn't say the word to her, not when she'd take it as a confession. Ellen returned to her stretches, her red hair falling forward to hide her face as she bent to touch her toes. She began humming to herself, pointedly ignoring me. I watched for a minute more, then left her to it.

There were still fifteen minutes before the show was due to start. I took up my usual spot in the wings and peeped out from behind the curtain for the final time. The front rows were already filled, with the women on one side and the men on the other as usual. It looked like there'd be an especially big crowd in tonight. All the better. With what I'd planned they'd more than get their money's worth.

A man in waistcoat and flat cap shuffled down the main aisle on his way to his seat. He had his hands full balancing three pints of beer. Lily, one of the dancers, made a bit extra by selling the sweetmeats and show pamphlets. She was doing a roaring trade, but I noticed her glance up at the clock that hung over the bar, knowing that it was time for her to be backstage. *Come on, where are you?* I muttered. Then, out of the corner of my eye, I saw a woman wave. It was Ethel. That meant that Crillick had received her note and come to the theatre expecting to meet an admirer. The first part of our plan—to get him away from Northumberland Avenue and into his box—had succeeded. After my performance he'd have to stay here to deal with the mess I'd unleashed, but there was more to it than that. Amazonia had been his idea, after all. He should be there for her final turn. *Time to get ready, Zillah.* But I lingered to watch the audience for a minute. There was a part of me that had thought I might miss it—the bustle of the audience, the anticipation in the air—but now I'd come to see the damage that my act was doing, I knew it would be a long time before I set foot inside another theatre.

I made my way back to my dressing room. This was the time I would usually start getting ready, but there was no need for that. Tonight I was going to be doing a very different kind of show. I cast my eyes around to see if there was anything I should take with me and they landed on a perfume bottle on the dressing table. I picked it up and had it halfway to my pocket before realizing that I didn't want it after all. It belonged to this part of my life. I would leave it all behind me.

There was a knock on my door. So, Ellen had softened. I turned with a smile, but it was Barky. I hadn't seen him this morning, as I'd hoped, so there'd been no time to tell him what I'd planned. Could I explain it all now? No. He hadn't quite forgiven me for questioning him about where he went late at night and was all business.

"You saw the list tonight, Zillah? You're down for the sacrifice scene."

Though I hadn't bothered to check, I nodded. It was fitting that it would be that scene. The one I'd performed the first night Lucien had come to watch me.

"You won't be late?"

"Not tonight."

He turned to leave but I couldn't let him go without saying something. It was his livelihood too, and he'd done a lot for me.

"You won't hang around tonight, will you? If anything kicks off, you'll get out sharpish? And make sure the dancers and all the other performers do too."

"Got something planned, have you? You don't think it's best to have a clean break?"

Of course he'd guessed there was something afoot. *Come on, Zillah, you know not much gets by him.* But what I had planned *was* my clean break. It was why I was here. I needed this. In some ways I was doing it for him as much as me. Maybe a part of him knew that too.

"I hope you know what you're doing," Barky said.

He looked tired, and I felt a pang of guilt. It wasn't only Crillick that would be affected by my actions, after all, but even so I knew it was the right decision.

"No one knows I've been staying with you, do they?"

He shook his head. "Don't you worry about old Barky. I can look after myself. I've been in this game for a long time, maybe too long."

He gave me a weary smile and it took away the final few nerves that I'd felt. He hadn't quite given me his blessing—he might not be cheering me on, but he wasn't going to stop me.

"I'll see you in the wings in twenty minutes, then?"

"I'll be there, Barky," I said.

Once he'd gone, I shrugged off my coat and replaced it with Amazonia's cape. The door was half-ajar and I could hear the opening music. Dancers first, then the comedian, and Aldous with his white rabbits, and then it would be my turn. I thought back to my first day at Crillick's. How far I had come. But there was no more time for that. I rolled my coat up into a ball and stuffed it just behind the door that opened out into the foyer, ready to collect once my performance was over.

ও

Ellen was already hovering in the wings, watching as Aldous took his bow. She'd painted on her burnt cork and the big red smile. Bouncer, sprawled on his tummy beside her, waved his tail as I came up behind them, but Ellen started when I said her name. She turned around with a sneer, but her curled lip dropped in surprise when she took me in and saw my bare face.

"You haven't done your makeup," she hissed. "Do you even have your costume on under that cape?"

"I have something a little different in mind for tonight," I said.

"You wouldn't dare! Barky," she called out, "Zillah's after sabotaging our performance," but he was already there.

"What's all this, Zillah? Is what Ellen says true?"

The anger in his voice gave no hint that we'd not long spoken, and I was relieved. There was little chance that anyone would suspect his involvement if he seemed as shocked as everyone else when I started my final performance.

The row had taken us a little closer to the stage. Someone in the audience must've seen a flash of my cape.

"It's her. It's Amazonia!" he called out and a cheer went up.

"My public want me, wish me luck," I said, taking my first step onto the stage, leaving Ellen dumbfounded and Barky wringing his hands. My moment had come. Surely the nerves would kick in now, but no. I felt completely calm and I smiled to myself. It was the final sign I needed that I was doing the right thing.

The compère had been speaking to the crowd, keeping them entertained. As he sensed me walking on, he switched to his usual patter about my jungle upbringing, my warrior-queen status, but he sounded rattled. I wasn't due to appear until the drums began, so he knew something was up. I reckoned I had about ten minutes before my plan succeeded or I was hauled away. I brushed past the compère, his voice falling away in confusion, and planted myself center stage. In all the commotion of my early arrival, there'd been no chance to put down the lights. I was glad of it. It was long past time for me to look my audience in the eye. Row upon row of confused white faces craned up at me. The one thing they had in common was that they didn't know what was coming.

"I am Zillah," I announced.

The compère shuffled offstage. *That's right, go. From now on I'll be speaking for myself.*

"Get off" came a cry from my left. I turned, but I wasn't quick enough to see who had shouted. I waited, daring whoever said it to repeat themselves. But all I saw were sullen stares.

"Where's Amazonia?" another man called out, but I ignored him. Amazonia was gone. It was my show now.

With the lights up and the anticipation of what I was about to do, everything felt bright, sharp. There was no music. The drummer must've been as stunned as the audience. In the silence, I took off my hat and let it fall to the floor. I took the pins out of my hair and the two long plaits fell past my shoulders. Next off was the cape. This was the moment that the audience usually gasped to see Amazonia in her skins. Now they saw Zillah dressed much as they were. A dress made of plain cotton. The shade of it somewhere between green and brown with matching buttons. A glimpse of grey stockings, chosen because they were likely to wear well, and sturdy brown boots on my feet. No cavorting, no hollering or whooping. Just me, Zillah, for all the world to see.

"Where's the dancing?" a woman called. A murmuring broke out as the audience whispered to one another, and a half-eaten roll flew past my head.

"There never was an Amazonia," I declared. "You've all been taken in by that man up there."

I pointed to Crillick, where he sat at the front of his box, and there was a shuffling sound as the audience turned to look up at him. Give him his due, he didn't back away. He stood up, as though he would face them down.

"That's the owner of this place, Marcus Crillick. He's been cheating you, laughing at you with his fancy friends. I've never even been to Africa; I was born in St. Giles, just down the road from here."

A tankard arced up toward Crillick's box, and beer dregs rained down on the stalls. Another missile meant for me landed short and caught a man on the head, knocking off his hat. Pushing and shoving and a man in the second row fell onto the people in front of him. His friends turned to find the culprits and the first punches were thrown. There were screams from the women's side of the theatre and others joined in the fray, egging on the men as they traded blows. Glass bottles, plates, and even a chair went flying through the air, thrown with no thought for where they might land. Another scuffle broke out in the seated area, and then another. Within minutes the whole audience was fighting or fleeing, scrambling over each other to leave or to land a blow.

It was glorious, but I knew I didn't have long before they turned on me too. I moved to the back of the stage, out of range of their projectiles. I looked up to the left and saw a movement at Crillick's box. It was too far away to make out the expression on his face, but how perfect that he'd had a front-row seat to see his house of lies come crashing down. For a brief moment, I soaked it all in, the shouting and the grunts of men and women fighting. Now there was the splintering of wood as benches and tables were upended and stamped on. I'd seen enough. I turned on my heel and left the stage.

Barky was gone. I knew he'd have moved straightaway to get the other performers to safety like I'd asked, but Ellen was still standing in the wings, her mouth half-open; she'd seen it all.

"Goodbye, Ellen," I said as I pushed past her.

I set my shoulders and walked down the corridor. Nothing left in the dressing room for me, but I did want to go to the foyer. I went straight to the Amazonia poster, reached up and tore out one long strip. *From the nave to the chaps.* The expression came to me and I tore another strip and then another, growing more and more frenzied until the poster was in shreds.

My coat was still in a ball where I'd left it behind the door that opened out into the foyer. I could hear the sounds of fighting as I eased it on and popped the collar. No more back alley for me. I walked straight out of the front entrance and left Crillick's theatre and the Great Amazonia behind me.

XXX

Within the Odditorium

I strode down the middle of the Strand, swinging my arms and with my head held high. The faces of the audience. They'd been a picture. There'd be a few broken heads when all was done. Who were the savages now?

"Psst, Zillah!"

Ethel stepped out from a shop doorway and beckoned me to join her. She must've waited for me.

"Here, take this. You need to make sure no one sees you."

Of course she was right. What had I been thinking of? I ducked into the doorway beside her and took the heavy cloak that she held out to me. It was big enough to go over my old coat and had a large hood beside.

"Your hands are shaking," Ethel said. "Take a deep breath or two, won't you?"

I did as she said and felt better. A rush had come over me as I walked out of Crillick's, but my evening's work had only just begun and it was more important than ever that I wasn't seen or recognised. I tucked my hair beneath the hood. The cloak covered me so well that no one would notice me.

"Are you ready, Zillah?"

I squeezed Ethel's hands, grateful to have her support.

"Let's go," I said.

Together, Ethel and I stepped back out onto the pavement and made our way toward Northumberland Avenue, talking as we weaved through the evening crowds.

"Crillick fell for your ruse, just as you said."

Ethel laughed. "I never doubted he would. I followed him to the theatre to make sure he didn't turn back and he was whistling to himself the whole way. It was so busy in there, I was relieved when you saw me wave. I knew you had something up your sleeve, but I wasn't expecting that."

"You didn't get caught up in it at all, did you?"

"Oh, no, I stayed well back."

"Is Elvira on her way?"

"If she's not there already, she soon will be."

It took us fifteen minutes to reach Northumberland Avenue, walking as fast as we dared. The enormity of what I had done was starting to catch up with me, but I forced myself to think only of the Leopard Lady. As we turned the corner, there was no sign of Elvira's carriage and my heart sank. There wasn't time to wait for her.

Number 25 gave no sign of the horrors that occurred beneath its roof.

"Will you wait here and keep a lookout until Elvira comes?" I asked Ethel. I'd have been glad to have her in there with me, but I'd taken another look at the blue paper I'd stolen from Crillick's office and had a good idea of the number of rooms within the Odditorium.

I pressed her hands, ready to approach the house, when we heard a grunt and saw the outline of a large man lurking by the side entrance. Ethel and I looked at each other.

"A guard?" she whispered.

I should have thought of that. The Odditorium might be in Crillick's house, but with his exhibits so valuable, of course he'd hired extra protection to prevent them from escaping.

"What'll we do now?" I hissed.

"Leave it to me," Ethel said. She was a slight girl—she must have weighed half what the guard did—but something in her eye told me she could handle herself.

"Be careful, won't you?"

"I'll distract him first; when he moves away from the house, you go in and I'll take it from there."

I walked a little farther down the road and heard Ethel start to sing as though she were drunk. I turned to see her weaving toward the guard, calling out lewdly to him, then I heard his shout of surprise before I doubled back and ran down the stairs that led to the kitchen entrance. I pounded on the back door with my fists. It was Grace who answered and I pushed past her to get inside.

"Where are you going, miss?" she asked. But I saw from the fear in her face that she knew. It may even have been her who ushered in the so-called gentlemen who came to experience the Odditorium. Crillick had forced her to hold the Leopard Lady's rope that first night in the library, but I knew her to be a kind girl. Maybe she thought she was protecting me when she denied hearing the sounds of carpentry that had bothered me while I recovered after my trip to the docks.

Black Bill had said he thought the Odditorium must be in the cellar, and the blue paper had proved him right. I looked around the kitchen for a door that would lead belowground and then I saw it. Before it had been hidden behind the tall dresser; that was why I'd not noticed it. I walked over to the door and wrenched it open. I'd expected a cold, dank passage, but though the way was narrow, Crillick and his builders had been busy. A series of nooks had been carved into the stone walls, and each had been filled with a gas lamp. Their combined glow showed that the thick carpet underfoot was a rich, deep red and trimmed with golden braid. The smell of damp was present but oh so faint, covered by something else that I couldn't quite work out. A few yards ahead, the passage descended into a flight of stairs. I looked back to Grace, but she'd stayed within the kitchen as if she feared to cross the threshold.

"Are there more guards?"

Grace shook her head. "Please don't, miss," she called.

I walked to the top of the stairs that led down into the Odditorium. Grace was staring after me, twisting her hands together in her apron. She hadn't run for help yet, but I knew she would. She had to if she was to keep her job. I didn't blame her, but that meant there was not much time. I lifted my chin for courage and moved forward.

Each step down the curved stairway was an effort. When the light from the open door behind me faded, I realised I could still see my way. There were more gas lamps, and these had red shades. They threw out a pinkish light and I clung onto the metal handrail as I descended ever further. The sound of my footsteps was swallowed by the carpet and I braced myself to hear the cries of Crillick's prisoners.

The bottom of the stairs was like an anteroom, long and low. If I stood on tiptoe and raised my hand, I'd be able to touch the ceiling. There was little furniture, but I did see a stand to hang hats and store umbrellas. Did someone wait here to greet the men when they came, to take their outer garments? A bar had been built and on the countertop was a silver filigree tray arranged with whisky glasses. Twelve of them. I could imagine Crillick handing them out. "A snifter to get the evening started."

I needed to get a move on. The Peelers would have arrived at Crillick's to break up the fight; they might even have arrested him, but there were no guarantees, and if he did return home, I couldn't have him catch me here. In any case, Elvira must come along with her carriage soon. I wanted Crillick's prisoners to be ready to go as soon as she arrived. There'd be no point in helping them escape the Odditorium if we couldn't get them out of Westminster. There was a door ahead of me. I took a deep breath and pulled it open.

The room was empty. This must be where the Leopard Lady and her child and the others were exhibited during the shows. Before me was a small circular stage with chairs all around. When I'd seen her in the library, she'd averted her eyes while the show was at its worst, but in this setup there'd be curious stares whichever way she turned. Beyond the stage, toward the back of the room, I counted eight metal cages. They barely looked big enough to house a greyhound and I shuddered at the thought of grown men and women forced to crouch down in them. They were lined with clean straw. If one of the poor souls wet themselves with fear, it would soak in. Turn dark and sodden. Attached to each cage was a collection of restraints. I counted three to each. Their occupants would be secured by their neck always and either hands or feet. A card was pinned to each cage. I couldn't bring myself to read them; I knew they would tell a tale about a savage, a beast, a monster. How they'd been captured and subdued so they could be studied. There was no pretense here of consent, like they had in the theatres, like I had offered with my own damnable act. I could hear the squeak of a cage door being pulled back, an exhibit shuffling out, Crillick's voice declaring him dangerous, even deadly, while he stood there in his smalls and shivered. But it was all in my mind. The silence crept back in, and in some ways, it was even more threatening to be alone in the room with only my thoughts.

Where could she be? Black Bill had promised I would find her here. I looked around, and then I saw it: another door to go through. Awful as it was, the exhibition part was just the surface. I hadn't reached the heart of the Odditorium yet.

Behind the next door was a glaring light. Where the anteroom and exhibition spaces were dim and red, this place was clean and bright. It smelt fresh, like lemon and vinegar, but the familiar smells which should have given some relief made it all the more ominous. There were two rows of wooden benches, giant steps big enough for men to sit on. That would explain the sounds of hammering and sawing, then. The benches looked down on a large wooden table, its top scarred but well scrubbed. Again, there were the iron cuffs. Crillick's captives would be strapped down while the gentlemen looked on.

There was a book opened, its middle pages inked with tiny drawings of the human figure, and a sketch that might have been a man, might have been a monkey, or might have been something in between, like the Missing Link or so-called Nondescript that had been displayed in London a few years ago. Beyond was a wall lined with shelves and stocked with stoppered bottles and things in jars. Each was labeled—Latin words I knew nothing of, but I took care not to look too closely. There was Crillick's white coat hanging up, others too, and I remembered a conversation about one of Crillick and Vincent's friends who was an amateur in something they'd called ethnology. Had he been one of those three men who had debated, calm as you like, the best means of removing the Leopard Lady's colour?

I looked around, listening intently. I was yet to find a soul, had not heard a sound. A coldness washed over me that Black Bill had been wrong, and that Crillick didn't keep his prisoners here after all, and then I smelt something rotten beneath the freshness. I followed the smell to the far side of the room, where an intricately woven tapestry hung from the wall. I still couldn't quite put my finger on what it was, but this was definitely where it was coming from. I pulled at the tapestry and it came away in my hand. At last, I had found out where they were keeping her!

The stench as I yanked open the final door was like when I walked into St. Giles, but worse for being all the more concentrated. Human beings in cramped conditions, mingled with excrement and layered with fear. And there was a sort of sweetness to it too. The night I had visited the West India Docks, this is what it had been like. The room was small, about twelve feet long and narrow with it. There were bunks on either side. As I walked along, I saw hunched forms in them. It wasn't late, but down here with no windows there was no way to tell day from night. Maybe that's why they slept. Each bunk had room for two and there was one more cage.

I began walking among the beds, peering at the oddly still faces of the poor souls trapped here, desperate for the sight of her streak of white hair. If I wanted any of these people to follow me, to trust me, I needed to find the Leopard Lady first. *"Sisi wami kunjani?"* — how are you, my sister — I whispered, and the thing in the cage awakened and began to throw itself from side to side before holding out an imploring hand to me. Good God, it was a child: the Leopard Lady's son. The Zulu must have been a burst of familiarity and hope to him. I ran to him, but when I knelt before the cage he retreated, his brown eyes wary. He was clothed in a grubby nightshirt but from what I could see there were no patches on his skin, which was the same light brown as my own. I reached through the bars of the cage, hoping he'd realise he could trust me and wishing I knew the Zulu word for *friend*.

He came a little closer and I guessed he was three or maybe four years old, but it was hard to tell when the size of the cage made it impossible for him to stand. Other than the sores from the rope at his wrists, there were no signs that he'd been harmed. Not on the outside at least.

"I'll get you out of here," I said, knowing he wouldn't understand but hoping he'd take strength from the fervor in my voice. There must be keys, a wrench, something that would allow me to free him.

Knowing that help was close, the child wailed all the louder. I had to get him out, but I couldn't do it alone. None of the bundles in the bunks around me stirred. Gathering my courage, I shook one by the shoulder and jumped when the man rolled over, his arm dangling into space. His breathing was even, and at last, I recognised the sweetness. He'd been given opium. They all had.

"Wake up," I shouted. "Please wake up."

One of the bundles stirred and sat up. The bedclothes fell away from her. It was the Leopard Lady.

"*Sisi*, sister, I came here for you," I said.

I pointed to the cage.

"I came here to free you, to free your son."

She must have understood me, for she held up her hands which were bound with rope. So she was tied to the bed. That's why she hadn't been able to comfort her boy. I picked and pulled until the knot had loosened and she was able to throw off the restraints. She hauled herself out of the bunk and dropped down onto the floor. When she rose, I saw her eyes were clouded. Did she recognise me? She looked thinner than before, her body wasted and hunched. The white patches had spread and those on her arms had merged into one another.

"The key, where is the key?" I began, but she was already dragging herself toward the far side of the room. I turned in the direction of where she was headed. Yes—why hadn't I seen it?—a single key hanging from the wall on a dirty string. I raced to collect it and went to the cage. At the sight of his mother the child had become calmer and watched me, wide-eyed, as I turned the key and the cage door swung open. I reached inside and he took my hand so I could draw him out. He was covered in his own filth. Only someone truly evil could have done this to him. I picked the boy up and placed him in his mother's outstretched arms. Weak as my sister was, I knew she'd have all the strength she needed to bear him out of here.

I touched my fingertips to my chest. "Zillah," I said.

She mimicked my actions. "Nosizwe," she said.

"I want to get you out of here, Nosizwe." I reached out my hand to her. "Come with me, please."

"*Ngisacela ungcede nalaba enginabo?*" she said. She looked around at the other captives drugged in their bunks. What about them?

"Yes, I have come here to help all of you. My friend will take you somewhere safe, she will be waiting for you outside, but we must go now."

Nosizwe turned away from me. I didn't understand why until she leant down and started to rouse her fellow prisoners. She whispered to them, words I didn't catch. Her tone was reassuring. I realised she was telling them that if they went with me, they would be safe. I ran into the bright room and took one of the scalpels. They could saw through their bonds quicker with this. I should have thought of it sooner.

"We must go," I urged Nosizwe again when everyone had been woken.

Nosizwe followed me out, the child clinging to her. Back we went through the brightly lit room. I grabbed a second scalpel as we passed the scrubbed wooden table. Ethel had said she'd distract the guard, but if she'd had any trouble I wanted to be prepared. We passed through the room with the exhibition stage and out into the anteroom until we were at the foot of the stairs. All the time Nosizwe had trained her gaze on the floor, but now she stopped.

"We're nearly there," I encouraged her, but she refused to move forward, her eyes staring past me. I turned and there stood Vincent at the top of the steps that led back into the house.

We locked eyes, but instead of speaking to him, I turned back to her.

"Come, Nosizwe, he won't hurt you," I said. I tugged on her arm.

"He *won't* hurt you," I said again, a warning for him as much as encouragement for her. She trailed me up the stairs. I kept my eyes on Vincent, but he said nothing and he didn't stop us. When we reached the doorway into the kitchen, I pushed Nosizwe out ahead of me. Vincent hadn't followed us; he remained where he stood, transfixed.

"You have been down there?" I asked.

He shook his head.

"Help me, Vincent. Help me free them."

He mumbled something that I couldn't make out. I didn't want to leave Nosizwe on her own for too long, but I needed to look him in the eye to understand how much he had known. To think, until recently, I'd been here in this house with him, and such horror downstairs the whole time. Had there been a showing in the Odditorium while I was living here?

"I can't go down there."

"You knew all along?"

He shuddered. "I can't go down there."

He might not have known, but only because he chose not to see it. He'd had enough warnings about Crillick but he'd ignored them. Now when it came to it, he was too much of a coward to confront what was happening, or even to do anything to help. All his noble intentions. It meant nothing if he was willing to avert his eyes from what he knew to be wrong. I curled my lip in disgust, but his gaze was fixed on the stairwell and he didn't even notice.

&

I'd expected to see Elvira's carriage, but it was only Nosizwe waiting when I came out of the house. I looked up the road toward the noise and traffic of Trafalgar Square, which was busy with cabs and horses. One of those vehicles must be Elvira's, but it was too far for me to see. Why was it taking her so long? Nosizwe stood on the pavement holding her son tightly, her eyes blinking rapidly under the glare of the streetlamps. She shivered in the cold night air and I shrugged off the cloak that Ethel had given to me and helped her to put it on.

"It's safer to stand here," I said, pulling her to one side.

Northumberland Avenue was quiet for now, but if someone came past and saw us standing here, they'd think something was up and I had no plan for what to do. *Come on, Elvira*, I muttered to myself. *Please don't let us down.*

I sent up a small prayer of thanks when, three minutes later, Elvira's carriage arrived. She was leaning out apologizing before the horses had come to a complete stop.

"A cart overturned and we had to change our route," she explained. "Where's Ethel?"

"I've not seen her. When we arrived, there was a guard. She said she'd distract him. But that was twenty minutes ago at least."

"Everything has gone to plan otherwise?"

So far it had. I didn't count Vincent. I knew he wouldn't stop us.

"How many prisoners are there?" Elvira asked.

"Seven more. They have been drugged, so I won't be able to get them out alone."

I looked back toward the house.

"You should go, Zillah," Elvira said. "Gregory, my footman, is here also. He will bring out the rest of them, and I have a second carriage on the way, but it'll be another fifteen minutes at least. I had thought to have you with us too, but it's more important you leave straightaway, before Crillick returns. He won't come after me, but you are vulnerable if he knows you had anything to do with this."

"What about Ethel?"

"I'm here," Ethel called, walking out from the side entrance of Crillick's house. Her hair had come loose from its bun and she rubbed her knuckles as though they were sore.

"What happened to the guard?"

"Dealt with," said Ethel. Her eyes were hard, challenging me to ask how, but she'd get no judgment from me. I'd come to the Odditorium prepared to do whatever was needed to free Crillick's prisoners.

Ethel and the footman headed into the house. They had bolt cutters and a knife. That would make short work of the restraints.

"Is Crillick still at the theatre?" Elvira said. "Either way, you must not take any more chances," she continued, when I indicated I didn't know. "You have done what you set out to do. This woman and her son are safe."

She was right, but still I felt I could not leave.

"You still intend to take her back to your home tonight?"

"Yes, Zillah, I will take her there now, but I want to get her out of London tonight if I can, and the others too. I was thinking overnight. Crillick will have contracts saying they are bound to him, and the moment he arrives he will have the legal right to take them back. You didn't rescue the Leopard Lady to have him reclaim her, did you?"

I put my hands on Nosizwe's shoulders and looked at her closely.

"This is Elvira," I said. "Please go with her. She will keep you safe."

I backed away, wanting so much to talk with her, this woman who I had searched so long and hard for, but knowing that with every minute that passed I was jeopardizing her chance of freedom. I turned away from deep brown eyes that pierced me and then she called my name.

"Zillah," she said, *"indodana yami,"* and she held out the child to me.

My stomach convulsed. In this moment when freedom was so close, why would she give away her child? She was asking me to look after him for her, but how could a mother bear to choose a life apart from her baby? *Because she trusts you. She thinks that you will have a better chance of keeping him safe.* Of course. Nosizwe didn't know Elvira, but she did remember me. She knew I had tried to speak her language. I embraced her, and the child too. Squeezing as hard as I dared so she could feel all the love and compassion and solidarity I felt for her.

"*Sisi*, you will both be safe now," I said, wondering if she could make out the words through my tears.

Elvira hovered at my side, not understanding the exchange but not wanting to interrupt. When at last I let Nosizwe go, she gave me a brief hug.

"You must leave, Zillah. God be with you. When you have reached safety, you must write to me," Elvira said.

She ushered Nosizwe into the carriage and I turned to see Ethel bringing out the first of the men. I set off down the road, but instead of crossing over and heading for Barky's, I turned left toward St. James's. There was one final thing I had to do.

XXXI

An Unexpected Visitor

It didn't take me long to get to Charles II Street, but when I reached the grocer's it was in darkness. *Silly girl. Didn't think of that, did you?* I'd been so keen to get here, to see Lucien, that I hadn't considered that the shop would be shut. I tapped lightly on the door. If Lucien was upstairs or in the back, he probably wouldn't hear me, but I didn't want to bang too loudly and draw attention. Not in this sort of neighborhood. No answer. I couldn't stay outside, though. The whole way here I'd been looking over my shoulder, waiting for someone to come after me. *Lucien will understand*, I told myself as I withdrew one of my hairpins and forced the lock.

"Lucien, are you there? It's me, Zillah," I called out as I entered, closing the door behind me.

The shop floor had been swept down and the counters gleamed with polish. The jars of tea and spices had been filled and the displays of candles and lampblack replenished. I lifted the counter and stepped behind it. I couldn't resist turning and facing the shop as though I owned it. Were African shops the same as British ones? The thought of all that I didn't know made me anxious.

But what choice did I have? After what I'd done tonight it would be too tough to stay in London.

I parted the beaded curtain that led to the back room and walked through. Here all was spick-and-span too, and just as I remembered it, with its bookshelves that reached from floor to ceiling and took up the whole of one wall. The only other furniture was a dining table and two easy chairs before the fire. There was a pamphlet on the table. The very one that had been given out when we went to Exeter Hall. I sat down in the chintz-covered chair that faced the flames and yawned. Now that Nosizwe was safe with Elvira, the evening's events were slowly catching up with me. I thought of the shock on the faces of the audience when I'd exposed the Great Amazonia as a fake, the pain of seeing Nosizwe's son trapped inside the cage, and then her smile of relief when she held him in her arms. I'd burnt all my bridges, but for that moment, and knowing she'd gotten away, it was worth it. I leant back and closed my eyes, thinking now of Lucien. I imagined him calling my name, touching me lightly on the arm.

"Zillah, what are you doing here? Wake up."

I opened my eyes and there Lucien was before me. I jumped up, still drowsy. What must he think, to come down and find me asleep in his armchair? As usual he wore a crisp white shirt, but his cravat had been loosened and I caught a glimpse of his chest beneath. I felt a sharp pang of longing and it only added to my confusion.

"Forgive me, the door was open. I called out to you."

"I don't care about that. Elvira sent me a note to say that all had gone well and she was headed for Dover. She must be halfway to the coast by now, but I didn't know where you were. I thought you were going to stay with your friend?"

"I wanted to see you first, Lucien."

"You've taken a grave risk, Zillah. Anyone could have seen you."

I recognised in his tone the angry relief of someone who has been worried.

"I couldn't go straight to Barky's. He'll be at the theatre for a while yet, I'm sure, and I didn't want to hang around outside for him."

"Are you sure Crillick won't think to look for you there?"

"No one knows that we are friends. I'll be safe there for a few days at least, but I didn't come here to speak of that. Last night, Lucien, you asked me a question."

"I did, and you said you weren't ready to give me your answer."

"I wasn't then. You surprised me and I had to put Nosizwe first, but I'm ready now. Will you ask me again?"

"I will, I will do it now." He half turned. "Let me find my coat."

"No, don't. You are fine as you are. I like you like this," I said and dropped my eyes, not wanting to seem too forward. We stood face-to-face and he took my hands in his.

"Zillah, the first time I saw you I was intrigued by you. When we spoke, I did not expect you to be so confident, so sure of yourself. I am a quiet man—you might say an overly serious one. For some time now I have been looking for someone to share my life with, but it wasn't until we met that I could begin to believe I'd met my match."

He waved a hand that took in not only the room where we stood but the shop beyond.

"As I told you before, it may look as though my life has been an easy one, but having the patron that I had, the education he gave me, and now this business has separated me from my earliest experiences. I cannot deny that I have had privileges that many of my countrymen haven't, but it has made me lonely. I need someone I can confide in, a wife I can trust."

He felt more deeply than I had given him credit for. I had indeed fallen into the trap of thinking he had few problems because he'd done well for himself, but of course he was lonely, and I knew well enough what that was like. The very first time I'd walked down Charles II Street, I'd felt out of place and wondered how he managed it, day in and day out. He'd called me confident and sure of myself. I'd thought the same of him, but it turned out there was a bit of front to both of us.

I leant in to him, and when he closed his eyes I did the same, concentrating on the places our bodies touched. My hands on his shoulders, his fingertips featherlight on my face. He raised my chin to bring my lips to his and we kissed. Lightly at first, then deeper, until he caught himself and stepped back before things could go too far. I had felt how his heart raced, knew that stopping cost him some effort.

"Will you marry me, Zillah?" he said.

"Yes, Lucien, my answer is yes."

⁓

I spent the next three days holed up at Barky's. I knew Crillick would never think to look for me there, and it meant I could keep abreast of what was happening since the stunt I'd pulled for my final performance. The main thing on my mind, though, was Nosizwe's safety. I thought constantly about where she might be, whether Elvira had gotten her onto a boat, how her son was doing. The moment she had tried to hand him to me played again and again in my mind. The fierce look in my sister's eyes was a mother's love. I'd never seen it before—or rather I had, that day when Mama took me to St. Giles, but I hadn't recognised it. I'd been too young to understand why she'd asked Mrs. Bradley to take care of me. Finally, I got it. Her only desire was to keep me safe, and as a mother, she'd been prepared to do whatever it took to achieve that, even if it meant never seeing me again.

Over the years it had plagued me. When she'd told me to be strong, I took it to heart, thinking that somehow I'd shown weakness and that's why she'd abandoned me. But no. She knew that as a former slave and now a servant in a so-called gentleman's house, she couldn't protect me, and it was a duty she took too seriously not to do something about it. I thought of the occasions when Mrs. Bradley had tried to talk to me about her but I hadn't wanted to hear it. If only I could go back in time. I'd give both women my heartfelt thanks for all the care they'd taken of me.

It would've helped if I knew that wherever she was, Nosizwe was safe, but I'd heard nothing from Elvira. It wasn't too surprising, as she didn't know where I was staying, but I thought Lucien might have managed to get a message to me. We'd not spoken since I'd accepted him and it made me feel uneasy. I'd kissed him —did he think I was too forward? He'd made it clear that traveling together to Sierra Leone would not compromise me. Before the ship started its journey proper, it would pause for a night at Liverpool to pick up further passengers, and that is where Lucien and I would be married. He'd promised to write and apply for our license the day after I accepted him. Barky wasn't too sympathetic when I voiced my worries about it—he'd disliked Lucien from the first. I was just grateful that he'd let me stay. Though no one at Crillick's knew of our friendship, it was still a big risk, and thanks to my final performance, he was no longer certain of his job at the theatre. If he was a bit short with me from time to time, I really couldn't blame him.

I didn't dare dwell on what Crillick would do if he found me, but I knew it would be violent. I'd always worried about being thrown in prison if my secret was discovered, but I'd hurt Crillick's business—the thing he most cared about. A cell was probably the least-worst option if he caught up with me. Exposing the Great Amazonia as a fraud had literally brought the house down. When all was said and done, there'd been around nine hundred pounds' worth of damage. Crillick might have been doing well, but I doubted he had that sort of cash to spare. Barky had told me that the Peelers had taken him down to the station on Wednesday night, but he hadn't been kept in. No doubt he'd greased a palm or two to convince them to let him go. He wouldn't get off scot-free, though. Barky said he'd been summoned to court next month to appear before the beak, so it would be a while yet before things died down.

Too many people had heard about what had happened, and it wasn't just Crillick they were asking questions of either. There were freaks at half the variety shows in London, and now the punters were paying far more attention. Already there'd been pieces in three of the evening papers asking which of London's freaks were gaffed, and how many hardworking men and women had been gulled by their performances. Each article had been illustrated with the Amazonia handbills that Crillick had printed to drum up business. That wasn't so good. It meant that, as well as Crillick and the Peelers, there were a handful of journalists looking for me too, and now that I'd said it in front of everyone, they knew my real name as well as my face. I had to trust the Blackbirds wouldn't turn me in—Black Bill was likely the only man in London smart enough to find me, but he would have little interest in helping the Peelers.

Now it was Sunday, the last day before our ship sailed on the sixteenth of October and I could begin a new life with Lucien. As far as I was concerned, it couldn't come quick enough.

Barky, back from the theatre, had gone into his room to get changed and I'd made him a cup of tea. I'd gone right off the taste of it, but the least I could do was have something ready for him after making his life so much harder. I knew he was concerned for me. Apart from his work at Crillick's, he hadn't been going out, saying he was tired, but I guessed that he didn't want to leave me on my own any more than he had to. I wondered if he was missed at the place he went to late at night. I hoped I hadn't spoiled things for him there. That was the very last thing I wanted.

"Was it still bad when you went in today?" I said as he sat down.

Really I knew it must be if he felt he had to go in on a Sunday. He drank the tea in two gulps and I poured him another from the pot.

"The cleanup's mostly done now. Crillick's had the dancers doing most of it."

I couldn't feel too sorry for them. They'd treated me pretty badly in the days before I'd left.

"What about Ellen? Has she been helping?"

"Can't say I've seen too much of her. She's a sharp one. I wouldn't be surprised if she's been touting herself around to the other shows for a job."

"She loves Crillick. She wouldn't leave him in his hour of need," I said. But Barky only gave one of his snorts and I changed tack to the thing that had been uppermost in my mind all day.

"Why won't he come to me?"

"Maybe he knows he's not welcome here," Barky said.

Whenever I talked about Lucien, he tried to close it down. I hadn't forgotten how Barky had threatened him. It was why I hadn't begged him to go to Charles II Street, even if only to look through the shop window. I couldn't help but be on edge.

"We're supposed to be getting married on Tuesday."

"Well, you know what I think of that too. He must be at least fifteen years older than you."

"He's thirty-two. I told you that already."

"That's as may be. But you'd have been better off with His Lordship."

If I could have mimicked Barky's snort, I would have done. He always stuck up for Vincent, but the idea was laughable.

"I can't see how that would've gone down with Crillick," I said.

"Fair enough, but I still don't think he knew as much as you say."

I wasn't going to get into this again. Now I'd explained everything to Barky about the Leopard Lady and what Crillick had put her and her little boy through, not to mention the other captives, the only bit he had trouble believing was Vincent's part in it. I sometimes wondered whose side he was on.

As Barky drained his second cup of tea, there was a knock at the front door. I leapt up.

"Do you think it's him?"

There had been other visitors in the past few days—a deliveryman, a neighbor in need of milk—and I always made myself scarce. But something told me that this was Lucien. It had to be.

"You want to hope so," Barky said. "I'll go down and answer it myself, and if I bring someone up, you stay in my bedroom until I tell you it's safe to come out."

I waited impatiently. At last, I heard two sets of footsteps climbing the stairs to Barky's rooms. It must be Lucien with him— Barky wouldn't risk letting in a stranger who might betray me. I smoothed down my hair; there was no looking glass, so I could do nothing about the bags that had formed beneath my eyes from the sleepless nights spent worrying. Barky had urged me to wash and change this morning. How I regretted ignoring him now, but my navy dirndl skirt and cream blouse would have to be good enough.

"Someone to see you, Zillah," Barky called out to me as he came in.

I stepped out of his bedroom and down the passage, but the smile on my lips died as I entered the kitchen, for it was not Lucien with him at all, but Vincent.

~

It was strange to see Vincent in Barky's tiny kitchen. His head almost brushed the ceiling and he hovered, unsure of whether to sit or stand.

"May I get you something, milord?" Barky said.

"Thank you, but I won't stay." He turned to me. "I came to warn you, Zillah, is all. Crillick is looking for you."

"I know that," I said ungraciously. "I hope you haven't led him here."

Vincent looked shocked and I remembered that I'd cheeked him very rarely when we were together. I hadn't known then about his family's slave-trading history, nor that he allowed Crillick to use his father's warehouse and not bothered to inquire what for. I still wasn't sure if I believed he hadn't known the Leopard Lady had been kept there. He'd known more about the Odditorium than he'd admitted, after all.

"He's not discovered Zillah's here?" Barky said.

Vincent shook his head. "He doesn't know and you can rely on me not to tell him. It's lucky that before I went to Surrey he knew Zillah and I had parted ways, otherwise he might have suspected me of knowing, but as it is she's safe for the time being. He is paying some undesirables to track her down, though. I'm sure that comes as no surprise."

"How did you manage to find us, then?"

"Zillah had spoken fondly of you to me."

I cleared my throat, irritated that they spoke over me as though I wasn't there.

Vincent looked in my direction. "Did you know about Grace?"

"Is she well?" I asked warily, remembering her panicked face when I'd demanded to know if there were more guards.

"She's gone. No one knows exactly where she went, but she left a note on the same night that you freed the freaks, saying something about going to care for her sick mother."

I knew Grace had been a foundling. Did that mean she might have gotten away with Elvira and Ethel? I fervently hoped so. She was a sweet girl and had been as true a friend to me as she could while we all lived under Crillick's roof.

"You don't need to worry about me, Vincent. I'll be leaving soon enough," I said.

"To go where?"

"Sierra Leone." I felt it was far enough away that it wouldn't hurt if he knew.

"When do you leave?" Vincent said.

"Tomorrow morning."

"Tonight would be better, but that's close enough."

"There's nothing in particular you're afraid of?" Barky said.

"Nothing specific, but I've never seen Crillick so furious," Vincent said. "All he talks of is how the affair has damaged his standing at Pascoe's. Alexander cut him there the other night and George Fayers took him to one side and told him he might want to keep away for a few months. None of the members want to associate with him. It's not just money that he's lost. As much as that would anger him, I think he'd know he could make it back. But influence can't be so easily replaced."

"At least he's got you to stick by him," I said.

Barky glared at me in warning, but I didn't care.

"I understand why you would be angry with me, Zillah, but you must believe that I knew nothing of that business in the cellar, his 'Odditorium.' I tried to tell you that, but you ran off."

Hateful word. Even the sound of it made me flinch. As long as I lived, I would never forget what I had seen in Crillick's cellar. Vincent may not have known the full extent of it but many of his acquaintances did. Alexander and Fayers—all his cronies from the club. God knew what they had been party to in that time.

Vincent looked sincere. This was a man I had given myself to. I badly wanted to believe him . . . and yet.

"You heard him talk about it, same as I did. I saw you looking at the blueprints, remember?"

And that wasn't forgetting that Vincent's own warehouse had played host to a show too, however briefly.

"I didn't know," Vincent insisted. "He asked me if he could use the warehouse. You know how much I hate it and why, so I said yes. He told me some of the things he'd seen when he went to the Continent. I had no reason to believe he'd try to re-create them here."

Vincent had been to the finest schools in England. He wasn't a stupid man, but he was expecting me to believe that he couldn't put two and two together. Once again, it came down to what he chose to know and what he didn't. I had no doubt he wanted to do good, but until he was willing to admit the part that he himself played with his inaction, he'd never be able to.

"It was good of you to warn us, milord," Barky said, interrupting us before the conversation turned even more bitter.

"I only ever wanted to help," Vincent said. "But I'll go now. I wish nothing but the best for you, Zillah. However angry you are with me now, I hope one day you realise that."

Barky followed him out and I heard him bidding Vincent farewell at the street door. When he came back, he sat down opposite me at the table. He took a long breath and then let it whistle out through his teeth.

"He didn't need to do that."

"It was the least he could've done."

"Come off it, girl. There's not many a lord who'd chase 'round after his fancy piece like this. He owes Crillick and he risked a lot to come here."

Barky was right, but I was stubborn and so I didn't reply. He shook his head at me.

"I just hope you know what you're doing," he said.

I started to speak when he held up a finger.

"Do you hear that?"

There was nothing, and then the sound of scraping and the door opening. A ragged cheer went up.

"What is it?"

"Everything and nothing, most probably," Barky said. He made to return to his seat at the table but we heard the upstairs door bang again.

"Fight, fight," a childish voice yelled.

We looked at one another. Barky pulled open his own front door onto the landing, and his upstairs neighbor brushed past.

"Two fancy gents going at it down the road, would you believe it? I just saw it out the window—I can't think what this neighborhood is coming to."

"What do they look like?" I asked.

"Get back, Zillah!" Barky said, but it was too late. The neighbor's face made an O of shock to see me and I cursed myself for my stupidity. Barky had helped me so much and the one thing he had asked was that I keep a low profile. I would not have exposed him like this for the world. Especially if Crillick had goons going around asking questions about any sightings of a Black girl. The neighbor hurried on, but as she went she cast a look back over her shoulder. I'd put us both in danger.

"Barky, I'm so sorry."

"That'll be all around town tomorrow," he said.

His voice was flat; he sounded tired. I couldn't blame him for being worried.

"You'd better get out of here. If Crillick did follow Vincent and they're fighting now, this will be your best chance to get away."

"But what about—"

"Go, Zillah. Above all else, you've got to keep safe."

I pulled on my scarf and coat and hurried out of the door. There wasn't time for goodbyes.

ॐ

A ring of people had formed in the middle of the street. Others leant out of their windows and shouted encouragement. Lamb's Conduit Street may have been a respectable thoroughfare, but that didn't mean its residents didn't enjoy a good brawl now and again. My best chance of getting away quickly was to get to High Holborn. It meant weaving through the onlookers, but I had to hope they wouldn't notice me flee if they were fighting. *Please let Vincent be all right,* I prayed as I worked my way through the crowd. I'd been angry and sharp with him today but he'd only sought to protect me, and if he was fighting now it was for my sake.

Vincent and Crillick were going at it hard. I heard the grunts but couldn't see them until the crowd shifted. The action had turned and all of a sudden I found myself close to the front. What I saw was a complete shock to me. Vincent's opponent wasn't Crillick at all. It was Lucien.

"What are you doing?" I cried.

At the sound of my voice, Vincent looked up.

"Vincent, be careful," I shouted, and in that moment Lucien landed a punch to his face. Sensing a new twist in the drama, the crowd quieted and looked from me to Vincent to Lucien. The two men were breathing heavily. Vincent's eye was swelling and Lucien's lip was cut.

"She knows 'em!" came the gleeful shout from a woman stood next to me. "It was your one what started it," she said. That meant Lucien.

I looked from one man to the other. The feeling of relief that had flared in me to see Lucien's face was rapidly replaced with dread. There was only one way this could go, and though I no longer loved Vincent, I didn't want to see him hurt. Foolish of me to shout out to him. I'd meant for both of them not to hurt one another, but would Lucien understand that? I hoped I hadn't given myself away.

The two men paced 'round each other. I'd seen prize fights where the men sized each other up in this way, but there was none of the banter that accompanied those occasions. What I saw in Lucien's eyes and reflected in Vincent's was deadly intent.

Barky appeared at my side.

"They say Lucien threw the first punch. His Lordship walked past him and something made Lucien take exception to his face."

"They met before. You remember?"

I'd never been quite sure if Lucien realised I'd been with Vincent, but seeing him that very first night at the theatre, and again walking away from Barky's, he must have guessed. My head began to throb at the idea that he might think there was still something going on between us. What had he said when he proposed? That above all he wanted a wife he could trust.

"God help us. Is he handy?" Barky said.

"What do you reckon?"

Lucien was broad, but quick. On the other hand, Vincent had probably never had a fight in his life.

"If there's any sense of the African winning, someone will step in on His Lordship's side, I'm sure of it."

Barky was right and the thought made my blood run cold.

"Wait a minute, though." Barky jerked his head toward the opposite side of the circle, where three Black men had gathered. They weren't cheering like the rest of the crowd, just watching. "Maybe they'll want their say too."

They were Blackbirds; they had to be. I didn't want Lucien to be beaten, but better that than a riot. If the Blackbirds laid a hand on Vincent, the thought of what it might lead to was frightening. The law wouldn't let them get away with hurting a viscount.

"You've got to put a stop to this," I said.

"How?"

"Please, Barky."

Barky stepped forward. Neither Lucien nor Vincent noticed him. They were still eyeing each other, both injured but neither willing to walk away.

"Come on, gents, that's enough," Barky said. "Ladies and children present."

A laugh went up. The women and children had been cheering the fighters on louder than the men.

Barky turned around to the crowd. "Nothing to see here, folks. The entertainment's done for the day."

He sounded as good as the Crillick's compère; it was probably second nature to him after all those years working backstage.

"It's not over yet" came one voice.

"No, not yet" was its echo.

"Come on, they'll tickle each other and it'll be done. Dinnertime, ain't it?" Barky said.

He was right. It had gotten darker, couldn't be far off six o'clock. The gas lighter would soon be along. The fighters still breathed heavily but showed little spirit to resume. A whisper went 'round that the Peelers were on their way. The Blackbirds cleared out, and one by one, the remaining watchers melted away.

"Come on, milord, you're all right," Barky said and placed an arm around Vincent. "We'll get you cleaned up." I looked away as he supported Vincent past me and back toward the house. Vincent's eye was almost closed now. That left Lucien and me. I was on high alert. If the police really were coming, I couldn't hang around for long.

"Are you hurt?"

"He throws quite a punch. I would not have thought him capable of it."

"Can I bathe your lip for you?"

"There is no need to make a fuss, Zillah."

"You came to see me."

"Our boat is due to leave tomorrow," Lucien said, his voice a little thick. "I've been concerned for you staying with your friend and so I wanted to come and collect you. I didn't want to leave anything to chance."

All this time he'd been thinking of me. I needn't have worried that I'd put him off in some way. But what now? I'd done myself no favours by getting involved in their fight.

"I'm glad we're going to Sierra Leone together," I said.

"That's what you want, is it?"

"You know it is. I told you on Wednesday."

"You know, that's the second time I've seen that man and always when you're nearby. Why is that, I wonder?"

"He's friendly with Barky," I said. "Knows him from the theatre."

Lucien looked at me through narrowed eyes. I wasn't sure he believed me, but I could see that he wanted to. He would've accused me outright if not.

"Let's stick to our original plan. I will meet you at the docks in the morning?" I said.

"The ship will depart at eleven o'clock. If you get there at half past nine, that will give enough time for your bags to be loaded."

"Barky bought me some fabric to make clothes with, but I don't have much else. I was planning to pick up a few final things in Liverpool, after we get . . . married." The word stuck in my throat a little since Lucien looked so stern.

"Good. I will see you tomorrow morning, then."

"Lucien . . ." He'd started to walk away but now he turned back. "We're doing the right thing."

"I pray you are right," he said. I wanted to hold him, but something stopped me reaching out. I let him walk away, his hand pressed to his side. Vincent must have landed a tough blow, for he seemed to hobble slightly. I let out a sigh of relief. Only a few more hours and then we could put this whole thing behind us. *No need for him to be so cold, though.* Lucien had reached the end of the road now, but he didn't turn back. *What of it if I had been with Vincent?* We weren't engaged then. I still wanted things to work out between us, of course I did, but if he was having second thoughts, then so be it. I wasn't going to beg him. The most important thing was that I got my new start. If I could make my way in London, I could do the same in Freetown. It would probably be easier, if anything. There was a whole boatload of people looking to begin afresh. Maybe other girls like me. I could get friendly with them. I'd pulled myself up out of St. Giles once, I could do it again.

A wind whipped up and I realised I should get back inside. I couldn't face the thought of sitting there with Vincent, though, and Barky would need a while to clean him up. I'd wait it out until he'd gone. As long as I stuck to the shadows, with my headscarf, I'd probably be all right.

I walked and walked in no particular direction, but it wasn't long before I found myself at the top of Kingsway. For the first time, I felt a serious pang at the thought of leaving it all behind. Sierra Leone was what I wanted, but London was all I'd ever known. I went down High Holborn in the direction of St. Paul's, the tall spire calling to me. It was not too long ago that I'd been approaching it from Fleet Street as Lucien and I strolled arm in arm toward the Dog and Duck.

A thin drizzle started and increased to heavy drops. I meandered along, not caring that I was getting wet or that my skirts trailed on the pavement. What did a little muck matter now? Down one passage I went, where the houses on either side of the road were so close together that if I stretched out both arms, I could touch two doors that stood opposite each other. A candle glowed bravely on the third floor of one house and it made me think of a woman waiting up for her sweetheart. I'd waited for Lucien and he'd come eventually, but he'd been spiteful and I didn't deserve it. If he wasn't going to voice his suspicions, I couldn't even defend myself. I'd be able to explain away what it was between me and Vincent, but only if he gave me the chance. *He took a punch or two for you tonight. Give him time.* But I hadn't asked him to.

My thoughts turned once again to the next day's journey. By this time tomorrow I would be well on my way and London far behind. Would there be alleys like this in Sierra Leone? There was a beach, I knew that much, and the weather would be hot every day, but when I tried to imagine anything beyond this, I couldn't. I pictured Lucien on the beach but he was alone.

In the distance I heard a clock chime. It was time to get back; Vincent would be long gone by now.

I found the key in its usual place under the flowerpot and let myself in.

"His Lordship left two hours ago," Barky said. "You been walking around in the rain all this time?"

He disappeared for a moment and returned with a towel for me to dry my hair. I hadn't realised how wet I was or how hungry. My stomach clenched and I looked around, hoping that Barky had left a plate for me.

"I thought a turn would clear my head."

"Has it?"

I shrugged, not seeing the use in lying. Barky could read me anyhow.

"Were they fighting over me?"

"He didn't say. He does love you, though, Zillah."

"No point telling me now. I made my choice." I certainly wasn't going to admit to him how off Lucien had been with me. *Right or wrong about him, you'll have to get on with it now.*

Barky busied himself finding a knife and fork for me, and I sat down at the kitchen table. Steaming hot tea, two hard-boiled eggs, and bread and butter. I tucked in, while Barky looked on with troubled eyes.

"Out with it, if you have something to say," I said, but he shook his head.

"It's nothing. Good night, Zillah. I'll walk you down to Embankment when I get in. You'll need a hand with your bags."

I stood and threw my arms around him. We'd disagreed but he'd been a true friend to me in these past few weeks. I was going to miss him. Awkwardly he stroked my hair.

"There now. No need to cry. It's a big step you're taking. I don't judge you for it. You're braver than I am."

"You could come with us," I said into his shoulder, my words muffled with tears.

Barky patted my head.

"No, Zillah. You're not the only one who made a choice."

"Are you going to tell me about your mistress?" I said. If I was leaving anyway, he might as well satisfy my long-held curiosity.

For a moment Barky looked as if he was weighing how much to say. Then he snorted. "There's no mistress, Zillah. There never has been."

"But all your gifts, and the nights you've stayed out? Who is she, Barky?"

"There's no woman in my life. I won't say any more than that. I can't."

I didn't know what he meant by it, but he refused to say more. He moved into the next room. I heard him at his ablutions and prepared myself to sleep by the fire, a little irritated that he hadn't wanted to share his secret after we'd become so close. For once I couldn't quite get comfy in the chair, but it was only for one more night, my last night in England. The voyage across the sea would be far harder than this.

At least you'll have Lucien, I told myself. Even as it struck me, the thought was no longer the comfort I wanted it to be.

XXXII

A Scene at Embankment

The last time I was at Embankment, I'd collapsed after searching for Nosizwe. I didn't know where she was now. It was best that I didn't, but there was a contentment in knowing that she and her child were safe.

"Do you think that's my boat there?"

Barky looked in the direction of my pointed finger.

"Best hope not. The sails could do with a mend."

He was right. When I looked again, I saw that the great swathes of cloth bore rents and gashes.

"Would pirates have caused that?"

"A storm, more like. You all right, girl?" Barky asked. I'd stopped. "You look a bit green."

"I am doing the right thing, aren't I?"

"Not this again. Right or not, you've said you will, so you might as well get on with it."

"There's another reason why you don't like him, isn't there? It's not just because he knew you were, you know . . ."

"It's almost time, Zillah," Barky said.

Whatever his thoughts on Lucien, it was clear he wasn't going to share them with me. Maybe he was right not to. I knew, of the two, he preferred Vincent, but he would know as well as I did that Viscount Woodward was not a long-term option for a girl like me, however much he said he loved me, and however naively I had once imagined a life together for us. Colour wasn't the only barrier between Vincent and me; it had always been class too, and everyone knew that was even harder to overcome.

"Here we are," Barky said. He dropped my trunk to the ground with a thud.

"Careful! That's got to make it halfway around the world with me," I teased. "It can't be that heavy. It's not half-full yet."

The main thing in there was the dress I'd picked to wear for our wedding.

"Do you see Lucien?" I said.

"Not yet, but we're a little early."

"Will you make sure that we're definitely in the right place?"

Barky rolled his eyes but off he went to speak to an official-looking man dressed in a naval uniform and holding a long roll of paper. They spoke for a few minutes before Barky came back.

"Right place. That's your ship out there." He gestured to a massive vessel anchored in the middle of the river. It looked much more impressive than the first one I had noticed.

"What's it doing all the way out there?"

"They'll row you out to it in groups. From there, you'll dock at Liverpool—should get there in the early hours. You'll stay there overnight, take on more passengers, more supplies, and then you'll be on your way. I've told them you're here. They'll call you soon."

There was a group of Black men standing patiently in a line. They would be my fellow passengers, my neighbors when we reached Sierra Leone. Most looked like soldiers. I could hear the American twang as they spoke to each other. How many were Londoners born and bred, like me? Hopefully the women had boarded first, because at the moment it looked like I was the only one.

"I wish Lucien were here," I said.

Barky reached into his pocket and pulled out his watch. "He will be."

I sat down on my trunk. Barky kept looking around, like he wanted a get-out.

"You can go if you want, I'm fine to wait on my own," I said.

But I was glad when he shook his head at me. "I'll stay with you, at least until your fellow gets here."

As the minutes wore on, the hustle and bustle grew. Sailors called to one another and the queue of passengers dwindled as the man with the roll of paper checked off their names on his list. They were rowed out in tens to board ship, and still I sat there, perched on my trunk waiting for Lucien to arrive.

"There's not another place you can board, is there?"

Barky shrugged his shoulders.

The fear that he might have boarded without me was growing, and it tightened my throat, making it impossible to speak. *Surely he wouldn't leave me at risk of missing the boat while I waited for him?* He couldn't be that angry over the little that he knew for sure. Barky said reassuring things from time to time, and that the roads must be bad, but I could tell he was worried for me by the way he kept his head on the swivel for whatever direction Lucien might come in.

This wait was the last thing I needed. Ever since Lucien had proposed to me, I'd felt like I'd been swept onto a steam train. I'd liked the thought of speeding to a new life, but my final performance at Crillick's, freeing Nosizwe and her child, had all happened so quickly I'd started to feel more and more like it wasn't a machine I was on at all, but a runaway stagecoach. What did I know about Sierra Leone? It was only a few weeks ago that I'd heard of it at all. Some of the talk I'd overheard by more skeptical listeners at Exeter Hall came back to me. Slavers patrolling, arid ground. There were so many things that might go wrong, and Lucien, who'd made it all seem so exciting to me, was late. Shifts, six cotton; shoes, sturdy, two pairs; one straw hat; three nets to keep off mosquitoes—to stop myself from wondering if I was doing the right thing, I ran through the items I still needed to buy when we reached Liverpool.

"Here we go," Barky said. But when I looked up, it wasn't Lucien on his way toward us but Vincent.

"Is he coming?" Barky asked him.

Vincent nodded. I looked from one man to the other, confused. Vincent's cheeks were flushed and I sensed that he'd been running. He never ran.

Barky bent down so his eyes were level with mine.

"You're going to have to board now, Zillah. I know you wanted to wait for Lucien, but Crillick will be here any minute. We can't let him catch up to you."

I looked over to Vincent, who had his hands on his knees to catch his breath. That told me all I needed to know. I jumped up and tried to pull my trunk, but it was a dead weight.

"You'll have to leave it for now."

I ignored Barky, bending lower to really put my back into it. The trunk budged less than an inch and I cried out as I felt a twinge in my stomach.

"Leave it, Zillah."

"But it's got the fabric you bought me, my petticoats, and my wedding dress."

"We'll send them after you. The best thing you can do now is get on the boat. Go with Lord Woodward; he'll make sure you're next in the queue."

"You should leave too, Barky. He can't know that you've been helping me."

"Old Barky can look after himself, Zillah. I said I'd see you safely off and I will."

I held him tightly. I'd never be able to repay all he'd done for me. It was the story of my life: it wasn't until someone was taken away that I realised how much they meant to me. My mother, Eustace, Mrs. Bradley, and now Barky. The closest thing I'd had to a father.

Vincent stood up and held out his hand. "Come, Zillah."

He pulled me over to where the man with the list stood. They put their heads together and I saw money change hands. I looked behind me but there was no sign of Crillick, just Barky watching on anxiously.

"Go on, you can get on now."

"But Lucien isn't here yet."

"He'll be on his way. But you must leave now. If Crillick comes, there'll be little I can do for you."

My eyes were hot with tears. This was too many goodbyes, too quickly. Without thinking, I reached for Vincent for the last time. For a moment he did nothing and then I felt his arms close around me. He was my old life. Now that I had held it close, I could let it go.

I stepped back and there was Lucien watching us. His face was livid with anger. My embrace with Vincent had lasted no more than an instant, but I could tell it had confirmed all of Lucien's suspicions.

"Lucien . . ." I started but my voice petered away. There was nothing I could say that wouldn't make things worse. Once we were alone, I could explain, but this was neither the time nor the place. I looked at him with pleading eyes, willing him to understand that I no longer loved Vincent, if indeed I ever had. But his face remained stony.

"Winters. You're here. You must get Zillah aboard. Marcus Crillick is on his way and he'll have the police with him," Vincent said, his brusque tone belying the consciousness that reddened his face.

"Come here," Lucien said to me.

His tone gave me pause. I stood halfway between him and Vincent.

"I'm waiting," Lucien said.

Hang on, he was rebuking me when he was the one that was late? He'd not explained where he was or even said sorry. I glared at him, feeling angry and also embarrassed to have him speak to me like this with Vincent and Barky watching on.

"Zillah! Quickly, he's here."

Sure enough, there was Crillick, and behind him not the Peelers, but just one woman. Ellen. What was she doing here?

"Go, Zillah." Vincent pushed me toward the boat, where the man with the roll of paper was calling for me.

It was little more than a rowing boat. All the other passengers in my group had now boarded. There were just two spaces left: one for me and one for Lucien. Eight Black faces looked up at me, worried by the raised voices and clinging on to their luggage.

"It is not for you to command her," Lucien said.

"I am trying to save her."

"That is not your role either."

"There's no time for this," Barky interrupted, but it was too late.

"There you are, you little whore," Crillick bellowed. "Tried to run out on me, didn't you? But I've got you now." He turned to Barky. "Don't think I don't know your part in this. You won't get away with helping her. I'll make sure of it."

From squaring up to one another, Lucien and Vincent stepped closer together, shielding me from Crillick. He was angry, there was no doubt about it. His face was almost purple and his eyes were piggy with spite.

"Hand her over."

My two protectors made no movement so he shouted over them.

"You owe me, Jezebel. You thought to ruin me, didn't you, with your little stunt at the theatre? But the Peelers have been paid off."

He still didn't know for sure that I'd freed Nosizwe. In the midst of the chaos, the thought warmed me.

"Hand her over now or you'll be the one to pay," Crillick said.

"I will do no such thing," Lucien said. "We are leaving now. There is nothing you can do."

Crillick looked scornful but the mockery on his face died when he saw Lucien's clenched fists. There was no way he'd risk a fair fight with him.

"Is that what you think? That I can't call that dinghy back."

"You wouldn't dare," Vincent said.

"Pipe down, Woodward. How can you defend her when she left you for this monkey?"

Vincent blanched with fury. Crillick had got to him and Lucien saw our chance to slip away.

"Come, Zillah," Lucien said and I took his hand. Together we hurried over to the boat. A sailor now sat by the tiller and urged Lucien to climb in. The boat swayed in the water and Lucien took a moment to get his balance before reaching out both arms to me.

"Run away. You think you've won, but you're not out of England yet," Crillick shouted over Vincent, who barred his way to Lucien and me.

How long could he hold him off? Was Crillick angry enough to charge him?

The sailor looked worried by the developments. He had untied the rope on the rowing boat and the seated passengers were impatient to get going, away from the trouble that was rapidly escalating.

"He can look after himself, Zillah. You'll have to jump now," Barky said.

Lucien smiled at me encouragingly. There it was, that warmth. It said he wanted me still. I took a few steps back, ready to make a leap, as the boat started to drift away from the dockside.

"Look at you, taking His Lordship's castoffs," Ellen shouted at Lucien. "Do you know she's in the pudding club?"

Two words: not long words and yet they made time stand still. Had he heard? Understood? Yes, Lucien's arms fell away and it was only Barky grabbing me by the waist that stopped me from falling. Pregnant. How could Ellen know when I did not? But of course, she was right. I'd thought it was all the strain of the past two weeks that had made me both sick and yet hungrier than ever. But no. There was a tiny life growing inside me. I remembered Ellen making a comment about me getting fat as we'd gotten ready together. She must have known for a while now.

The rowing boat bobbed on the current, Lucien still standing, the oarsmen in shock, and the passengers growing increasingly annoyed at the delay. The look on Lucien's face was terrible to see.

"Row," he shouted.

It broke the spell. The oarsmen, directed by the sailor, fell to and Lucien sat down. I watched the boat make its way out to the ship that would have taken me safely away from England to a new life in Sierra Leone.

"Lucien," I called, but the wind snatched his name from my lips so it sounded like the cawing gulls that soared above us. My legs buckled and I felt Barky lower me to the quayside.

"Milord," he called out over his shoulder.

I waited for Vincent's arms to wrap around me. For him to hold me like I'd held him not twenty minutes before. A baby. This changed everything between us. He was shouting: him and Crillick and Ellen.

The tears flowed down my cheeks, and while Barky cradled my head to his bony chest, I placed my hands on my belly, in horror and awe. All this time I'd been so careful—how could this have happened to me? There was one time, only one: the night Vincent had comforted me when I first saw Nosizwe. Me, a mother? It couldn't be. My head swirled amid the shouting all around, as I contemplated that there were two of us now, inside this body.

We sat like that for a very long time, Barky and I, long enough for the yelling to die down. At last, he said, "We'd best be getting home, Zillah."

"Vincent's gone, hasn't he?"

"He has, girl. He has."

"He left us. He doesn't want her," I whispered to myself.

Somehow, I felt sure the baby I carried was a girl. Fortitude. The name came to me. I would call her Fortitude.

"For now, but he'll come back. We'll explain it to him."

"Lucien too?"

"That's right."

Vincent and Lucien, Lucien and Vincent. So different and yet, in this moment, their actions had been the same. This was why my choice had been so hard. Vincent was wrong for me, always had been. Society was not ready for a couple like us; there was nowhere we could safely be together, and he was not a strong enough man, for all his good intentions. I'd thought the answer was Lucien, but in his own way he too was wrong. He'd taught me to take pride in being Black but he forgot that I was British too, a Londoner who'd fought her way out of St. Giles, and that meant that, as much as I didn't belong in Vincent's world, I didn't fully belong in Lucien's either. I had sensed a bitterness in him toward England, which I did not, could not feel when this was all the home I had ever known. With Eustace so long gone, I'd thought I had to choose between them, and in doing so I had tried to choose between the two sides of who I was. But what was it that I had told Barky about cakes and gin fizz? It was not so simple as that. I may have been half-Black and half-white but I was wholly Zillah. That was the choice I would make. Not Vincent, not Lucien. I chose myself.

I thought of the child growing in my stomach. Vincent's daughter. She would be fair, like Barky, but I would make it so that she never felt she had to pass. That she could honor every bit of who she was, and in the meantime, I'd do whatever I could to help make a world where that was possible.

"We best be getting home, Zillah," Barky said again.

"Yes, home," I said. Home was London and it would always be that way: for myself and for my daughter and for her children and for her children's children too.

Seven Years Later

Epilogue

Go to the theatre much? No, nor me. I hear it's not what it used to be. I went down to the Strand a week or so back — the urge came over me to remember that wild year that brought Fortitude to me — and there was a sign saying that Crillick's Variety was due to be knocked down. I don't think of it often, but once it's gone, there'll be no cause to. It will be almost as though it never existed, and perhaps that's for the best. There was a stink around its owner some years back. He had a lead act — the Great Amazonia, a freak from darkest Africa — but now they say she was gaffed, not a savage at all, just a girl from the East End. Still, Marcus Crillick carries on. From time to time I hear he's working on a new show, but without his venue and his fancy friends, it's unlikely that anything will come of it. The scandal made him unclubbable, and he lost quite a bit of money on imperial railways too. But I haven't seen him myself so I couldn't swear to it. I never knew what happened to Ellen, but now, after so much time has passed, I can honestly say I hope she made it to America just like she wanted.

It's Elvira that brings me all the gossip. She goes to parties at least twice a week, but mainly to find subscribers for her causes.

She's got hundreds and I help her with them—Ethel too. Saving
Nosizwe gave me a taste for doing good, and with what Elvira pays
me to scribe for her and help administer her foundation, there's
no better way to earn a living. I was grateful to accept when she
offered me a home too. Together, the three of us write letters and
collect funds. But we go out onto the streets as well, to help the
working girls plying their trade, and into the prisons and asylums
likewise, for those who've decided to kick hard against the hand
that life has dealt them. We've raised a thousand pounds already
this year and it's only October. We send money to Sierra Leone
and all over Africa. There are many who mistake Elvira's intentions. Mr. Dickens sent her up in his latest and now some call her
Mrs. Jellyby behind her back, but she should worry.

One of the events Elvira attended most recently was the mar-
riage of the Viscount Woodward to Miss Dorothea Reed, a min-
ing heiress. She didn't tell me too much about it, but there was a
write-up of their wedding in the society pages and it didn't hurt
me to read it. I wish them both well. When Vincent found out
that Fortitude was his child, he wrote to me from his new home
in Pimlico. He said he was sorry, that his family would take her in,
but I never wrote back. I think he's seen her. Once, when I went
to St. James's Park and watched her play, there was a carriage that
parked up close by. I saw it a couple of times after that, but I never
marked the livery or tried to find out who was in it. Sometimes,
if it's raining and I feel a little down, I do wonder to myself what
her life could have been like. Gowns and parties, yes, but what if
they'd have steamed out her curls and bid her keep out of the sun?
No. I want her to be proud of who she is, and for that reason I
can't help but feel she's better off with her mama. But I'm equally
confident that, if living with Vincent was the best thing for her, I
would've known it and not hesitated to give her to him. Nosizwe
and my own mother taught me that.

I'm in my bedroom now, looking out of the window while my
little girl plays in the garden. I was never sure I wanted to be a

mother, but the moment I laid eyes on her, I knew she'd be my greatest love. Sometimes, I wonder if ever there's been a child that is so adored as she is. Elvira and Ethel both dote on her, and she's got her uncle Barky around too. Of course, I tell her all about her grandmother and the sacrifices that she made for us both, and Mrs. Bradley who did so much for me as well. It's important to me that she grows up with both of them in her heart. When she gets a little older, I'll tell her about her uncle Eustace. Of all the trouble we used to get into together and how deeply we loved one another. I wish she could have known him, but if I tell her all the stories, maybe it will feel as though, in some way, he's here with us.

Fortitude and I see Barky at least once a week. He left the theatre game a few years ago and now runs a school teaching actors and actresses their craft. There's a job for me there if I want it, but I much prefer working with Elvira. It's by far the thing I'm best at. I'm not sure I ever was much cop as an actress. There comes a time in life when you have to stop pretending.

Acknowledgments

My heartfelt thanks to everyone who has supported and encouraged me with the writing of this novel. Firstly to my agent Juliet Mushens, for believing in me, championing my work, and making all my writing dreams come true, and to Jenny Bent, for all her help and support in the US; to my editors Emily Griffin and Millicent Bennett and their teams at Hutchinson Heineman and Mariner Books, for all the love and care that went into making the manuscript the best it could be; to my fellow writers, Hattie Clarke, the very first person to read Zillah's story, as well as Julia Barrett, Madeline Dewhurst, Ian Hamilton, Eyre Kurasawa, and Natasha Stokes, who were there from the very beginning; to my SI Leeds shortlist sisters; to the 2022 Debut Stars Twitter group—it's been wonderful to share the publishing experience with you over the past year; to my London Lit Lab and Jericho Writers workshop buddies; to Hajira Mahomed, Victoria and David Dillsworth, and Nikki May for help with translation; and to all those who have been part of the journey to helping me find my voice and to become a better writer: Nikita Lalwani, Eley Williams, Susanna Jones, Claire Berliner, Fiona Goh, Debi Alper, Emma Darwin, and all those involved with the London Library Emerging Writers Programme and the SI Leeds Literary Prize. And to my family for the tricky feat of simultaneously lifting me up and keeping me grounded: Giselle Dillsworth and Catherine Dillsworth, the bestest mama and nana a girl could ever have, and to my aunties, Mary Leeds and Therésè Luck, for being there to support and encourage and to take the strain during the most difficult of times so I could seek refuge in my writing.

The majority of this novel was written between 2020 and 2021. My final thanks go to Dr. Melanie Powell, Mr. Stefano Andreani, and Dr. Sarah Slater, to their teams, and to everyone who works for our wonderful NHS, who kept those dearest to me safe and well during this time. I appreciate you.